THE SECOND BOOK OF THE CROWN COLONIES

OF *Limited Loyalty*

Other books by Michael A. Stackpole:

DragonCrown War:
The Dark Glory War
Fortress Draconis
When Dragons Rage
The Grand Crusade

Age of Discovery:
A Secret Atlas
Cartomancy
A New World

BattleTech: Warrior:
Warrior: En Garde
Warrior: Riposte
Warrior: Coupé

BattleTech: Blood of Kerensky:
Lethal Heritage
Blood Legacy
Lost Destiny

BattleTech Core Novels:
Natural Selection
Assumption of Risk
Bred for War
Malicious Intent
Grave Covenant
Prince of Havoc

MechWarrior: Dark Age:
Ghost War
Masters of War

Star Wars:
X-Wing: Rogue Squadron
X-Wing: Wedge's Gamble
X-Wing: The Krytos Trap
X-Wing: The Bacta War
I, Jedi
X-Wing: Isard's Revenge
The New Jedi Order: Dark Tide I:
    Onslaught
The New Jedi Order: Dark Tide II:
    Ruin

Dark Conspiracy:
A Gathering Evil
Evil Ascending
Evil Triumphant

Once a Hero
Dementia
Talion: Revenant
A Hero Born
An Enemy Reborn
Wolf and Raven
Eyes of Silver

Crown Colonies:
Book 1: At the Queen's Command
Book 2: Of Limited Loyalty
Book 3: Ungrateful Rabble (forth-
    coming)

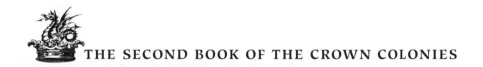

THE SECOND BOOK OF THE CROWN COLONIES

OF *Limited Loyalty*

MICHAEL A.
STACKPOLE

NIGHT SHADE BOOKS
SAN FRANCISCO

First Printing

ISBN: 978-1-59780-205-5

Night Shade Books
Please visit us on the web at
http://www.nightshadebooks.com

To my lovely and talented nieces,
Faith and Clare

Acknowledgements

The author would like to thank the following individuals for their help and support with this book. Kat Klaybourne, her daughter Carly Klaybourne for naming Peregrine and championing the cause of wooly rhinoceri, the folks at Night Shade Books for indulging me in my side trip into the Hyborean Age, my agents Howard Morhaim and Danny Baror, Janna Silverstein for translating me into English again, and Reinhold Mai for translating me into German.

Mike would especially like to thank all the wonderful people who said so many great things about *At the Queen's Command* on the Internet and in person. Authors work in isolation and the editorial process is centered on fixing things that were wrong. Hearing that folks really enjoyed the story and have recommended it to others really pushed me to make this volume the best it could possibly be.

1767

CHAPTER ONE

27 March 1767
Temperance Bay, Mystria

Owen Strake leaned on tea crates, watching sea gulls wheel and listening to them shriek above the wharf. One landed not twelve feel away, eying him suspiciously from atop a weathered piling. The bird adjusted its feathers with a quick nip, then brought its head up warily as waves slapped pilings, spraying a salty mist into the air.

Owen smiled as the cool droplets drifted over his face, looking past the gull toward the rowboats tugging the *Sea Mistress* toward the docks. Anxious passengers stood on deck, centermost among them a portly man clutching an oilskin parcel. Owen took the general pallor of the passengers and the fact that their clothes hung loosely as a sign that the crossing from Norisle had not been kind or calm.

A tow-headed young man trotted over to Owen, his brown eyes filled with mischief. As did Owen, the young man wore a white shirt, black breeches over white stockings, and low shoes. They both wore dark woolen jackets against the breeze. Neither wore wigs and the younger man had eschewed wearing a hat. "Looks like Horace Wattling can't wait to be on solid ground again."

Owen nodded. "It would appear he's looking for the coach he ordered. Its absence isn't going to help his disposition."

"I don't figure much could." Caleb Frost smiled broadly. "I've got a crown says he just gets back on the ship and sails for Norisle."

"Your mother would not be pleased with your gambling." Owen laughed. "And it's for fear of her I don't take your money."

He turned back and watched the ship bobbing in the bay. Out at the headland, the *Mistress'* captain had sent word for a harbormaster to

1

2 MICHAEL A. STACKPOLE

guide him in, had passed on some news, and had relayed orders from passengers. Wattling's request for a coach had been delivered to his printing company and subsequently transferred into Caleb's hands. Caleb had sent word to Owen's estate and Owen had ridden in earlier that morning to await Wattling.

As much as Owen looked forward to dealing with him, his thoughts flew back three years to when he'd been on a similar ship making the crossing to the colonies. Even when in the field, fighting the Tharyngians, being rained upon, frozen, and shot, he'd never been so miserable. The sight of the Mystrian coast had been incredibly welcome, but even as grateful as he had been then, he never would have imagined he'd come to love the land as he did now.

I will never sail back to Norisle. Owen shook his head. The nation he had once considered his home now no longer had any allure for him. Mystria provided him distance and sanctuary from his stepfather's family. Were it within his power to widen the ocean, Owen would have done it in a heartbeat. *There's nothing there for me.*

Longshoremen made the *Sea Mistress* fast and raised a gangway. Wattling elbowed his way past a family and bounded down to the dock. His knees almost buckled when he hit the pier, but he caught himself and stormed toward the shore.

Caleb intercepted him. "Good morning, Horace."

Wattling stopped and stared, his piggish eyes narrowing. "Frost, isn't it? Good day to you. Where is that blasted coach? I'll have Redland flogged if he's forgotten me."

"William sends his regards, and he goes by Scrivener now."

Wattling's head came up, his jowls quivering. "What?"

"It's Mystrian custom to change your name when you begin a new life." Caleb nodded solemnly. "He thought Inkhand would suit him, but we convinced him Scrivener sounded better."

"I am aware of the abominable custom, Mr. Frost, but he is a redemptioneer. He cannot change his name, he cannot do anything, until his term of service to me is up." Wattling stamped a foot. "And that term is getting longer with every minute I wait here. Where is my coach?"

"This is what we need to speak to you about." Caleb turned and indicated Owen with a quick nod.

Wattling followed his gaze and paled. "Captain Strake. What have you done?"

Owen shook his head. "It's not what I've done, Mr. Wattling; it's what you've done. You called a tune, and now you'll pay the piper."

"I have no idea what you are suggesting."

Caleb took a step toward Wattling. "I think you do, but you have no idea what the consequences of your action have been. While you were in Norisle, in the company of Lord Rivendell, preparing his book on military theory, you obtained a copy of Captain Strake's account of the expedition to Anvil Lake. You rewrote the book, injecting yourself into the narrative as if you had joined us. You also wove in an inordinate amount of praise for Lord Rivendell, painting him as the savior of Mystria, and completely discounted Mystrian accomplishments. You made Captain Strake appear to be a mutinous renegade. You cast the Mystrian Rangers as bumbling amateurs, failed to mention Count von Metternin, and reduced Prince Vlad to a fop who took his wurm for a swim while the battle raged."

Wattling took a step back. "You must understand, gentlemen, that I had instructed Redland to obtain permission to prepare a Norillian edition of Captain Strake's book…"

Owen's eyes narrowed. "Permission, which was denied."

"I never got…"

Owen crossed his arms. "I sent my own man to hand-deliver the message. He traveled back with you on the *Mistress*."

Wattling's shoulders began to sink. "You don't understand. Lord Rivendell was being slow, so very slow, with his book. He would constantly revise. I was going broke waiting for him, but he could not be rushed and there was a hunger for news. The '65 campaign on the continent was a disaster. The people hungered for a tale of victory—which they'd not get for a year until the issue was settled at Rondeville… But no one would have believed your account, so I *had* to take liberties. It's just a thing which is done."

"I'm afraid it's not, Horace. Not in Temperance Bay. Doing what you did, you unleashed forces which would make demons quail."

Owen shivered involuntarily. His wife, Catherine, loathed Mystria and had only intended to remain long enough to give birth to their daughter, Miranda. She dreamed of returning to Norisle and resuming her place in society. Toward this end she urged Owen to write his memoirs of the Anvil Lake campaign and had even consented to Caleb's sister, Bethany, editing it. Though Catherine barely skimmed a page or two, she was overjoyed with Temperance College's willingness to print the book. She trusted that some publisher in Norisle would subsequently be willing to print it to great acclaim, allowing her to return home covered in glory.

Horrible weather and sickness prevented Catherine from traveling to Norisle through the summer of 1765. She longed so to return that Owen even maintained an apartment in Temperance so she could feel she was that much closer. Then, in August, she received a copy of Wattling's book, sent by a woman who had been a social rival. The accompanying note, while polite in form, ridiculed Catherine and suggested that anyone she had once counted as a friend in Norisle was greatly amused by the match she had made in Owen.

Caleb stabbed a finger against Wattling's breastbone. "Catherine Strake gathered together the women of Temperance and convinced them that your book amounted to high theft, extreme defamation, and blasphemy. Princess Gisella, who was likewise displeased with how you treated her friend, Count von Metternin, and her husband, Prince Vlad, pushed for and caused to be passed through our assembly fairly strict laws against what you had done. By December 1765, you had been tried, fined, and your property seized to satisfy your civil debt."

"What? That is outrageous!"

Caleb held a hand up. "Your assets were purchased at sheriff's auction. My uncle, Balthazar, purchased everything, lock, stock, and barrel. He opened the Frost Press. We publish the *Frost Weekly Gazette*, as well as books and pamphlets by Captain Strake and Samuel Haste. We also did an edition of your book, *To the Fortress of Death*."

"Ah ha!" Wattling shot a finger into the air. "You commit the very crime you have accused me of committing."

Owen snorted. "The court found that your book was *my* book, so all rights to it are mine."

"And here, Horace, is what will really turn your stomach." Caleb chuckled coldly. "We sent your book to the Mystrian Rangers, along with a copy of Captain Strake's book. Both have gone all over Mystria. Your book so outrages people, they buy dozens of copies of Captain

Strake's book. William, who is now our pressman, can barely keep up with demand."

"This will not stand!" Frothed spittle collected at the corners of his mouth. "This will be overturned and you will be paying me for the work of mine you have stolen."

Owen now stepped forward. "Caleb has not told you the worst of it."

"How can it be any worse?"

"Your property was forfeit to satisfy civil penalties. The *criminal* penalties, however, are still to be addressed." Owen opened his hands. "You stand convicted, but have yet to be sentenced. The court is willing to listen to witnesses who swear to your character. If you show signs of contrition, if you have work, and are a man of substance, the judge may be inclined to pass a very light sentence."

Wattling's knees gave way. Owen caught him before he went down. Caleb rescued the parcel. Hodge Dunsby, Owen's messenger, came up on Wattling's right and helped Owen straighten him.

"Good to see you, Mr. Dunsby."

"And you, Captain, Mr. Frost."

"You're looking good, Hodge." Caleb tucked Wattling's parcel under his arm. "The thing of it is this, Horace: Frost Press needs another pressman. You can have that job. You'll live above the press. You'll be in charge of getting out the *Gazette*."

"A pressman? I am an editor."

"My sister is the editor."

"A woman?"

Owen smiled. "The passages she worked hardest on in my book are the only ones you refrained from editing, Mr. Wattling."

"That is immaterial, sir. No woman has the proper temperament or intellect to deal with the nuances of words."

Caleb's eyes and voice tightened. "Are you saying my sister is stupid?"

Wattling appeared, for a moment, inclined to reply in the affirmative, but the fire in Caleb's eyes sent a shiver through him. He shook both Owen and Hodge off. "Gentlemen, this whole problem is because of the involvement of women. Captain Strake, had you kept proper control of your wife, none of this ever would have happened."

"You say that, but you have left your own wife back in Norisle, if I am informed correctly." Owen clasped his hands behind his back. He feigned indignation because, in reality, he owed Wattling a debt. Catherine's pride at Owen's book had quickly evaporated. She had not spared him the sharper side of her tongue when telling him everything that was wrong with Mystria. Doctor Frost, Caleb's father, suggested some women had such moods after they'd borne a child and urged Owen to endure. Owen did, devoting himself to their daughter and hoping for leavening in his wife's demeanor. Until Wattling made himself a target of her ire, however, she had been content to gnaw on Owen.

"You leave my wife out of this."

"You should have left mine out, Mr. Wattling."

Wattling snorted. "My portrait of you is not wrong. Were you a true man, you would have her under control."

Caleb stepped back, his expression slackened with astonishment. Before he could offer a comment, however, Hodge Dunsby hauled off and cuffed Wattling in the back of the head, knocking him a step forward. "You listen here, Horace Wattling. I don't got too many letters, but some as do read me what you said about Captain Strake. I was there, right before that Fortress of Death, and I'd have been dead long since but for Captain Strake ordering me to my feet. He led me through fire and shot, through Tharyngian regiments into the lair of Guy du Malphias his own self. Now maybe he gone and done married himself a willful woman. That marks him a braver man than you will ever be. And what he did out there to Anvil Lake confirms it."

"I will not be lectured to by some gutter-spawn coward!"

The young, brown-haired man spat at Wattling's feet. "Then take some advice. You call Captain Strake a coward around here, there's men what'll dispute that with switch, sword, or shot. And if that isn't enough, you'll like as not make his wife mad all over again."

Owen raised both hands. "Thank you, Hodge. Here's the thing of it, Mr. Wattling: I'll speak for you to the judge. The Prince will as well. The judge will suspend your sentence. Spend a year or two working hard, and you'll be free to do your own business. Take Caleb's offer. You really don't want to see the inside of what passes for a prison in Mystria."

Wattling's lower lip began to quiver. Owen feared he would cry. "It isn't fair, what you've done. It's counter to Norillian law."

"But, Horace, you're no longer in Norisle." Caleb patted him on the shoulder. "Back there you'd already be in irons. We're offering you a chance, just like all of our ancestors had. What you did was wrong, but it doesn't have to haunt you forever."

"I'm too old to start over."

"Better that than jail, isn't it?" Caleb shrugged. "Two years, you can change your name and…"

"No, *never!*" Wattling shook his head vehemently. "I may be trapped into being your servant, but I shall never become one of *you*. You're all the spawn of criminals. Over here, given a society of your peers, it's no wonder you are able to twist the laws to mock honest men. Well, you have me. You've robbed me of my resources, you have stacked the courts against me, I have no choice but to bow to your will. It does not mean, however, that I accept your warped concept of justice. I shall make certain people know what you have done."

Caleb smiled. "Write it down. If my sister likes it, we'll even publish it."

Various emotions fought across Wattling's face, and the battlefield reddened. Before he could explode, however, a tall, strongly built blond man wearing a Norillian Army uniform came up the gangway and paused between Caleb and Hodge. "Are you well, Mr. Wattling?"

Wattling nodded quickly. "As best I can be, Colonel."

The man's red coat had black facings with two red stripes. The black vest beneath likewise had the stripes. Owen recognized the regiment easily. *Fifth Northland Cavalry.* Two curled dragon ensigns in silver decorated each black lapel, marking the man as having been afforded the courtesy rank of wurmrider. Had they been gold, it would have meant he'd been assigned one of the wingless dragons for combat.

Owen offered the man his hand. "I'm Owen Strake. This is Caleb Frost, and you traveled with Hodge Dunsby. Mr. Wattling you already know."

The officer, being slightly taller and heavier than Owen, met him with a firm grip, yet did not try to overpower him. "Strake, formerly of the Queen's Own Wurm Guards?"

"The same." Owen freed his hand from the other man's. "And you are?"

"Ian Rathfield." The Queen's officer smiled easily. "Your uncle sent me to finish the job he'd given you."

CHAPTER TWO

27 March 1767
Government House,
Temperance Bay, Mystria

Prince Vlad stuffed the last of his soiled clothes into the portmanteau and began to buckle it closed when Chandler, his aide, entered his chambers. "Is the cart here already?"

"No, Highness." Chandler closed the oaken wardrobe's doors as he moved past. "Captain Strake has arrived with a Colonel Rathfield to see you. The Colonel came in on the *Sea Mistress.*"

Him, here? What is my aunt up to? Vlad ran a hand over his chin. "Describe the man."

"Captain Strake's size perhaps, blond. He wears the Fifth Northland Cavalry uniform, with wurmrider badges."

"Very good. See them into the audience chamber… what is it?"

The aide glanced down. "The Colonel insisted that he see you in private."

"I see. Send him to me in the audience chamber. Tell Captain Strake to wait outside." Vlad pointed at the well-worn, brown leather case. "Finish up with this and get it into the cart, whenever it arrives."

"As you wish, Highness."

His aide withdrew and Vlad crossed to the wardrobe. Within it hung several coats. For official business he often chose a red-and-gold brocade—a gift from his aunt, the Queen, after the Anvil Lake affair. The gold threads had been worked in a wurm design. It impressed visitors, though tended to make Mystrians of Virtuan stock uneasy because of its sheer ostentation.

No, that won't do for this man. Instead he selected a forest green woolen jacket, cut after the military style, with black facings. This, too, he'd been awarded after the Anvil Lake campaign, and he prized it much more highly than his aunt's gift. The Mystrian Rangers had all voted him the rank of Colonel and presented him with the coat on the first anniversary of the battle. Within two weeks, his son Richard had been born, making August 1765 the single best month of his life.

Vlad had instantly recognized his visitor's name. Scant few would not. The Battle of Rondeville nine months previously had ended the long war between Norisle and Tharyngia. Colonel Rathfield—then Major—had been sent into the city by Richard Ventnor, Duke Deathridge, to offer the Tharyngian commanders a chance to surrender. Laureate-General Philippe de Toron laughed at the suggestion, accused him of being a spy, and imprisoned him. Rathfield escaped and killed de Toron and his command staff. Without leadership, the Tharyngian forces collapsed and the war ended.

Norillian forces entering the city found Rathfield seriously wounded and barely alive. He managed to recover and became the sort of hero Norisle desperately needed.

Vlad frowned. *The Crown must have had a very good reason for sending him here. I don't think any good will come from this at all.*

Pulling the Ranger coat on, he entered the audience chamber through a side door. When the Colonial assembly was in session, wooden desks filled the room and a podium occupied the same spot as his throne. Because of his royal blood he was permitted such and, occasionally, in his role as the Mystrian Governor-General, he used it. He opted against it with Colonel Rathfield and hoped he would not regret that decision.

The double doors at the room's far end opened. Sunlight from the windows in the hallway opposite poured in, initially reducing Rathfield to a tall slender silhouette. He moved easily and powerfully into the room, the squeaking groans of floorboards seeming muted by his steady tread. He came with hat in hand, his face impassive and noble. The only visible scar ran from forehead to right cheek, over his eye and splitting the brow, but the eye had suffered no apparent damage.

Rathfield paused a dozen feet before Vlad, then dropped to a knee and bowed his head. "Highness, please forgive my interruption. I am…"

"I am well aware of who you are, Colonel Rathfield. News of your heroism has spread even here." Vlad stepped forward, offering his hand.

"Please, rise."

Rathfield came up and shook the Prince's hand firmly. The man looked the Prince up and down. A slight tremor rippled through the Colonel's grip as puzzlement faded into a hint of shock on his face. He let Vlad's hand drop, then drew himself up and clasped his hands at the small of his back.

"If I might be given leave to report, Highness."

Vlad purposefully delayed his reply. His wife often chided him for playing games with people as he did the unexpected and gauged the results. Rathfield expected more formality, clearly, and Vlad's wearing a colonial militia uniform surprised him. The Mystrian Rangers' reputation had suffered horribly because of the Battle of Villerupt in 1760. The victory at Anvil Lake in 1764, being an action in the colonies misreported back in Norisle, had done little to rehabilitate it. Vlad took the man's reaction and behavior to mark him as somewhat vain. This tallied with the story of his heroism, and would be a factor to temper Vlad's reading of anything he said.

"Yes, please, Colonel. Report." Vlad turned, took a step toward the throne, but did not mount the dais before turning back. "I'm anxious to hear news of court."

"I have little of that, Highness. I am a mere soldier acting under orders. I have written copies of them in my luggage." He reached inside his jacket. "I was, however, asked to personally convey a letter from your father."

Vlad accepted it, turning the yellowed package over to verify the red wax seal, then tucked it into a pocket. "Thank you. Now, if you would not mind communicating that which my aunt or her advisors feared to consign to writing."

Rathfield almost covered his surprise at Vlad's deduction.

Ah, his vanity extends to thinking he is more intelligent than most.

"As you wish, Highness. The Crown has received a petition for the charter of a new colony. It calls itself Postsylvania. The petitioners are vague about the location of their colony because, it appears, they already have founded several towns. What they ask for—demand really—is a claim which runs from the Gulf in the south, north to the Argent River, and from west of the mountains to what they refer to as land's end. We do not know if this means the Misaawa River or the far coast."

Vlad's brown eyes narrowed. Aside from the characterization of the petition as a demand, he instantly recognized two problems with the claim. The first was that by either measure, the petitioners were requesting a vast amount of territory—virtually all of it unknown to Mystrians. While ships had circumnavigated the world, inaccuracies with measuring longitude meant that no one could reliably state how far away the continent's west coast actually lay. The Queen, even on her least lucid day, would never consent to such a concession.

More immediately, however, the claim would overlap with Tharyngian territorial claims. Having just ended a war, the Crown would never grant a charter for a colony that would immediately reignite that war.

Vlad nodded slowly. "You were sent to assess how far settlers have gone in the mountains and beyond?"

"Yes, Highness. Toward that end…"

"There is more, isn't there, Colonel?" Vlad killed a smile prompted by the flicker of distress on the man's face. "You betrayed nothing, sir. You described the petition as a demand, which my aunt saw as mutiny or treason or worse. Given the colonial reaction to last year's document tax and resentment over the Crown's refusal to compensate the colonials for expenses incurred during the Anvil Lake expedition, she wants you to assess the level of loyalty among her subjects."

Rathfield's hands appeared open from behind his back. "You understand the situation very well, Highness. Queen Margaret became quite alarmed when Lord Rivendell read from Samuel Haste's *A Continent's Calling* in the House of Lords. He said it was a seditious document, claimed the colonials revered it more than they did the Good Book, and suggested certain passages advocated regicide."

"That's a bit hyperbolic, but this is Rivendell we're talking about."

"True, Highness. By your remark, I take it you've read the book?"

"Several times, in several editions." Again Vlad reveled in the surprise on Rathfield's face. *I hope you do not gamble, sir, for you certainly will lose.* "I suspect my aunt would be even less enamored of Haste's latest pamphlet *The Blood of Liberty.*"

"He has new work available? You've seized it, of course, and destroyed the press."

"Hardly." Vlad refrained from mentioning he'd financed the first print run. "One cannot kill an idea by suppressing its publication, Colonel. One can merely mount a counter-offensive through reasoned discussion. This, however, is a point we may debate more fully at a later time."

"Yes, Highness."

"If you don't mind, I will invite Captain Strake to join us. Your mission will require an expedition, and he has particular insights into these things."

"Highness, I was told this information is to be held in the utmost secrecy."

Vlad smiled easily. "I know, Colonel, that you do not mean to suggest you doubt the soundness of my judgment as to Captain Strake's character or intellect, nor that you understand the administration of Her Majesty's affairs here in Mystria better than I do."

"No, Highness." Rathfield half-turned back toward the closed doors. "Shall I fetch him?"

"You're very kind."

Within three steps toward the doors, Rathfield had regained his composure. He strode with a certain grace, reminding Vlad of the effortless power with which a jeopard moved through the Mystrian forests. *Perhaps he is like the saber-toothed cat, strong enough to be deadly and, therefore, not required to be too clever.* If the story of Rondeville was even half-true, the man would be implacable in combat, and just intelligent enough to learn what his masters wanted, yet not so bright as to question their need for that information.

The two men returned, Rathfield a half a step ahead of Owen. Vlad offered his friend his hand, then clasped Owen's in both of his. "Wonderful to see you again, Owen. I didn't realize you were in town."

"I rode in this morning. There was the Wattling affair to take care of."

"Resolved satisfactorily?"

"I hope so. I left him with Caleb. Mr. Dunsby and I escorted Colonel Rathfield here."

"Please tell Mr. Dunsby I am pleased to learn he has returned. Baker will be happy to have his help with Mugwump again." Vlad slapped Owen on the shoulder, then released his hand. "Colonel Rathfield tells me that there has been a petition sent to the Queen concerning a new settlement in the west. Colonel, what do you know of the petitioners?"

Rathfield again hid his hands at the small of his back. "Highness, we know very little. No one signed the petition per se. It was signed in the name of the True Oriental Church of the Lord. No one in Launston seems to know who or what that organization is."

"Owen, have you any insights?"

"Nothing about that group, Highness, but most of the villages and towns in Temperance Bay and Bounty started when churches had doctrinal splits and half the people moved away. Caleb once mentioned that he had second cousins who helped found the town Humility over in Bounty. I also seem to recall Makepeace Bone mentioning a group heading west a couple years ago—'62 maybe, or '61—to escape the corruption of the coast."

"How long would it take to mount an expedition to survey such settlements?"

Owen frowned. "No honest way of knowing, Highness, without a clue as to where to start looking."

"They want to call their settlement Postsylvania, and want it to run from the Argent to the coast, west of the mountains until they hit water."

Owen nibbled his lower lip. "I see the problem. That narrows it down slightly. A month to the mountains, perhaps, several more hunting, then a month back. Head out in two weeks, be back in time for your son's birthday. Six men, including the Colonel here: Hodge, Makepeace, Nathaniel, Kamiskwa, and me."

Vlad nodded. "I believe we have a working plan. Would it inconvenience you, Captain, to host Colonel Rathfield? Given the confidential nature of his mission, housing him on your estate would be prudent. It makes him easily accessible to me. And while I am certain Mr. Dunsby will acquit himself well, might I suggest you offer Count von Metternin a chance to join you?"

"Of course, Highness. I should have thought of that."

Rathfield lifted his chin. "Highness, I'm not certain that this expedition, as outlined, fulfills the dictates of my orders. Horse Guards and the Queen were most keen on the idea of bringing any settlement back within chartered territories. I was thinking I could take a company of the Life Guards and that you might scare up a company of colonial scouts and skirmishers to guide us."

"I will certainly read your orders carefully, Colonel, to make certain we are not in violation of them. Captain, would you care to explain to Colonel Rathfield how long his expedition would take?"

Owen shrugged easily—a mannerism he'd picked up while living in Mystria. "We'd be wintering somewhere out in the mountains, and be lucky to make it back here by spring. Folks in the settlements would agree to head back to the coast, but would just reoccupy things after we left for the next settlement."

"Then we should have to burn their settlements."

Owen shook his head. "You don't understand. You're thinking of towns in Tharyngia or Norisle, but settlements out here aren't like that. Folks will have cabins spread all over, five to ten miles from the church, trading post, or tavern they consider the heart of their settlement. You'd never find them all, and they'd warn others. You'd grow more settlements than you'd stomp out."

"I believe, Captain, your assessment misses the fact that I act with the Crown's authority."

Vlad held up a hand. "Gentlemen, this is a subject we can discuss on the road west. I have a cart coming at noon. Colonel, if you and Mr. Dunsby see to your luggage, it can be loaded into the cart. Captain Strake's home is adjacent to mine. We will ride ahead and see if we can settle things."

"As you wish, Highness."

"Good. Please, you'll find Mr. Dunsby waiting outside, won't he, Captain?"

"Yes, Highness."

"Tell him to collect your things. Godspeed." Vlad nodded toward the door. "And, Owen, a word, if I might."

"Of course, Highness."

Rathfield saluted the Prince smartly, then turned on his heel and marched from the chamber. Vlad waited until the door closed behind him, then looked at Owen.

"Tell me, Owen, truthfully. Do you want to go on this expedition because you wish to guarantee success, or do you just want to get away from your wife?"

CHAPTER THREE

27 March 1767
Government House,
Temperance Bay, Mystria

Owen hesitated before he answered, less because of the question's direct nature than the insight behind it. "My only wish, Highness, is to be of service."

The Prince smiled. "I hoped that was the case. I asked because you are a friend. I wish you only the best."

Owen glanced toward the floor. "I know that. Had you not asked, I would have convinced myself that service to the Crown is my *only* concern. However, it *is*…"

"The sailing season, I know."

Catherine Strake had never abandoned the idea of returning to Norisle, even when she was told she would be friendless and humiliated. If anything, that seemed to heighten her desire to go back. As spring gave way to summer, she would spend more time in their rooms in Temperance and become increasingly insistent that she be allowed to leave. The edge in her voice would grow, and her glances would become more venomous.

Owen sighed. "It's the sailing season to everyone else, but I know it as the *insane* season. I had so hoped she would come to love the land as I do, as our daughter does."

"Miranda's a bit young to ascribe such feelings to her, don't you think?"

"Is she, Highness?" He smiled. "You've not seen it with your children yet, but to hear Miranda laugh toddling after butterflies, or sticking her nose in flowers, I have no question that she loves her home. Her mother thinks I let her run wild and wants me to hire a governess from Norisle to raise her properly. This is this year's ploy, to be allowed to go back to Norisle to find someone suitable."

Vlad nodded thoughtfully. "When she says it, it's always a return *home*, yes?"

"Yes." Owen rubbed a hand over his face. "Why she can't see the beauty of this place, why she can't come to love it, I don't understand."

Vlad laid a hand on Owen's shoulder. "I have come to realize that some people can love what is, and others can only love what they *control*. You and I can marvel at the wonders of this land, and take comfort in its mysteries. Your wife sees it as hostile and chaotic. Had you remained in Norisle, you likely never would have been given cause to notice this difference. Here, you could not possibly escape it."

And this would mean that she loved me because she could control me. But here, no more. Owen's shoulders slumped. "You'll not have me go, then?"

"Regardless of your answer, I have no choice but to send you. That die was cast before Rathfield ever sailed from Launston." Vlad frowned. "The only reason to send a hero to Mystria is to lose him, or to use his notoriety to validate whatever news he sends back. Without Tharyngia to worry about, my aunt now has time to concern herself with Mystria. I have no doubt that your uncle and Johnny Rivendell have convinced her the colonies are festering pits of rebellion, so she's sent Colonel Rathfield to deal with it.

"I would have assigned the same men to the expedition as you suggested. You may not recall how Nathaniel and you got on at first, but can you imagine how he would treat Rathfield if you weren't along?"

"Abandon him in Hattersburg, I'd imagine."

"If he didn't trade him to the Ungarikii for a polecat pelt sooner."

"True." Nathaniel Woods, arguably the best Mystrian scout, had little tolerance for Norillian imperiousness. His association with Lord Rivendell during the Anvil Lake campaign had made his negative attitude even worse. "Do you think he could get that much for him?"

The Prince raised a finger. "I don't find myself much inclined to like Colonel Rathfield either, Owen, but I am forced to respect him. What he did at Rondeville was commendable, and the tragedy he suffered after nearly unendurable."

Owen nodded. Word had gone from the Continent back to Rathfield's wife, mistakenly informing her that her husband had been killed. Though she was joyful when he returned home, apparently the specter of his death haunted her. In November of 1766, she died of "a broken heart," which Catherine informed Owen meant she'd killed herself.

"I suspect he accepted this assignment for similar reasons to your doing the same three years ago, Owen. He's far away from home and will rigidly adhere to his orders. You were intelligent enough to be flexible. I am not certain he is. You will have to watch him carefully."

Owen frowned. "What is it you're not telling me, Highness?"

Vlad opened his hands. "I know nothing substantive, but since the end of the war, Ryngian correspondents of mine have hinted at dark rumors about Colonel Rathfield. Don't ask me for details—there are none. There have been more reliable rumors about Rufus Branch's location than there are about the hero of Rondeville."

"Understood, Highness." Owen scratched at the back of his neck. "If he insists on meting out the Queen's justice in the back country?"

"If it is warranted, allow it; if not, suggest the case be appealed to the Governor-General." Vlad walked with Owen to the door. "I trust your discretion, Captain. And I do want a full report of everything. You're used to that, however."

"Thank you, Highness."

As the men descended the wooden stairs, Owen once again could scarcely believe he was walking beside an heir to the throne. His disbelief grew out of equal parts of Prince Vlad acting entirely common and Owen's not feeling worthy of the man's friendship and trust. He had no doubt that things like Vlad's friendship with him or Nathaniel Woods became the source of many crude jests at the Queen's Court. The same qualities that endeared the Prince to the people of Mystria would make him the object of ridicule in Launston.

Indeed, Vlad's openness and friendship had been the sole reason why Catherine had initially remained in Temperance Bay. Catherine and Princess Gisella became fast friends and, Owen subsequently realized, Catherine had believed this friendship would place her at the top of Mystrian society. She'd been right. In Norisle she would have been the equivalent of one of the Queen's Ladies, making her the envy of millions. In Mystria, however, her status placed her only a class or two above barmaids. While their deference amused Catherine, her enjoyment did not last long. Mystria's virtually classless society came to repulse her.

She doesn't understand that only because of it was she able to become so close to the Princess. Owen reveled in the same simple social structure, but he had connections into it that she did not. His actions at Anvil Lake, and the time he'd spent with Nathaniel and Kamiskwa, had solidified his position in Mystria.

Owen also realized that he didn't need society or its approval the way his wife did. In Mystria people were judged largely on what they made of themselves, not who their parents had been. The point of coming to Mystria and changing their names had been to cut themselves off from the past. Many Norillians saw it as a move to spare their families embarrassment, but Owen realized it went further. Unencumbered by eons-old expectations, individuals could become the people Mystria needed them to be.

The two men exited Government House and headed north on Generosity to the livery. While the winter had been cold, it had not produced a great deal of snow in Temperance. As a result, the streets remained in fairly good shape. They made it easily to the stable, greeting many people with a nod or wave on their journey.

Rathfield awaited them. "Your man has taken the cart to gather my baggage after he gets yours, Highness. As you suggested, we can ride ahead."

Owen collected his horse—a brown gelding—and saddled it. He pulled a horse-pistol from the saddle-scabbard, checked it, and rotated the firestone. Satisfied, he returned it to the scabbard.

"For the savages?" Rathfield studied the street. "I thought I saw one a bit ago. Can you allow them into town if they're dangerous?"

Owen shook his head. "You'll not want to call them savages. They're the Twilight People to most, Shedashee as a whole, then there's the tribes and nations among them."

"But they *are* savages." Rathfield mounted the saddle on a grey stallion. "I am aware there is a certain affection for them in some parts, but I also have read reports of atrocities committed by them."

"Don't believe everything you read." Many of the reports to which Rathfield referred had been written by Colonel Langford to explain expenditures of materials from Norillian armories. These false reports covered his wholesale theft of the same items, like brimstone and firestones that he sold to colonists, enriching himself.

Vlad swung into his black gelding's saddle. "You'll find, Colonel Rathfield, that the only way you'll see the Shedashee is if they want you to see them. Owen's pistol is just to frighten off any predator we might encounter."

The Norillian chuckled. "Surely we have nothing to fear from animals."

Owen led the way back along Generosity, then turned west on Kindness. "Not much to fear, really. The wolves mostly have gone back up-country. Bears are heading into the mountains. We're too far north for axebeaks." Owen shot a sidelong glance at the Prince. "I don't recall many signs of a jeopard this winter."

Vlad shrugged. "One rarely sees a jeopard before it's too late."

"True."

Rathfield looked from one man to the other and back again. "I do believe you are having me on. Wolves? Jeopards? You've made them up to frighten visitors. You'll find I do not frighten easily."

Vlad shot a quick salute to the sentries at Westgate. "I assure you, Colonel, we would not attempt to frighten a man of your obvious bravery. However, wolves are far from extinct here in Mystria. In fact, they appear to be considerably larger than the variety that has been hunted out in Norisle. And they do exist. The winter of '65, just like that of '63, came on quickly and very harshly. We had wolves at the doorstep. Captain Strake and his wife were staying with me until their home was built. On the very night his daughter was born, he killed three dire wolves."

Owen nodded. "Shot two, killed the last with an ax."

"Really?" Rathfield studied Owen a bit more intently for a moment. "And jeopards?"

"Biggest cat you'll ever see, Colonel. Long curved fangs, very sharp claws. Brown or grey in the summer, winter coat grows in thick and white. Big enough to take one of these horses down, and fast enough in a sprint to catch it." Owen patted the pistol. "Not very fond of loud noises, which is why I keep this with me."

"I see."

Vlad laughed. "Not likely. Nor will you hear it, save screaming in the distance. If it's close, you might smell it."

As they rode west along the Bounty Trail, Owen tried looking at it with the same eyes as Colonel Rathfield. Things had already changed significantly in the four years since the first time Owen had made the same ride. More houses had been raised, more land cleared, and stone bridges had been built over a few streams. Still, to Norillian eyes, the place would seem largely wild and sparsely populated.

For Owen it remained a land that surprised and delighted him. Going on an expedition thrilled him, and not just for it getting him away from his wife. Mystria had so many wonders and secrets that he wished to see. The whisper of wind through pines, the lonely call of loons in the night, the scent of a field of bright daisies, and even the chill of seeing where a jeopard had sharpened its claws on a tree made him smile. He'd spent too long on his estate and in town—he needed to get back to the land he loved. That this might be an opportunity to save it from Crown foolishness only made the expedition that much better.

As they rode, Prince Vlad played host and guide, pointing out the natural features and commenting on interesting tidbits his researches had discovered about a variety of the plants. "Of course, Colonel, for your expedition, I shall prepare you a list of plants and animals of which, if you are able, I should be most pleased to have samples."

"A jeopard among them?"

"We have one, but more are welcome." The Prince smiled. "And we mounted the wolves Captain Strake killed. I'd be delighted to show them to you. They are in my laboratory."

"It would be an honor, Highness."

You have no idea. Owen watched Rathfield from the corner of his eye. The man looked at the landscape much as Owen had, judging it by its suitability for waging war. He'd been told that two companies of men would be slow, and he measured that claim against everything he saw. Initially he discounted that idea, but as the forest closed around the trail, and the trail wound itself uphill and down, his assessment shifted. His concentration suggested he was compiling recommendations that would allow him to fulfill his mission.

Owen found that particular idea unsettling. Having been raised in Norisle, he found himself more reluctant than most Mystrians to ascribe hostile motives to the Crown. Still, when he'd come this way looking to move troops along, it was to bring a war to Tharyngian forces. Rathfield intended the same thing, but that the troops be used against Mystrians.

And yet, four years ago, I would have accepted that same mission. Now the idea of doing that sent a shiver down Owen's spine. Unbidden came the memory of his uncle asking him to pass along the true identity of the writer known as Samuel Haste. Owen harbored no illusions that the request was born simply of his uncle's idle curiosity.

Just because Owen wasn't automatically inclined to think badly of the Norillian court, it didn't mean he didn't understand why others did. Just a year previously, Parliament had passed the document tax, which not only imposed a duty on imported paper, but also required payment for any transaction involving papers—from the production of a Will to the printing of the *Frost Weekly Gazette*. Mystrians flat refused to pay it and sent the Queen a petition of protest on a sheepskin. Tax collectors—locals who had hired on for a portion of the taxes collected—got run out of town and had their businesses boycotted. Before the petition reached Launston, the document tax had died.

Three months after news of the tax had reached Mystria, reports of its repeal arrived from Norisle. The bill repealing the tax had been greeted happily, but men like Caleb Frost and his father carefully pointed out that the bill affirmed the right of Parliament to impose future taxes on the Crown's citizens no matter where they lived.

Most Mystrians dismissed that idea saying, "I'll be paying ole Queen Mags when she comes to me with her hand out." They assumed the ocean insulated them from her wrath, but Colonel Rathfield's presence suggested otherwise. *How long until refusal to pay taxes is seen as sedition?*

Rathfield rode ahead and, for a heartbeat, unbridled fury raced through Owen. What if Rathfield *was* a precursor? What if the information he'd gather would convince the Queen to send troops to Mystria? *If I knew it would, if I knew that was his intention, what would I do?*

He glanced at the pistol. Mystria was a vast place, full of all manner of dangers. Would leaving a man in an unmarked grave be so hideous a sin if it saved countless lives?

Owen shivered, and hoped he would never have to answer that question.

CHAPTER FOUR

27 March 1767
Prince Haven,
Temperance Bay, Mystria

P rince Vlad bid his traveling companions farewell at the drive leading to Owen's home, then continued on the extra two miles to his estate. He scribbled notes about how far the snow had receded on the southern side of hills versus the northern into his notebook, and looked for anything else remarkable. He was certain there were things, but the import of Colonel Rathfield's arrival distracted him.

Since the founding of the colonies, Norisle had treated Mystria with benign neglect. The Colonists paid duties and tariffs, accepting them as part of doing business with their mother country. Mystrians made few demands on Norisle and because most of the Norillian nobility saw the Mystrians as criminals and cowards, they certainly would never allow themselves to think they might actually need them.

The long and expensive war with Tharyngia had changed things. Norisle had, effectively, bankrupted itself prosecuting the war and, after ten long years, ended up with some of Tharyngia's holdings in the new world. While the Spice Island acquisitions were immediately lucrative and New Tharyngia was an untapped resource, neither was sufficient to staunch the economic wounds suffered from the war.

The imposition of the document tax heightened tensions and built resentment. Mystrians didn't believe the Crown had any right to tax their internal affairs—a position which, to the Crown, made Mystrians once again sound like criminals and rebels. Couple with that the antics of men like Lord Rivendell claiming credit for a victory against the Tharyngians in Mystria, and the Mystrians were feeling unappreciated and abused.

Sending Ian Rathfield to conduct a mission into the interior to bring unruly subjects back into the fold would not be taken well. People had fled to Mystria to avoid Norillian oppression or seek freedom. And they moved into the interior of Mystria to avoid further oppression or seek freedom from the coastal society. Rathfield would be lucky if those people acknowledged his existence, much less were impressed by his status as a hero. They certainly weren't going to reverse life decisions based on his say-so alone.

Vlad turned down the roadway to his home and smiled. Baker, the wurmwright, was up on a tall berm, forking hay from a hayrick into a large, round enclosure with ten-foot-high, sheer sides on the interior. The wurmwright waved, then turned back to his task.

The Prince returned the wave and rode over, dismounting and letting his horse nibble hay. He climbed up the berm, his smile growing. "He looks content."

"He does, Highness. Weathers the cold right nice, but seems to like a bit of warmth."

Below them the wooly rhinoceros named Peregrine happily grazed on hay. Over fourteen feet long, and half that high at the shoulder, the beast appeared placid and even uncaring about his being watched. Thick brown fur covered his forelimbs and aft but was darker on his chest and abdomen. A single horn nearly two and a half feet in length curved up from his nose.

In the year and a half since Peregrine had been bestowed upon him, Prince Vlad had spent a great deal of time studying the beast. In many ways the wooly rhinoceros struck him as being a perfect heraldic animal for Mystria. Largely docile, but very industrious, capable of fierce fighting and with a preference for being left alone, Peregrine reminded him of many a Mystrian. The fact that the creature was very short-sighted and ignorant of politics reinforced the impression. Which was not to say that he found either to be stupid.

The most curious thing he'd learned about the rhinoceros was discovered completely by chance. Peregrine's enclosure required mucking out from time to time, but the beast was reluctant to allow anyone in to do the job. One of the stable boys had gone straight from helping clean out Mugwump's pit, and had been thoroughly splashed with wurm mud. As the boy approached Peregrine's enclosure, he expected the beast to charge at him. Instead, the rhino trotted over, nose high, nostrils flared, then reacted much as a puppy might. Given his gigantic size, this proved problematic in other ways, but was an amazing discovery nonetheless.

The Prince himself had experimented using soiled clothes and found that Peregrine appeared quite happy to be around people smelling of wurm mud. When they deposited wurm mud in the rhino enclosure, Peregrine was more than happy to roll around in it. Wearing just a pinch of dried wurm mud in a sachet around the neck was enough to calm the beast and a number of discussions had covered whether or not Peregrine could be ridden. Most agreed it was possible, but no one volunteered to be first.

When the Prince had brought Mugwump to the enclosure, neither beast showed much of an interest in the other, akin to the way that cattle and sheep could graze in the same field without difficulty. Prince Vlad had yet to work out the significance of that discovery, but this was because he had other distractions to deal with at home. With them in mind, he patted Baker on the shoulder, remounted his horse, and continued the ride to his home.

Prince Haven consisted of a large, rectangular main house with two wings, one at each end, which extended south toward the river. The easternmost one had originally been his laboratory prior to his marriage. He raised a new, larger laboratory further to the east, back behind the barn, and had converted that wing into rooms for his children, his wife's servants, and a day room for his wife.

Opposite the new laboratory, down by the Benjamin River, lay the wurmrest. Up the lawn from it, a storage building had been added for canoes and other watercraft, as well as some half-built experiments too large for his laboratory.

Prince Vlad tossed the reins to a stable boy and entered his house. It remained one of the largest homes in the colonies, and one of the finest, but it paled in comparison to the refinements of a palatial estate in Norisle or on the Continent. The daub-and-wattle walls lacked murals or gilt-edged mirrors, but the warmth of wooden floors and exposed beams and posts provided an atmosphere that he loved, even though Norillians would dismiss it as rustic. The furnishings had all been crafted locally, as evidenced by their sturdy, blocky nature. He'd made the table in the dining room himself and his bed. The other items he'd purchased in Temperance.

His reasons had been simple: he saw no virtue in paying ridiculous prices for spindly chairs from far away that would break easily when perfectly good work could be had nearby. Men who had visited—and many of the survivors from the Anvil Lake expedition had visited down through the years—took it as a sign that he'd rejected fancy notions from Norisle. Prince Vlad feared that some of his aunt's advisors might well believe the same.

Princess Gisella had changed some of that perception. She added things here and there—a picture on a wall, a tea service, seasonal decorations—which transformed his dark and masculine domain. He'd never seen the need for such before, since he mostly spent his time in the laboratory. Having a wife and family drew him out from what Gisella lovingly called his "Cavern of Science" and into their home.

The door had barely closed behind him when a squealing peal of laughter started from the east. He darted forward into the corridor running the width of the house and scooped up his son. The boy, his blue eyes shining, giggled even more loudly, reaching out to his father. Soaking wet and utterly naked, Richard steamed in the cool air.

Tucking his son under his arm, Vlad waved off the serving girl bearing a towel. "It's fine, Madeline. I'll take him back."

"Yes, Highness."

Vlad looked down at his son. "Aren't you cold?"

"Birdie, birdie, birdie." The boy pointed off somewhere. "Birdie."

"What kind?"

"Red." His eyes widened. "With *feathers*. Feathers. Feathers."

"Red with feathers, very good."

He entered the bathing room and held his son upside down by the ankles, eliciting a delighted shriek. Madeline followed through the door and took the boy from the Prince. She drew the boy to the side and toweled him off. The way he squirmed suggested that getting him into clothes would be an epic battle.

He crossed to where his wife sat, holding their six-month-old daughter to her breast. He leaned down and kissed Gisella on the top of her head. "You are the two most beautiful women in Mystria."

She looked up, her blue eyes focusing, her smile broadening. "I did not expect you back so soon. This is wonderful."

"I hope." He dropped to a knee and caressed Rowena's cheek with a finger. "She'll look just like you, which is a blessing."

"I care only that she is as brilliant as you, my darling."

"If our children combine our brilliance, we are truly in trouble." He kissed his wife on the cheek, then stood. "I take it 'feathers' is our new word for the day?"

"Yes, he was collecting them earlier, clutching them in his hands, and trying to fly."

"I'll make certain there's no access to the roofs." Vlad shook his head. "I do have some news from town. We are going to have guests for dinner. Captain Strake, his wife, and Colonel Ian Rathfield."

Gisella looked up, surprise widening her blue eyes. "The hero of Rondeville? He's here? Why?"

"Purportedly on a similar mission to Owen's, but of much greater potential trouble." Vlad sighed wearily. "At least with Owen there was a very distinct threat, a very visible enemy. Rathfield has been sent out to see how far west colonists have gotten, with an eye toward returning with them to chartered colonies."

Gisella stroked Rowena's brow. "It will be a long expedition. You'll send Owen and Nathaniel. Will you be joining them?"

"No."

"But you would like to." She smiled openly. "No, Vladimir, do not protest to the contrary. The man I love loves this land very much, and wishes to know more about it. You would gladly head west with the least bit of provocation. I only wish I could go with you."

He laughed lightly, then frowned. "I will make you a promise, beloved, that we shall go west. We, together, will see sights no other human beings have seen. The only thing I love more than this land and our children is you, and I can think of no greater joy than sharing Mystria's wonders with you."

"Then you will go on this expedition."

He shook his head. "Were it possible, perhaps, but it is not. The Temperance Bay Colonial assembly will be meeting come May, and I need to be here to support the cooler heads among then. I've already had petitions from other legislatures requesting things from the Crown."

"And there is training."

He smiled back over his shoulder at his son who was struggling mightily to get back out of his clothes. "There is that, too. My uncle, his namesake, was said to be able to read at three."

"That's not what I meant, husband."

He nodded. "Yes, there will be the spring militia muster, and I need to be here for that. 'Twould be good if Nathaniel was here as well, of course."

Gisella reached up and tugged his shirt once, sharply. "My dearest love, our children you will *educate*. Soldiers you will *drill*. Mugwump requires *training*."

"I am sorry, my dear. I'll pay more attention to semantics in future. Yes, Mugwump does need *training*." Vlad smiled to himself. In many ways the wurm—despite his having wings, Vlad had studiously avoided calling Mugwump a dragon—resembled Richard in terms of energy and determination to go exploring. The successful molt had imbued the wurm with a puppyish sense of wonder about the world. This included wing-assisted flying hops, which clearly presaged full flight, but growth of the wings had not caught up with the body, making the short flights end prematurely and somewhat comically.

"I am going to ask Count von Metternin to travel west. He will be able to mediate between Colonel Rathfield and the others."

"Will you invite him to dinner this evening?"

Vlad thought for a moment, then shook his head. "I'd rather have a chance to brief your countryman before he meets Rathfield. I'll have to go over documents from Launston before I can do that."

His wife nodded, then handed him their daughter before adjusting her gown and standing. "Will you want Catherine Strake and me involved in any discussions?"

He cradled Rowena in his left arm, then reached up and stroked his wife's cheek. "I would welcome your insight, beloved, but I fear her reaction. Owen *must* go, but that means that she cannot sail back to Norisle this year. The girl is too young to make the voyage."

Gisella kissed his hand. "I would gladly keep Miranda here, if it would grant Catherine the chance to leave."

"I can't imagine she would abandon her child." Vlad wasn't sure if he was saying that because he thought Catherine loved the child, or because she was aware that no matter how disagreeable her position in Mystria, deserting her husband and child would hold her up to the sort of social ridicule that she hated. *She is ruled by her own ambition and the judgment of others. She is caught within miseries of her own making.*

"I think you're right about her, dearest. Regardless, I shall arrange for us to be able to take tea and work at needlepoint while you discuss substantive matters." Gisella smiled. "Perhaps it will be a good night for her and she can contribute. She can be quite clever."

"I would tell you that I will make it up to you if she is in a mood, but I'm not certain that is within my power."

"We'll keep her glass full during dinner, and ply her with port afterward." His wife's eyes twinkled. "She is not the only clever one here."

"Oh, how well I know that." Vlad kissed her again, then handed her their daughter. "The people of Mystria do not know how much they owe to you. You keep me sane."

"No, darling, I just let you be you." Reaching up, she squeezed his shoulder as she slipped past. "And you being you is what will be their salvation."

CHAPTER FIVE

27 March 1767
Strake House,
Temperance Bay, Mystria

Owen waited for Prince Vlad to fade from view before turning his horse down the drive to Strake House. Rathfield said nothing while they waited. Owen expected him to fall in for the short ride to the house, but the Norillian officer remained where he was. Owen reined about again. "Is there something you wish to say, Colonel?"

Rathfield squared his shoulders. "There are a few things I do think you should know, Mr. Strake."

"I may have resigned my commission, Colonel, but were we in Norisle, you would still afford me the courtesy of addressing me by rank." Owen's eyes tightened. "And, for the record, I currently hold the rank of Captain in the Mystrian Rangers."

"I was aware of that, sir, and wished to avoid the embarrassment of reminding you how far you had fallen." Rathfield snorted. "I understand why you might have resigned your commission. Were I in your position, I might well have done so myself. I would have respected that. But to so thoroughly and scurrilously besmirch the reputation of a well-respected commander who snatched victory from the jaws of defeat at Anvil Lake; that, sir, is an offense which cannot be forgiven."

Owen arched an eyebrow. "By what account, save for any fantasy which Lord Rivendell wrote up and submitted to Horse Guards himself, do you mark Rivendell as being respected or the victor at Anvil Lake? Have you read my account of the battle, or only Wattling's fantasy based upon it? Have you had private correspondence from soldiers who were there and thoroughly embarrassed by their failure, or have you some more objective account? Perhaps you've read Laureate du Malphias' account of the battle."

"Do not think me a fool, Strake. I've read Wattling's book, and I can read between the lines. I know John Rivendell is not a genius, but I also know it was a matter of numbers. Victory was inevitable."

Owen drew in a breath slowly and forced himself to tamp down his rising anger. Though born of a Mystrian father, he had been raised in Norisle on his stepfather's family estate. He had faced the Norillian prejudices that came with his obviously Mystrian surname. In the Tharyngian War he'd seen Mystrian soldiers go toe-to-toe with the best Ryngian forces in the field, yet the loss of battles were blamed on them. And the battle of Anvil Lake had been one in which Prince Vlad had led Mystrian troops to rout Ryngian forces, yet Lord Rivendell and his Norillian troops claimed the victory for their own.

"Colonel, you may think that numbers made victory inevitable, but history is rife with examples where a handful of men have fought and successfully defied the might of empires. You judge Mystrian troops and their performance based on stories told by those who have a vested interest in denying how good Mystrian troops really are. Rivendell may claim the victory at Anvil Lake, but he never mentions the taking of Fort Cuivre by an inferior Mystrian force."

Owen held a hand up to forestall a comment. "More to your point: yes, I dared tell the truth about Anvil Lake. I told it for one specific reason—had Rivendell listened to his advisors, he would have lost far fewer men. You've been in combat, Colonel. You know the horrors of men torn asunder. Is not saving their lives worth exposing incompetence?"

"You forget yourself, Strake." Rathfield shook his head slowly, as if speaking to an idiot child. "The decisions to promote or remove an officer are made by Generals, not subordinate officers. If they chose to leave Lord Rivendell in place, this is their right. And those men in the ranks sign up fully aware of the risks their duty to the Crown entails. They march into battle proud of their service. You suggest they are cowards."

Owen laughed. "No, sir, I suggest they are a limited resource and should be preserved." Guy du Malphias had realized this very thing. Because Tharyngia's colonies in the new world had fewer people than Norisle's colonies, New Tharyngia was doomed. To even things up he had created the *pasmortes*—reanimated corpses that, depending on their level of decay, could serve as everything from slave labor to skilled, autonomous agents. The fortress at Anvil Lake had been packed with them, and killing them was no simple thing. Had Prince Vlad not intervened to turn the tide of battle, the Norillian troops that had been sent to destroy the fortress would have become its new generation of defenders.

"You speak like a merchant, sir, not a soldier—a tradesman devoid of honor."

"Perhaps it is because I think more of war as a trade than an honor."

"That trade would have included following orders, I believe."

Owen nodded. Rathfield's lips were moving, but Owen heard his uncle's words coming out of his mouth. Richard Ventnor, Duke Deathridge, had ordered Owen to secure all of du Malphias' papers from Anvil Lake. Owen had recovered them, but had not turned them over to his uncle. He'd been certain that the papers included the secrets of raising the dead. That was not information Owen wanted to see in his uncle's hands.

"You refer to the recovery of du Malphias' papers, I believe. My uncle knows I found them and immediately turned them over to the Crown. It was my assumption then, and yet is, that Prince Vlad would make them available to Norillian authorities as soon as possible." Owen shrugged. "Or did I misinterpret what my uncle requested of me?"

"I would hardly know your uncle's mind."

"But you've spoken to him more recently than I."

"True. I sought him out when I was given this assignment." Rathfield tapped a gloved finger against his chin. "He suggested that you had forgotten that duty to family is exceedingly important."

"I could take that as a suborning of treason."

"Your uncle?" Rathfield threw his head back in a genuine laugh. "My dear boy, you have no idea how far he has risen, do you? Because of his victory on the Continent, the Queen trusts him most highly. He is her right-hand man on all things international."

Owen stroked a hand along his jaw. Not knowing his uncle as well as Owen did, Rathfield likely believed that the Crown was simply considering Mystria as part of the empire and, therefore, warding it against external predation. Owen could see a deeper game. While learning the magick that created *pasmortes* would be a powerful thing to use against Tharyngia, likewise it would be a splendid tool a man could use to carve his own empire out of Mystria. Du Malphias had intended to do that, and Owen could see his uncle using the same opportunity.

My having given the documents to Prince Vlad would be seen as a step toward independence for Mystria if the Queen no longer trusted her nephew. Owen forced himself to smile. "I'm pleased to hear my uncle is doing so well. My choice was the expedient one and, truly, the only one possible. The papers would have to be copied here to prevent their being lost in transit to Norisle. Who better to trust with that job?"

"You may have a point, but the Prince's lack of alacrity is the cause for some concern."

"Would you like me to mention this to the Prince?"

"You shouldn't bother him with it. I believe he has had correspondence from the court as regards it."

So, the answer is yes, *but you don't want to admit to it.* Owen leaned forward in the saddle, both hands on the horn. "Is there anything else you wished to address before you enjoy the hospitality of my home?"

"I would not address it, save that you seem to have adopted the frighteningly annoying custom of Mystrians to be abrupt, inappropriate, and direct. The fact of the matter is simple, Strake: you're not truly of my class and you've risen well above what ought to be your station. I say this with all due respect to your mother and her fine lineage. Blood will out, and your Mystrian blood is telling in you. This expedition is at the behest of the Crown. I am in command. Things will be done as I direct, when I direct them, and I shall tolerate no insubordination. I will hold you to a higher standard than any of the Mystrian miscreants with whom I am saddled. Are we clear on this?"

Owen could not help himself. He began to laugh.

Rathfield stiffened. "You have been warned, Strake."

Owen stopped laughing, but his smile would not die. "Understand something, Colonel. The Crown's authority extends only in so far as you can enforce it. Here in Temperance Bay or Bounty or south—that's pretty far. Two days' ride from here there are whole villages populated by people who've never seen Norisle and who think the Queen is something out of a faery story. When we get further out, you'll see places where there aren't many people, and where the only law is Nature's law. You think Mystrians won't care about the Crown? Jeopards and wolves will care even less."

Owen straightened up in the saddle and opened his hands. "As for your holding me to a high standard, understand what that means. You can write me up in reports and say bad things, but everyone will expect that. If you try to flog me—flog any of us—it won't be tolerated. If you choose to demand satisfaction of me, I'll decline as the Prince doesn't favor dueling. Others who will be joining us, however, have different opinions, and they're a lot deadlier than I am.

"So, Colonel, your being here is pretty much like your being in Rondeville. You're on your own. How you best decide to proceed is up to you."

Rathfield considered for a moment, and then nodded. "I see. I will take your words under advisement, though I warn you that I meant what I said."

"I understand that."

"Good. As long as we understand each other, I believe we can work together." Rathfield pointed south. "Shall we?"

"By all means." Owen gave his horse a touch of the heel. "Welcome to my home."

The drive to Strake House snaked through woods, which had been thinned of larger trees. The road worked its way around hills simply because that had been less expensive than digging through them—and level roads were more practical in the winter when the snow came. The serpentine track opened onto a wide lot with a barn on the left, smoke-house to the right, and the main house in the middle. Beyond the main house, down by the Benjamin River, stood a small boathouse and dock.

"I know it's not much, but…"

"It is impressive."

The main house had been built on a stone foundation. They'd excavated down to bedrock, which gave the house an eight-foot-high cellar for food storage in winter. The rectangular building rose to two stories, with chimneys at either end and fireplaces sufficient to heat four upstairs bedrooms. The pitched roof hid an attic. The main floor boasted a kitchen toward the back on the right side, a dining room to the front on that side, a sewing room back left, and a library and parlor left front. Stones finished the corners, but clapboards otherwise covered the house, and the roof had been done in cedar shingles.

Owen snuck a look at Rathfield's face and suppressed a smile. In Norisle, even a man with Rathfield's money could barely have afforded a house such as that. Because Mystria had so much land and so many resources abundantly available, the construction had cost a fraction of what it might have in Norisle. Owen could afford to build a house that was much larger than the equivalent in Norisle, and in Norisle would have had to be a minor noble to afford an estate that size.

As they rode toward the stables, James the stable boy emerged to take their horses. The two men dusted themselves off. Before they could reach the front door, however, it opened a crack, then a little, black-haired girl with bright hazel eyes slipped through. Giggling gaily, she ran toward her father, hands extended, then stopped and looked up at Rathfield.

Her smile died and her hands disappeared behind her back.

Owen scooped her up and kissed her cheek. "Colonel Rathfield, this is my daughter, Miranda."

Rathfield drew off his hat with a flourish and bowed solemnly—a bit of playful whimsy that Owen would never have credited as possible. "Pleased to make your acquaintance, Miranda."

The beautiful little girl stared at him wide-eyed for a moment, then buried her face against her father's neck. Owen shook his head. "She tends to be shy around strangers. Normally she is quite happy and talks all the time."

The main house door opened and a woman appeared, though she still faced back into the house. "Let that happen again, Agnes, and I shall get the strop!" She turned, looking over the yard for her daughter—there was no mistaking the resemblance in the nose and the chin—then she stopped. "Owen, I hadn't…"

"We have a visitor. Colonel Ian Rathfield, may I present my wife, Catherine."

Catherine stiffened, then pressed her brown hair into place and straightened her dress. "Please forgive me, Colonel."

Rathfield took her hand and raised it to his lips. "My pleasure, Madame."

Catherine covered that hand with her other, then her brown eyes narrowed. "Are you? Yes, your uniform, the Fifth Northland Cavalry. You're Ian Rathfield, the hero of Rondeville."

"You are very kind, Madame."

"Catherine, you must call me Catherine, Colonel."

Owen watched his wife transform herself into the woman of the manner, with a small hint of the flirtatiousness he'd enjoyed when they first met. He'd not seen it in so long, it surprised him that it still existed. He found her a bit silly, but dared not laugh, and welcomed the change.

Catherine raised a hand to tuck a stray lock of brown hair away." It will be an honor to have you here. How long will you be staying?"

"I shall do my best not to inconvenience you for long, Catherine. I hope to take rooms in Temperance soon enough." Rathfield smiled. "I've been sent by the Crown for a specific mission. I am afraid, however, I shall have to take your husband with me. I hope you won't mind."

Her eyes flashed. "Not at all. I live to serve the Crown."

"It's good to hear that in the Colonies, Catherine."

Owen looked at his wife. "The Prince has invited us to dine with him this evening. Hodge will be up with the Colonel's things. I imagine we will head out inside the fortnight."

Miranda clutched his neck. "No, Daddy, don't go!"

Owen rubbed her back and kissed her head. "It will be okay, Miranda. I'll be back before you know it."

"I get scared."

"I know, honey. More nightmares?"

Catherine folded her arms across her chest. "Yes, during her nap. The shadows in the woods are back."

Rathfield smiled. "I'm certain there is nothing to fear out there, Miranda."

The little girl hid her face against her father's neck again and shivered. *Oh, Colonel, you have no idea what lurks out there in the woods.* Owen nodded. "You're probably right, Colonel. But, for now, no shadows, Miranda. Just friends—friends from far away."

CHAPTER SIX

27 March 1767
Prince Haven,
Temperance Bay, Mystria

Prince Vlad retreated to his laboratory to open the packet from his father. When he'd built the new laboratory, he'd started with a barn so he had a massive open room that featured two lofts. The main floor contained his desk and drafting tables, dissection tables, closets for maps, charts, and equipment, and the largest or most recent of his specimens from around Mystria. The first loft had been ringed with bookshelves, which he had filled almost halfway with volumes from all over the world. A smaller bookshelf near his desk contained books he needed for current study, and piles of books supplemented its capacity. The highest loft, which he referred to as the attic, had a pulley and winch system on the main roof beam to help haul heavier items into the darkness. He'd thought he might store seasonal things there, like canoes, but he couldn't fit them through the lower door and hadn't yet opened a wall that high.

He sat at his desk, and turned up the wick on a lamp. He pinched the wick much as he might do to snuff a flame, then invoked a spell, and pulled his hand back. The wick caught quickly and burned yellow-gold. The spell—a variation of that used to ignite brimstone in the breech of a gun—was common enough, but those who could not use magick were often wary of those who did, so the Prince did not indulge himself over much.

Vlad turned the packet over and took a good look at the red wax seal. It bore the mark of his father's ring, but he'd long suspected that the Queen had had the ring duplicated so she could read their correspondence. The outer packet showed no sign of tampering. Had agents softened the wax and scraped beneath the seal, the paper would be discolored around the seal itself. This did not surprise Vlad, since he doubted his father had packed the letters up anyway.

The packet contained four letters, each folded, sealed, addressed, and dated. Vlad laid them out in order, then looked again at each seal. These *did* show signs of tampering. A heated knife blade had been slid under the flap and used to lift the seal, then a drop of wax had been applied to reseal the letter later. Those doing the reading, however, had no way of knowing how much information the seal itself provided.

Around the edge of the seal ten symbols had been inscribed, appearing there similarly to the way numbers would have been displayed on the face of a clock. The symbols were astrological in origin, but only represented numbers. The number that stood on a line drawn vertically from the top of the letter to the bottom gave Vlad the cipher offset. A line drawn at right angles to that line at the level of the flap's point would intersect two symbols. Their values would provide the word offset.

In the case of the first letter he examined, the cipher offset was a four. He took a clean piece of paper and drew a five-by-five grid. He put the numbers zero through four across the top and five through nine down the left side. Then beginning with the fourth letter, D, he filled in the grid. He finished with the letter C, which also substituted freely for the letter K. This provided him the first key for the cipher.

The word offset value came to eight. This meant every eighth word would contain the hidden message from his father—if there was one. If the date on the letter's interior matched that of the outside, there was no message. The first two messages and the last had dates which matched, and Vlad chose to read them first.

They were as many of his father's messages: encouraging and positive, but not in the manner of a man advising his son. They came more in the style of a priest advising a parishioner in a difficult time. Vlad, who had not seen his father in over a quarter century, had come to expect such missives. Still, it bothered him that his father remained distant even when Vlad shared details about the man's grandchildren.

Then again, he is always guarded.

He had to be. Prince John had never been suited to the throne, and had willingly entered a monastery in his youth. When it became apparent that King Richard was unable to father children, John was recalled from the monastery, married to a Princess of Strana, and sent to Mystria to act as Governor-General. Vlad suspected this was less to teach his father to govern than it was to keep him free of court intrigues. When Richard died in 1740 while campaigning in Tharyngia, Margaret—the youngest of the three siblings—assumed the throne and sent for John. He returned to Norisle, abdicated in her favor, and again entered the monastery.

And Vlad, at the age of twenty-four, was made Governor-General in his place.

These letters, as with many others, amounted to sermons on the virtue of service to the Crown. While suspicious men might think John wrote them to disguise a loathing for the woman who usurped his rightful place, Vlad was convinced of their sincerity. His father would have ruled had he been forced to, but he truly welcomed a chance to return to the monastery where he could resume his theological studies. Moreover, the fact that the Queen had produced five children, all of whom had lived to adulthood, meant that Vlad would be saved the burden of ruling. That fact made Prince John—whom many referred to as Saint John—very happy.

The third letter contained a hidden message, so he refigured the keys and began to coax information out of the note. He picked out the words involved in the code, then broke them down, letter by letter, replacing them with the numbers from the key. Each word produced a three-number combination which corresponded to the page, paragraph, and word in a particular book. His father's choices were limited, and after a couple of test runs, Vlad realized that *A Treatise on Magick* was the volume his father had chosen. The resulting note, while not wholly grammatical, managed to convey its intent.

"Sun, no word of dead walking. Proof required. Ranged magick whispers. Church rules black art. Eye shall learn more as directed. Instructions required."

Vlad's flesh puckered as he read. The message confirmed two things, and neither of them brought him joy. The first was that the code he shared with his father was compromised and that this third letter, though written in his father's hand, had been composed and dictated by others. While the covering message matched his father for style, the coded message did not. His father was a passive being. He would have urged caution. Use of the word *required* wouldn't occur to his father, neither would making a strong declaration as he did with *Eye shall learn more*. The request for direction was a clear solicitation of treason. The warning about the Church's opinion about ranged magick would have been couched in terms of his beseeching Vlad to return to the ways of the Church.

The warning confirmed hunches Vlad had harbored of a conspiracy so monumental that it forced him to see the world in an entirely new but hardly flattering light. His researches, including the study of the du Malphias papers, confirmed what he'd have dismissed as insanity had another tried to convince him of its veracity.

Until the advent of brimstone and guns, magick had been severely limited and of little power. Because magick could only work by touch, and because iron and steel completely deadened magick, a man armed with a sword could easily kill a witch, warlock, or sorcerer no matter how powerful. Magick would have been rooted out of the Auropean population entirely down through the years, save that most who revealed talent—oddly enough referred to as "the curse"—exiled themselves to the fringes of society and did their best to appease those inclined to dislike them. The Church, while condemning the sin, bestowed charity upon the sinners and invited back into their ranks those who promised to refrain from using magick.

Once brimstone had made magick useful in the theatre of war, the Church reinterpreted certain teachings, and then condoned the use of magick. Most people who could use it were not terribly powerful, and magick use had its price. The Prince's indulging himself in lighting the lamp through a spell would raise a little blood beneath his thumbnail. When he'd fought at Anvil Lake, he'd been black and blue to the elbows because of his efforts.

But then, he was of royal blood. It seemed to him rather curious that within a generation of the Church sanctioning the use of magick, all the royal houses of Auropa revealed strains of strong magick use among their scions. Soldiers were ranked by how many shots they could get off before exhausting their magickal ability. Most were twos or threes, yet the majority of nobles ranked five and above.

Marry all that to the fact that the miracles performed by saints in service to the Church could be duplicated by spells, and add in the fact that the Church often accepted into its ranks the lesser sons and daughters of nobility, and it suggested that the Church had, down through the centuries, secretly enshrined magick and preserved it. A case could be made for their having used it to influence world events.

While a prisoner of Guy du Malphias, Owen Strake had witnessed the Tharyngian Laureate using magick in a manner that did not require direct contact. The Shedashee Mystrian natives likewise did things with magick that appeared to circumvent the need for direct touch. Du Malphias had told Owen that when the Tharyngian Revolution overthrew the King and destroyed the Church's power in Tharyngia, they uncovered evidence of the Church's conspiracy.

Vlad might have considered that all fanciful save for a few chance comments his Norillian magick tutors had made. He'd begun instruction at the age of eight and progressed quickly. He'd been a keen learner and having inherited his father's studiousness helped him greatly. His tutors had praised him lavishly for his abilities and hinted at his being able to work great magicks. And then, when he turned ten, those tutors departed for Norisle, and the others sent out were neither so enthusiastic nor intelligent. Vlad already knew more than they did, so they remained for a year, declared him hopeless, and left Mystria.

Vlad had always consigned his memories of the first tutors to fantasy. Even when he noted that their recall coincided with the birth of his cousin, Edward, he'd not suspected anything sinister in it. But with evidence that greater magicks existed and the knowledge that the Church and Crown both had a vested interest in keeping them secret, he began to wonder. He began to question his father about things, gently, and the directness of the replies had kindled one other memory.

It had been back when Vlad was twenty-three and just returned from what the family referred to as his pirate adventure. He'd awakened one evening and found his father pacing in the library of their home in Fairlee. John would walk, then try to write something, get up to walk again, then sit to write. Vlad watched him, then just took up his father's place at the desk and told him to dictate.

The resulting message, though lacking in specifics, was his father at his most direct. The letter was to his brother, King Richard. John urged him to abandon his foolish quest. He predicted dire consequences for them all if Richard persisted. He begged his brother to reconsider and refused to tell Vlad what it was all about. "For your own good, Vlad, you should forget this evening."

And so I would have if they had not chosen to use you against me, Father. To engage Vlad through his father, someone hoped to trap him into revealing a plot against either the Church or the Crown—perhaps both. His inquiries, however, had not involved politics and certainly were within the bounds of normal curiosity. To someone who had something to hide, however, even the most innocent question invited suspicion, and his father might be an unwitting dupe in the entire plot.

At another time, in another place, Vlad might not have cared at all about the plot. After all, weren't the nobility proven superior to the common man? Were they not ordained by God to rule? That was certainly what the Church taught—which was quite a trick if the Church and nobility were an oligarchy of magicians. If they were not the best, would not God strike them down?

Vlad would have accepted that as the truth, and likely taken his place among them, save for his time in Mystria. The colonists had been the dregs of society, cast onto a far shore to live or die. They didn't die; they thrived. They created a vibrant society that encouraged free thinking and exploration. Their energy created an economy that kept Mystria alive. At Anvil Lake they proved themselves the equal of Norillian troops in terms of courage, and perhaps just a little bit better in terms of warfare in the New World.

Isn't that proof that they are the better men?

A hand tapped lightly on his door, bringing him out of his thoughts. "Yes, beloved."

"Your guests, darling, have arrived." Gisella came to his desk, picked up a brush, and removed the dust from his coat. "Your good shoes are just inside the house. I think you will be fine otherwise."

"Owen's wife?"

Gisella smiled and gave her husband a quick kiss. "In Colonel Rathfield, she has a distraction. I gather he is willing to indulge her taste for court gossip."

"I'm sure."

She stepped back, eying him carefully. "Out with it."

Vlad laughed. "Forgive me. I grow suspicious in my old age."

"You are not old." She playfully threatened him with the brush. "What are you thinking?"

"I am thinking that Colonel Rathfield is here to observe more than the land to the west. If anything amiss is said about my aunt, he'll relay it to her. Likewise any news about Owen will reach his uncle. I'm not certain whether Rathfield is playing at politics, or just trying to do his duty as he sees it. Either way, he could cause trouble."

Gisella applied the brush to his shoulder, then slipped her arms around his neck. "But you are loyal to the Crown, my Prince. The Queen has nothing to fear from you, so you have nothing to fear from her."

Vlad hugged his wife tightly. "Let's hope it is as you say or, my dear, that the ocean can insulate us from her baseless wrath."

CHAPTER SEVEN

5 April 1767
Prince Haven,
Temperance Bay, Mystria

As the members of the expedition gathered on the lawn near the wurmrest, Owen could not help but smile. Seven men of disparate backgrounds and inclinations were bound for lands unknown to them, in service to a distant ruler that none, save one, had ever met in person. It took Owen back four years. *A journey measured in more than miles or time.*

Nathaniel Woods, slender and of above average height, with long brown hair ungathered and light brown eyes, would lead the expedition no matter what Colonel Rathfield believed. Born in Mystria and more at home in the forests than in town, Nathaniel had a keen love for the land. He wore beaded buckskin leggings and a loincloth, moccasins and a leather tunic with fringed sleeves. The knife at his belt was the only weapon on him; his rifle and a tomahawk had already been stowed in his canoe.

With him stood Kamiskwa, a prince of the Altashee, one of the Twilight People. Rathfield tried not to stare at him, but to no avail. Owen could understand, as the Mystrian native looked unlike any human being in Auropa. Shorter yet more heavily muscled than Nathaniel, Kamiskwa's flesh had a gray cast to it with greenish undertones, which all but made him invisible in the forest. His long, evergreen hair had been braided and knotted off with a beaded leather cord. Restless amber eyes moved quickly, as might those of a predator. Like Nathaniel, he wore moccasins, leggings, and a loincloth, the latter woven with a bear-paw design that proclaimed his descent from Msitazi, the leader of the Altashee. He wore a knife and had a warclub slung over his back. A variety of tattoos and scars marked him, but his coloration made them difficult to see.

Count Joachim von Metternin of Kesse-Saxeburg had attired himself most ostentatiously. He wore bleached buckskins as close to white as possible. The tunic had been beaded in the Shedashee style by Ishikis, one of Kamiskwa's sisters, but the image was of lion rampant in coral—the von Metternin family crest. Perched on his head, hiding all but a few errant locks of brown hair, was a white foxskin cap with the ears still upthrust and the tail dangling at the back of the neck. The Count had shot the fox himself and was inordinately proud of that fact, so he wore the cap at every suitable opportunity.

Though von Metternin was not a small man, Makepeace Bone dwarfed him. Tall and powerfully built, the first thing anyone noticed was a trio of scars raking forward from his crown to his left eyebrow. They were a memento of an encounter with an angry bear that Makepeace managed to kill with his bare hands. Born of a family professing the Virtuan faith, Makepeace, along with two of his brothers—Tribulation and Justice—had helped win the battle at Anvil Lake. Makepeace wore buckskins with no decoration and, save for the smile splitting a thick brown beard, one might have thought he would be given to considerable melancholy.

Owen and Hodge Dunsby had also donned skins for traveling. Owen chose to wear the leggings, loincloth, and tunic given to him by Msitazi. His tunic featured a beaded bear paw. Hodge's clothes were more modest but he'd killed the deer himself, tanned the hides, cut and sewed them together with minimal help. Though his inexperience showed, his pride in self-sufficiency lit his face brightly.

Owen found Rathfield's outfit distressing. When Owen had headed out for the first time, he'd insisted on wearing his uniform. Beginning with his boots, it had begun to deteriorate almost immediately. Nathaniel and Kamiskwa managed to convince him to adopt more practical attire. *I was a complete fool, and had they not coerced me into sensible clothes, I should have been naked and humiliated three weeks out of Temperance.* Owen had been hoping that Rathfield would be as foolish and arrogant as he'd been—a petty desire, he acknowledged, but he'd revel in the man's ignorance.

Rathfield, however, had arrived in Mystria prepared for his journey. He wore buckskins and moccasins similar to those the others wore, save that these had been tailored in Launston, based on a drawing of Mystrian native garb. Rathfield had also specified that the leather be dyed such that two broad black stripes ran from shoulder to waist in the front, and two red stripes angled up from his breastbone toward the shoulders, mirroring the pattern on the Fifth Northlands Cavalry uniform.

Prince Vlad stepped forward to make the final introductions. "Colonel, I believe you have yet to meet Mr. Nathaniel Woods, Mr. Makepeace Bone, and Prince Kamiskwa."

Rathfield offered Nathaniel and Makepeace both his hand, but after they shook, he clasped both hands behind his back and bowed his head toward Kamiskwa, in the Shedashee style of greeting. *Since magick works at a touch, the Shedashee see a handshake as a potential attack.* Owen wasn't certain how Rathfield had learned that much about the Shedashee, but was getting a sinking feeling that it was through having read Owen's book.

That didn't please Owen, but nothing about Rathfield had. Having housed Rathfield for over a week had not improved the situation. Owen knew he'd been arrogant when he came to Mystria, but he hadn't been *that* arrogant. That Rathfield would be learning from mistakes that had cost Owen dearly hardly seemed fair. And though Rathfield's very presence had lightened Catherine's mood substantially, Owen still didn't like him.

Nathaniel looked Rathfield up and down. "I'm wondering, Colonel, iffen all your clothes got them stripes on them."

Rathfield smiled proudly. "Horse Guards issued a special order adopting this as an official uniform. Why do you ask?"

The scout stepped forward and poked the man in the chest, right where the red stripes would have converged. "I'm just thinking this draws the eye to a mighty good spot for shooting."

"Indeed." Rathfield looked down at Nathaniel. "Then I would suggest, Mr. Woods, that it is your job to alert me if anyone is close enough to make that shot."

"I reckon it is, Colonel."

The Prince clapped his hands. "I want you to know that I dearly wish I was going with you. Please, Colonel Rathfield and Captain Strake, promise you'll let me make copies of your expedition journals."

"A pleasure, Highness."

"As Horse Guards allow, Highness, yes, of course."

"Thank you. I won't keep you." The Prince waved them toward the three canoes tied to the dock. "Owen, a quick word, if I might?"

"Yes, Highness."

They withdrew up the lawn a bit and the Prince pulled a folded piece of paper from his pocket. "I have a list for you. Wouldn't be an expedition if I didn't, would it?"

Owen unfolded it and read quickly. "I'll bring samples back if possible, Highness, and let hunters know you're looking for some of these things. A dwarf mastodon?"

"A correspondent in Auropa suggests that high mountain valleys might create the same effect as isolated islands—which is to encourage dwarfism in larger creatures. Think of the valleys as islands in the sky, if you will." Vlad smiled encouragingly. "I know bringing one back would be difficult, but were you to describe one in the detail you've put into previous reports, it would enrich the world of science. We could, in fact, name the species after your daughter."

That brought a smile to Owen's face. "If it is possible, Highness, it will be done."

The Prince's smile shrank. "Did you happen to pack a copy of *A Continent's Calling?*"

"No, Highness, I brought Haste's new book. I thought Caleb gave you a copy."

"He did. He did. Very good. We shall use *The Blood of Liberty.* As needed."

"Yes, Highness." Owen shivered. Prince Vlad had instructed Owen on how to use a book to encode messages. Establishing a protocol for doing so on this trip meant the Prince did not wholly trust Rathfield. If he saw anything odd, Owen would send word to the Prince.

Prince Vlad slipped an arm over the man's shoulder and led him further up the lawn to where Catherine and Miranda stood with Princess Gisella. "I was just saying to Captain Strake, Mrs. Strake, that I am very pleased you've consented to join our household here while your husband is away in service to the Crown."

Catherine curtsied. "Your invitation was an honor I could not refuse."

Gisella took her arm. "Catherine, you are doing me the biggest favor.

My husband, when he sends men off and would rather be with them, can be a frightful bore. Our children shall play together and we shall have good companionship for the summer."

Owen crouched and held his hands out. "Miranda, come give your father a hug."

The little girl flew into his arms and hugged his neck tightly. He embraced her and could feel her little body throbbing with unvoiced sobs. "It will be fine, Miranda. I love you and I will be back very soon."

"Don't go, Papa."

"Shhhh. Miranda, you're three and a half years old. Do you know what that means?"

Her hair brushed his hands as she shook her head.

"It means you're a big girl now. You're almost four. So, I need you to do big girl things. Can you do that for me?"

The girl pulled back and looked up at him with big eyes brimming with tears. "What?"

"I need you to help Agnes and Madeline to take care of Prince Richard and Princess Rowena. And I need you to be quiet and good in case your mother gets a headache. Can you do that?"

Miranda's face scrunched up. "Richard plays like a boy."

"That's because he is a boy, darling." Owen kissed her on the top of her head. "You do the best you can."

"When will you be back?"

Owen held a hand up, fingers splayed. "Five full moons. You can count them. It won't be long at all."

The little girl looked at his hand, then touched each of his fingers in turn. "Okay. I will count."

"I love you, Miranda."

"I love you, Papa."

Owen slipped from her embrace and took her hand, walking her over to Catherine. "Five months at the most. Back sooner, I hope."

Catherine folded her arms over her chest. "As quickly as you can."

"Of course."

"Owen, this is another grand adventure for you. You've wanted to be off with your friends again since the last time you returned. You have responsibilities."

"To the Crown, as well as my family. I know that, Catherine."

"There are times, Owen, when you need to get those responsibilities properly ordered." She smiled. "Miranda, be a good girl and find Agnes, please."

"Yes, Mama."

As the girl departed, Catherine's eyes narrowed and ice entered her voice. "You may think this is all grand good fun, but I do not appreciate being abandoned. Not in the least. Don't be surprised if Miranda and I are in Norisle when you return."

He reached out to caress her cheek, but she turned her face away. "Catherine, do not do anything rash. When I return, I promise you, we will go to Norisle together. As a family."

"For good?"

"Catherine, let's not make decisions until we know what is best for us."

"That's how it always is with you, Owen. You know what is best for *you*. You never consider what might be best for *me*." She poked a finger against his chest. "Whatever you do, Owen, see to it that no harm comes to Colonel Rathfield."

"I think he's quite capable of taking care of himself."

Her nostrils flared. "You know that is not true, not in this savage land. I shall hold you personally responsible for anything untoward which befalls him. I will not have his death or injury besmirching our name, do you understand me?"

"Yes, Catherine." Owen forced his right hand open, then leaned in and kissed her cheek. "No matter what you think, Catherine, I love you and I love Miranda, and I would do neither of you any harm. I go because I *must*, but I return because I wish to be no place else than with my family."

He turned, and Catherine reached for his hand. She brought it to her cheek and he felt a warm tear against his flesh. "Owen, I am sorry. I worry so."

"Hush, my dear. See to our daughter and I shall be home soon." He drew her hands to his and kissed them, then headed down the lawn to the canoes. He listened to the delighted shrieking of children, but didn't turn to see them at play. He would have lingered and watched them for far too long.

The expedition had been fitted out with three fifteen-foot-long birch-bark canoes of Altashee manufacture. Nathaniel and Kamiskwa had the first one, and filled the middle with cargo. Likewise the third would carry cargo and had Count von Metternin and Hodge crewing it. That left Owen and Makepeace to handle the second one, with Rathfield reduced to the role of self-loading cargo. He helped Makepeace steady the canoe as Rathfield got in, then Owen took up his position in the bow, and Makepeace sat in the stern.

As they moved out onto the water, Owen looked back and waved. The watchers waved back, though his wife less enthusiastically than the others. Quickly riverbank brush stole them from sight. Owen bent to paddling and slid in behind the lead canoe. His muscles protested at first—it had been a while since he'd been out in a canoe—but as he warmed up, the tightness eased.

They left in mid-morning, so only the last tenuous threads of mist clung to the shadows along the riverbanks. The Benjamin River flowed slowly and serenely to the sea, but as broad as it was, the current did not flow fast enough to make them work terribly hard to go upstream. Cattails lined the banks, and tall grasses filled the fields. Yellow, red, and orange wildflowers bloomed here and there. Dragonflies zigzagged above the water and bald eagles perched high in trees surveyed their party as they rowed past.

Owen glanced over his shoulder. "What do you think, Colonel?"

"It is a vast land, Strake, no doubt about it. A farm here and there, but untrammeled otherwise." He shrugged. "I'm certain poets would be given to excess in describing it, the bucolic beauty, the unspoiled, virginal nature of things. That's not quite how I see it, I am afraid."

Makepeace spat over the side. "How would you be seeing it, Colonel?"

"What others see as unspoiled, I see as untamed. As the Good Book tells us, man was given dominion over the world. It is up to us to impose order on the world. The natural order."

The larger man grunted. "And this natural order is…?"

"Man over animals, greater men over lesser, noble over peasant." Rathfield smiled in a way that made Owen think it would be a frighteningly long journey. "To bring that order over those who defy the Crown is the soul of my mission. It is one from which I shall not shrink nor surrender."

CHAPTER EIGHT

10 April 1767
Prince Haven,
Temperance Bay, Mystria

"Are you certain, Highness, that this is wise?"

Prince Vlad scratched the side of his head, then righted his floppy-brimmed hat again. "I'm more convinced it isn't entirely stupid. If it works, it will be wise."

Mugwump, the Prince's dragon, blinked a golden eye. When Mugwump had arrived in Mystria with Prince Vlad's father, he'd been a thickly constructed, dull black beast. The wurm's official portrait confirmed his appearance. As with all wurms, he'd been largely seen as a giant gecko, save for claws, horns, and a mouth full of ivory teeth. As wurms went, he had been unremarkable.

Since living in Mystria he had changed. His skin had become very shiny. Gold and scarlet stripes and spots had risen to make him appear festive. And then, in 1764, he'd undergone a molt and chrysalis which, instead of killing him as the Prince had expected, had transformed him into a dragon. His head had narrowed and his neck grew longer. His tail had similarly slimmed down and lengthened as a counter-balance. He grew ears, which swiveled about freely, suggesting great auditory acuity. Mugwump, while being leaner and lighter than before, had become far more supple and strong.

And then there was the matter of his wings. When he first emerged from the cocoon, the wings appeared underdeveloped and clearly never meant to sustain flight. But stories of old had told of dragons cruising high through the clouds. Over the next three years, the wings had become stronger. Using a long lead, the Prince had tried to encourage Mugwump to hop about or glide—efforts the dragon took with seeming equal parts amusement and disdain.

Before he'd gotten his wings, Mugwump had been an avid swimmer. As his wings developed, he took to the water less and less. Though he had not spun another cocoon, he did regularly shed scales bilaterally—much as a bird sheds feathers—leaving Vlad with little doubt that the dragon was meant to fly.

Unable to come up with any other way to convince the dragon to test out his wings, Prince Vlad reconfigured the saddle he'd used for swimming with Mugwump and cinched it into place. He added a bridle with no bit to provide a suggestion of direction—the Prince never could have wrestled the beast's head around. He attached a second set of reins to Mugwump's horns hoping again that tugging on them might convince the dragon to climb.

Prince Vlad hauled himself into the saddle. "Now, Mr. Baker, I want you to pay close attention to what happens."

"So I'll know where to find you when you fall off?"

"Let us hope it doesn't come to that." Vlad forced himself to smile. "I want you to note how much Mugwump spreads his wings when we go over the jumps."

"Yes, sire."

The Prince started the dragon off at a slow pace, heading up the drive, past Peregrine's enclosure, then toward the west to a five-acre lot he'd decided to leave fallow. With the help of Baker and Owen's man, James, they'd harvested wood and created four log walls roughly six feet high. They placed them at the cardinal points around an imaginary circle. The Prince intended to ride Mugwump toward one and encourage him to jump over it. The walls would prove little obstacle as the dragon's playful pouncing upon game had previously showed. Primarily Vlad hoped that Mugwump would associate a tug on his horns with leaping.

Vlad settled goggles over his eyes. Mid-April and it was already warm. Trees had budded and farmers were predicting a good harvest if they got some rain at the right time. Only a few clouds threaded themselves through the blue sky, drifting slowly with warm breezes. Prince Vlad closed his eyes for a moment, drinking in the warmth and doing his best to relax.

Mugwump's transformation from wingless wurm to dragon was the most closely held secret in Mystria. Fewer than a dozen people knew it had happened and all of them had been sworn to secrecy. To further obscure things, Vlad caused to be circulated a number of very fanciful stories about fantastic creatures to be found in Mystria. Within these were absurd stories about dragon colonies living in caverns dug into mountains in the far west. While a few inquiries came back from Norisle and elsewhere asking him what he knew, he promised to check, then later declared all of them lies. Were someone to learn the truth about Mugwump and report it back to Norisle, it would be assumed to be another fantasy and dismissed out of hand.

Wurms were not common back across the ocean. Every nation had a regiment or two of wurmriders to play off against each other. Since the advent of brimstone, the nature of warfare had shifted away from a basis where wurms could completely dominate battle. While cannon and muskets couldn't easily kill a wurm, they could kill riders and hurt the beasts, so wurm regiments paraded more than they fought. But when they did fight, they could still be terribly effective.

Vlad reached down and patted Mugwump on the neck. "Take the jumps easily, just one after the other."

One ear flicked back at him, then both flattened against the wedge-shaped skull. The dragon began running through the grasses, less as a lizard might than with the power of a great cat gathering speed to pounce. Mugwump stretched his neck out, heading straight for the first fence. Prince Vlad tugged back on the horn-reins and Mugwump left the ground, but only cleared the fence by inches.

Now apparently aware of what the game was, the dragon hit the ground without losing any speed and sprinted toward the next fence. Vlad tugged harder on the reins and again the dragon leaped into the air. His wings began to spread just a bit, but then he was down again and running. They approached the third fence even faster than the first two. Vlad yanked hard, but the dragon's breastbone grazed the top log.

They turned and made for the last fence in the circuit. Vlad quickly wrapped the reins around his hands and stood in the stirrups. The moment Mugwump's nose neared the fence, Vlad hauled back for all he was worth. Mugwump's head came up. He leaped, his tail lashing the fence to splinters.

"Up! Up!" Vlad held on tight.

Mugwump's wings spread, fluttering weakly and out of synch. They started to dip to the right. His tail went left, then down, dragging like an anchor. That brought his bottom down and threatened to flip him over onto his back. So his wings spread fully, in complete, batlike glory, catching enough air to slow his speed. He landed hard on his haunches, tossing Vlad back and down into the saddle, then his forelimbs came down and his wings furled again.

The Prince took a moment, shifting in the saddle and rubbing his buttocks. Then he patted the dragon on the neck again. "You're getting it."

Mugwump's head came around. The dragon stared at him with a single golden eye. It seemed to Vlad as if the beast was saying, "Was that it? Was *that* what this is all about?"

The Prince found himself nodding. "Yes, that's what I want. We need to get your wings strong so you can fly."

As if he understood, the dragon loped off toward the first wall, barely faster than a man could trot, and leaped high. His wings snapped out. His tail twisted. He soared over the wall and flapped his wings to slow his descent. He landed hard again on his haunches, but he'd managed to stay level. Vlad had braced for the landing, so he didn't slam into the saddle again.

From that point forward Mugwump needed no encouragement, but followed no direction. He wandered through the field, sometimes taking the fences, other times just leaping into the air as if a cat pouncing on a mouse. He'd stop, nibble the forward edge of a wing, then trot off again. His behavior bordered on playful, but he pursued it with a concentration that bespoke far greater intelligence than most people knowledgeable about wurms would allow.

Perhaps wurms are intelligent, or, rather, dragons *are.* Most wurm-wrights considered wurms to be on an intellectual par with draft horses. For as long as Mugwump had been in his care, Vlad would have pegged him as being a bit smarter than that. Since the chrysalis, however, the dragon had been brighter. Prince Vlad would have matched him to a dog and yet, the way he approached testing his wings, took him further than that. Vlad had seen his son exhibiting similar self-awareness.

Vlad flicked the reins. "Time to go home, Mugwump."

The dragon came about and started trotting back toward the wurmrest. As he went he would spread his wings and give one solid beat. His body rocked and got a little lift, but not nearly enough to sustain flight. He stopped trying to fly as he came back into the yard and he shied from where Miranda and Richard were running around—something not terribly easy for a sixty-foot-long lizard to manage.

Prince Vlad remained in the saddle until Baker caught up and took charge of the dragon. He watched the dragon return to the wurmrest, then began to think. At the battle of Anvil Lake, Mugwump had scaled a sheer cliff as if it was nothing. If he were to gain height that way, then leap into the air, he might be able to glide or actually fly. Bats, who had similar wing designs, roosted upside down in attics and caves, allowing them to drop into the air before they had to begin flying.

That gave the Prince one area of inquiry to pursue. Then he turned back to the question of intelligence. At the time Mugwump had entered his cocoon, Msitazi of the Altashee had arrived with a gift to celebrate the dragon's birthday. That day, correctly predicted, was really the day he emerged from the cocoon. It occurred to the Prince that he'd been judging intelligence incorrectly simply because the wurm was almost seven centuries old. In any other creature, that would have established his being an adult and fully grown.

But what if the clock started anew when he emerged from the cocoon? If that were true, then Mugwump was, in effect, only three years old. Given the likely timescale of a dragon's life, he was, for all intents and purposes, still an infant. Assuming his intelligence was developing at a rate that roughly paralleled that of his physical development, he might quickly work his way past the intelligence of a dog and on up to a small ape. *Or even a man?*

Part of Vlad wanted to dismiss that idea out of hand, but another more tantalizing thought tempted him to go beyond it. No one truly knew the limits of a dragon's lifespan. While stories told of repeated raids by the same dragons over a number of centuries, old bards' tales were hardly reliable sources of empirical data. Still, if dragons could outlive men by a factor of ten, who was to say that they could not also become ten times smarter than a man? Judging by skull volume alone, Mugwump's brain had to be at least ten times the size of a man's.

The implications of what he'd seen and was thinking made Prince Vlad want to retreat to his laboratory and scribble copious notes. He wanted to set up some experiments to determine just how smart Mugwump really was. He had Richard for comparison, and Miranda. He could pose problems for them, measure how well they solved them, then offer the same problems to the dragon. He would do these things. Science demanded it.

Then he stopped. He could gather his data, test his theories, but then what? He couldn't possibly share them with anyone else. Others would want to duplicate what he had done, which meant creating more dragons, or having Mugwump taken away from him. An intelligent creature, capable of flight, capable of carrying small swivel guns could terrorize cities and towns. People feared wurmriders and they would find dragonriders infinitely more terrifying.

The greater moral dilemma struck him. He *owned* Mugwump. The dragon was chattel. But if Mugwump proved to be as intelligent as a man, or even more intelligent, did Prince Vlad have any right to own him? The Prince and all civilized nations had long since repudiated the horror of slavery. Indentured servitude often amounted to the same thing, though the contract did contain limitations which, in theory, prevented abuse. And what would become of all the wurms whose growth and development had been stunted by their long captivity? Could a thinking man condone their enforced infantilization?

He looked up and saw his wife out with the children. She'd told him that he'd train Mugwump, but would educate his children. *How will you take it, my dear, if Mugwump needs educating?*

A cold chill ran through him. He wished, just for a moment, that both he and dragon were stupid. He literally had no choice. He had to educate Mugwump and determine just how smart he truly was. He would have to encrypt all the records, and likely needed to create two sets containing disparate data that he could untangle with the proper key. They would send anyone who stole his information off in the wrong direction.

Gisella approached him, her brow furrowed. "What worries you? Have you had bad news?"

"No, good news, I think." *I think. Is that what Mugwump can do?* He slipped an arm around her slender waist and watched his son bend down to pick something off the lawn. It appeared to be a twig, which the boy peered at closely, then immediately attempted to stick into his nose. Madeline took it from him, which appeared on the cusp of starting him crying, but Miranda presented him with a yellow flower, which distracted him.

"Are you going to tell me, husband?"

He smiled. "Nothing to tell yet, darling. When there is, I will let you know."

She leaned her head on his shoulder. "And did Mugwump take well to his training?"

"Dashed one fence to pieces, and did more hopping than flying, but his landings became less and less jarring." He kissed the top of her head. "Which reminds me that I'll likely need a pillow on my chair for the next several days. If a bruise comes up, you must promise not to laugh."

Her blue eyes flicked up and she smiled. "I would never…"

"…laugh aloud?" He squeezed her tightly. "As long as you keep it a secret, darling, I think we will do just fine."

CHAPTER NINE

18 April 1767
Plentiful, Richlan
Mystria

Out of respect for Prince Vlad, Nathaniel Woods had done his best to reserve judgment on Colonel Rathfield. The Norillian officer didn't shy from hard work and took to paddling a canoe pretty easily. Even though he carried a smooth-bore musket, he proved a fairly good shot with it. Of course, that meant he was still the worst shot on the expedition, but he was worlds-away better than most Norillians straight off the boat.

There were things about him, however, that just stuck in Nathaniel's craw. One was how he addressed all of them by their last names, save for Count von Metternin and Kamiskwa. Those two he treated with a certain amount of deference, but he still spoke down to them. And he treated Hodge Dunsby as his own personal servant. Hodge didn't seem to mind very much, his having been a soldier in the Queen's Army until not long ago, but it didn't sit right with Nathaniel.

Still, if Hodge had no complaints, Nathaniel wasn't going to step in for him. Hodge had been in Mystria long enough to know that he could speak his mind. Nathaniel and the others would back him in that. Nathaniel figured that until Hodge decided to change his family name to something more Mystrian perhaps that message hadn't quite sunk fully in. Still, he was willing to bet Hodge would take a stand before the journey was up.

The expedition had worked its way west to Grand Falls, then started an overland trek toward the southwest. The journey took them across countless small lakes and small rivers, all part of the watershed of the Westridge Mountains. The mountains began roughly where the Bounty and Richlan Colony borders met at the western edge of their grants, and extended off to the southwest and northwest. They cut the coast off from the Misaawa River valley, which, if Tharyngian and Shedashee tales were correct, roughly split the continent in half.

Within the first two days they'd left most Colonial settlements behind. Rathfield had referred to it as "abandoning civilization." Nathaniel and Kamiskwa had exchanged glances, since the Shedashee had nations and tribes all throughout the land. Nathaniel had found them much more civilized than most Mystrians, and figured he might make that point to Rathfield. Then he figured that Rathfield wasn't ever going to understand, so he resolved to hold his tongue.

As they traveled toward the mountains and into Richlan, they came across scattered settlements in small valleys with good water and fields. The people generally had constructed a big log blockhouse in the center, with a town green that they jointly worked. Barns had been raised and flocks of sheep wandered over hillsides. The individual homes appeared small, but clustered in small groups.

Plentiful was such a town and fairly new. At the last town, Wisdom, they'd been encouraged to bypass Plentiful since the people there had split from Wisdom over doctrinal issues a decade earlier. While the people of Wisdom had been full of forgiveness for their former colleagues and family members, the word "wicked" got thrown around a lot more than made Nathaniel comfortable.

The expedition entered the small valley on foot, having abandoned canoes on the shores of the last lake. The Snake River, which eventually caught up with King's River to the east and flowed to the sea at Kingstown, ran too shallow in the foothills to be navigable. The people of Plentiful found it a convenient source of fresh water and had built closely on both sides of it. They'd even raised a couple of footbridges, though most folks just happily splashed through it at low points.

Nathaniel and the others had walked a day and a half in, and brought with them a ten-point buck, which Rathfield had shot and insisted on carrying after basic field dressing—as opposed to butchering it and letting each man carry a piece. Nathaniel figured that was the man trying to show how strong he was. The Mystrian would have been more impressed if the load had been shared out, since that was the smarter way to travel.

A man in the valley rang the alarm bell in front of the blockhouse when they came out of the woods, but without the enthusiasm of someone reporting real danger. A large man wearing a white shirt, black woolen pants, and a tall, round-brimmed hat with a buckled hatband emerged from the blockhouse and headed toward them, cutting around the green. Nathaniel stayed on the road and raised his right hand, keeping it away from his rifle's firestone, in a sign of peace.

The man bowed and spread open hands. "God bless you and welcome you to Plentiful, friends. I am the Shepherd, Arise Faith."

Makepeace Bone stepped up. "I am your servant, Makepeace Bone. My companions and I would welcome comfort and counsel, as the Good Book dictates."

Faith's blossoming smile set Nathaniel's stomach at ease. "Please, friends, know you are welcome. It is fortunate you arrived when you did, for the Sabbath begins at sunset, and we would have been forbidden even greeting you until Monday dawn."

Nathaniel nodded. "We're truly grateful for your welcoming, Shepherd Faith. I'm Nathaniel Woods. This here is Kamiskwa of the Altashee. Count von Metternin is from Kesse-Saxeburg only four years back. That's Hodge Dunsby and the man with the deer is Colonel Rathfield. The Queen done sent him. And that there is Captain Owen Strake, hero of Anvil Lake."

Faith nodded to each man in turn, but his face betrayed zero recognition. He covered himself well, but Nathaniel found him as easy to read as fresh tracks in stiff mud. While Faith knew there was a Queen, he didn't know a place called Kesse-Saxeburg existed. Nathaniel caught a flicker that suggested he'd heard of Anvil Lake, but whatever he knew didn't have Owen's name attached to it.

Plentiful's Shepherd pointed toward the blockhouse. "You will be quite welcome to stay in our Spiritual Hall, but you must understand that no profane or lascivious behavior will be tolerated. There is no hard liquor allowed. We will have services, and you are welcome to attend, and then we shall have our communal meal after that. You are welcome to share, though this early in the year the fare can be somewhat meager."

Rathfield stepped up and dumped the buck at Faith's feet. "Please, Goodman, accept this meat as a gift from Her Imperial Majesty, Queen Margaret. She wishes the best for all of her subjects."

Faith looked down, and then back up. "Are you certain, Colonel? I would not have thought the Queen…"

Rathfield smiled. "My dear sir, by my reckoning, Plentiful is still within the bounds of Richlan, which marks you as loyal subjects of the Crown. If she cannot show her beneficence here, at the very edges of the empire God has granted her, to God's most faithful servants, what kind of a ruler would she be?"

"I see. This is most unexpected but most welcome." He clasped his hands together. "Please, friends, I will see to your accommodation and get people to prepare your gift. Follow me."

Shepherd Faith led them to the blockhouse, which had been solidly built of logs. Longer than it was wide, it rose to two stories, with a loft that extended halfway in from the door. Bark had been skinned from the interior, making the room appear lighter and larger than it might have otherwise. The far end had a small pulpit carved from a single log. Trestle tables and benches filled the main floor, but people had already begun to break most of the tables down and arrange the benches for the coming service.

Faith took them up the steps to the loft, which clearly served as community storage during the winter. A few sacks of grain remained, along with a collection of items from spinning wheels to scythes that required repair or sharpening.

"Please, friends, make yourselves at home."

Nathaniel smiled. "Already feel at home, but I reckon you can do me a favor."

"Yes?"

"Point me to an ax and a pile of wood that needs splitting. I hain't worked an ax good in a while, and I am sadly feeling the need of that exercise."

"Of course. Around back is our shed. You can chop all you want until sundown."

"Much obliged."

Nathaniel waited for Shepherd Faith to descend from the loft before he turned to Colonel Rathfield. "Mighty nice of you just to up and give them your deer."

"Calculated risk, really. Thank goodness they were not like that other place several days back—Restraint, was it?—which had its list of proscribed foods. I determined it was a good way to gain entry and a certain amount of trust."

Owen, who crouched over a pack, glanced back at them. "But offering it in the Queen's name could have caused a problem."

"You think so, Strake, really?" Rathfield snorted. "Thing of it is this: either they are loyal subjects or they are subjects who have to be reminded that they are subjects. Let us face facts. While many of these settlements are based in religion, and the Virtuans came to Mystria to escape the wrath of the Church, these settlements are not fleeing the Queen's power, but the perfidy of the settlements from which they have split. The Shepherd of Wisdom suggested the people of Plentiful were cannibalistic slave-drivers who believed in plural marriage and baptism in blood. I'd be concerned, but that's what the people of Contentment said of the people of Wisdom, and everyone has said of the people of Restraint."

Owen straightened up, his journal in hand. "I think you're missing my point, Colonel. We're a long way away from any Norillian troops. If we faced opposition…"

Rathfield laughed. "Surely you jest. Why Dunsby and I could pacify this settlement without blackening a firestone."

"I ain't so sure you're right, Colonel." Nathaniel pointed at the nearest window, which stood four times as tall as it was wide, and it was fairly narrow to begin with. "These windows ain't just for letting light in. Get all your people in here with muskets and short of bringing up some cannon, you ain't dislodging them."

"And if they chose to defy the Crown, I would just order the building fired." Rathfield raised his chin. "It would be a prelude to the hellfire reserved for those who defy God and oppose his anointed one."

"I reckon that might be one way of handling it." Nathaniel shucked his tunic and left the loft, making his way to the woodshed out back of the blockhouse. Logs had been dragged from wood yards and piled up. Residents had sawed many of them down into foot and a half lengths. Nathaniel hauled one of them onto a chopping block, split it with a hammer and wedge, then used an ax to cut it down further.

It wasn't easy work, but wasn't terribly complicated, either. He worked up a sweat quickly enough, and attracted the attention of a few young boys whom Shepherd Faith scattered to chores quickly enough. That behavior didn't surprise him. Nathaniel likely had more scars on him than could be found in the whole of Plentiful. His long hair and the beadwork on his clothes marked him as an intimate of the Shedashee. Woods wasn't a recognizable Virtuan name and though Nathaniel could be found in the Good Book, it wasn't common among Virtuans either. Shepherd Faith likely didn't see Nathaniel as being as bad as a horde of demons, but he reckoned the older man didn't see him as being far off from that, either.

Shadows crept through the valley as the sun began to set. Nathaniel buried the ax in the chopping block and started to stack wood. Shepherd Faith summoned the boys back to help in that task, then tried to pull the ax from the block. Nathaniel helped him before the boys could begin to laugh at his struggles.

The red-faced man smiled. "It might seem a little thing, but we let our tools rest on the Sabbath, too. There it was working, but here, hung on the wall, it enjoys rest."

"Pardon my ignorance."

"No pardon needed." Shepherd Faith smiled. "I know that you travel with Friend Makepeace, but clearly you are not of the faith."

Nathaniel ran a long-fingered hand over unshaven jaw. "Well, my pa lived far from a church, and the missionaries what visited the Altashee didn't take much notice of me. But Makepeace, he's a fine example of a man. Saved my life a time or three."

"I hope, Friend Nathaniel, he will save your soul as well."

"Truth be told, Shepherd, my ears is pricked and my eyes is open."

"Then I shall hope and pray the Lord's Word lodges in your heart tonight."

Nathaniel joined the others in the loft as Plentiful's residents filed in. Everyone brought a pot, a crock, a jar, basket, or a cauldron and set them on the few tables that had been dragged to the walls. The scent of venison stew, baked beans, and oven-hot bread filled the hall. Nathaniel rubbed his belly to keep it quiet. While they'd not had trouble finding food on the journey, it was mostly fish here, berries there, being gathered as they went. This would be the most complete meal they'd enjoyed since leaving Temperance Bay.

Owen sat toward the back of the loft, making notes in his journal. The fact that he had a smaller book beside him and referenced it meant he was composing a message for the Prince. None of them could be certain how long it would take letters to make it back to Temperance, but every village sent someone down-river to trade skins and locally produced goods for sugar, salt, and anything which Mystria didn't provide. That included firestones and brimstone for muskets, both of which could only be purchased through a government-licensed dealer.

In studying Rathfield, Nathaniel was able to pinpoint that which he found most unsettling about the man. When Owen had first come out to do the survey during which they'd discovered du Malphias' fortress at Anvil Lake, he'd taken all sorts of notes and sent all manner of messages back to Prince Vlad. Rathfield, who said he was on a mission of similar import, seldom wrote anything down. Since Nathaniel had only begun to learn to read and write, he wasn't about to fault a man for being illiterate. But he supposed an officer and a hero in the Queen's Army would be able to read, and would have better sense than to believe his notes might not be valuable in the event he didn't make it back from the journey.

He just ain't taking this serious. Nathaniel frowned. If the man wasn't devoted to his mission, either he was a fool, or the mission they'd been told he was on was just a story to cover what he was really doing.

Nathaniel had half a mind to ask Rathfield about that, but the hundred or so people that called Plentiful home had filed into the blockhouse and taken their places. They wore standard Virtuan garb, darkly colored, which covered the women from floor to wrists and throat, with a bonnet tossed on to hide their hair. Nothing decorative or unique about their clothes helped tell them apart. The men all wore hats and dark trousers, white shirts and long-tailed black coats pulled on over them. The hats remained on, with the brim lowered to modestly shade the eyes.

Arise Faith came to the front of the congregation and murmured a greeting, which the people returned. "We have among us some visitors who have chosen to share the bounty of their journey with us." He looked up toward the loft, but no one turned around to look.

The Shepherd smiled. "I had intended on delivering a message on the virtues of chastity as all nature blossoms with fecundity around us, but after conversing with one of the visitors, I have decided to ask him to speak to you."

Nathaniel's stomach knotted for a moment. *Ain't no way...*

Rathfield stood. "It would be my pleasure, Shepherd." He pulled on a hat that clearly had been borrowed for the occasion, and stalked down the stairs to address the people of Plentiful.

CHAPTER TEN

19 April 1767
Plentiful, Richlan
Mystria

What on earth is he doing? Owen slid forward to the loft railing, standing beside Nathaniel, as Rathfield strode up the center aisle. The others joined them at the railing, equally curious. Given Rathfield's arrogance, Owen did not anticipate a happy ending to this bit of theatre.

While Rathfield had attended church services in Temperance with Owen and his family, on the trail he'd not seemed particularly religious. He'd not discussed the Good Book with Makepeace, nor paid much attention when Makepeace offered a lesson. At least once he'd heard Rathfield refer to a village Shepherd as a simpleton—a sobriquet commonly used by Norillians to ridicule Virtuans for the way they had simplified worship ceremonies.

Rathfield replaced Shepherd Faith at the pulpit and lowered his eyes. His lips moved, but Owen couldn't make out any words. Then the man rested his hands on the lectern and glanced up briefly. "I asked Shepherd Faith to allow me to speak with you. Though I am very far from home, here I feel at home. Your simple settlement, clearly created with love and devotion for each other and Our Lord, feels like home. Not my home specifically, you understand, but a place where I am welcome. I feel welcome because we share something very dear: our faith. And I wanted to share with you part of my journey in faith."

Again he looked down, drawing in a mighty breath as if setting himself in the traces to drag an incredible burden along. "I am a simple soldier in service to our Queen. It has been my honor to serve her. Prior to being sent here to you, I fought for her in Tharyngia, against the godless Laureates. You've likely never heard of the Battle of Rondeville which, not even two years ago, ended the long war we'd fought with our ancestral enemies. Some people have even referred to me as the *hero* of Rondeville—but you should know, Friends, that the true hero was Our Lord.

"Duke Deathridge had positioned his men around the town of Rondeville such that the slaughter the coming day would be frightful. Imagine an ocean of blood and fire just sweeping through this valley. It would have been a terrible, terrible thing. Victory was assured, but Duke Deathridge did not want to take any chances in case the Ryngians had somehow set a trap. He sent me to infiltrate their position. It was my pleasure to serve my Queen and Our Lord on so dangerous a mission."

Rathfield sighed. "I was proud. I admit to that sin, and Our Lord saw fit in his wisdom to chasten me for my pride. I was discovered and brought before Laureate-General Philippe de Toron, the Tharyngian commander. The man had me clapped in chains, then beaten and tortured so I would reveal what I knew of our plans. I said nothing. Did not modesty prevent it, I would show you my scars. The one on the right side of my face is the first among many I received that night. And when they saw I would not be broken, they threw me into the wine cellar beneath their headquarters. They promised they would return after they crushed our army, and would execute me along with any other survivors.

"So there I was, locked in a dungeon. The only light came from the full moon, just as it comes tonight, through these narrow windows. And I knelt in the moonlight and prayed, Friends, prayed fervently. I begged forgiveness for my sin of pride and rededicated my life to the service of Our Lord. I told Him that if it was His will for me to die there, I would go happily. But if He had another mission for me, He should show me a sign and I would do whatever He required of me."

Rathfield allowed himself the ghost of a smile. "And, yes, Friends, I thought that even my prayer might be prideful. Contemplation of the consequences worried me, but Our Lord did have another mission for me. I shant go into the sordid details. Suffice it to say I emerged from the dungeon as Our Lord's avenging angel. I stalked through the tavern that morning and killed every man I could find—including the Laureate-General. By the time I escaped, the battle had commenced, but in slaying de Toron I had struck the head from the serpent. He never got to spring his trap. Our men were saved and the atheists were sent to Perdition."

He hung his head for a moment as if exhausted, then looked up, his blue eyes bright. "I did not share my story so that you would know who I am. I am but a sinner who is unworthy of Our Lord's favor. I merely wished to show you that though we come from distant places, though the role Our Lord asks of us can be anything and different, we are the same. Our hearts beat by His Grace, to be full of His Grace. Though you may find yourself here, thinking you are at the edge of the world, remember that He has placed you here so that no matter how far a man has traveled, he will forever be reminded that Our Lord blesses his life daily."

Owen leaned heavily on the railing. He wanted, very much, to believe Rathfield was a fraud. In Restraint, Makepeace had similarly given his testimony about the bear who attacked him and the Lord healing him. That had shifted attitudes toward them. He wanted to assume that Rathfield, having studied Makepeace's performance, sought to duplicate it here.

He would have been happy to think ill of Rathfield, but the man's voice had rung with sincerity. The story's details seemed largely consistent with versions he'd heard before. Catherine had regaled him with several retellings. And Rathfield's humility came through so strongly that Owen found himself disarmed by it. The man might be arrogance personified on the trail—and had been so in Wisdom and Contentment—but here he shrank back.

Hodge and Makepeace descended to join the congregation in thanking Rathfield and resetting the main floor. Owen, shaking his head, looked at Nathaniel. "What do you think?"

The lean man shifted his shoulders. "Seems as like he tells a good story. I reckon if he did what he said he did, it would be easy for men to call him a hero."

"Little doubt of that. I seem to recall that troops found him half dead in de Toron's headquarters. They expected him to die and someone even sent a dispatch back to the main army reporting his death. His wife took the shock badly and never recovered. I believe my wife said she died several months later—and hinted she may have taken her own life."

Nathaniel leaned his hip against the rail. "That so."

"If you choose to believe gossip." Owen smiled. "So do you believe what you just heard?"

"When exactly did this here battle take place?"

"16-17 July, 1765."

Nathaniel frowned. "Well, I reckon things must have unfolded pretty much as he said, what with other folks being around to save him after, but I do believe I'll puzzle about one thing for a mite."

"Yes?"

"He amembers praying in a puddle of moonlight, which makes a powerful image, specially on a night like this." Nathaniel shook his head. "Fact is, however, mid-July two years ago, weren't no moon in the sky that night."

The call to supper precluded Owen thinking too much about Nathaniel's revelation. He couldn't be certain if the people of Plentiful regularly set such a wonderful table, did it in honor of their visit, or simply in recompense for the venison. Shepherd Faith had said fare might be meager, but Owen found it generous by most any standard—and he'd eaten often at Prince Vlad's table. Even Count von Metternin praised the meal, comparing it to the best he'd ever eaten on the Continent.

Venison stew formed the central portion of the meal, with some potatoes and beans added in. The Virtuans hadn't used any spices in the stew. Not only would they be expensive and difficult to obtain, but they might prove to excite the blood more than was good for a healthy spiritual life. Maple sugar sweetened the baked beans. Honey had been whipped into butter and then spread on bread and biscuits, which were proof enough to Owen that there was a God and that Heaven would be a place of many delights. Pickled beans and cucumbers rounded things out, and apple pies finished them off.

All of the travelers restrained themselves. They lingered over their food, knowing it would be a long while before they'd likely enjoy such a meal. Makepeace commented about stopping back through as they returned, and Owen was willing to grant the wisdom of that idea.

Over supper they got a chance to speak with Shepherd Faith about other settlements in the area. He had nothing bad to say about the people of Wisdom, but said he didn't know much about any other settlements. "Trappers come through and talk. There are valleys in the mountains, so there may be smaller settlements from elsewhere."

Makepeace leaned forward. "Going on four-five year ago, I heard tell of a man was leading a flock out here. Was going to establish the City of God. Said he'd had a revelation."

Faith's face closed down. "The Simonites. We don't hold with the True Oriental Church of the Lord."

Owen's eyes narrowed. "What do you know of them? Do they call their settlement Postsylvania?"

"They are heretics. They claim that when Our Lord gave his apostle Peter the new name Simon, it was a clue to a mystery in the Good Book. They say he is one in the same with the sorcerer Simon Magus. They claim that magick is not the *gift* of God, but the gift of *becoming* God. They point to the Books of Acts and how the Apostles were able to perform the same miracles as Our Lord, and how many magicks are able to imitate the miracles. They claim that great magick and glory awaits them across the mountains. Whether or not they call their holdings Postsylvania, I do not know, but I will tell you this: the men and women that have come this way looking for them have been anything *but* virtuous."

"You think they are out there?"

"Not think, Captain, *know*." Shepherd Faith sighed. "We are simple people. We pray for the Lord's Blessing every day. We also pray for His Justice, and for Him to smite His enemies. We can feel it, Captain, the blight upon the earth. It is out there. Beware if you seek it, and linger not long. Our Lord will rain down cleansing fire and you, most assuredly, do not wish to be consumed."

The people of Plentiful spent the Sabbath in quiet contemplation of all things Godly and glorious. Owen and the others kept to themselves and spent much of the time sleeping. The journey inland had been tiring, and moving into the mountains would make the trip more difficult. Not wishing to upset their hosts by resuming their work on Sunday seemed a good excuse to recover.

On Monday morning they packed up their gear and prepared to leave. Nathaniel chopped more wood, Count von Metternin managed to repair a broken spinning wheel, and Hodge put a keen edge on every scythe in the loft. The residents prepared small packages of dried sausage, cheese, and bread to take with them. Rathfield bade them keep the deerskin and Owen gave Shepherd Faith's wife a small packet of needles from Temperance—a gift which was very well received.

Its reception brought a smile to Owen's face. Bethany Frost had suggested it and Owen availed himself of her wisdom. Bethany had nursed Owen back to health after his escape from Anvil Lake, and had done a splendid job of editing his book. Because of Catherine's jealousy, Owen usually refrained from meeting with Bethany outside of group affairs, but she'd managed to get him alone in Temperance before the expedition departed.

He thanked her for the gift of the needles. "What can I do for you in return?"

The beautiful young woman had smiled warmly, then averted her eyes downward. "In return, you *will* return and let me read your journal of the expedition. Just like last time."

He had agreed and faithfully recorded most details of the trip. He thought about including Nathaniel's comment concerning Rathfield's story, but held off. He was certain Nathaniel was right and knew Prince Vlad could confirm it, but perhaps Rathfield had been mistaken. *Perhaps he added that detail for effect given where we were.* Owen still couldn't shake the impression of sincerity.

The land determined their course to the west. Because the Snake River came out of the mountains through a high gorge, they left it and followed a smaller tributary, angling to the southwest to reach the mountains through a series of forested hills. As they entered the foothills they saw no obvious pass to the west, so began the trip up toward the ridgeline a day out of Plentiful.

Kamiskwa, who was in the lead, called for them to stop on a promontory overlooking a small teardrop-shaped lake. Owen studied it, looking for any signs of dwarf mastodons living amid the underbrush and evergreens. Ahead, to the southwest, clouds still shrouded the highest peaks.

The Altashee crouched and pressed his left palm to the ground. "This is an evil place."

Rathfield frowned. "What are you talking about?"

"Can't you feel it?"

Rathfield folded his arms across his chest, but Owen went to a knee and touched the ground. He wasn't sure what he was feeling. He wasn't sure he'd ever paid attention to what the ground felt like, but there did seem to be something odd. His fingers tingled the way they did when thawing out after a long winter walk. "It *is* different, Colonel."

"Are you having me on?"

Nathaniel tipped his floppy-brimmed hat back. "I don't reckon they are. Been stories told of these mountains. Shedashee have 'em. There's things what lurk where folks might not want them lurking."

"So, because of some faery stories told to frighten children, we're going to stop?"

"This ain't the onliest way through here, Colonel." Nathaniel pointed off south. "Backtrack a day, cross the Snake, head on in that way."

"We already lost a day in Plentiful, Woods. I see no reason we shouldn't just continue on through."

Count von Metternin shrugged off his pack. "In the four years I've been here, Colonel, I have learned that time sacrificed in the name of safety is seldom wasted—unless there is some urgency to your mission of which I am not privy."

"With all due respect, my lord, there are aspects of this journey which are known only to those who gave me the assignment."

Then it began, a rumble which shook them much as thunder close by would—made all the more remarkable because only the barest wisp of clouds existed from horizon to horizon. The vibrations pounded through Owen's chest and, as they continued, he realized they had nothing to do with thunder. The vibrations were coming up through the ground, causing the earth to shift and trees to sway as if caught in a gale.

His guts knotted and he got down on all fours. A ripple ran through the lake below, starting at the broad end and racing northeast toward the narrows. As the rising wave approached the promontory it picked up speed. Water withdrew from the near shore, curling into a fluid wall. The wave crested, splashing up over the narrow beach and into the wood. The water just kept going, picking up deadfall logs and bashing them against other trees. Taller trees, with their roots already shaken, succumbed to the flood and fell. A second and third wave hit the shore, neither going as far as the first, but when the water calmed itself again, what had once been beach lay beneath twenty feet of water, and what had been a teardrop now better resembled an egg.

Kamiskwa rose and offered a hand to help Rathfield up off the ground. "As I said, it is an evil place." He pointed toward the tallest peaks, two of which, Owen was willing to swear, stood further apart than they had. "The evil is concentrated up there. A wise man would run."

Rathfield dusted himself off. "I have my orders."

Nathaniel shook his head. "Follow 'em and you'll likely have more scars, too."

The Norillian lifted his chin. "Are you brave enough a man to follow me, Woods?"

"Iffen you ever do see the far side of those mountains, it ain't because I been *following*." The scout shrugged. "I reckon I can stand a couple more scars. So long as I live to tell the tale, I ain't got call to complain."

CHAPTER ELEVEN

23 April 1767
Government House, Temperance
Temperance Bay, Mystria

Prince Vlad hated finishing the day off with a lie. "Very pleased to have you here, Bishop Bumble. I hope the late hour has not inconvenienced you." *So that was* two *lies.*

The stocky little man limped his way into the Prince's private office. He shifted a heavy walking-stick from right to left and offered his hand. "So kind of you to see me, Highness. And on such short notice. I'd not expected to see you so quickly."

"I hardly wished to waste your time, Excellency." Vlad shook the man's clammy hand. "Your gout is acting up?"

The man patted his bulbous stomach. "I fear I like rich food too much. It is a curse, but I endure."

The Prince waved him toward a sitting nook near the fireplace where two chairs flanked a tiny table. A small fire had been laid to take an edge off the evening's chill, and to heat water in a pot. A silver tea service on a tray, with fine ceramic cups from the far east and a small dish of biscuits beside it, sat on the table. He waited for Bumble to sit, and took secret pleasure in his servant, Chandler, having given the cleric a chair that wobbled beneath the man's weight. It was a petty victory, but likely the only one he'd see in their meeting.

"You will take tea, of course."

"You are so very kind."

Prince Vlad poured each of them a cup, then sat. He did so gingerly, his hindquarter still being a bit sensitive. Mugwump, while doing better when it came to flight training, still landed hard. "Your note said you had urgent business. As this is the only opening in my schedule…"

"Yes, I shan't keep you over long, Highness." Bumble smiled, excess flesh piling up around the edges of his mouth. "I wanted to ask after the disposition of the Rathfield Expedition."

Vlad raised his cup and sipped, burning his tongue, and using that sensation to cover his surprise. "Beg pardon?"

The white-haired man blew on his tea before sipping. "I only know the barest of details, Highness. I'd had a note from the Archbishop that arrived with Colonel Rathfield. Before he departed he attended services here at St. Martin's and sought some spiritual counseling."

"Indeed."

Bumble returned his cup and saucer to the table. "I would not be breaking a confidence to note that he had reservations about how his mission should be acquitted. You see, on one hand, the Crown gave him free rein to do what was necessary to bring the people of Postsylvania to justice. He felt, however, that if they had moved away because of religious motivation, temporal remedies might not be appropriate."

The Prince nodded. It seemed both a logical conclusion and one in keeping with Rathfield's character. "What did you advise, if I may ask?"

Bumble took a biscuit and nibbled. "These are very good."

"Chandler's wife bakes them. Her brother and sister-in-law own the bakery on Friendship, just south of Prudence."

"Prosperity Baker and his wife, Lisbet." The bishop nodded. "I shall visit and even recommend them."

"Very kind." The prince snapped a biscuit in half. "You were saying?"

"Oh, my, yes, was I? Quite. I suggested that a devout man—and he is quite devout you know—might be able to serve both spiritual and temporal realms by returning the leader of Postsylvania to Temperance for a trial. It would let the people see that we are quite fair, and would point out the logical consequences of defiance against heavenly ordained authority."

"An interesting idea, but the charges laid against the Postsylvanians would be treason. They'd have to be sent to Launston to be tried." Vlad shrugged. "Your plan had merit."

"It yet does." Bumble brushed crumbs from his shirt. "You see, I knew about the treason charges. I was thinking of heresy, and a court ecclesiastical. The end result would, of course, be the same."

Vlad's eyes narrowed. "But we have a question of jurisdiction, don't we? Postsylvania is well beyond the borders of Temperance Bay."

"I've already taken the liberty, Highness, of securing the agreement of my counterparts in Richlan and Bounty. My aide, Mr. Beecher, is bound for Rivertown in Fairlee even now. I really anticipate no difficulty in getting the other bishops to agree to holding the trial here. In fact, I would expect two of them to join me on the Tribunal."

"And if the Postsylvanians are found guilty?"

"They will burn at the stake, of course." He sipped more tea. "All of their property would be forfeit to the state."

The Prince sat back in his chair, his mind racing. For Bumble to already have an agreement from Bishop Hereford in Kingstown, he must have sent his agent off before the expedition departed. He likely sent a number of men south on a ship. One landed in Kingstown, Beecher would land in Fairlee, and so on. Given that Bumble had a reputation as a powerful orator and leading theologian, getting support out of the other bishops would not be difficult. *Nor is his action inappropriate from their point of view.*

What surprised and concerned Vlad was Bumble's mentioning the forfeiture aspect of the heresy laws. The Postsylvanians had violated the law by moving outside colonies sanctioned under official charters. The Crown had granted no charters west of the mountains because the land beyond it lay in the Tharyngian sphere of influence. If property the Postsylvanians claimed as their own ended up being forfeit to the Crown, it could be given out to a variety of supporters, effectively extending Mystria's border into the area claimed by the Tharyngians. That would either result in another war immediately, or lay the groundwork for something even worse, later. Moreover, he got the sense that Bumble pointed this out as a way that the Prince might enrich himself—in effect offering him a bribe for his compliance with the Church's plan.

Something else niggled at the back of the Prince's mind. "You mentioned the Postsylvanians having a leader. Their petition mentioned no single person as the leader of the True Oriental Church of the Lord. What do you know of the congregation?"

"I would never spread gossip, Highness."

"Indulge me. The welfare of the expedition is my responsibility. If you knew something that hinted at danger, and I was not able to act to prevent it, the consequences could be dire."

Bumble glanced down at his fat fingers as he rubbed crumbs from them. "I doubt you will recall him, but twenty years ago I had a young prelate join St. Martins. Mystrian, he had been sent to seminary in Norisle. I paid for him to go. I had high hopes. Ephraim Fox was his name. He returned full of God's fire, or so it seemed, and then, at times, would sink into so deep a melancholy that he could barely rouse himself. I did all I could to counsel him. My wife and I prayed with and for him, but something had gotten into him. He began to see things in the Good Book. He found patterns, you see, codes. He claimed that there was another Revelation due the Church, and he had been chosen to deliver it."

Prince Vlad shook his head. "I don't recall any of that."

"I tried to save him, but it was of no use. The demons in him were too strong. He fled Temperance. I would hear nothing for years, then would occasionally get thick missives delivered. It was all nonsense. He'd press a leaf into a page and draw diagrams and show how they were related to Scripture. It proved nothing, but he said it proved everything."

So, what did Fox think he'd discovered, and why are you so anxious that it should remain hidden? Vlad could not help but think of the possible conspiracy concerning magick and the Church. "You received more than one of these documents? Do you still have them?"

"Yes, and no, I had them consigned to the flames. They were the devil's work."

Vlad stood and began pacing. "You don't understand what you've done, do you? With just one of those leaves and my library, I could pinpoint where he'd been when he wrote you. I've had Nathaniel and Kamiskwa and Owen collecting hundreds of samples. The Shedashee regularly bring me things that I could have used to place him. Postsylvania could be anywhere, and his messages could have told me exactly where."

Bumble's face closed. "I understand that you take great pride in what you learn through these Tharyngian methods of study, Highness, but I warn you that you put your immortal soul in peril by continuing them."

"And I fail to see how compiling a catalog of God's creation does anything to diminish the glory of the Creator." Vlad sighed. "You're certain you have nothing?"

"The last thing came months ago, before December."

"About the time the petition would have gone to Launston. No chance it was saved?"

"I gave it to my wife to destroy."

"Ask her, please if, by accident…"

"This is my wife, Highness. She obeys me in everything. It's gone, I assure you."

"Yes, of course. Still, it could be very important." Vlad gave him an open glance. "I would be in your debt."

"I shall make inquiries." He held a hand up. "And if anything else comes, I shall turn it over to you."

"Thank you."

Before the Prince could return to his chair, the teacups began to rattle in their saucers. The small mound of biscuits collapsed. They rolled off the table's edge, eluding Bishop Bumble's clumsy attempts at catching them. The silver teapot danced across the tray, the lid bouncing up and down. Then Bumble's chair cracked, spilling the cleric to the ground.

Vlad ignored him and his plight. He stared at the tea in his cup, memorizing how high waves rose. He began counting to himself, slowly, measuring the time. His heart pounded as the floor shifted and the building creaked. Little dust falls shot down from rafters, spreading through the air like ink disappearing into a glass of clear water.

After twenty seconds the ground stopped moving. Vlad waited, still counting, just to be certain.

Bumble, florid-faced and fumbling to return the biscuits to the plate, stared up at him from the floor. "There, you see, God does not approve of your Tharyngian studies."

"Quiet, man." The Prince crossed to his desk and noted the time. He wrote down the duration, then found a ruler and returned to his teacup. He measured the difference between the settled level and the high point. At his desk again, he wrote the numbers down, estimated the volume of liquid that had been moving, then sat.

"Would you say it was more a shaking motion or a rolling one?"

"Shaking."

"We agree." Vlad left his chair and sprinted across the chamber to the eastern door. He threw it open and ran into the corridor, all the way to the windows looking toward the bay. Ships rocked at anchor, but not extraordinarily so, and the people in the street carried on normally. A few folks were picking up dropped packages, and a grocer restacked potatoes in a box, but otherwise it would appear that no serious damage had been done.

The Prince had started back toward his office by the time Bumble caught up to him. "Highness, do not mock me or God."

"I assure you, Bishop Bumble, I would never mock God. Or his servant." Vlad led him back into the office. "That was an earth tremor—not unknown in these parts, but rare according to the Shedashee. They usually presage disaster, at least in their folktales. Dark times come after them."

Bumble snorted. "Yes, you have crumbs on the floor, and could have lost some very nice porcelain."

Prince Vlad turned and jabbed the cleric in the chest with a finger. "You, sir, are unaware of what all this means. For us to have felt a tremor here, one which, if my reading of the du Malphias scale for earthquakes is correct, would measure 3.2; there must have been a tremendous event somewhere else. And you may damn my Tharyngian methods, but natural philosophers from around the world—some of them clerics like yourself—have noticed a correlation between earth tremors and tidal waves. If, by the top of the hour, we see water recede from the shore here, we could be looking at a wall of water that would wash away the entire city, including your cathedral. If it occurred to the west, we could experience a surge coming down the rivers that could be far worse than spring flooding. This is to say nothing of what has happened in communities closer to the site of the earthquake. The devastation there could be utter and complete."

Vlad pointed at the tray and tea pot. "If you look at the scratches, the tea pot moved from the southwest to northeast. This might suggest that the earthquake took place out in the direction of Postsylvania."

"It would be God's judgment upon them."

"I care less about His judgment of them than the welfare of the expedition."

"A very good point, Highness." Bumble straightened his frock coat. "I shall return to the cathedral and pray for them."

"No, you won't."

The small man's dark eyes blinked with surprise. "I do not believe,

Highness, that you wish to tell me when I can and cannot do God's work."

"And I thought you understood God's intention for you in all this." Vlad pointed toward the bay. "You'll ring the bells and when people respond, you will send some of them to watch the bay to see if it recedes. If it does, you will ring the bells again and urge people to get to high ground—Virtue Street or Blessedness. You'll also ask them to watch for signs of fire.

"If the water does not recede, you will offer a service for those who might be affected and will begin to collect things like clothes and anything else people can spare. God help us if the Benjamin River overflows. We will have things ready to send to Kingstown or Fairlee, since refugees will follow the rivers."

"That would defy God's judgment."

"But did not Our Lord demand forgiveness and charity? 'Respect the demands of the Father, but temper your response with the demands of the Son.' Don't I recall you having said that in your sermon *The Lantern Held High?*"

"You would be taking that out of context, Highness. Even the devil can quote the Good Book for his own purposes."

Prince Vlad forced his face to blank, and let a hurt tone enter into his voice. "How can you ever believe, Bishop Bumble, that I would be doing the devil's work? I was merely suggesting that you organize among your flock as I shall organize the Mystrian Militia. As your people are able to organize supplies, we can take able-bodied young men and deploy them to survey the damage and rebuild. While God may have visited his judgment on a people, could not the devil have used the consequences of that just punishment to hurt others in an attempt to drive them from God's bosom? If the devil can use the Good Book, surely he could use divine acts for that same purpose. This was what I meant, Bishop, and if I was so abrupt that my intentions unclear, please forgive me."

The look of puzzlement on Bumble's face revealed much to Vlad. The man knew he was trapped, but not quite how he had been trapped. For him to refuse to organize when the Prince did would leave Bumble in an inferior position. Just as he had laid the groundwork for the court ecclesiastic to elevate himself, now he found himself with another op-portunity to raise himself in the esteem of others. He couldn't pass it up, but he also couldn't shake the knowledge that he'd been manipulated for his own gain.

He also won't like that I was able to quote both his sermons and the Good Book back to him. It was a sin Vlad was certain he'd pay for, but that mattered little at the moment. "Please tell me you understand, Bishop."

"I do, Highness. Of course I shall do my utmost to help in these dire times."

"Good. And you will send me the Postsylvania manuscript."

"Yes, Highness." Bumble bowed his head. "I shall do God's bidding for the exaltation of His family here on Earth."

CHAPTER TWELVE

Nathaniel looked back at the others following behind him along the game trail. "Another turn around and we should have a pretty good vantage point."

The others grumbled and laughed in equal measure, since he'd been making that promise for most of the morning. Since the earthquake, they had moved slowly onward and upward along the eastern ridgeline. What they had taken from the distance to be a single mountain chain actually had multiple rows of saw-toothed ridges running in parallel. They could see two over to what was the tallest, but had no idea how many rows stood on the western side of the tall peaks. They also could see no obvious passes through to the west.

When the earthquake hit, their natural inclination had been to descend to the lake, but Kamiskwa stopped them. He pointed to the great eruptions of bubbles across the lake, which churned the placid waters into a turgid gray-green sludge. Having a source of fresh water so clearly fouled was enough to slow them, but when an eagle dove to pluck a dead fish from the surface, and plunged into the water without appearing again, they stopped cold.

Count von Metternin produced a spyglass and studied the lake. "This is not unknown in some swamps and lakes. Yearly sediment covers over decaying plants and animals. It traps gasses which suffocate the unsuspecting."

Kamiskwa nodded. "Our people are told that when the ground shakes, or a lake bubbles, we should seek high ground. In the wake will come the dark wind."

"But a dark wind? It is so primitive." Rathfield stood tall, his arms folded across his chest. "This land is sorely lacking civilization, and would be better for it."

Nathaniel had stood at that point. "I might be taking exception to the notion that my brother is lying, or that his story ain't as good as the Count's on account of his telling it."

Rathfield looked down his nose at Nathaniel. "I think even you would agree that the considered opinion of a noble from Auropa carries more weight than a tale of fancy from an uneducated savage."

"I might agree iffen we was talking things all noble and Auropy, but this here is Mystria and ain't nobody gonna be knowing more about it than the Shedashee." He raised a hand. "Hold on up, now, I ain't done my piece. I been out here on this land for thirty years. I felt a tremble or two, but ain't never I felt nothing like we just did. And I ain't never seed a lake bubble like that, or an eagle die like that. Now, iffen you're of a mind to go down there and bring some of your civilization to that lake, I ain't gonna stop you. I jes want you to know you'll be walking alone."

Owen looked up from where he'd been writing in a notebook. "What do you think we ought to do?"

Nathaniel looked at Kamiskwa, then pointed further up into the mountains. "We ain't exactly at the highest point around here. I reckon we get there, then we figure out what else to do."

Kamiskwa led the way and Nathaniel remained at the rear. He wasn't concerned with anyone coming up on them; he just didn't want to be leading. The ground shaking the way it had wasn't right. The ground had always been solid, then it just turned into jelly. He wasn't sure how long it had been shaking, but how ever much time it was, it was more than he wanted to experience.

More than that, the lake bothered him. He couldn't count the number of similar lakes he'd crossed or camped beside in his life. Had the party been making camp on the shore, he'd have had them set up right where the outlet stream had been trickling to the north. By the time the earth had stopped shaking, the wave would have washed them all away without warning. If someone survived, the dark wind would have taken him.

They stopped on a shelf overlooking the lake, but not high enough to see to the next valley. They supposed there was a lake up there, too, since a stream spilled down a rock face, and a ruin of trees showed where some water had pitched giant stones from above down to the lake and forest below. It didn't look to Nathaniel that a great volume of water had flowed down—a sentiment that Owen and von Metternin agreed with when he mentioned it.

None of them slept very well that night and, with dawn, they gathered their things to move on. They did so sluggishly, as the lake below them still burped here and there, and the water still possessed the appearance of a rancid pea soup. They debated whether or not to make a fire and cook breakfast, and Nathaniel helped the debate rage by advocating sloth simply because Rathfield wanted to get going.

Then, just after dawn, the dark wind came. Hodge noticed it in the way that the trees at the edge of the upper valley started rustling, then how the trees below bent as if being hit with an invisible river. More trees shook, then the lake's surface rippled. Clearly wind was moving over it, but the explorers felt nothing. They smelled nothing unusual, either. It was as if a ghost stalked the valley.

And that ghost killed. Birds that had nested high enough to avoid the effects of the lake gasses had descended to feed on dead fish. As the dark wind passed, they keeled over. One tried to get airborne, but in mid-flight simply folded its wings and crashed onto a small stretch of beach. The dark wind killed everything, including their debate on whether to stay or go.

They all agreed to move on, wanting to be well shed of the place. They began working up along the ridge and aiming to go further up. This course of action made sense in a couple of ways. The dark wind appeared to be heavier than air, and moved along quickly. Kamiskwa pointed out that it had not shaken boughs in the upper third of the forest, so as long as they stayed higher than that, they should be fine. If they came to a place where safety was questionable, they'd put a rope on a man, let him go, and pull him back if there was any trouble.

To his credit, Rathfield volunteered to be that man, overruling Hodge Dunsby. Hodge had advanced himself because he was the smallest, lowest to the ground, and the lightest for pulling back. Rathfield countered that this was his expedition and would accept no counter to that argument. With him leading them through the most dangerous places, it took another week to get past two higher mountain valleys and reach the overlook.

The valley had once been home to a large lake. It normally drained to the east, but the earthquake had shattered that edge of its basin, creating a giant rupture. The draining water had carved a deep channel through the sediments and the lake itself had been reduced to a small pond. To the southwest, another higher valley poured water into it through a spectacular, slender waterfall which appeared to have been born of the quake.

Owen had produced a map and annotated it. He showed it to Nathaniel and shook his head. "I hope I am wrong, but I think this lake was the headwater of the Snake River. It probably flooded every spring after snow melted, but nothing like this."

Flesh tightened on Nathaniel's arms. He didn't know how to do the math that Owen and Count von Metternin would do to determine the volume of water pouring down from the mountain. He didn't need to. He just knew it was a lot. *And down there in Plentiful, they built a lot on the banks of that river.*

He looked at Owen. "Reckon there's anything left of Plentiful?"

Owen flipped back several pages in his notebook. He'd mapped the village accurately. He looked up at the muddy expanse that marked the lake's original shore. "Not much of it. Nor of many other places along the Snake. Kingstown might even be in trouble."

Rathfield came over and glanced at the map. "Spot of bad luck for Shepherd Faith and his flock."

Owen frowned. "That's cold blooded."

"Hardly, Strake."

"It's hardly charitable."

"Neither does it lack charity." Rathfield pointed off along the unseen river. "Standing here we can do absolutely nothing for them. Whatever fate overtook them did so a week ago. I fervently believe that because of their faith, God will call them to Him. In fact, calling them to Him may have been the reason this all happened."

Nathaniel's eyes narrowed. "You're 'specting me to believe your God would cause all this destruction for to harvest nine dozen folks what see Him as their salvation?"

"I am not a theologian, Woods, just a man who believes what he is told. I am not wise enough to figure out the mind of God."

"But you're willing to suggest He's sloppy when it comes to doing a job."

Before Rathfield could respond, Hodge Dunsby came running over from the west. "Captain Strake, you'll want to see what Count von Metternin has found."

The rest of the party followed Dunsby around what had once been the shore and off into a small canyon to the west. Water seeped down from the higher walls and drained through the middle. It created a lush grassland with a few wide trails through the shoulder-height growth.

Count von Metternin crouched over the body of a creature roughly the size of a dairy cow. It had a shaggy grey coat, though the coat was thinning in patches as the beast lost its winter fur. Its skull had a high crown and featured a pair of ivory tusks about as long as a man's forearm. It had a long snakelike nose, and something—a crow most likely—had taken the upward-facing eye.

Nathaniel dropped to a knee. "Looks like one of them mastodons what will be migrating north soon."

Owen pulled a piece of paper from his notebook and unfolded it. "Pygmy mastodon. It's on the Prince's list. He said they might be in an island in the sky."

Owen and the others fanned out through the grasses to look for more bodies. They took to counting and measuring the carcasses. As they went to work, Nathaniel grabbed Kamiskwa and headed down to the pond to refill canteens and waterskins. The water had cleared and the presence of wading birds hunting on the new shore suggested the water was safe for drinking.

"Did you know these was up here?"

Kamiskwa sank a bubbling canteen into the water. "The Altashee do not hunt in these lands."

"Doesn't answer my question."

"I do not believe every story I hear."

Nathaniel caught an odd note in his voice. "Are you a-scared?"

Kamiskwa's hand dropped to the hilt of his obsidian knife. "I am a Prince of the Altashee."

"Then you're damned lucky, on account of I am *terrified*." Nathaniel sat and sighed. "Ain't enough we're out here visiting villages where all these people professing to believe in the same Good Book use it to justify all manner of different things. You've been acting queer since we climbed into the mountains, and more so since the ground shook. I ain't been no great shakes since then, neither. And now you not telling me the truth."

The Altashee grunted, then sat. "I do not know what the truth is. We have stories, Nathaniel, many old stories. Some told of creatures like Mugwump, and I did not believe them until I saw him. But those were good stories, for the most part. But here, do you know what we call these mountains? *Nesgagoquina.*"

Nathaniel scratched at the back of his neck. "Wall of the other men?"

"More *fortress.* They are monsters, Nathaniel, like the *wendigo*, but many, many times worse. There were once many stories of them, horrible stories. Not even my father knows many of them. He says his grandfather refused to tell him all he knew, because *his* grandfather had refused to tell all he knew, and so on. They come and kill silently—and an earthquake presages their arrival."

Nathaniel frowned. Kamiskwa wasn't given to panic, but something about the mountains was clearly getting under his skin. He figured that these other men could just be a story made up to explain the dark wind, but if that were true, why would there be anything called the dark wind in the first place? Just because he'd never seen one of these other men didn't mean they didn't exist. Nathaniel believed in the Queen of Norisle, even though he'd never clapped eyes on her.

"Well now, what *has* Msitazi told you 'bout them?"

"Nothing good. He says the spirits of the winding path bow before them. It's why none of the Shedashee hunt in these mountains."

Nathaniel ran a hand over his jaw. "I reckon I hain't never been steered wrong listening to Shedashee wisdom. I also reckon that if Prince Vlad knew about these other men, he'd have them on his list. And if they's as nasty as you're letting on that they are, we're going to need to learn a mite more about them. In the stories, can they die?"

Kamiskwa thought for a moment, then nodded. "There are warriors who have slain them. They always pay a terrible price."

"Shoot 'em or what?"

"It was before we had brimstone."

Nathaniel forced a smile on his face. "I reckon I like the sound of that."

The Altashee nodded, then looked over. "Nathaniel, what if my coming into the mountains awakened the other men?"

"Somehow I don't see that a-happening." Nathaniel began filling a waterskin. "First, I don't imagine you is the first Shedashee to set foot in these mountains since your grandfathers stopped telling some stories. Second, I would be thinking that the tramp of some hunter's boot, or the sound of some preacher hollering the gospel would have gone and did wake anything in these here mountains. Lastly, Colonel Rathfield reckons it was his God what split the earth. It's His responsibility, then, not yours."

Kamiskwa gathered the canteens and stood. "And you were not lying about being afraid?"

"Just to make you feel good? Iffen I thought it would make you feel better, I still wouldn't do it. I ain't never going to lie to you, Kamiskwa. If a lie would make you feel better, you ain't worth having as a friend. And if you was dumb enough to believe a lie, ain't no sense in having you as a friend."

"Thank you." The Altashee's amber eyes tightened. "And it is not just the earth shaking that scares you, is it?"

"Don't reckon it is." Nathaniel stood and slung the waterskins over his shoulder. "Even after the shaking, this land is beautiful, but the others, they don't notice it. I love Owen and Prince Vlad, but all their measuring and taking of samples and all, it just steals the beauty. And once a man puts a number on something, another man equates it to money, then the spoiling really begins."

He shook his head. "What I'm afraid of, my friend, is that this land is going to be dying, and that there ain't a damned thing I can do about it."

CHAPTER THIRTEEN

1 May 1767
Westridge Mountains, Mystria

In the highest valley, rising from the sediments of what had been a deep and forbidding lake, lay an unearthly settlement the very sight of which froze Owen's blood in his veins. The scale of buildings mocked that of even the grandest place in Temperance, and rivaled that of palaces and Parliament back in Norisle. Though the walls surrounding the town had been largely destroyed—*melted* from the way they sagged between towers which resembled half-burned candles—details remained here and there to hint at great artistry.

The expedition had taken three days at what they called Little Elephant Lake to catalogue specimens and smoke as much of the mastodon meat as they could. They hid tusks in a small cave for retrieval on their return trip. Rathfield had protested at the delay, but only half-heartedly. Thousands of animals had died when the dark wind rose from that lake. The sheer magnitude of the slaughter demanded exploration.

And then they moved on and discovered something even stranger. Owen had been in the lead when a treefall gave him a clear view of the city. Even at dusk, as they approached, its terrible majesty slowed their steps. Kamiskwa visibly hung back. Nathaniel moved up with Owen. Rathfield, who had asserted leadership in other times where enthusiasm had flagged, did not push past either of them and stripped the deerskin scabbard from his musket.

Makepeace broke the silence. "I may not be knowing what it is, but I know it ain't holy. And I ain't afraid of saying this is about as close as I want to get in the dark."

Nathaniel agreed. "I reckon we should set up camp over yonder, up by that outcropping of rock. Me and Owen will look around a bit, then join you."

The Altashee grunted. "Cold camp."

"Much as I might be wanting fire, I ain't thinking I want a beacon." Nathaniel unsheathed his rifle. "Let's go, Captain Strake. I reckon the Prince is going to want to know all there is to know about this place."

Owen took a deep breath, then shucked his pack. Hodge offered to carry it to their camp. Freeing his rifle, Owen fell into step with Nathaniel. As much as he didn't want to be going any closer to the strange ruins, he took a perverse joy in the fact that Rathfield retreated to set up camp.

Did you leave your courage behind in Rondeville, Colonel? Owen blushed the second the thought occurred to him, but didn't find himself particularly sorry for having thought it.

"I hain't never seen nothing like this."

"Nor have I." Owen pointed to a single tower that had somehow escaped destruction. "There are towers that high in Launston, but you can see where the stones are fitted together. Here, no seams, no mortar."

"And the color, milky white like a blind man's eyes. Little bits of color where the sun is touching the top there."

"Like an opal." Owen shivered. "There, at the tower's base."

The closest thing he could think of to remind him of the statue at the tower's base was *gargoyle*, but somehow that didn't seem right. The sediments, which had dried and cracked, revealed little bits of the statue. It had been carved of a pale green stone and had a massively bulbous head that sagged back away from deep, empty eye-sockets. The creature's face had no nose, just a pair of vertical slits, and no ears. While dirt covered the lower half of the face, stone tentacles emerged as if some obscene parody of a moustache or beard.

"I reckon that when the Good Book talks about graven images, this is what them prophets and all had in mind."

The two men moved toward the north, giving the half-buried statue a wide berth. From their new vantage point they looked into the city. Most of the buildings had the same seamless construction, and were quite modest. Two of the three larger buildings had sustained significant damage. A third, set into the mountain's flesh on the western side of the valley, was by far the largest and appeared intact. In fact, the center of the settlement appeared to be much lower than all of the surrounding area, and buildings leaned toward it as if being drawn down into it. Even so, the stresses that would entail had not cracked any stone.

Owen had only enough sunlight left to make a basic sketch of the settlement. He chose not to draw the statue. He told himself this was because it was largely hidden, but he knew it wasn't true. It would take more time to sketch it than he wanted to spend around it.

Owen and Nathaniel made their way to the camp. They supped on smoked mastodon meat, which benefited from the applewood they'd use dto smoke it, though it still tasted gamey. Rathfield set up watches, and they all agreed to his schedule. No one believed they'd be sleeping much. Makepeace read Scripture aloud—Hodge and Rathfield chose to listen.

Owen momentarily wished for moonlight, but then decided having a dark sky was better. The city would glow in moonlight, like a ghost from some ancient time. The mountain's peak eclipsed a wedge of the night sky, which prevented the towers from being silhouetted against stars. He hoped that not being able to see the city would help him relax, but he could *feel* it lurking there, as if it were an infection in the earth, giving off heat.

He decided it was best that he had no light, for he would be compelled to note all of his observation in his journal. He certainly would make complete notes, as he had at Little Elephant Lake, but were there light he would have put down more of his feelings—admitting to fear and dread. While he was not worried about such admissions casting aspersions upon his manhood, he wasn't sure he wanted them set so raw on the page. He had, after all, promised Bethany Frost he would let her read what he wrote.

Fear of what she would think of him didn't give him pause. She had seen him at his utter worst, and had gotten him through it. She had edited the memoir of his previous adventures, and had even suggested cutting or modifying certain passages she felt might be open to misinterpretation. She had read more of his adventures than anyone else save for Prince Vlad, and had protected his interests through her editing.

But here he could protect her, for nothing he had seen before had ever felt as wrong as this place did. He didn't want her terrified. The second that thought burst into his brain, he had to smile. If he had told her that, she'd have scolded him. She was much stronger than she might have appeared—and much smarter. But in many ways he felt that what the dawn would reveal was something against which intellect could provide scant armor.

Though he had not thought he would be able to sleep, when he finally stretched out, he dropped off immediately. He didn't wake up until the first rays of dawn painted themselves against the gray spearhead of the mountain summit stabbing into thin clouds above. He sat up immediately and the world swam, as if he'd drunk far too much the night before. He remembered no dreams, and found that fact as unsettling as he did his companions' pale complexions.

Nathaniel reached his feet first and hefted his rifle.

"'Pears to me that this here place is a mite unsettling for all of us. Colonel Rathfield was sent out here to find Postsylvania. I reckon that still needs to be done, but I also figger that this here place needs some going over. I hain't got no book learning, but I'm thinking that those what does among us hain't seen none of this before, neither."

Every one turned toward Count von Metternin. The small man smiled, but opened his hands. "You do me credit, my friends. I have traveled extensively, at war and in peace. I have read the Remian historians and attended lectures by those who have traveled to places I have not. Though my glimpse of this place was brief, I know of nothing like it."

Nathaniel nodded. "Colonel?"

Rathfield shook his head. "I recall nothing like it, Woods."

"No disrespect intended to anyone else, but I reckon that's as good as we'll do on the book-learning front. So what I propose is this. We start looking this place over, but we do it the way Prince Vlad would do. And I reckon we can start with anything you've noticed already."

Hodge raised a hand. "Look around. I don't see any sign of beavers, and there were a number at Little Elephant Lake. They should be here, shouldn't they?"

"Good point, Hodge." Nathaniel scratched at his jaw. "Fact is, I don't see no birds' nests, no dead fish, no signs of raccoons or bears or anything else scavenging here. No claw marks on trees, neither. I don't reckon much lived up here."

Kamiskwa stood, his expression as hard and eyes as tight as Owen had ever seen. "It's the magick. Very bad magick. I can feel it."

Owen looked at him. "Like the heat from an infection?"

Surprise lifted the Altashee's brows for a second. "A bit more than that, but yes."

Nathaniel nodded once, strongly. "Good. I reckon you'll want to be making notes, Captain. Let's start in. Once we learn something gots some heft to it, we can figger if this is more important than Postsylvania and plan accordingly."

Their survey produced a great deal of information that led to speculation, the contemplation of which introduced a tremor into Owen's handwriting. The statue, when excavated, showed a man crouched beneath the figure, wearing the tentacled monstrosity as a mask. Lettering ran all the way around the statue's square base. No one had seen anything like it and none of them could decipher it. The serpentine lettering seemed to shift when he stared at it, frustrating any attempt to make an accurate record of the words. At least, it did before Owen had Hodge cover the writing up, then only reveal a handful of letters at a time.

And while he was writing, Owen checked often to see if the infectious heat was coming up from his facsimile, but it was not.

The intact tower provided a second set of revelations that set everyone on edge. A stairway spiraled up inside the walls all the way to the flat roof. The stairway had two sets of risers, with the smaller running right up the middle and adding two steps to the other set. The taller stairs rose eighteen inches between courses, while the smaller only six. Owen could take the larger steps, but not conveniently. Missing floor beams and planking hinted at tall ceilings and suggested that whatever used them stood ten or twelve feet tall. The lower steps suggested creatures smaller than men, but how much smaller he had no way to gauge.

More importantly, while the windows in the tower's lower reaches amounted to little more than slits, up top they broadened and had a wide sill at the bottom. While that sill would provide cover against shots from below, the window width made no sense unless man-sized creatures were meant to move in and out. Owen ran his hand over the sill's smooth, cold stone and could detect no scratches or other clues as to its purpose.

The need to accommodate giants became evident elsewhere, as did provisions made for smaller creatures. Large doorways opened into houses with no inner partitions or decorations. For all intents and purposes, they were warehouses into which creatures were marched and stored. The lake's water had long since washed away any murals or other paintings. Though he looked closely, he couldn't even find signs of where someone had scratched marks corresponding to days on the walls, or carved his name for posterity.

Count von Metternin found that odd. "I once heard that even in the Tombs of Kings in far Aegeptos, grave robbers scrawled their names. Men wished to be remembered."

Owen sighed. "I don't think these were men. I'm not even sure they had names."

"Their names are here." Kamiskwa ran a hand over the smooth stone. In its wake, letters glowed violet for a handful of heartbeats. Rendered in the same lettering as on the statue's base, but more crudely so, they overlapped in some places, and in others had extra letters squeezed into place to correct an error. "But these are names that should be forgotten."

Owen raised his hand to the wall and concentrated. He didn't feel anything at first, then, in his fingertips, he caught the same tug as a nettle might cause when brushing the flesh. Nothing glowed as his hand passed over it. He pulled in all fingers but one and began tracing invisible letters.

Kamiskwa's hand closed on his wrist with an iron grip. "Owen, stop."

Owen blinked his eyes. He stood a dozen feet from where he had begun and could not remember taking a single step. "I don't understand."

"The winding path, you remember."

He nodded. "I *do* remember the winding path. That's what's odd. I don't remember what I just did here."

The Altashee shook his head. "This magick is that much stronger precisely so you cannot remember."

Count von Metternin's eyes narrowed. "You will forgive my impudence, Prince Kamiskwa, but your knowledge of magick could be taken as a knowledge of this place and the people who were once here."

Kamiskwa released Owen's hand. "I wish I knew more magick and less of what these people were. To know less would be difficult, for what I know is echoes of whispers of stories half-heard in days long dead. None of it is good. Until I saw this place, I had no reason to believe any of the stories."

"What do you know?"

The Altashee opened his arms. "There are creatures that come in the night to steal children and to crush and kill. Sometimes they are giants. Sometimes they are smaller fiends."

Von Metternin smiled. "Not so unlike the trolls and goblins of my nation's folklore."

Owen frowned. "But I don't remember you saying anything of lost cities like this in Kesse."

"True, Owen, but then we have not drained our deep lakes. There are glaciers which could bury a thousand of these settlements and we would never know." He narrowed his eyes. "These creatures appear to be very reliant on magick, and this may, too, be a part of why we have no ruins for them.

"In the Good Book we have the flood, which God used to wash away evil from His creation. What if this is a place that survived the flood? We could be standing in the last outpost of an Antediluvian civilization. I believe the Good Book even mentions giants on the earth. Mr. Bone would know. Perhaps we can consult him and…"

A gunshot rang through the ruins. The three of them sprinted from the giant house, and a second gunshot turned them west toward the edifice they had taken to calling the Temple. They ran toward where Hodge and Nathaniel knelt on one knee on a patch of dried mud.

There was no mistaking the clear moccasin print, now days old, in the middle of it.

Nathaniel glanced toward the Temple. "'Pears we weren't the first to find this place, and those what was here before us, they weren't of a mind to be scientific about their exploring."

CHAPTER FOURTEEN

1 May 1767
Prince Haven
Temperance Bay, Mystria

Prince Vlad sat back, removed his glasses, and scrubbed hands over his face. *How can my eyes burn when my blood is running cold?*

Documents and books lay strewn over his desk as if it were debris washed down the Benjamin River after the earthquake. The damage in Temperance Bay and Bounty was not severe, though requests for supplies had been sent down river and goods started back up in the hands of the militia. Prince Vlad had given Caleb Frost the responsibility for organizing a company of men to make the trip. Caleb, he trusted, would make sure the supplies reached those who needed them and would resist the temptation of profiteering along the way.

Princess Gisella and Owen's wife had spearheaded relief efforts in Temperance Bay. They solicited donations, sorted them, and arranged for them to be shipped south to Kingstown. Though Catherine Strake hated being in Mystria, she did enjoy exercising unfettered power. This made her very useful in dealing with the current crisis.

Their efforts bought Prince Vlad time to work on two projects. One was Mugwump's flight training. The Prince was proud of his effort; the dragon was flying short distances without tiring quickly and appearing to gain strength and confidence each day. He, as yet, did not have the agility to pluck a bird out of the air, but he enjoyed flying enough to chase after wood doves. Vlad had cousins who were devoted to the art of falconry, and the Prince entertained fantasies of bringing Mugwump to one of their hunting jaunts.

The only thing the Prince did not like about the flight training was that he had no parameters for knowing how much dragons flew or pretty much anything else about the demands this would be making on Mugwump. The thing that troubled him the most was that Mugwump appeared to tolerate directions, but really didn't enjoy them. The dragon had never given him a glance that suggested he was thinking of just devouring the Prince—more of a look that said, "I know what I'm doing," which reflected a bit more annoyance than amusement.

Prince Vlad generally ended training sessions shortly after such looks. Mugwump was content to eat his fill and sleep for a long time after his flights. Not only did this give the Prince a chance to recover from his own aches and pains, but to work on his second problem—the problem that had sent a chill through him.

Bishop Bumble had sadly reported that none of the missives from Ephraim Fox survived. Within twelve hours of that message being delivered, however, a burlap satchel full letters and manuscripts appeared on the Frosts' doorstep. Dr. Frost had brought them to the Prince, and Vlad had retreated to his laboratory to study them.

They were remarkable in two ways. First, Ephraim Fox, or Ezekiel Fire as he had begun to call himself when he created the True Oriental Church of the Lord, had done an incredible job of cataloguing plants and animals in Mystria. The details he provided on each rivaled those recorded by the most careful of Tharyngian naturalists. His early work referenced some of their work and referenced journals that he appeared to have made of his observations of natural phenomena while studying in Norisle. Had the Prince known of the man and his passion for precision, he'd have hired him to travel with Nathaniel on expeditions.

Unfortunately, as brilliant as the observations were, the conclusions drawn from them were utterly and completely insane. Right next to a traced outline of a leaf, onto which had been drawn the veins and to which had been added a host of critical details, would be a long list of Scriptural references. Some clearly related to the ratios of leaf length to width, or the number of ribs and veins, or the number of points or petals on a flower. Others were abstracted through more arcane formulae, most of which the Prince could not intuit. The Norisle journals appeared to be the key to deciphering some of the material.

Prince Vlad tucked himself into Ezekiel Fire's world so deeply he began to see things through the man's eyes. He pulled out his own journals to double-check the man's observations. He crawled around outside, looking for new samples which he could measure and test against Fire's work. Before very long, Vlad began to see patterns in nature—very much the same patterns Fire did.

And, unfortunately, he saw more.

It all boiled down to the question of whether or not magick had predated the ability of men to read and write. Clearly it had. Illiterate men like Nathaniel Woods could be taught to use magick, so reading and writing were not necessary, but an ability to reason was. Prince Vlad's initial instructions in magick had involved reading the formula for a spell, memorizing it, transforming it into a symbol or concept, and then invoking that concept. His instructor had mentioned, for example, that some men think of a torch when igniting brimstone, and others the sun. That symbolic representation allowed them to focus magickal energy for the desired result.

As a teaching method, that made sense, but it didn't point out how preliterate people learned that they could access magick or how they trained themselves to focus it. One of the basic laws of magick, the Law of Sympathy, suggested that like objects could have a similar effect on a target. In preparing medicines for the heart, the foxglove, because of its heart-shaped blossom, was considered extremely valuable. Such linkages would have been obvious to the preliterate. In fact, as Fire had appeared to discover, many of the measurements in nature encouraged abstraction, which generated a symbol, upon which focus could be devoted to attain a desired magickal result. The idea, then, that early magicians had learned how to do magick based on things they saw in nature, made perfect sense.

Where Fire pushed it further was that he linked these measurements to scattered Scriptural verses. When Prince Vlad began playing with them, pulling them together and ordering the sentences, he immediately noticed two things. First, the words had the same sort of rhythm and cadence as offered in spell formulations. Second, and this had taken closer reading, the verses differed from the original Achean and Phaonaean verses. They were not so different as to be wholly incorrect, but the use of unsuitable or inexact synonyms for the original words made the translation more difficult than it needed to be.

Which made no sense. Prince Vlad sighed. It made no sense unless an entrenched group of magickers within the Church of Norisle had conspired with King Robert in creating his version of the Good Book. It seemed so monstrous and yet elegant a plan that Vlad did not know whether to be horrified or pleased with the work done by his ancestor. It appeared that the Church might have turned the Good Book into a grimoire. This put the key to magickal power into the hands of everyone, since the book had been printed and widely distributed. As primitive as Mystria was, Vlad doubted there was a village where at least one copy of the Good Book couldn't be found, and many were the families who cherished their own heirloom copies.

He rubbed his eyes. How often had he seen the sign in the cathedral, where Bishop Bumble had posted a list of Scriptures to be read and contemplated during the week? His sermons were liberally sprinkled with Scriptural references—some of which made no sense to Vlad, and now he understood why. The printed version of those same sermons often included footnotes that referenced yet other passages.

Anyone who knew the key to deciphering the verses could learn new magicks. The Church had, in essence, adopted the same sort of book-based code that the Prince shared with his father and with Owen, but in this case the key was also the message. And since books and verses were independent of page counts, any Good Book, big or small, in multiple volumes, would serve, provided it faithfully reproduced the King Robert Version text.

It seemed clear from Fire's writing that he felt his discovery of these spells within Scripture were confirmation of God's hand in their original transcription and in the KRV translation. Prince Vlad had no difficulty seeing the Church having a different reaction—primarily one of panic to learn that a madman had somehow cracked their code. This meant that anyone who learned it could use their grimoire, even Tharyngians. And some Church officials must have seen the even greater ramifications of Fire's work. He'd discovered the key by looking at nature, which meant *anyone* could rediscover the key.

Vlad shivered. The implications of all that were beyond his ability to fully comprehend. He wondered, however, if basic magick principles worked in ways he'd not considered before. The Law of Sympathy, for example, or the Law of Contagion. Could the Church use a person of a certain bloodline to control others in that bloodline? The Church encouraged—and often selected—members of noble families to enter its ranks. Vlad had seen that as a measure the nobility had taken to guarantee that the Church would not betray political leaders, but what if it was reversed? What if his father, for example, was a means through which King Richard could be controlled? And not just because he might be a hostage, but through some sorcerous influence that Prince John might not even understand. *What if my father's prayers for his brother constituted a formula through which the King was magically controlled?*

Though that thought disturbed Vlad the most—primarily for its implication for his children—he set it aside for the consideration of a greater issue. He went back to Fire's texts. Fire had used his observations of the natural world as confirmation of patterns in Scripture. Prince Vlad reversed that. He found a formulation that most closely approximated the words used to teach him to shoot a musket. He copied out the lines and included the numbers. The jumble of verses read, "The sun stood still and lit the way, shadows growing small."

He compared the words and data to plants, animals, and anything else he could think to use. Correlation escaped him at first, then he closed his eyes and composed a mental picture of what the words suggested. The sun was standing still, so he visualized it at its zenith. That would naturally make shadows small, but not completely invisible. Depending upon how far north one was from the equator, the angle of the shadow to the base of a rod would vary. It struck Vlad that while the image mirrored the noonday sun, it did so without invoking the sun directly. He suspected it did so because the image created would trigger magick sufficient for lighting brimstone and because, somewhere lost in the annals of time, a sorcerer invoking the power unleashed by the sun's direct image had accessed incredible power or caused a disaster, or perhaps both.

So the image we are trained to focus upon limits *us.* Prince Vlad frowned. The reason a musket spat fire when shot was because not all of the brimstone used in the charge was consumed before the ball left the muzzle. More powerful magicks might consume the brimstone completely, creating more pressure. That might burst a gun barrel, but were the breech strong enough, the greater propulsion would make a bullet go further and faster.

The reverse engineering of the spell cracked the door on an area of study that was at the root of all magick. The Tharyngians, when they overthrew the King and Church during their revolution, had begun to use scientific methods of measurement and observation to study and quantify the basic principles of magick. Had they had Fire's notes, they might well have understood everything and be so far beyond any other nation in the ability to control magick that they would be unstoppable. There was no doubt that the infinite power granted through magick could so thoroughly corrupt one that he might attempt to take over the world—and make him believe he might be successful in that attempt.

The Tharyngians' study had uncovered several things. Guy du Malphias had been able to reanimate the dead. Owen's reportage about what Prince Vlad took to be a control center suggested the Laureate could control his *pasmortes* at range. Owen had also seen du Malphias move objects with magick. This meant that either the dictum that magick only worked by touch was wrong or that du Malphias had managed to redefine touch. The idea that magicians were taught that magick only worked at touch certainly limited their ability to use it, but exactly how one could redefine touch escaped the Prince.

And then he heard Mugwump give his usual trumpeted bellow to welcome the wurmwright and dinner. In his laboratory, the sound came muted because it had to travel through the wall. *Outside it would be crisp and clear and in the wurmrest it would be deafening.* Then he remembered the times he'd ridden Mugwump while the dragon dove for fish in the river, and how the bellow had sounded different in water. Then it struck him.

Magick *did* only work by touch. The key was in defining the *medium* through which it moved. Just as water and the wall changed the nature of the sound so, too, might magick be changed by communication through another medium. Depending upon range and air pressure one might have to adjust a spell, just as one would have to speak louder to be heard over a storm. The cost paid for invoking such a spell might well be greater, too, so that limiting spells used at range would be a way to guarantee that magicians did not exhaust or kill themselves.

And using little devices, as du Malphias did for controlling his pasmortes, that used the laws of magick might make invoking those spells easier. If like spoke to like through channels that didn't involve air or, somehow, the intervening space, then magick might become even easier at range. Two halves of the same stone, no matter how far apart, might react within magick as if they were still part of a whole.

Vlad closed his eyes. Tangents and angles, symbols and their duplications, and the implications of all that spread through his mind. He could see the spells he knew lining up in a new order. If the spell to shoot a gun was near the top of the sun spells, then the spell to light a candle would be much lower. And, not surprisingly, he'd always visualized that spell as the sun dawning. The spell to extinguish such a flame he saw as the sun setting.

He saw what Ezekiel Fire had seen, though he doubted Fire had completely understood what he discovered. Prince Vlad could peel the limitations that clothed magick and take it back to its most raw and powerful form. He could provide greater access more simply for more people, which would make their lives infinitely easier.

And give everyone the chance to be corrupted by that power. In a heartbeat he understood why the Church had done what it did. In the next he feared what their knowledge would allow them to do. They had distributed grimoires so their selected agents would have access to advanced magicks as needed. Until Vlad knew who those people were, and why they were being given knowledge forbidden to the average man, he couldn't judge whether their effort should be encouraged or destroyed.

And he wondered, as he opened a blank notebook and began to outline his own system of magick, if he would fall victim to infinite power or if his purpose—balancing the Church's tyranny—might somehow save him from magick's corrupting influence.

CHAPTER FIFTEEN

1 May 1767
Antediluvian Ruins
Westridge Mountains, Mystria

"I hain't never seen the like." Nathaniel stared up at the edifice carved into the side of the mountain. The arches over doorways were formed by squids linking tentacles. More tentacles dangled from atop pillars. Even the way the stones had been carved to sluice away rain water had a tentacular pattern. Nathaniel had never much taken to the sea and sea life, and was more than happy nothing squidlike inhabited lakes and rivers.

Even odder than the general theme of the architecture were the two figures decorating the twenty-foot-tall and half-opened bronze doors. Age had imbued the doors with a green patina, but they didn't appear to be weathered nearly enough for having existed under the water for more than a couple of years. The nearby mud didn't have the sour stink of age, either. Given that he'd never heard of the place in Shedashee tales—and some of them recounted events centuries old—something definitely strange was going on.

The figures were male and female, right and left as one looked at them. The female, on the lean side, had ample curves to her and wasn't wearing much more than the bronze patina. Aside from her being nearly naked, she could have walked down any street in Temperance Bay without attracting a considerable amount of notice. Her strong jaw, noble nose, and deep-set eyes suggested she'd be a hatchet-faced crone by the time she got old, but in her youth, she definitely presented a handsome image that any man would be happy to have enter a dream.

The male, on the other hand, would have attracted notice and most of it hostile. Despite being clothed in something falling halfway between a fancy gown and the sort of vestments Bishop Bumble wore on high Holy Days, there was no mistaking the fact that the man was skinny to the point of looking consumptive. If there was an ounce of fat on him it was because he pulled it out of some animal's carcass and tucked it in a pocket. His long-fingered hands rested on the head of a staff. It rose to the middle of his belly, making it a bit longer than a gentleman's walking stick. Though it wasn't easy to see, the stick had a squidlike thing worked at the head, and that design matched the ring on the man's left hand.

His face and expression concerned Nathaniel more than anything else. He had more chin than he did nose, and that wasn't because his jaw was particularly strong. His nostrils tended more toward slits, and his nose looked closer to that of a bat than it did of the woman. Sharp angles defined his face, including cheekbones and peg-teeth seen between half-opened lips. His ears sharpened and his hair had been pulled back tight to his head. Had the patina been any thinner, Nathaniel would have assumed he was bald. The eyes, sunken back, projected a venomous glance.

Owen started up the steps. "Not the welcoming type, are they?"

"I reckon not." Nathaniel bent over and wiped a finger on the Temple steps. "No grit here, no mud."

Kamiskwa pointed to a rough semicircle that ran around that end of the courtyard and then on up to the mountainside. "A dome protected this place. I can feel the residual magick and see traces of it still."

Makepeace crossed himself. "I reckon I'll not be going in. I'll just keep watch out here."

Rathfield looked at him. "I would have hardly thought you susceptible to cowardice."

The Virtuan drew himself up to his full height. "Don't take a coward to recognize that this here is an unholy place. The Good Lord wants me going in there, He'll give me a sign. Until that point I ain't seeing why I should risk Perdition right here and now."

Nathaniel smiled. "Ain't no reason you should. Fact is, I was gonna ask you and Hodge to stay out here to keep an eye on things. See anything, fire a shot and we'll come running."

Hodge nodded and Makepeace moved off in the direction the footprint had pointed toward.

Owen stepped up first and entered the Temple, with Kamiskwa close behind him. Rathfield and Count von Metternin went next, and Nathaniel brought up the rear. He kept his rifle cradled in his arms and forced himself to watch their backtrail. He checked on the doors, visually measuring the opening, and dreaded seeing them close.

The doorway opened into a tall and long corridor carved from the native granite. At least that's what Nathaniel wanted to believe, but he couldn't see any chisel marks. As with the statues outside and the settlement's building blocks, everything had been joined seamlessly. Just the way Kamiskwa kept to the middle of the corridor, as far from the walls as he could, suggested he was feeling magick coming off the stones. Nathaniel didn't want to be thinking about what kind of power it would take to have shaped what he saw.

Owen rubbed his nose. "Dry, musty air; not at all what I'd expect."

Every ten yards or so a pair of statues had been placed to support the walls. They alternated male and female, repeating the figures from outside, save that all of them held a glowing stone ball about a yard in diameter. The stone looked similar to those used to build the settlement, and yet was a thin-enough shell that Nathaniel imagined he could see shadowy creatures swimming through the interior. He took comfort in the fact that he didn't see anything at all squidlike, but he didn't enjoy the fact that something lived inside those stones.

Halfway into the structure the corridor widened, quadrupling in size to create a cavernous room. Statues continued at regular intervals, now freestanding pairs back to back, holding more lights. At the far end they discovered a raised dais, an altar and a tabernacle structure, the latter of which lay open. Something had once resided in there, but since the Temple's interior showed no sign of decay, Nathaniel couldn't begin to guess how long the tabernacle had been empty.

Nathaniel smiled at Count von Metternin. "You seen its like in Auropa?"

The Kessian frowned. "For scale, yes, but..." He pointed to vast expanses of blank wall. "Any cathedral would have murals there and in the ceiling vaults. In the building outside the water washed images away, but here they should have been intact."

Owen shook his head. "Maybe the water didn't wash things away. Maybe they were all rendered in magick. Kamiskwa, can you feel it?"

The Altashee brave nodded slowly, and Nathaniel recognized how much conscious control his friend was exerting. *Only seen that a time or two, when he's been in powerful-bad pain.*

"Yes, it is magick. The walls tell stories." Kamiskwa exhaled slowly. "What you would *see* in a painting, the magick makes you feel. Over there, it must be a battle. I can feel the wounds. Screams are whispers, but they are there."

Rathfield turned and stared toward the panel Kamiskwa faced. "Impossible. You would have to be touching that to get any magick sense from it."

"The Shedashee, Colonel, they don't exactly cotton to the rules of Norillian magick."

"Do you, Woods, feel what he feels?"

"No, but that don't mean what he feels ain't true." Nathaniel's eyes narrowed. "You just think of him as someone what was born to magick the way you was born to reading Norillian. You had to learn and got good at it. I 'spect iffen we done learned the right magick, we'd be feeling the same thing. And if we learned more we'd be seeing and hearing and maybe smelling what was coming off them walls. Ain't something I'd be looking forward to, mind, but I reckon it could be done."

Rathfield chuckled. "I envy you the innocence of your world view, Woods. This couldn't have been raised by magick."

"And you know that exactly how?" Nathaniel looked around. "I seen some darn good masons working in Temperance Bay, and hain't nothing they done been even close to this. That the same in Auropa, my lord?"

"I am forced, Colonel, to agree with Mr. Woods."

"But the Church, gentlemen, instructs me that such uses of magick are quite impossible."

Owen laughed. "And you would know if they had decided that you needed know whether or not it *was* possible."

"Careful, Strake, you approach blasphemy."

"I reckon, Colonel, it ain't blasphemy he approaches, but common sense. We know this ain't natural. We cain't see no sign that masons did this. Kamiskwa says he can feel the magick, and we ain't got no cause to question his judgment. That leads toward a powerful conclusion. You need to think on this, Colonel…"

"Yes, Woods?"

"Mayhap be that your Church done told you what they thought was true, but this here settlement and what it represents is outside their knowing."

Rathfield folded his arms across his chest. "It is a point worth considering."

"Well, here's another two. Ain't but one entrance here, and that strikes me as peculiar. There has to be other ways in and out. And the other thing is this: we don't know what made this place, but we know it look powerful magick. That being so, I'm of a mind to wonder, just what in the name of Heaven was powerful enough to *melt* the city out there."

The latter thought sobered them for a moment. Nathaniel moved off and started looking for anything like a door or perhaps a place where a door had been sealed over. He found nothing until he met Owen over by the right side of the dais. "What have you got?"

Owen, on a knee, traced a fingernail along an almost invisible seam in the floor. "It's fitted flush. I cannot find anything to open it. Magick would seem to make sense."

"I hope not."

Owen frowned. "I don't follow."

"Perhaps I do, Owen." Count von Metternin ran a hand over his jaw. "Supposing Nathaniel's observations are correct, likewise that what Kamiskwa is reporting is correct. We would have a settlement that was created through the use of magick. Imagine for a moment what it means for a people to see magick as so common and so simple to do that they use it *in preference* to manual labor. Imagine a people who, instead of splitting wood with an ax, just touched a tree and had it fly apart into a cord of wood."

"More to the point, my lord, I ain't noticed no fireplaces or chimneys here, and we know they didn't need no lanterns, candles, or torches for light."

"An even better point, Nathaniel." The Count shook his head. "They might use magick to warm themselves instead of such large structures. Magick might cook their food for them, much as an apothecary invokes magick to create tinctures and unguents. For us, of course, doing that is very difficult, but if it is not for them…"

Owen stood slowly. "Magick of that magnitude would make them very dangerous."

The Count smiled. "If we are lucky, they are long since dead. Perhaps this was an outpost of Aliantis, which slipped beneath the waves eons ago. It would explain the decorative motif they enjoy."

"Nice thinking, but I don't reckon that's it. I don't reckon they's dead."

Owen frowned. "Why not?"

"Well, there was a bubble what was keeping this Temple safe whilst it was underwater. And them doors, ain't no way the man what left the track we found could have pushed them open. Then there's that empty tabernacle and this here passage below." Nathaniel scratched at the back of his neck. "Imagine what ever it was built this place went and laid itself down for a nap after something melted the settlement. The earthquake might have waked it up. It comes up, don't see nothing, ain't sure if it is safe, so opens the doors, opens the Temple, and maybe even puts something in that tabernacle there that the Colonel's giving the once over."

The Kessian arched an eyebrow. "Bait?"

"Something on that order. It just waits and someone comes along and takes the bait. And our thing waits, most likely to see if whatever melted the settlement is still out there. So that bait would attract it."

The three of them began to look around the Temple. Hair rose at the back of Nathaniel's neck. If something had set a trap, they were square in the middle of it.

He put fingers to his mouth and whistled. Rathfield and Kamiskwa came at a run, shifting their course as the other three moved toward the entrance. "What is it, Woods?"

"We're getting on out of here. Ain't nothing good coming from this place."

Irritation flashed over Rathfield's face, but vanished in an instant. "Very well." It seemed clear he didn't want to spend more time in the Temple alone, but he clearly had a desire to see more. "I suggest we return to camp, then explore in the afternoon."

Nathaniel didn't say anything to that until they reached camp. "I reckon Makepeace has it right. That there is an unholy place. I figure whoever left that track done come in, found something valuable, and headed out. If that track is right, he's heading west, maybe to Postsylvania. I'm thinking we need to be finding out what it was he took."

Rathfield shook his head. "There are mysteries here to be solved, Woods."

"I don't reckon we'll be the ones a-solving them, unless you've a might more magick than you let on. I ain't sure there's that much magick on this side of the ocean 'cepting among the Shedashee."

Kamiskwa, who sat back against a rock, facing away from the settlement, nodded. "None of the Shedashee will come here. I won't again, and I will undergo *kenatomis* before I return home."

Rathfield frowned. "What?"

"Cleansing ritual. Bath for the soul." Nathaniel nodded. "I'm thinking sweating out the evil of this place ain't a bad idea, neither."

Owen snapped his journal shut. "Not only do I think we need to follow whoever left that track in the mud, I think we need to send word back to Prince Vlad about what we have found."

Rathfield shook his head. "That won't be necessary."

"I think it is."

"Think all you like, Strake, but this is my expedition. I forbid it."

Count von Metternin sat down on the ground rather unceremoniously. "I do fear, gentlemen, that this whole ordeal has greatly fatigued me. I do not believe my system, which I thought much stronger, can take more shocks. I feel the need to return to my home. I hate abandoning you and, with no disrespect intended, Colonel Rathfield, but your orders do not pertain to me. I would also take Mr. Dunsby with me, as I have need of his skills. There would be no objections, correct?"

Rathfield blinked, his jaw opening and closing several times in rapid succession. "I really cannot... I..."

Owen cut him off. "I'll have a message or three for you to carry back to my wife, if you would be so kind, my lord."

"My pleasure, Captain Strake. If any of you would entrust me with your messages, I would consider it a sacred duty to carry them for you. We shall fetch some of the ivory and samples for the Prince on our way."

Rathfield's mouth closed for a moment. "I will remind the rest of you that I am in charge here. I will permit Dunsby to go, only as a courtesy to you, my lord. But from this point forward, I expect my orders to be carried out without question, and immediately."

I already know one secret you got. 'Pears there might be another one. Nathaniel smiled. He wasn't much of a one for following orders, but he did enjoy a good hunt. *And before we're done, I'll have your secrets, Colonel. Every last one of them.*

CHAPTER SIXTEEN

1 May 1767
Antediluvian Ruins
Westridge Mountains, Mystria

Owen wrote as quickly as he could to create messages for Prince Vlad—though he placed them in a folded sheet of paper which he sealed and addressed to his wife. Rathfield didn't like it, and clearly knew the information would be going to the Prince, but there was nothing he could do to prevent it. Count von Metternin and Hodge Dunsby packed their things up and headed out by mid-afternoon. While Owen had hoped they'd stay and leave the next morning, he couldn't blame them for wanting to get away from the ruins as swiftly as possible.

Owen had noted the change in Rathfield after Nathaniel had suggested the ruins were of a settlement created by a people powerful in magick. Whereas before Rathfield had just not listened to anyone else or reacted to them—save for the occasional sneer—now he worked hard at not seeming to listen. Owen was fairly certain, based on the man's reaction, that he had not expected what they found, but that he'd been prepared to find something in the west that was more than a settlement wishing to break away from Norillian rule.

As night came on, Owen began to wonder about Rathfield. Nathaniel had noted that Rathfield's recollection of the battle at Rondeville had gotten the phase of the moon wrong. What if Colonel Rathfield was not actually Colonel Rathfield? What if he was another man traveling under that name. Owen had never met the man in the service and since his uncle had selected him for the mission to Mystria, any trickery would be possible. Who might the man be?

He smiled to himself. In reality, no substitution was really necessary. Rathfield easily could have been given a secret set of orders. He probably

did have some political orders to be followed, and it almost made sense
that Deathridge would brief him on magick, since Deathridge had also
wanted Owen to give him the secrets of what du Malphias had been doing.

The idea, however, that Rathfield might know more about magick and
was hiding that fact did not make it easy for Owen to fall asleep. As the
outpost showed, magick could be incredibly powerful. Du Malphias had
used it to animate an army of the undead. If Rathfield not only knew
more about it, but could control more of it than anyone else, he posed a
danger that Owen wasn't sure any of them could handle. That thought
kept sleep at bay, then proved an ally to nightmares.

Dawn did not come early enough for any of them. They packed up
quickly and circled around the settlement. At the far side, they picked
up a trail roughly six days old. Nathaniel studied it closely, then nodded.
"Two men, one big, one more Hodge's size. Something familiar about the
big man's track, though he don't leave much. The other man don't know
the woods so good. He's slowing them down. They was both up in the
area when the earthquake hit. Maybe we'll find traplines to explain why.
Didn't spend more than a night here, though, and weren't in too much
of a hurry to cover their tracks when they left."

The expedition followed, but took its time. No one wanted to say
anything, but the ruins had left them unsettled enough that they watched
for booby-traps along the line of march, and for anything deciding to trail
them. Makepeace and Owen shared the rearguard duty, while Nathaniel
and Kamiskwa took point. Rathfield didn't like having to remain in the
middle, but he accepted that role without any obvious complaint.

As they were closing in on mid-afternoon, the trail led to a rock
chimney descending into a canyon similar to the one where they'd located
the pygmy mastodons. It presented no problem for them, but the high
walls meant dusk had settled in the canyon by the time they reached the
bottom. A trickle of water in the north wall fed a decent-sized pool, so
they decided to camp there.

Owen shucked his gear and headed out to gather wood for a fire. Low
bushes formed a webwork of isolated patches of grass and the occasional
copse, but well-worn game trails provided easy access to them. Before
they climbed down, they'd seen plenty of birds active in the area, so

they weren't afraid of the dark wind getting them. Still, it didn't surprise Owen to find a small mastodon dead at the edge of a meadow and a half-dozen crows perched on it, feeding gluttonously. He gave it a wide berth, remaining upwind, and began gathering fallen tree branches.

With an explosion of outraged cawing, the crows shot from the carcass to the tree above. Owen spun, dropping the armful of wood, immediately reaching for the rifle slung across his back. He crouched as he shucked the covering, hoping somehow he could remain unnoticed. The clatter of falling wood made that impossible, which he recognized immediately.

Two dire wolves had trotted into the clearing. Five feet long, almost four high at the shoulder, they had broad chests and short, thick legs. Owen brought his rifle up and covered the firestone at the base of the barrel with his right thumb. Had the wolves remained intent on the carcass, they would have been beyond his gun's lethal range. He'd have retreated and left them in peace. Unfortunately, the sound of branches hitting the ground had pricked up their ears, and they made straight for him.

Owen took a deep breath and let it out slowly. The wolves trotted toward him, now eighty yards away. Had he a smoothbore musket, they would have been at the edge of its range, and the ball wouldn't have gotten through their thick grey fur. If he was lucky, he could shoot one at fifty yards, kill it, and frighten the other one off. Then he'd have a chance to reload or just run.

But they don't frighten, and if I run, they'll just chase me. He swallowed hard. *And they come in packs.*

Sixty yards, fifty. He let the lead wolf come closer. He wanted it dead. It would be one less for the others to kill. Forty yards.

Now.

Owen invoked magick. The spell flew from his thumb and into the firestone, through it, and into the brimstone charge at the base of the rifle's barrel. The powder ignited, thrusting an ovoid bullet into the barrel. The lans and grooves sheered off a thin layer of lead as the bullet accelerated through the metal cylinder. It emerged, born of thunder, chased by fire, spinning much as an arrow might, but so much faster.

The bullet slammed into the dire wolf's breastbone, shattering bone and cartilage. Bone splinters sprayed through the creature's body cavity, severing an artery. The beast would bleed out from that wound alone.

The bullet, however, continued on, bursting out through the wolf's spine. The shot's force lifted the creature and twisted it around. It yelped, more surprised than hurt or angry, then flopped onto its side and spasmodically clawed the ground with its forepaws.

The second wolf never paused, but broke into a sprint. Owen rose, brought his tomahawk to hand and hurled it. He had no hope that it would hit the beast, much less kill it. It did, however, make the wolf swerve. That gave Owen time enough to club his rifle and swing as the dire wolf leaped.

His swing connected, catching the beast hard in the neck. The wolf slew around in the air, slamming its ribs into Owen's chest. Owen flew from his feet and hit hard, with the dire wolf on top of him. He shoved it away to the left, then rolled to his right. He slid a knife from his belt, then pounced on the stunned animal, stabbing it again and again in the chest. Blood gushed, painting his face red as the beast struggled from beneath him. It snapped at him once, weakly, then crumpled, leaving him drenched in its blood.

Owen grabbed for his rifle and began to reload. He worked a lever to the right, which slid the breech assembly back. The brimstone cup rotated up. He pulled a paper-wrapped cartridge from a belt pouch, pinched the bullet off the one end, then poured the brimstone into the cup. He used the paper for wadding and tamped it down with the bullet. He put the bullet in the top of the cup, which tipped it back over again, and worked the lever back to slide bullet into the chamber and seal the breech.

Even though that operation had only taken ten seconds, it was enough time for three more dire wolves to enter the clearing. Noses to the wind, they caught the scent of fresh blood immediately. They looked at him, lips peeling back from very sharp and long teeth. They started toward him, then hesitated.

Barely a step into the clearing, Nathaniel Woods brought rifle to shoulder and cracked off a shot. At twice the distance Owen had taken his shot, Nathaniel's bullet struck a wolf in its skull, blowing an ear off. The beast staggered drunkenly, then collapsed and thrashed. The other two sniffed the air and slunk back through the brush.

Nathaniel ran over to Owen, with Kamiskwa trailing in his wake. "You got two, good."

"That was a hell of a shot."

The Mystrian reloaded. "The white of his teeth just made an arrow pointing at his head. Weren't nothing."

Kamiskwa returned the tomahawk to Owen. "You're unhurt."

Owen shifted his shoulders. "Two hundred fifty pounds of wolf land on you, you get some aches. I'll be fine."

Nathaniel levered his rifle's breech closed again. "Better get moving. I'm going to guess the pack of these things ain't going to take nicely to our camping in their larder. It's going to be a long night."

The trio retreated to the pool. They told the others what had happened. Rathfield didn't believe but Makepeace just started shifting rocks around to build a small wall. The rest helped, raising it to a height of three feet. It wouldn't stop the dire wolves, but with their short legs and heavy builds, they'd think twice before trying to take it at a leap.

As darkness fell, Rathfield fitted a bayonet onto his musket, adding eighteen inches of steel to it. "I shall take the first watch."

"Not alone you ain't." Makepeace hunkered down behind the wall. "Being as how you're disbelieving these wolves even exist, having you keep an eye out for 'em is just asking for trouble."

Owen pulled back, settling down beside the small fire. He pulled out a journal and chronicled his encounter with the dire wolves. He kept the description fairly spare, but filled it with the sort of information Prince Vlad would love. Try as he might to focus, however, he couldn't help but remember killing the dire wolves at Prince Haven, on the night when Miranda was born.

Just as with this battle, he didn't have time to be scared. That came later—and could be seen in the tremors running through the words on his journal pages. That night the wolves had been bold. They probably caught scent of Miranda's birth. He'd gotten three, the Prince and servants one apiece, which was enough to drive the pack away. It was only later they learned that the wolves had moved upriver, gotten into a barn, and killed two cows and a milkmaid.

Owen didn't remember the details of the fight, and knew he'd soon forget these. What he did remember, however, was being covered in wolf's blood when Princess Gisella handed him his daughter for the first time. How tiny she had been, bare wisps of black hair on her head, her face flushed. He'd been fighting for her even without having seen her, and he smiled.

Then he saw Catherine looking at him, pure loathing in her eyes. He'd known she did not want to be in Mystria. She'd not spared him the sharp side of her tongue when discussing their new home. It always seemed it was the land she hated, not him. But that night, as she glowered at him, he knew he'd never see love in her eyes again.

That should have saddened him, but it didn't. There he'd stood, covered in blood, his heart pounding from the fight and from the excitement of seeing his child. He was proud of himself and Mystria, of the people he'd come to love and the opportunity the land provided. His daughter—and in that moment he'd stopped thinking of Miranda as *their* daughter— would grow up in a place where the measure of her worth would not come from her bloodlines but from what she could do. And while Mystrian society still did view a woman as an extension of her husband—often as property of her husband—no one made the mistake of believing that was *all* a woman could be.

Bethany Frost, for example, served as an editor for the *Frost Weekly Gazette*. While there were those who would grumble about how that wasn't a job for a woman, they were just as likely to argue that she did a damned fine job of editing when outsiders would comment to the contrary. That she edited his book, and Samuel Haste's most recent—at each author's personal request, it was known—furthered the esteem in which she was held. Some people did think it a pity that she'd not found herself a husband and hadn't produced a brood of children—at twenty-five she should have had at least a half-dozen—very few voiced that opinion aloud, and fewer tried to find her a husband. The few suitors who came to pay her court found her to be headstrong and too quick for them.

Catherine, on the other hand, was more than content to define her status based on Owen's position within Mystria. That became the nugget of her hatred for the new world. In Mystria he was Prince Vlad's friend, and she was a confidant of Princess Gisella. One could rise no higher in society. But in the eyes of her friends and rivals in Norisle, this meant little. After all, a scullery maid in some Launston pub warranted higher social standing than anyone in Mystria. Their colonial cousins were to be humored and tolerated or pitied and despised. While Catherine reveled in the status she did possess in Mystria, she hated that it meant her standing had fallen below where it had in Norisle when she'd married him.

He turned to a fresh page in his journal, and began writing her a letter. He wasn't certain that it would ever be found if the wolves got them, or that he would ever let her read it if they didn't. Still, he had much to say to her. He would make one last attempt to let her know why he loved her and Miranda and Mystria.

He hoped she would understand.

CHAPTER SEVENTEEN

1 May 1767
Prince Haven
Temperance Bay, Mystria

Prince Vlad's spirits soared with Mugwump. Firmly lodged in the saddle, his goggles in place and gloves on his hands, the Prince could not help but smile as the dragon flew lazily over fields and back toward the wurmrest. Mugwump showed no inclination to descend and instead raised his head and gave voice to his joy.

At least, that's what Prince Vlad assumed he was doing. Since midday, right after Vlad had stopped working on his Mystrian thaumaturgy, Mugwump had begun an odd series of vocalizations. They tended to break at odd places for Vlad, but the howling of dogs and Richard's putting his hands over his ears suggested the sound just moved into higher registers than Vlad could hear. The string of sounds—and the calls seemed the same every time, deliberately repeated—ended on a rising note making it sound as if the dragon was asking a question. Vlad even timed the intervals between calls, as best he could. They ran roughly a minute, which meant the sound had thirty seconds to travel out and a reply to come back. If Mugwump was asking questions, he was expecting an answer from a creature roughly six and a half miles away.

No replies came, however, and as nearly as Prince Vlad could see, the silence had no effect on Mugwump's mood. In fact, were he to compare the dragon's reaction to the call and lack of reply, it would mirror Richard's concern over something one moment, then his utterly carefree response to something else the next. Still, while they flew, Mugwump tended to vocalize toward the west, with more of a challenging tone to his voice.

During those vocalizations, Mugwump tended to be gliding, and lost altitude. Aside from the first time, the loss was neither abrupt nor quick, but it did seem to surprise the dragon. He flapped his wings a couple of times and they regained the distance they'd lost. Beneath them the buildings had shrunk to something roughly the size of Vlad's thumbnail. He took note of that fact, even stripping off a glove to make sure the comparison was close to exact. Later he rode out from Prince Haven, took proper measurements of ground features, and calculated how high they actually had flown.

Making observations about distance were about as far as Prince Vlad got. The exhilaration of flying so far exceeded the thrill he'd felt when swimming with the dragon that he could scarce compare them. Granted, the thought of drowning had always dampened the thrill—and the inability to holler happily likewise caused problems—but flying combined freedom and speed with placement in a realm where men were not meant to go. Even the knowledge that were he to fall off or Mugwump to plunge from the sky, he would die, could not kill the happiness bursting within him.

He kept his hands very light on the reins, but Mugwump responded when he tugged. The only time he had difficulty was after Mugwump had shrieked toward the west and awaited a reply. After the requisite interval, however, Mugwump turned, swooping or climbing, drifting over the broad river which flashed silver in the sunlight.

It was in crossing the river that Prince Vlad realized something had changed in how Mugwump approached flying. When flying over warm land, thermal updrafts helped Mugwump maintain altitude. As he passed over the river, he'd descend. His descent, however, was a fraction of what it had been before and didn't provoke a need to flap his wings. His wingspan had not grown significantly, so it had to be something else.

The dragon is using magick.

The thought came to Prince Vlad unbidden, and he tried to dismiss it as a hangover from his morning's considerations. It presented him with two problems, neither of which he liked. The first was that there was magick that would allow heavier-than-air creatures to fly. While no man might be able to discover, master, or power the exact nature of that spell, the Prince found himself making a mental list of every story in the Good Book that involved angels or other people flying and levitating. Adding in every saint who had been said to have managed it swelled the list enormously. Vlad transformed that into a battalion of flying soldiers armed with rifles and didn't like the implications at all. That the Church might know of that magick and might have incorporated it into their grimoire frightened him.

On top of that, the idea that a dragon could work magick caused all sorts of philosophical problems. Men spoke proudly about their ability to reason as being what differentiated them from beasts. Use of magick was but one example of the fruits of reasoning. Men used the ability to reason in conjunction with passages from the Good Book to justify the subjugation of every other creature in the world—as well as their fellow men.

If a dragon could use magick—and magick use was a sign of the ability to reason—then there could be no moral justification for treating a dragon as chattel. Could he actually own a creature that had its own mind? Society would agree that he could—indentured servitude was an example of an acceptable form of it, and even the Good Book failed to condemn slavery. But Vlad had never bought a man's contract, and the idea of owning slaves repulsed him. *Yet if Mugwump is a reasoning creature, can I pretend to own him?*

Prince Vlad's eyes tightened. "How much do you know, Mugwump? How much can you understand me?"

The dragon looked back at him, then opened his mouth as if to smile and dove. He plunged head-first toward the ground, wings tight in. Vlad held on to the saddle and leaned back, forced into that posture by air resistance. Then Mugwump's wings came out and his head came up. His tail went down, then twisted. The dragon came up and over in a somersault, then rolled over and soared back the way they had come.

Vlad's heart pounded in his chest. "I hope to God you can understand me. Do not do that again."

The dragon frowned.

"At least, not without warning."

Mugwump raised his head and trumpeted proudly.

Vlad laughed, then something wet hit his face. He looked up, seeing not a single cloud in the sky. Then he looked at his shirt and saw a red splotch, as big around as his fist. He swiped a glove against his face and it glistened.

He pulled back on the reins. "To the ground, now, Mugwump. *Now!*"

The beast glanced back at him and more blood flew from his nostrils to strike Vlad in the chest. A shiver ran through the dragon, then he dove toward the ground. He unfurled his wings at the last moment and slowed, but not enough. They hit the ground heavily, though Mugwump's powerful arms and legs cushioned the landing somewhat.

Vlad vaulted from the saddle and ran to the dragon's head. He was bleeding from the nostrils and this confirmed what Vlad had wondered. Use of magick demanded a price of the user. Blood would seep beneath Vlad's thumbnail when he shot. Likewise Mugwump's use of magick had taken its toll on the dragon. Whether his nasal passages had begun to bleed, or the blood came from his lungs, Vlad couldn't be certain—though Mugwump's lack of distress and the regularity of his breathing suggested the former case was true.

Baker came running over. "Are you hurt, Highness?"

"Not my blood. His. Nosebleed."

"Nosebleed?" The wurmwright frowned. "Can't imagine what would cause that."

"I believe he may have snorted a sparrow, much like one of us getting a gnat up the nose."

"I hate noseeums." Baker frowned. "I could swab out his nose, but I don't imagine he'd like it. Ruin a mop and I'm not sure I'd get the bird out."

Vlad smiled. "I think you should just let Mugwump rest for a bit. Stand clear in case he sneezes it back out. Then lead him home, let him eat his fill. He's earned his rest."

"As you wish, Highness."

Prince Vlad patted the dragon below his left eye. "Take it easy, my friend. We'll take a week, then try this again."

The dragon made no sound, but his golden eyes seemed to reflect understanding.

Vlad headed off across the field to cut through the narrow strip of woods. He damned himself for not having at least a pistol with him. He didn't really imagine that a jeopard would hunt something reeking of dragon's blood, but the scientist in him could not discount that possibility. That same scientist also knew that a pistol wouldn't be of much use, nor would running, since that would only attract the beast's attention.

Remaining as vigilant as he could, then, he headed home.

As he emerged, he caught sight of a young man on a horse, riding up toward the front of the house. He waved. "Is that Caleb Frost?"

Caleb reined around and rode toward him. He vaulted from the saddle, concern evident on his face. "Are you hurt, Highness?"

"Not any part of me you'd care to see. Not my blood." Vlad stripped off a glove and shook Caleb's hand. "What brings you out here?"

Caleb fell into step with the Prince, his horse trailing behind. "Fast packet boat came in this morning. Rumor from certain parts reports that Parliament has come up with a new scheme for collecting revenue. Since taxing our economy directly didn't work previously, they are intent on creating a series of licenses and permits which one must purchase to hunt and harvest here in the Colonies. If you pay for a trapper's license, for example, you will pay a much lower price for brimstone and firestones. Goods produced by a licensed person will pass through Customs faster, likewise products being released to licensed merchants. If you refuse to obtain a license, your goods can be confiscated, you can be fined or even sentenced to jail or servitude."

As the Prince walked with Caleb toward the stables, his stomach tightened. He'd always known Parliament would retaliate for the Colonies' protest against the document tax. Requiring licenses would generate income, and soon after would come fees which were, *de facto*, taxes. That Norisle needed the money was not in question, nor was the Mystrian resistance to sending money east over the ocean.

Caleb handed his horse over to the stable boy and Vlad washed up in a water trough. He raked wet, brown locks from his face and relished the tickle of cool water running down his back.

"Someone in Launston is being very clever. This plan forces merchants to become the tax collectors. They'll have to pay less for unlicensed merchandise to cover the cost of their own licenses. Plus increasing the prices of brimstone and firestones guarantees that most people will buy licenses." Vlad frowned. "Instead of taxing our economy everywhere, they put the pressure on the people at the point of contact with the Norillian economy."

Caleb nodded. "It's also selective. For someone like me, the licenses and fees mean nothing, since I only sell within the colonies."

"Still, the added fees will get passed on to you when you buy anything that comes from Norisle, or through the hands of someone who has paid for a license. And what man in Mystria is not going to face higher prices for brimstone and firestones?"

"Men dealing with smugglers. Ryngian powder sends a ball just as far, just as straight."

"True, but if you're caught with it, you can get your thumbs ringed in iron or taken off entirely."

Caleb held his hands up. "I understand that, Highness, but there are those who will see these licenses as being different than the document tax. That affected everyone and almost immediately. This will affect everyone, but more slowly. And once outrage about this dies down, the licenses get expanded, fees get raised. And even then we lose sight of what's really going on. This set of fees is being bundled under what is known as the Shipping and Control Acts. The legislation will assert as its justification that the Crown owns everything in Mystria. Not just the land and the raw materials it produces, but the products all men create. There is nothing and no one who will not be touched by it."

Vlad nodded. "You may have even seen where that can go in the future. If the Crown can license your livelihood, they can go further and restrict where it is that you may practice your trade. You'll be forced to carry papers that agree that you can work, and specifying where you can work. In essence, people will be tied to a specific place for life, or can be uprooted and sent to another place at the Crown's whim. There could even be wedding licenses and fees for children. It is serfdom reborn. You said this was rumor. I take it, then, that the Shipping and Control Acts have not yet been passed?"

Caleb shook his head. "The packet boat left before Parliament voted. There didn't seem to be an overwhelming majority in favor, at least not in Commons, but there *was* a majority. Most who opposed it were afraid that the Control Acts would get established in Norisle if they were successful here."

No doubt a very real fear. Vlad's mouth soured. "What will you do with this information?"

The young publisher sighed. "It would be irresponsible to print notice of what, right now, is speculation. Unless the Crown is going to send us their copy of the Control Acts along with thousands of soldiers to enforce them, we will have ample time to respond in a way that makes the Crown reconsider. Our response would take six weeks to get to Norisle, and we'd not hear back for at least another six weeks. If a ship arrives with the Acts tomorrow, it would be September before the Queen could respond to our reaction, and that really means this time next year, if she is planning an armed intervention."

"You've told me what you're *not* going to do, and I applaud your caution." Vlad patted the man on the shoulder. "Now, what *will* you do?"

"Highness, you know I have the utmost respect for you."

"I consider us friends, Caleb, and no matter what you say, our friendship will not be affected by it."

"Even if it is treason?"

"Let's see how far down that road you are going to travel." Vlad threw his arm over Caleb's shoulder and guided him back around toward the new laboratory. "As you did me a favor to inform me what is happening, so shall I keep what you tell me in confidence."

"Thank you. Highness, the Control Acts cannot be allowed to stand. A copy of the message we received will be in Samuel Haste's hands before the week is out. I'm sure he'll write another book and it will influence many people. We will also support and print notices for community meetings and debates on the Control Acts if they pass. We will print stories of how the acts are enforced. We will not advocate armed resistance to the Acts. We might report about same, but we will not glorify what happens."

"This is all assuming the Control Acts are real."

"Yes, Highness." Caleb shrugged. "If they are not, the alarm is for nothing."

"It's not for nothing, Caleb. It never is." Prince Vlad smiled. "As a friend, thank you for telling me all this. As Governor-General, I am pleased that you bear your responsibility to the community so highly."

"You don't think anything I would do is treason?"

"It might border on it, but only just." Vlad nodded solemnly. "As long as I am Governor-General, speaking the honest truth about injustice will never rise to the level of treason. And if my aunt doesn't like that, she can recall me and I shall explain it to her, face to face."

CHAPTER EIGHTEEN

2 May 1767
Dire Wolf Draw
Westridge Mountains, Mystria

The wolves came after darkness fell, silent as death, dark as shadows, only betrayed by sparks of firelight glinting in amber eyes. Nathaniel couldn't figure out why they'd come. Growls and snarls in the distance had communicated the fate of the three they'd already killed. If the valley was at all like Little Elephant Lake, they should have had more than enough to feed on. Could have been they didn't like the intrusion. In his experience, however, despite their fearlessness, they'd always been inclined to let men pass unless someone was bleeding or food was scarce.

The meager fire provided a sphere of light just less than thirty yards in diameter, so when they came, the dire wolves came fast. Nathaniel, crouching behind the low wall, tracked the biggest of them and shot. The bullet caught it square in the chest, dropping it. Other wolves leaped over it, giving him just enough time to club his rifle before they hit.

Other shots had killed wolves, but the holes in their line closed fast. Rathfield hit another with a pistol-shot, then cast aside the handgun and stabbed with his rifle. The bayonet was almost long enough to go clean through a dire wolf's chest. The beast's momentum and weight forced Rathfield to raise it, thrashing, as if his rifle was a pitchfork, tumbling him back from the line.

Makepeace, roaring like the bear that had once mauled him, stepped up with a long knife in one hand and short ax in the other. He split a skull with an overhand blow and buried his knife in a wolf's breast. The stabbed beast twisted, ripping the knife from Makepeace's hand, then closed its jaw on his left forearm.

Beyond him Kamiskwa brandished his warclub, in the half-light looking every bit the sort of demon that preachers warned would torture the unworthy in Hell. The heavy wooden club came up and around in an arc that crushed skulls. Blood sprayed from the obsidian blade as it slashed through thickly matted fur. Kamiskwa matched the wolves' snarls with curses and challenges, then broke those that came at him.

Owen fixed a bayonet to his rifle, just as had Rathfield. Owen benefited, however, from having had years dealing with wild creatures. Instead of stabbing heavily as one might with a man, intent on driving him into the ground, Owen's strokes came quickly. He slid steel into their breasts, then pulled it free. His rifle butt came around to fend them off, driving them back so they could bleed out.

Two wolves came over the wall at Nathaniel. He caught one with his rifle's butt, hitting it a straight-on blow right between the eyes. It fell back, twitching. The other one came on and bit him in the leg. It tugged, teeth finally piercing deerskin and the flesh beneath, and pulled Nathaniel down to one knee. He drew his tomahawk and killed it, but it took four blows to sever its spine, and that didn't loosen its jaws.

The wolves kept coming. The low wall had done its part, but had collapsed near the middle. The wolves leaped over the dead and through the gap. They turned left and right, snapping at men's flanks and legs. The fight might have been lost there, save for Ian Rathfield.

If Kamiskwa had been a demon, Rathfield returned to the line a man possessed by demons. He shrieked inhumanly, his face a mask of fury. He waded into the wolves, heedless of their worrying his legs, and smashed them with his musket. He knocked two flying, then a third, and shattered his musket's butt on a fourth's skull. That didn't matter, however, because he just reversed the weapon and stabbed with the speed of a scorpion. When a wolf finally got hold of his rifle's sling and tugged it out of his grasp, he bent down, grabbed one of the stones that had been in the wall, and hurled it two-handed, splattering that wolf's brains.

Screaming defiantly, he stepped over the wall, kicking dire wolf bodies out of the way. Makepeace came quickly up beside him, but the wolves had already decided to retreat. A handful limped away into the darkness, their howls short and pain-filled.

Owen and Makepeace sorted out the bodies, slitting throats. Kamiskwa, using an obsidian knife, cut the jaw muscles of the beast with its teeth in Nathaniel's leg. As he did that, Nathaniel reloaded his rifle—both because it needed to be done and it let him think about something other than the pain.

Rathfield, fists balled, stared into the darkness after the wolves.

Nathaniel nodded to Kamiskwa. "Thanks. We'll be needing to find us some *mogiqua*."

"I have dried leaves I can make into a tea. After brewing, we can use the wet leaves for a poultice."

"Best be getting Colonel Rathfield on the outside of a swallow or three."

"Agreed. He is *tired*."

The way he said it, Kamiskwa meant the man was in shock. Nathaniel guessed it was the simple ferocity of the fight more than it was pain. Everyone save for Kamiskwa had gotten gnawed on, but none of the others were still locked in the fight.

"Colonel."

No response.

"Colonel Rathfield, sir." Nathaniel slowly stood. "Colonel, I've got me the first watch. You go and rest now."

Rathfield turned slowly, his eyes eventually focusing on Nathaniel's face. He looked him up and down. "Woods, you're wounded. Get that taken care of."

"Begging your pardon, sir, but you're more gnawed on than I am, and I have a rifle. Kamiskwa will fix you up."

Rathfield looked down at his empty hands then found the splintered remains of his musket on the ground. "It will take some work to fix that."

"We'll see to it, sir."

The Norillian nodded torpidly. He turned and watched Owen and Makepeace stretch the wolves out and begin skinning them. "Is this a time to be taking trophies?"

"Ain't quite looting the dead." Nathaniel jerked a thumb toward the bodies. "Iffen they'da kilt us, they'd have eaten what they could, left the rest for crows and the like. I ain't much for eating wolf—don't know many who is—but them furs is worth something. So we'll take what we can use, leave the rest for the scavengers. It's the way things is done here."

"I see." Rathfield pointed to the wolf he'd brained with a rock. It had been one of the larger ones, and had a coat that ran more to black than gray. "Please, save me that one, and the one I broke my musket on. I will do the skinning if you'll show me the proper way. I think the Prince would like a specimen. And there are men of my acquaintance in Norisle who'd not believe lest they run their fingers through the pelt."

"I reckon we can do that."

By the time Owen and Makepeace had finished skinning the wolves and dragging the carcasses away from the campsite, Kamiskwa had bandaged Rathfield's wounds and made him drink *mogiqua* tea. That put the Norillian to sleep, so the others skinned the two wolves he wanted saved for himself and piled the skins near the fire. They'd killed seventeen of the animals, which made it the largest pack Nathaniel had ever heard of, and that wasn't including the three killed previously.

Owen took over for Nathaniel. "If he complains we skinned his kills when he wakes up, we'll tell him we wanted to get the carrion away from camp."

"I don't reckon he'll remember much."

Owen raised an eyebrow. "You're smiling, and I'm guessing your amusement is at my expense."

"Ain't it at all, Owen." Nathaniel shook his head. "I was just remembering what I thought of you when I met you and how that changed. The Colonel, he done changed my mind a bit this here night. I kinda figured that once he went down, that was all the fight he had."

Owen glanced over at where the tall man lay stretched out. "Given what they say about him being a hero, I shouldn't be surprised, but had you asked me before how he'd act, it wouldn't have been like that."

"I agree." The Mystrian hunter frowned. "You remember Rufus Branch?"

Owen rubbed at the back of his head. "Tried to crack my skull with a musket and tried to murder you. Makepeace's brother shot him in his hindquarters. He's long gone."

"Three year now, and ain't lamented." Nathaniel's eyes narrowed. "Thing of it was that he was sneaky and more inclined toward lazy and coward than otherwise, but the few times he got into the thick of it, he'd fight like he weren't human. Reminded me of the Colonel."

"What do you think does that?"

Nathaniel shrugged. "Used to think it was what a coward does when he just cain't be no more scared. I mean, some of 'em, they'll just curl up in a ball and whimper. But there's a set—always the ones who don't seem to have a terrible great liking for themselves—just lose their minds. I ain't much for that, even if they're on my side in a fight. Don't mind a man killing a lot, just want him thinking while he does it."

"You think Rathfield a coward? Deep down? That doesn't make any sense. He won the battle of Rondeville all by himself."

"Did he? Or is that just the way the story gets told?" Nathaniel scratched at his throat. "He didn't seem to remember how the moon was that night. I reckon if you don't write down the details of this little set-to, ain't none of us gonna remember it none too good, neither. And the way he told it at the meeting, he was all but dead when they found him. He'd not amember nothing. What if the men who found him made up their own story and when he done waked up, he just went along with it?"

"Rather than be labeled a coward?" Owen's eyes narrowed. "But if that's true, why would my uncle send... No, never mind. The question is, why did my uncle hope he'd die out here?"

"I reckon there ain't but one man can answer that question, and he's a mite far away for the asking."

"I have no complaint about that." Owen forced a small smile. "You go get yourself some sleep."

The next morning Nathaniel woke up stiff and sore, but not nearly as bad off as he expected. He made sure not to let Rathfield get any clue as to how achy he was, since the Norillian wasn't moving very quickly himself and appeared disinclined to want to talk much. Rathfield said nothing about the wolves and agreed to help Kamiskwa harvest *mogiqua* for poultices and more tea.

The others set to preparing the wolfskins for preservation. Using dull knives and stone scrapers, they took off every bit of flesh they could find, then lay the skins out to dry in the sun. Because of the canyon's orientation and depth, they didn't get nearly enough sunlight, and they didn't have enough salt to even begin to cure the skins, but they did what they could.

When they finally lost useful sunlight for drying, they explored and discovered that about five hundred yards toward the southwest, the canyon narrowed considerably. Wide enough to allow a pygmy mastodon through, or a couple of wolves shoulder to shoulder, the canyon would have caught a wooly rhino fast. They set about harvesting small trees, trimming them, sharpening the ends and sticking them into the ground, pointing to the southwest. They cross-braced them so even seriously determined dire wolves couldn't drag them out of place. While a jeopard would have leaped over the triple rank of spears without a thought, the barricade would be enough to keep the wolves out.

They spent three more days in the canyon. An abundance of the fern called *mogiqua* by the Shedashee encouraged their decision to remain. As a tea, or just chewed raw, it had a bitter taste and numbed aches and pains. *Mogiqua* poultices did the trick on wounds, preventing infection. The bites closed quickly and it didn't appear as if they would scar too badly.

By the morning of the sixth day, everyone was ready to head out. Because the skins had not had time to properly cure, they opted to bind them up tightly and stash them in a small cave on the south side of the canyon. It never got any sun and would stay cool at least until their return trip. They blocked the entrance with stones and defecated nearby to keep animals away.

Though the trail they'd started following had become older, it hadn't become any more difficult to read. The two men they were pursuing were making no effort to hide their trail, and were moving on with a fair amount of haste. While they found campsites with cold ashes, their quarry hadn't left behind any bones to indicate that they'd hunted or trapped while traveling.

Nathaniel straightened up from where he'd been examining a footprint. "We hain't gained nothing on them, but over that next rise, I reckon we might get a gander at where they're heading."

Rathfield, who carried the remains of his musket slung over his back, nodded. "Then, by all means, let us not waste the rest of the day."

They came up through a narrow valley and at the highest point, where it opened widely to the west, they all stopped. The mountains gently merged with forested hills, which gave way to flat plains covered in lush green grasses. Nathaniel thought it might have been a trick of his vision that he saw black dots on the plains, but were that true, and at that distance, they would have had to be full-grown mammoths or wooly rhinoceri. The plains faded endless into the distance and Nathaniel suddenly felt very small.

Kamiskwa came up beside him and rested a hand on his shoulder. "There are stories of *Gushneypak*."

"Green Ocean?"

"Yes. There are Shedashee tribes living out there. We call them the foolish ones, *Torenkii*. They are always on the move, following the herds."

"You have to go where the prey is."

"That's not why they are foolish." Kamiskwa rested a hand on the knife at his belt. "They consider their villages to be islands in the ocean, but they forget what lives under the green."

"What?"

The Altashee sighed. "The reason these mountains were raised, my friend, was to keep what lurks out there from bursting free. You think that the city we found was their furthest outpost, but you mark the distance from Aliantis and where it sank in the ocean. But you're wrong."

He pointed off toward the west. "They came from out there, and this is as far as they got, before the land itself swallowed them, and the grasses wove a net that would forever keep them buried."

CHAPTER NINETEEN

10 May 1767
Happy Valley
Postsylvania, Mystria

Two days further on through the forest, they reached a broad valley within the hill country. A river ran through it, heading toward the southwest and, presumably, the Misaawa River in the middle of Tharyngian territory. How far away that was Owen couldn't begin to guess. Just the idea that it might be as unspoiled as the land they'd traveled through filled him with awe and a little bit of dread.

When he'd first come to Mystria, the untouched nature of the land had surprised him. In Norisle and on the Auropean continent all the prime land had been lived on for centuries. Certainly there were wastes and barrens, salt marshes and tall mountains where none but the insane or shunned lived. Otherwise, one could not travel more than a mile without spotting a sign of human habitation and five miles without finding a village of some sort. Aside from the Shedashee, few humans had seen these lands and fewer still dwelt in them.

His dread came from knowing how the hand of man would transform the land. Though he had lived in Mystria only three years, he'd already seen what had once been wooded vales clear-cut to feed the need for building materials and firewood. Elsewhere he found abandoned homes near exhausted fields. When the land would not produce anymore, people just loaded up wagons and moved west. Though the Westridge Mountains created a huge obstacle, men would find their way past it and the virgin landscape would suffer.

Happy Valley surprised him because it didn't display the same sorts of signs he'd expected of human habitation. Down in the valley itself lay an orderly collection of small houses surrounding a village green. At the eastern end stood a rectangular, palisaded fort, but no one watched from the walls or the tower built atop the main building. The gates stood open and the way weeds had grown up, Owen didn't imagine the gates were closed all that often. The hillsides had been terraced and cultivated, but some fields had clearly been allowed to lie fallow. He couldn't see any clear-cut tracts in the surrounding woods, and a series of canals had been dug to carry wastewater from the fields to the river well downstream of the village itself.

Owen cradled his rifle in his arms. "What do you think?"

Nathaniel shook his head. "I reckon they went in there. Don't know if they stayed, but the people will know."

"Makes sense." The village's people went about their daily lives without any apparent concern. A small mill sat beside the river toward the southwest, and the village smith opposite. A stable and paddocks had been built there as well. A large barnlike structure stood beside the stables, but Owen couldn't make its purpose out, even though people regularly went in and came out. Shepherds and sheep dotted the hillsides, grazing on open land between the terraces. Dairy cattle grazed closer to home on the green. Another oblong building with two smoking chimneys had been built near one of the waste canals. Owen took it for a laundry because of the lines strung out from around it where sheets and clothes flapped in the light breeze.

Rathfield came up beside the two of them. "I suggest we go down and make ourselves known. This might be our Postsylvania or not, but regardless, it should not be here so I shall have to speak with them."

Nathaniel ran a hand over his chin. "Seems to me, Colonel, that given them a talking-to might wait for until a return trip, or leastways until we have knowledge of the men we're trailing. We don't know what they took from the ruins, but I do think finding out would be a good idea."

Rathfield frowned for a moment, then nodded. "Splendid point, Woods. Perhaps you or Strake might address them. If they are religious, Bone could do it."

"I reckon that would be the thing."

Owen turned back toward the village so Rathfield couldn't read his smile. While he wasn't completely certain Nathaniel's observation about the source of Rathfield's heroism was correct, there was no denying that the man had returned to his annoying habits once he began to feel better. Owen did believe, however, it wasn't because he wanted to irritate his fellow travelers. It felt more as if Rathfield believed that by rebuilding himself as a Crown officer, he could distance himself from the creature he'd been during the fight.

They set off again.

Owen, though he felt no desire to do so, sympathized with Rathfield. When he'd been captured by Guy du Malphias, his host had tortured him. Owen had always thought of himself as being brave and stoic, but the Ryngian subjected him to tortures beyond countenance. However brave Owen had thought himself, whatever courage he thought he possessed, du Malphias had stripped it away. He had no idea how long the man tortured him, but he did know two things. First, it wasn't as long as he would have hoped and second, in the end, he'd told du Malphias everything he wanted to know.

The only way Owen had been able to recover himself was to escape. Because he'd been successful, his escape appeared to be a story of incredible fortitude and bravery. In reality, it had been foolhardy and, save for the working of Mystria's ancient magicks, he would have died and no trace of him ever would have been found. Had it not been for his companion, a *pasmorte* known only as Quarante-neuf, he never would have made it, and he'd not seen his friend since.

Is that what Rathfield is doing? It seemed so and Owen almost pitied the man. If things had happened at Rondeville as Nathaniel had speculated, then Rathfield awoke fearing he would be thought a coward, and found himself being lionized as a hero. The temptation to keep the truth hidden would be incalculable. In whom could he confide? His wife? Owen recalled Catherine's whisper that Rathfield's wife had taken her own life. Had she known the truth of his situation and been unable to live with the disgrace?

Or had she threatened to expose him and he killed her? Owen glanced back and couldn't see a murderer in the man. Then again, the man who fought back mindlessly against the wolves would have been capable of anything.

They came up over the last hill and cut across empty fields toward the road paralleling the river. It really wasn't much more than a cow path that led nowhere, since there was nowhere to go outside the valley. A couple of shepherds saw them and waved, but made no move to intercept them. Others below noticed them, however, and a reception committee formed itself up. Three men straddled the track near the edge of the village. Boys and girls hung back about another twenty yards, and an old man started across the green toward them.

Nathaniel slowed their advance to allow the old man to reach the others before they did. As the visitor approached, Nathaniel kept his rifle cradled, but raised an open hand. "Greetings. Whereabouts is this place?"

The older man—older appearing, anyway, because of the grey shot through his hair—opened his arms. "Welcome, travelers. This is Happy Valley, in Postsylvania. You've come far."

"We have." Nathaniel looked back toward the mountains. "Cut some tracks up there, followed 'em down here. Two men. If I don't miss my guess, sir, given the look of your shoes, you was one of them."

The older man smiled. "I was indeed. God had sent me into the mountains with one of my deacons, then He shook the earth to show me His grace and power. He led us to a vast Temple, where we found golden tablets, upon which He has inscribed His *new* commandments."

Owen nodded. "We saw the Temple."

The other three men exchanged glances and smiled.

The older man laughed. "You see, I told you there would be pilgrims come to verify what we told you. Gentlemen, please. I am Ezekiel Fire. Happy Valley is the home of the True Oriental Church of the Lord. We are God-fearing people who live in harmony with the land and the precepts God has laid down in the Good Book. He has favored us with further Revelations, which we are translating now."

Owen arched an eyebrow. "A new revelation? That's interesting, Reverend."

"No Reverend here, no Bishops. I have no title, though many call me the Steward. I have deacons, but they are chosen by their fellows for specific tasks, then they surrender power until called upon again to serve."

"Beg pardon, then." Nathaniel nodded. "I'm Nathaniel Woods. This here is Makepeace Bone, Captain Owen Strake, Kamiskwa of the Altashee, and Colonel Ian Rathfield. The Colonel, he done come out here all the way to jaw with you about the petition you sent to the Queen."

For Owen it was like watching Miranda's smile the first time a butterfly fluttered down and landed on her finger. Ezekiel's face opened up, displaying such innocent joy as Owen had never seen on another adult's face. "That is wonderful, Colonel; our prayers have been answered. Please, let me show you our settlement. I guarantee our sister settlements are very similar. You can report back to the Queen about us, and she'll know that granting us a charter was the perfect thing to do. God's work, truly."

Rathfield smiled. "Please, lead on."

Ezekiel guided them through the village, naming the families who lived in each home. Though he did not come out and say it, his liberal use of the term "sister-wife" led Owen to believe the Orientalists practiced plural marriage. A fair number of children six years and younger played in and around the homes, and that surprised Owen. While working a farm usually required a good-sized family, rare were those who'd not lost children in their early years. Granted he couldn't know how many children *had* died, but he didn't see any graveyards and the children especially looked healthy.

The one barnlike building Owen had not been able to figure out from the hilltop turned out to be the village workshop and school. The Orientalists had harvested the wood from the nearby forests and had fitted broad planks over a stout lattice to create a solid structure. They'd put a thatched roof on it, fitted it with windows for light—though no glass had made it that far west. The whole thing had been painted red on the outside, with the pigment coming from rusty earth.

Ezekiel proudly waved them through the broad doors. "Each of us shares what we can with each other and the children. Here they can learn to read, write, and cipher. They learn to carve wood and make furniture or weave, sew, and quilt."

"Even the boys?" Rathfield looked over at a young man patching a pair of homespun pants, his tongue poking out of his mouth as he concentrated. "That's women's work."

"Is it?" The older man smiled carefully. "In the Good Book, you'll find Our Lord healing those who are sick, and yet that task usually falls to women. And His cloak was described as being seamless—meaning *perfect*. So He must have made it, since no one but God could create something perfect. Yet you would tell me that weaving and sewing are work meant for women. But if Our Lord could do them, are they not fit for men?"

Rathfield stared, but behind him Makepeace breathed a single word. "Amen."

Ezekiel tousled the boy's hair. "We have found, Colonel, that people tend to do a better job when they enjoy what they do. God lets us know what He wants us to do by the pleasure it brings us and that may change as time goes on. Out here we don't always have the luxury of having someone to do a task for us, so we find that letting everyone learn a little bit of everything, then concentrate on what brings them joy works best. It's one of the messages that God has for His people."

Rathfield looked around, then frowned. "You don't appear to have a gunsmith. I should think that would be a very vital trade out here."

The Steward smiled. "Guns are not mentioned in the Good Book, so we prefer not to use them. Our people are quite proficient in using slings, bows, and even spears if we must hunt. As it is, God has blessed us with this land of incredible bounty."

Owen looked up from where a man was using a draw-knife to scrape down what would become the seat of a chair. "How long has Happy Valley been here?"

"Ten years. It was only after Green River and Piety became established that we sent our petition to the Queen." Ezekiel clapped his hands. "I hardly expected the Queen would actually send someone to us. But, please, come along, you must see our most important work."

He waved them out of the workshop and toward the log fort. "Reading the Good Book led me to this place. I only had a handful of people with me, but others came out and joined us once they understood what our work entails. You see, the Good Book tells us that God has given us dominion over the entire world, but there are those who interpret this to mean they can despoil and ruin as they will. We, instead, choose to live in harmony with the land, much as the Twilight People do."

Owen's eyes narrowed. "How is that, exactly?"

Ezekiel stopped and swept a hand toward the terraces. "Each morning we collect nightsoil and use it to fertilize the fields. We start at the top. As the rain comes and water washes down to the lower fields, the nightsoil is not wasted. And when the water comes off the last field, it flows into the river below the settlement. In another two years we intend to dig out and reinforce the hilltops, then fill the basins with water. We will stock them with fish, and use the water there to irrigate the fields.

"And you may have noticed that we have no timber yards. We go into the forests and select the trees that need to be thinned. We take only what we need as we need it. In the workshop, as you saw, we would rather repair something than harvest new wood. We do not require much. Because we live in harmony with God's Creation, He provides for us."

Kamiskwa looked over at the Steward. "How is it you know which trees must be taken?"

The older man's smile broadened. "When a deacon is called for such work, God blesses him with a *knowing*. He can walk through the woods and pick out the trees to take. God is very generous that way."

Owen nodded. "So the bounty of your community would attest."

"God is pleased. This is why He has granted us another great gift." Ezekiel headed for the fort. "This is why He brought you to us."

The five of them caught up with him, Rathfield in the lead. "If you don't mind, Steward, what are you talking about?"

Ezekiel giggled, and were his voice not so full of delight, Owen would have thought him completely mad. "Up there, when God drained the lake, He did so to give us a great teaching. Two tablets, there in the tabernacle. Gold, written in His own hand."

The man threw open the door to the fort's main building. "I cannot translate them—I cannot even lift them, but my deacon, he can do both and is even now writing down what God wishes us to know."

As they entered the room, a hulking man with a shock of red hair looked up from a table and the twin golden tablets thereupon. "Nathaniel Woods, as I live and breath."

Nathaniel swung his rifle around with one easy motion. "That won't be for long, Rufus Branch, not long at all."

CHAPTER TWENTY

10 May 1767
Prince Haven
Temperance Bay, Mystria

Prince Vlad ushered his wife into his laboratory and bade her sit at a small table. It had been cleared entirely of books and specimen jars. Instead it had a wooden panel two feet tall clamped to the middle, and two small blocks of wood set between it and the chair Gisella lowered herself into. Each of those blocks had a small brass firestone retention collar fitted to it, and firestones trapped beneath the collars, ruby on the right, amber on the left.

She smiled up at him. "I am certain this will work."

"As am I, which terrifies me." The Prince pulled a blindfold from his pocket. "It is not that I don't trust you…"

Gisella laughed. "Despite my father's best efforts to keep me ignorant, I do understand certain things about the manner of Ryngian science. You must blindfold me so I cannot possibly react to anything I see."

He kissed the top of her head. "Thank you." He slipped the blindfold over her eyes and knotted it at the back of her head, being careful not to tangle any of her golden hair in the knot. "There, right hand on this block, left hand there."

"I know, husband. When I feel heat beneath my palm, I am to raise that hand."

"Perfect." Vlad retreated to another table, similarly shielded. Behind his shield he had corresponding blocks with identical firestones. He also had a quill, an inkpot, paper, and a die. He rolled the die and it came up a five. Since it was an odd number, he touched the amber stone on the left. He triggered the spell to light a candle and pushed it into the firestone. Then he waited.

137

About four seconds later, Gisella raised her left hand.

The Prince continued through twenty trials, randomizing each time. In seventeen of twenty tries his wife raised the correct hand. The only failures came in the last five attempts, when he was so excited he wasn't concentrating as well as he should have been. With shaking hands he capped the inkpot and set the quill down. "We're done."

She pulled off the blindfold, her blue eyes positively bright. "How did we do?"

"Seventeen of twenty."

"Oh, I'm sorry, I shall do better. May we go again?"

He stood and crossed to her, taking her hands in his. "No, darling, that is a very good result, better than I expected."

"Then what bothers you?"

He sighed, his shoulders slumping. "What bothers me, my love, is that in doing what we have done, we have invalidated a perceived truth of magick. As we are taught now, to make you feel heat, I would have to touch your hand and invoke a spell."

Gisella raised one of his hands to her lips. "You do not need magick to have that effect on me, beloved."

Vlad looked down upon her face, both unable and unwilling to hide his smile. How he had been so fortunate to have her chosen for him by his aunt was completely beyond him. She had become his partner in every way, sharing some tasks equally, but willingly shouldering some burdens alone while he handled yet others by himself.

He had not, in fact, intended to tell her at all about his discovery concerning the Good Book, but he had read the concern on her face as easily as he could read Scripture. She knew he was worried and asked if she could help. He confided in her and instead of recoiling in terror, she had smiled eagerly. "My ability to use magick is tiny, but it is at your disposal, beloved." And when he agreed to let her help him, he could scarce remember a time she had seemed so happy.

He nodded toward the wooden blocks with the firestones affixed to them. "I did what I could to eliminate some variables. The blocks and the brass fittings are all from different places and types of trees. The firestones are from the same lots and as close to a match in color, shape, and clarity as I could manage. Now it could be that the magick just passed through the air from one stone to the other, or through another channel, or that I directed it to the stone under your hand, since I knew what it looked like, without the stone under mine having anything to do with it."

Gisella's eyes narrowed. "We could blindfold you, too, and someone could mix up the blocks, so you only touch one. You'd not know what color firestone it was. I would still raise my hand. We'd need someone else to record the results. Caleb Frost, perhaps?"

"You're right—blindfolding both of us would work. As for an aide… I dearly wish Owen was here, or Count von Metternin. I trust Caleb, but he is still young and enthusiastic." Vlad frowned. "He might let things slip by accident. The fewer people who know, the better. If Bishop Bumble ever comes to suspect what we've learned, we're undone. The same is true of Colonel Rathfield."

"Do you truly think Colonel Rathfield was sent here to find Ezekiel Fire and destroy his settlement before he could share the secrets of the Good Book?"

Vlad slipped his hands from her and began to pace. "I'd not have thought so, save for Bishop Bumble wanting Fire returned here to stand trial for heresy. It also bothers me that papers which Bumble claims to have had destroyed have come into my possession anonymously. A second packet has been delivered, which confirms things in the first, and hints at Fire's having taken things further. Someone knows things that Bumble does not, and wants them shared on a limited basis. Or do I imagine that the notes were sent to me so they could be found on me, setting me up for a trial on the same heresy charges? What we have just done here would make a prima facie case against us."

"Will that concern stop you?"

"I would stop if you ask. For the sake of our children."

"But not otherwise?"

"How can I, really?" Vlad looked at her directly. "What we have discovered here must already be known in Tharyngia. Owen described as much in terms of things du Malphias was able to do. This means that failure to pursue studies would put Mystria at risk."

"Norisle, too."

"Yes, of course. I meant Norisle and her colonies." *Didn't I?* "The risks here, at least in the eyes of those like Bishop Bumble, would be that all controls over magick would vanish. We would end up with those who are strong magically carving out their own little empires and lording their power over others. This has not happened in Tharyngia, however, and when you look at it, has not the Church set itself up as the same sort of tyranny through magick, albeit covertly?"

"We may believe the Church has, beloved, but what proof have we of it?" She turned in her chair and smoothed her skirts. "Do you see Bishop Bumble as some sorcerer?"

Vlad remembered back to Bumble and his hardships on the way to Anvil Lake. "No, but if he were indeed one, and had been tasked with watching over magick in Mystria, would he be effective if he could be easily spotted? Were Richard Ventnor sent on that sort of mission, he would be suspect immediately."

Gisella shivered. "The idea that Duke Deathridge could wield powerful magicks frightens me."

"Heavens, you are a genius!"

Her face brightened. "I am?"

"You are."

"Tell me, beloved."

Vlad smiled. "Just as the first spell we all learn is how to extinguish a fire, so perhaps there needs to be magick developed which can extinguish or diminish other magick. Of course, that would only work if we can determine the medium through which magick travels. If it would require matched items, as we used here, then it would be difficult to employ. If it can travel through air, or some other unseen medium, then it might be more effective."

Gisella nodded. "Could it be that there is more than a single channel? Sound travels through air, and through water, but at different speeds, yes?"

"Excellent point. It could be that magick might travel faster or slower in some cases. It might be faster through linked items, and slower through air or water. And it might have range limitations based on the strength of the person using it." Vlad returned to his desk and began jotting notes. "We will have to devise a series of experiments to determine what we can. But, first, there is an even more important bit of work I need to do."

She smiled. "Yes, darling?"

"I need to create a spell which, to my knowledge, has never been created before. If I can do that, we open a world of possibilities, and will urgently need to explore them all."

After lunch Vlad returned to his laboratory. From the woodpile outside it, he chose a small stick of oak roughly two inches in diameter. Using a saw he sliced off two disks, each roughly a half inch in width. He sanded them down until smooth, then, using a stencil, he decorated each side with identical images of a bell. He heated a small iron rod in his stove and then used it to burn the image into the wood.

He set the disks aside and pulled a small brass bell from an upper shelf, blowing the dust and cobwebs from it. He hung it from a small wooden stand and used a tiny hammer to ring it. The tone pealed crisply. Closing his eyes, he struck it repeatedly, forcing himself to remember the sound. He listened to it rise, then fade and echo back from the walls. He focused on how he could feel it reverberate in his chest, and then rested a finger lightly on the top so he could feel the vibrations in the bell itself. He weighed the bell in his hand, sniffed it, and even licked it, getting as much sensory information about it as he could. He pressed the cool metal to his neck, memorizing that sensation as well, then hung it on the stand again.

He took one of the disks and crossed to the table his wife had used in the morning. He set the disk down and then placed on top of it a teacup and saucer. From a pitcher he filled the cup to the very brim with water. Careful not to jostle the table and spill anything, he returned to his desk and laid his right hand on the other wooden disk.

As he had been instructed to do when learning how to light a candle, he closed his eyes and focused on how a bell looked and sounded and felt when it rang. He visualized the bell he'd been experimenting with, knowing he could shift to the image of a massive bell in a cathedral steeple if needed. For his experiment, however, he felt that the immediacy of experience with the smaller bell made it perfect for his purposes. In his mind he drew an image of a bright, sunny day, cool and crisp like the sound of the bell. He thought about how the word *peal* seemed so perfect to describe a bell's sound.

He concentrated on that word, imbuing it with all the other sensations, and pushed magick into it. And then he shoved that magick through his hand and into the wooden disk.

Eight feet away, the teacup clattered in its saucer, and water spilled.

Vlad forced himself to measure the volume of water he had spilled, less because it was important, than it gave him sanctuary from considering what he had done. When he sat back down, the enormity of it hit him: he'd created a brand new spell where none had existed before. Even more amazing, it had not been that difficult. All he had done was to analyze one spell and how it had been taught to him, then he repeated that process with a parallel phenomenon.

But if it was so easy for me, why haven't others done it?

He shivered. Likely they had, hundreds if not thousands of times, perhaps tens of thousands of times. But just as with Mugwump using magick of which he had no clear understanding, a spell could drain a man, hurting him badly. In the battle for Fort Cuivre, Makepeace Bone had fired a swivel-gun, assuming it was, in essence, just a big musket. While that was true, the magick necessary to fire it off had bruised his arm to the elbow and left him completely exhausted. Had he been a smaller man and lacked the constitution of a mammoth, it likely would have killed him.

The Prince looked at his right palm. Blood had risen in tiny blisters, barely the size of freckles, in a circle the diameter of the disk. The presence of blood did not surprise him—but he *had* expected to see more. *Why would I get away so easily with a new spell?*

Vlad tapped a finger against his chin. It was easy enough to suppose that the Church began imposing limitations on magick as a way to prevent people from killing themselves. This would naturally lead to them refusing to teach spells or branches of magick that they found morally objectionable—necromancy being a case in point. That did not mean, however, that Church officials would not study it, or other things, in order to understand the true nature of the threat they imposed. From there, the creation of a self-perpetuating thaumagarchy would only make sense. It would have to destroy any threats to its monopoly on power and knowledge, and would do so behind the guise of preventing people from unleashing unspeakable evils.

The difficulty there was simple: they had no monopoly on magick, only a monopoly in Auropa and the Near East. The Twilight People had their own magickal traditions. Vlad assumed the same was true of the Far East and of the Dark Continent. The Tharyngians, since their revolution, had created yet another magickal tradition, the destruction of which could explain why Norisle was willing to bankrupt itself waging wars it could never be truly expected to win.

That thought brought him all the way back to Ezekiel Fire. Assuming the man knew at least as much as Vlad did, there seemed no question that Postsylvania could be home to its own, brand new, magickal tradition. Not only would it have the freedom of the Tharyngian system, but it would be paired with an absolute belief that God intended men to know this new way of magick. Power, when coupled with a vibrant theology, often wrought havoc.

Vlad rose and left the laboratory, walking down toward the river. He looked west. "If you find a new magick out there, my friends, I don't know whether I hope you bring it back, or destroy every trace of it. My fear is that if any of it is even rumored to exist, Norisle will feel forced to extinguish it, and I do not think the Crown will be particularly concerned with how many people die to make that happen."

CHAPTER TWENTY-ONE

10 May 1767
Happy Valley
Postsylvania, Mystria

The Steward gestured gently toward the ceiling. The rifle's muzzle rose accordingly, despite Nathaniel's valiant effort to keep it centered on Branch's chest. "You will find, gentlemen, that your guns will not fire within the precincts of Happy Valley."

Owen pointed his rifle at the floor and covered the firestone with his thumb. He invoked magick, but nothing happened. *How is that possible?* He let that question linger in his mind because du Malphias had moved Owen's own musket aside the same way Ezekiel had raised Nathaniel's. *With contempt on his face, not the Steward's kindness, but it was the same nonetheless.*

"I don't need no rifle to kill you, Branch."

Ezekiel raised a hand. "Please, Brother Nathaniel…"

"I ain't no member of your flock."

"But the Good Lord commanded us to consider all men our brothers." The Steward imposed himself between them and Rufus Branch. "Brother Rufus has been among us for over two years now. I have spent long hours with him, teaching him to read and write. He is a very peaceful man and has been of great help to me. He has borne witness to his sins, but they are in the past. They have been forgiven."

Nathaniel shook his head. "I ain't done no forgiving for his poisoning me, trying to murder me. Murder for hire, too. And I don't suppose his wife done forgive him none for abandoning her and a half-dozen halfwit children in Temperance."

The older man smiled indulgently. "You should understand that Brother Rufus was most candid about his misdeeds. We did not accept him im-

144

mediately. However, he worked with us and for us. He proved himself to us. Though we value children highly, because he has left a wife and children behind, we have not let him wed. Even so, he does his share of duty minding children. He also has not taken a drop of hard cider, ale, or whiskey since he has been with us."

Nathaniel let his rifle rest back on his shoulder. "I find that hard to believe."

"But you must believe it, or believe I am a liar."

"Begging your pardon, Steward, but I onliest got to believe you done been fooled."

Rathfield stepped up and laid a hand on Nathaniel's left shoulder. "I think, Mr. Woods, we should take the Steward at his word."

"Colonel, this man tried to murder me."

"I appreciate that, but I would point out that Colonial authority ended somewhere back at the crest of the Westridge Mountains." Rathfield addressed the Steward. "I would think, sir, that you would agree that Mr. Woods' grievances do deserve to be aired."

Ezekiel Fire nodded solemnly. "Confession is the first step to redemption. Brother Rufus, you will attend a council meeting this evening. We shall discuss your situation."

"Yes, Steward."

The way that Rufus bowed his head, and the respect in his voice, surprised Owen. Rufus Branch had been a loud, lazy, corrupt braggart who drank and brawled and ran a gang of ne'er-do-wells in Temperance Bay. Though he joined the Mystrian Rangers and fought valiantly at Fort Cuivre, he fled the Crown Colonies when he failed to murder Nathaniel. Save for a musket ball fired by Makepeace's little brother, Justice, he would have succeeded.

But the man before them was a man transformed. He clearly wasn't afraid of any of them, but neither was he defiant. He'd become passive and accepting. Owen had no idea what had happened to him, but the change was nothing he could have believed without seeing it with his own eyes.

And I am still not sure I believe it.

The older man smiled. "Until then, you will remain here and continue your translations. You'll have no supper, of course."

"You are very kind, Steward. Thank you."

Ezekiel guided them back out of the large building and back to the workshop. "You will understand if I have you stay in the workshop loft, rather than split you up and install you in our homes. No matter what verdict is rendered this evening, some hard feelings will result. If you do choose to wander the village, I would ask that you leave your guns in the loft. I promise no mischief will be done. It is just that guns do excite the blood of the young, and we would seek to avoid that."

Owen lifted a hand. "This evening, when Rufus stands before you, what might his punishment be?"

The older man clasped his hands behind his back. "He will atone for his sins, but please do not imagine that his punishment will be based on the need for anyone to be vengeful. I understand, Mr. Woods, that you are aggrieved, and rightly so. But I would ask you to understand that in committing the sins he did against you, that Brother Rufus removed himself from the state of God's Grace. Our punishment will be intended to bring him closer to God."

"Give me 'bout three minutes with him, Steward, and I can guarantee you he'll be as close to God as he'll ever get."

Ezekiel Fire glanced at the ground for a moment, unable to hide the hint of a smile which greeted Nathaniel's words. When he looked back up again, he'd composed his face in such a manner that it made Owen think of a kindly old man indulging an enthused child right before laying down the law. "God has clearly gifted you with a sharp mind, Mr. Woods, and a sense of responsibility. So, I ask you, would killing Rufus Branch undo any of the things he has done? Or, is it only by living a good and honest life that he will be able to make amends?"

Nathaniel frowned. "I can see the trail you're blazing here, but I gotta say, just because you ain't seen a dog bite no one ain't no reason to believe that dog's cured of biting."

"Brother Rufus is not a dog."

Owen touched Nathaniel's forearm. "You can understand, Steward, why Nathaniel is reluctant to accept what you're saying about Brother Rufus."

"I can, very easily." The old man smiled. "And this is why I believe, with my whole heart, that God brought you all here. He has great things in mind for you, and Brother Rufus' change of heart is clearly part of his plan."

They followed the Steward in silence to the workshop, which had been completely vacated, and climbed into the loft. There they made themselves at home. Owen sat down and retrieved a journal to start making notes. Nathaniel pulled the bullet from his rifle, scraped the powder out of the chamber, and fitted a new firestone into the firing assembly.

Makepeace leaned against the wall. "Seems to me, Nathaniel, you may owe Rufus an apology."

"How is that?"

"If Rufus has truly accepted the Lord and is living a holy life, then his sins have been forgiven."

Nathaniel's eyes narrowed. "And exactly how is we going to know he's being truthful? He could just be out there spinning a web of lies gonna come back and catch us all up."

Rathfield, seated against the loft railing, smiled indulgently. "You clearly don't understand the power of a conversion experience, Woods."

"I ain't saying it cain't happen. Makepeace here tells a powerful story about him and the Good Lord. What I want to know is how we know it's true what Rufus says."

Rathfield looked up. "It's true because God put it in Brother Rufus' heart to confess his sins and accept the Good Lord as his savior. And he could not say that he's done so, if God had not inspired him to do so."

Nathaniel set his rifle down. "Now, if I is hearing you right, you're telling me that you know he's not lying because he tells you he's not lying because God done spoke to him and told him not to lie?"

"Exactly."

"But what if he was lying about God speaking to him?"

"The Good Book says…"

The guide raised a finger. "How do you know that what the Good Book says ain't a lie neither?"

Rathfield blinked. "We know the Good Book is true because it was inspired by God, and God cannot lie. It says so right in the Good Book."

Nathaniel looked over at Owen. "Kinda convenient, ain't it, to have a book believed to be true simply because there's a verse in there somewhere what tells you it's true?"

Rathfield shot to his feet. "I will not tolerate blasphemy, Woods."

Nathaniel stood, but slowly and languidly. "Well now, I don't think I's blaspheming. I'm just pointing out what is what. Now God, He done made every animal under the sun afore a single jot or tittle of that Good Book was writ down. Ain't that so?"

Makepeace nodded. "The Scribes did come considerable later than events in the Garden."

"And that means that when I see a bird pretending to have a broken wing to lead a predator away from a nest, that I'm watching a God-given talent for deception on display. Ain't that so?"

Owen nodded. "He does have a point."

"Animals do not have souls, Strake. Men are not animals." Rathfield lifted his chin. "If God inspires a man to change his life, and that man shares the good news of his redemption, he is doing the work of God. When a man gives his testimony within a Fellowship, it is to confirm the faith of others and bring them closer to God. It is proof that God has touched them. Do you doubt Makepeace's story, Woods?"

"Never said I did, but that's on account of I knowed him before and after."

Rathfield smiled. "And yet you won't allow Brother Rufus to show you who he has become. I would have thought you were more fair-minded than that, Woods."

Kamiskwa made a comment in Altashee. Makepeace chuckled and the tips of Nathaniel's ears flushed with hot color. "I ain't saying he hasn't changed. I am just saying I am powerful disinclined to believe it. And as my brother has taken it upon himself to remind me, I have done me a bit of changing down through the years. Ain't never been because God paid me no never-mind, but I done changed."

Owen made a quick note in his journal. "Colonel Rathfield, might I ask you a question?"

"Of course, Strake." The man beamed. "How may I help you?"

"I just wanted to record your reaction to the fact that the Steward was able to move Nathaniel's rifle without touching it, and to prevent the rest of us from firing our own weapons."

"I have no idea what you are talking about."

"Did you see what happened in there?"

The blond man nodded solemnly. "The Steward gestured and Mr. Woods, being polite, followed the implied request."

"Ain't exactly how I remember it." Nathaniel sat back down again and began reloading his rifle.

"Me, neither." Owen looked up from the page. "Colonel, I was unable to fire my rifle."

Rathfield's face darkened. "Do you mean to tell me you actually *tried* to fire your rifle?"

"Yes." Owen looked at Makepeace and Kamiskwa. "Did you two try?"

Makepeace shook his head.

Kamiskwa shrugged. "It was not necessary."

"Try now."

Rathfield raised both hands. "Absolutely not. I forbid it. You took what the Steward said to be a declaration of his ability to stop your rifle from working. It was clearly a request for gentlemanly behavior which, I am pleased to see, at least two of my companions agreed to."

"This isn't the first time I've seen this sort of magick, Colonel. If you read the reports I sent to Horse Guards, you'd know that Guy du Malphias was able to do the same thing: to make magick work at range."

Rathfield exhaled slowly. "You'll be pleased to note, I believe, that certain officials were able to put your dubious observation into perspective, Strake. Your attempt to call undue attention to yourself was apparent, and treated properly. You alone saw du Malphias wield this sort of magick. None of your companions did, did they?"

Nathaniel laughed. "Someone has to have a fancy word for this. You is asking me to take the word of a drunken, murderous scoundrel that he ain't no more any of them things on one hand. and then suggesting that a friend who ain't never lied a day in his life is lying about something that important? That do beat all."

"The fact of the matter is, Woods, that we know, because of centuries of tradition, that magick only works through touch." Rathfield's eyes became angry slits. "You are asking me to accept Strake's word for something that contradicts hundreds of years of teachings by Church authorities. That's a rather tall order, don't you think?"

Nathaniel didn't even look up from his rifle's breech. "It might be, Colonel, but then, you might want to think on it this way. Just because a baby ain't never taken a step on its own, don't mean that someday it might not. Maybe all your tradition just speaks to times when men is crawling through magick, and Owen here, he done seen men beginning to stride proudly. Ain't no fault of your own that what you think you know is wrong."

Rathfield hesitated, then glanced down. "Your commentary warrants some thinking, Woods." His head came back up. "Regardless, I expect all of you to abide by the Steward's wishes. We leave our guns here. We leave *all* of our weapons here. We shall get to know these people and their customs."

Owen forced himself to nod and put on an angry expression. He knew that's what Rathfield expected. It gave him the opportunity to hide his true reaction, which was complete astonishment. Rathfield's command was at complete odds with the nature of his mission as stated back in Temperance Bay. And as the discovery of the Antediluvian ruins had led them to the golden tablets, Rathfield should have been demanding that they be turned over to him. And then he should have ordered the people back over the mountains.

I wonder if the petition was the only *missive sent to the Queen.* The Steward had welcomed Rathfield, which was an act that would seem to have been at odds with the nature of the petition. What had Rathfield expected to find in Postsylvania?

Owen began to write out a list of questions for which he would try to get answers, but he didn't get very far before a boy can running breathless into the workshop. "Please, come; the Steward wants you to come. Something's happened."

Rathfield looked down. "What, boy?"

The child shook his head. "I don't know, but it has to be bad. He said you should bring your guns."

CHAPTER TWENTY-TWO

10 May 1767
Prince Haven
Temperance Bay, Mystria

Prince Vlad's wife found him on the dock down by the wurmrest. He smiled at the softness of her tread and turned slowly to watch her. "Good afternoon."

"Good evening, you mean." She returned his smile, then caressed his arm. "You've been here for hours. I thought you were going to train Mugwump more but…"

He glanced over at the wurmrest and noticed that the building's shadow had almost reached him. *Has it really been that long?* "I was thinking."

"Apparently."

Vlad slipped an arm around her waist and pulled Gisella to him. "What we did this morning, and what I did after, it has me thinking so many things. I wanted to fly Mugwump, but then I got to thinking about a way I could direct his flight using what little I've learned. And that made me wonder so many other things."

She smiled and rested her head on his shoulder. "Such as?"

"You brought up the idea that we need to assess how fast magick can travel. If the speed is immediate, this has incredible implications for the future of the world. Imagine that I have a partner in Rivertown, down in Fairlee, and he tells me that the cotton harvest has been fantastic. The abundance means cotton is priced very low. With this knowledge I can solicit sales and contracts here in Temperance Bay, locking in what is, in Temperance Bay, a below-market price, but still considerably above the price in Fairlee. I tell my man in Rivertown how much to buy and to ship. Those waiting for the same information to come by land or ship, or those just waiting on the shipments themselves, will be at a severe disadvantage."

Gisella laughed. "You are far too kind in your example. Imagine a pirate learns what ship is sailing and what cargo it holds."

"Well, yes, that, too, would be an example. I got to thinking of how I could work with a series of disks to transmit numbers which would be keyed to coded phrases—much the kind of book cipher I use now—so transmission would be quick. So if magick travels faster than a man on foot, or a ship at sea—and if it is not subject to weather delays it would not have to be that much faster—it is incredibly useful. And this got me thinking about whether or not there are ways to speed it or disrupt it."

"Disrupt, how?"

He pointed toward the river. "Few people see the river for what it really is: a *lot* of energy. Could it be that the river itself has a presence not only in the natural world, but that it casts a shadow into the supernatural world? Might a message designed to flow along *with* the river travel faster than one going *against* it?"

Her brow wrinkled. "That is a good question."

"And there is another. In Norisle, and even here, there are places that people believe are sacred sites. Men who have studied them claim they are linked by straight lines that intersect at precise angles. Could it be that magick sent along those lines will travel faster? If so, it could be that a trading post built on one of those intersections could be more valuable than one built at the convergence of several rivers? Economic information that allows a downriver merchant to get a good price on furs would be more valuable than the furs themselves."

Gisella nodded and slipped from beneath his arm. "You avoid the obvious discussion. Is it to save me heartache?"

"The obvious, darling?"

She stared at him for a moment, then smiled. "From any other man, that would not have been an honest question. Husband, if magick can convey messages faster than a man can travel on foot, if it travels in a direct line, ignoring mountains and rivers, then it has most direct and terrible applications in *war*."

Vlad shivered, then pulled one of the wooden disks from his pocket, tracing a thumbnail over the design burned into it. "As I visualized the code wheel, I had seen it built into a desk, where the operator would have room to write out incoming messages. I had done that, I think, to make it seem impractical in the field. And it might yet be. It could be that it would take someone well-versed in magick, someone who would be invaluable on the line, able to fire many shots before tiring, to run it. The demands, therefore, might make it completely impractical for any tactical consideration. But strategically you would be right. A field device would need be no larger than this disk."

High above them a hawk glided lazily through the sky. "You avoid the other obvious implication, Vlad."

"That the Church already has discovered what I know, and that they have put it in place?" He shook his head. "Circumstance argues against its deployment. As you have noted, it would confer an incredible advantage in war, so would have been used against the Tharyngians. There seems no evidence of its use in the last war, or by agents of the Crown in communicating with Launston. While we have to assume that the Church has figured out at least as much as I have, it would not seem that they have the personnel capable of using it, nor have made the decision to use it so far."

"And if you are wrong?"

"There is the question, isn't it?" He clasped his hands at the small of his back. "Every advancement can be seen as a boon or a curse. Steel, when used as a plowshare, makes it easier for a farmer to till more acreage and raise more food. That same steel, shaped into a sword, makes it easier for someone else to take that food away from him. Faster communications might have let us know of the damage done to settlements near the earthquake faster, so we could send relief. By the same token, faster communications will allow those who possess it to cheat those who don't. It might even allow people in charge of armed forces to stifle the freedoms of others—perhaps just as easily as it would let news of their excesses spread far and wide."

Vlad brought his hands forward and stared at them. "The Crown already controls the supply of firestones and brimstone in the colonies. It is not hard to imagine that both will become scarce if the Crown feels there is any real chance of insurrection. If the Control Acts are actually put into place, they could add a provision to heavily tax any use of a thaumagraph."

"*Thaumagraph?*"

"From the Achean—it means miracle writing. I made it up to name my device."

Gisella laughed gaily and closed to kiss him on the cheek. "You are the most amazing man, Vladimir. You shoulder grave weight, and yet address tiny details with whimsy and perfection."

He laughed, embarrassed and proud at the same time. "Giving it a name makes it real—and yet we don't even know if it will be practical. The experiment I did earlier proved I could make the thing work. In fact, I was thinking that I could rig us a series of disks, suspending them from strings, and attach bells to them that would ring with different notes. By touching disks, or even keys similar to those on a pianoforte, I could easily communicate a message to anyone who was not tone deaf."

"As well as play music."

"Yes, that, too, provided the magick was not exhausting." Vlad sighed. "I was also thinking that a similar system could communicate simple commands to Mugwump in flight, obviating the need for reins and bridle. Of course, that assumes that the magick he's using in flight will not interfere. Just so many things, Gisella."

She took his hands in hers. "There are many things, yes, my love. You will attend to them, but first you shall come inside and join your family for supper. Your son had an exciting day. He caught a grasshopper. He wishes to show it to you."

Vlad arched an eyebrow. "He let it loose in the house, didn't he?"

"We believe so, yes."

Vlad squeezed his wife's hands. "Lead on, my darling, and thank you for saving me from myself."

Prince Vlad forced himself to pay attention over dinner, and then participated in the great, though fruitless, grasshopper hunt. Catherine and Miranda had kept Gisella company while father and son searched the house high and low for the grasshopper.

Richard had not yet grown out of that awkward phase where, from time to time, gravity got the best of him. The boy would bend over to peer under couches and hutches, rolling through somersaults. The results always seemed to surprise him but, being a happy child, they prompted giggles instead of tears.

Vlad, of course, had no real recollection of being that age though both his parents had told him he was precocious and always interested in the natural world. He supposed he'd gotten that interest from his mother, who had taken immediately to studying Mystrian flora. Some of his earliest memories were of accompanying her into the woods, looking for flowers and studying their life cycles. He couldn't help but notice the fauna as well and, with her encouragement, took to studying the natural world with the same concentration his father devoted to Scriptures.

Gisella appeared in the parlor's doorway. "It's time you put your son to bed."

Without giving it a second thought, Vlad scooped the boy into his arms, bid Catherine a good evening and carried Richard to his room. He let Madeline dress the boy for bed, but dismissed her and sat beside Richard's bed.

The boy smiled at him. "We find it tomorrow, Daddy."

Vlad nodded and brushed hair from the boy's forehead. He found it curious that he never recalled his father showing him even the least little bit of physical affection. The man must have done, but all of Vlad's memories were of his father being stiff and distant. His father existed in a different realm, a spiritual one, where he sought to distance himself from physical reality because those realities interfered with his ability to effectively worship God. Had the Good Book not called for men to be fruitful and multiply, Vlad doubted he would ever have been born.

He bent down and softly kissed his son's forehead. "We will. I may even have a little cage in which we can make it a home."

"No cage, Daddy." Richard's face scrunched down seriously. "He wants to be free."

"Does he?"

"Yes." The boy nodded solemnly. "He and Mugwump will be friends."

"I think that is a splendid idea." The Prince gave the boy's hand a squeeze. "Now, you get to sleep. We have to hunt tomorrow."

The boy smiled and closed his eyes, squirming to get comfortable.

Vlad pulled a light blanket over him and sat, watching, listening to the boy's breathing become regular as the shadows deepened in his room. It occurred to him, as he sat there, that both of his parents had spent their lives working to define the world. His father did it through reading

Scripture and philosophers and doing his best to make God's message understandable to all. And his mother had done the same thing with plants, bringing together as much knowledge as she could about each, so people could employ them in ways that would make life better. Even he had done similar things with his missions to explore Mystria and the way he catalogued the creatures.

But that carefree phase of his life had begun to change. He couldn't quite put a finger on when it had, though the battle at Anvil Lake was one likely candidate, and certainly Mugwump's emerging from his chrysalis was another. With both events he had moved out of the traditional realm of things that were known, into a new arena. His magickal discoveries were pushing him yet further into territories either unexplored, or jealously guarded by a tiny group of people that virtually no one outside their number even guessed they existed.

Or were allowed to live with the knowledge.

Just for a moment he considered abandoning his studies. Yes, he'd always wonder what he could have learned, what he could have created, but he could console himself with the belief that all of his experimentation would come to naught. After all, magick might have a very short range. His greatest discovery might be to create a magickal pianoforte that was notable for the fact that it exhausted the musician playing it before a single song was complete. To give up on his Mystrian thaumaturgy now meant he might never open a carefully guarded, secret door that could not be closed again.

If he *did* open that door, his would be the responsibility for everything that came through it. *And the forces that will be arrayed against me will be very powerful, indeed.*

He looked at his son again. It had been noted that when the discovery of brimstone fostered a need for *cursed* individuals to wield magick in combat, that after a generation or so, royal families through Auropa manifested the ability to use magick. It had been speculated that perhaps noble families had always had that ability, but had kept it hidden. Vlad, as he looked at his son, wondered if there might be another explanation— that it had taken a long time for noble families to produce magick-users of significant strength. It could be that with each new generation, the children were getting stronger. And if that were true, then while Vlad's magickal pianoforte might exhaust him, it might provide his son the ability to entertain others for an evening or more.

He harkened back to his wife's earlier comments and smiled as she appeared in the doorway. He got up, pressing a finger to his lips, and slipped from the room. "I think he'll be down for the night."

"And so up very early." She brushed a finger over his cheek. "And you'll likely be the night in your laboratory."

Vlad frowned. "I do recognize what you did in asking me to put Richard to bed. You wanted to remind me of my obligations to my family, and to remind me that I'm not my father. I cannot thank you enough. And, yes, I desperately want to be in my laboratory, working on the thaumagraph, but I won't. Not tonight."

"Vlad, this is very important work."

"It is important, yes, but not nearly as important as you are." He caught her hand in his and kissed her palm. "What happens here, in Mystria, in my laboratory, will shape the future for our children. It will shape it for all children. So, I ask you, my love, what think you of our trying for another child? Another child for whom and with whom, we can build that future?"

She reached up and drew his mouth down to hers. They kissed, his arms slipping around her, her body molding itself to his. Then she broke their embrace and took his hand, leading him deeper into their home, up to their bedroom, and into their future.

CHAPTER TWENTY-THREE

10 May 1767
Happy Valley
Postsylvania, Mystria

They exited the workshop and ran toward the west end of the settlement, past the fortress. A small group of people had gathered there and two men were dragging a cart over. The Steward knelt beside what appeared to be a bundle of bloody rags. As Nathaniel drew close, people moved back, revealing a second body, an adult, laying beside the child next to Ezekiel Fire.

The Steward rubbed his hands together, then laid them on the child's form. "Our Father, Almightly and Powerful in Heaven. As You look over us and guide us, please work through me to bring Your special blessing, a healing blessing, to this child, Becca Green. In Your wisdom You know she is an innocent. Thy will be done."

Fire hunched forward, firmly pressing his hands to the child's body. It looked, just for a moment, as if his hands glowed the color of blood. It didn't appear to be a trick of the light, but Nathaniel had never seen anything like it before. Then the girl gasped and struggled, kicking out. Though she couldn't have been any older than eight, and still appeared weak, one kick caught Fire in the ribs and knocked him down. He sagged as if he'd caught a rifle-butt to the head and lay very still on the ground.

And his hands had taken on the deep purple of bruising that came from powerful magick use.

One of the women gathered the girl into her arms and carried her to the cart. A couple others saw to the Steward. Nathaniel approached the other body and dropped to one knee beside it. Kamiskwa faced him on the other side, and Rathfield stood at the woman's head, staring down with his hands crossed over his chest.

Nathaniel knew the body was that of a woman more by her clothes than anything else. Homespun and grey, similar to those worn by the women of Happy Valley, they'd been shredded. Brush and brambles had done their work on the skirts, but the bodice had been rent by something nastier. A trio of claws had opened the woman from shoulder blade to buttocks, right to left, and again on her right flank.

Nathaniel shook his head. "Cain't say I find anything familiar about them claw marks."

Rathfield pointed. "Surely she must have been attacked by a jeopard."

Kamiskwa laid a hand on Nathaniel's arm. "Colonel, a jeopard has four claws. They use them to hold prey, not to slash them open. Once the prey is down, then they bite, very specifically and very precisely. This woman, had a jeopard taken her down, never would have gotten up again."

Nathaniel teased aside a bit of grey cloth. "And if you see here, she done used her underskirts to be binding up her wounds. I reckon she did the same for her child. Iffen jeopards was attacking her, they'da smelt her off miles. Wounds weren't deep enough to kill her, but exhaustion of hauling her child here was. How far is Piety? What direction?"

The people of Happy Valley looked at each other, but said nothing.

Then Rufus Branch shouldered his way through the small crowd. It might have been a trick of the light, but he'd grayed at the temples and his usually florid face had taken on a hint of grey, especially under his eyes. He pointed toward the northwest "Three days off. This time of year reckon on the bright star in the Big Dipper's handle."

Nathaniel stood, running a hand over his jaw. "Three days tore up like that? She had a lot of sand, that woman."

Rufus shook his head. "She had faith, Nathaniel. She believed in the Lord. She probably said a prayer with every step. That's how she got here."

Owen walked over to Nathaniel. "The little girl is terrified. It's all a nightmare. She said demons attacked Piety. They came at night, blotting out the stars. They flew down and slaughtered everyone. Her mother forced her to run. She doesn't think anyone else survived. Makepeace is going to talk with her, see if she remembers any details of the trip, but he doesn't think backtracking them would be difficult."

"I reckon we get some supper and we go."

Rathfield held a hand up. "You're going nowhere."

Nathaniel's eyes narrowed. "I don't reckon you have much say in the matter, Colonel."

"This is still my expedition, Woods."

"Is it, now?" Nathaniel looked around. "As I recollect, we was hired to get you to your Postsylvania, and we have. And we went hunting for whatever got stole from the mountains. We done found it. Now, whatever done attacked Piety, it's a bit of a worry for folks in these parts. As you so politely pointed out, your jurisdiction ended back in them mountains. I don't expect you to come, and we'll fetch you from here and back to Temperance when we return, but we's going to Piety and ain't you nor nobody else gonna stop us."

Owen and Kamiskwa stood by Nathaniel's sides.

Rathfield studied the trio, then slowly nodded. "Though I find it difficult to imagine, I believe you have the wrong impression of me. I fully understand and accept the nature of my mission, and my responsibility. I also recognize a greater responsibility. Dammit, man, I am an officer in Her Majesty's Army. I wear the uniform of the Fifth Northland Cavalry proudly. These people may have moved beyond the bounds of the charters granted by the Queen, but they *are* her subjects, and it is my duty to protect them."

He looked west. "You have no idea what you will find out there. It could be they were attacked by wild beasts. It could be that some tribe of the Twilight People has risen in war against us. There are doubtless Tharyngians to the west, and I am certain they would not welcome a Norillian settlement in territory they believe belongs to them. For all we know, some of them yet believe our nations are at war."

"And you reckon them reasons mean we need you?"

"No. I am pointing out why I must be going west. It's not *your* responsibility."

Nathaniel folded his arms across his chest. "And I reckon it is. I was born in Mystria, Colonel, just like most of these here folks. Rufus and me been fighting each other since before we could speak. You didn't know any of these people done existed, that this place existed, afore someone sent you west in a boat. Iffen anyone has responsibility for them, it's me."

Nathaniel thrust his chin out, just hoping Ian would swing a fist. His heart was pounding, not really from anger, but from surprise. He allowed as how if Rathfield said the sky was blue, he'd say it wasn't just to be contrary. Had he been asked to think about it in the past, he wouldn't have felt he owed the people of Happy Valley anything. If they were foolish enough to move as far west as they had, traipsing off after some half-mad preacher, he would have figured they got exactly what they deserved.

But that had changed, and it surprised Nathaniel how much it had changed. Before Anvil Lake and Fort Cuivre, he'd wanted as little to do with civilization as possible. The fact was, however, that men in his command had come to rely upon him. Nathaniel realized that he was very good at what he did and that, in part, included looking out for folks who couldn't look out for themselves. The people of Piety, damned fools though they might have been, hadn't deserved to be slaughtered no matter what the provocation.

If he hits me, maybe he'll knock some sense back into me.

Rathfield looked him up and down. "It would seem, then, Mister Woods, that we have an unity of purpose. I shall accompany you."

"You cain't. You don't have no musket."

"We can remedy that, Mr. Woods." Ezekiel Fire leaned heavily on Makepeace Bone as he joined the group. "Joseph Wright, can you shape a stock for Colonel Rathfield's musket before morning and get the hardware fitted to it?"

A burly man nodded and withdrew toward the workshop.

Fire turned toward Nathaniel. "You should leave at dawn. I will come with you."

"This here is going to be a war party, Ezekiel Fire. Ain't going to be time for preaching."

"I assure you, I will keep pace with you." The older man glanced down. "Those people were out there because of me. I must go to comfort any other survivors, and to see to it that the others are properly laid to rest."

"Then that's why you ought to be staying here, sending someone out to your other settlement, to warn them or bring them in. They'll need you here."

Fire shook his head. "No, I have someone who will lead in my absence."

The hair stood up at the back of Nathaniel's neck. "Who would that be?"

The Steward nodded to Rufus Branch. "God has spoken to me. This deacon will serve."

Nathaniel didn't like leaving Rufus Branch in charge, but he couldn't say anything about it. The Steward's word was law as far as Happy Valley was concerned. More importantly, the people knew Rufus better than they did Nathaniel. If he continued to say bad things about Branch, the citizens of Happy Valley would consider him mad or untrustworthy, which meant they'd side with Rufus if any showdown erupted.

By morning the Steward's hands had already begun to heal, having faded to a greenish-yellow with tinges of purple on the palms. The old man seemed to be quite chipper and shouldered a pack equal to that the others carried. What he wasn't hauling in brimstone and shot he replaced with food and some medical supplies. A small skinning knife was the closest thing to a weapon he carried, and Nathaniel figured it would only ever be used for eating.

Owen's assessment had been correct. Backtracking Gail Green and her daughter had been very easy. Nathaniel straightened up from where a footprint on a stream bank had dried. "Kamiskwa, Makepeace, you notice anything odd?"

Makepeace bent down to study it. "Looks about right for being a day and a half old."

The Shedashee grunted. "No other tracks."

"Right. Ripped up as the woman was, shoulda been dire wolves and pert near everything else a-hunting her."

Owen pointed to a long blade of saw-grass. "Blood here, and doesn't look as if anything has touched it. There's butterflies all over, but none on this?"

Kamiskwa nodded. "Bad blood."

Rathfield arched an eyebrow. "Meaning?"

Nathaniel scratched at an unshaved cheek. "Means that whatever done clawed her got the blood poison into her. Weren't nothing that cut her trail liked the smell of her."

"But that would hardly seem to make sense, Woods." Rathfield cradled his new musket in his arms. "Creatures don't kill for sport."

"But men do, Colonel." The Mystrian scout shook his head. "Could be whatever tried to kill her was a man, or least ways thought like one. I ain't sure which is worse."

They pushed on as quickly as they could and, despite racing toward a settlement that he expected to find in ruins, Nathaniel found himself enjoying the trip. The forests seemed older, with fewer varieties of trees. It struck him that some trees transplanted from Norisle had worked their way inland season by season. He knew from the Shedashee that they'd never raised wheat or rye, but the crops could be found up and down the Colonies. Not only had men invaded Mystria, but they'd brought green allies to exert dominance over the land.

Nathaniel knew that the Good Book gave man license to establish dominion over the world. He found himself wishing that the Good Lord had been a bit more specific with his instructions on how to do that. All too often he got the feeling that the Good Lord had said, "Yes, you may make light in the darkness," and most men figured that gave them license to burn down a forest.

He found himself walking behind the Steward as the second day stretched toward night. "Don't mind me asking, Ezekiel Fire, but what was it made you come on out here?"

The older man glanced back over his shoulder. "God gave man an unspoiled garden. He gave people everything they wanted, including the gift of magick. But men got greedy, and they spoiled the garden. So God exiled them and took away their gifts. Mostly He did, that was, but He's a loving God. He gave us a way to return to His grace. And it came upon me to realize that He wanted men to be back in that unspoiled garden. Now, truly, have you seen any other place that has done without man's spoiling hand since He created the world?"

"I don't reckon I have, but we ain't alone out here. There's Shedashee lives in these parts."

"But they live as God intended. They're innocents, of course, because they have not heard the Word and have not been saved, but their innocence and the way they live in harmony with the land makes them blessed. I believe, when the Good Lord comes again, He will reward them for their fidelity to His intention."

Nathaniel snorted. "That's a mite kinder assessment than I done heard coming out of some other preachers' pieholes."

Fire looked back, a wistful expression lighting his face. "That's because my brethren are frustrated. They hold the key to salvation in their hands every day, but they have failed to discern God's true plan, failed to have learned the lessons He set out for each of us."

Kamiskwa worked his way back along the trail. "We found where they probably spent their first morning. It has good water. We can't be more than four or five hours away now, so we might as well camp for the night."

"Agreed, iffen you're agreeable, Steward."

"Yes. I shall use the time to pray."

Neither man said it aloud, but they expected fighting the next day. Taking the evening to rest and prepare would not hurt.

"Now, Steward, when we head out tomorrow…"

Fire shook his head. "Son, do you think God has spared me a vision of what we will find?"

"Don't know if He has, sir, or not, but I don't know if you done ever seen a slaughter before. It's been going on a week since they died. Scavengers might not have been at them because of the blood poison, but the sun ain't going to have spared them none, and maggots, well, they tend to be hearty little beasts." Nathaniel pointed up and down the trail. "For us, they ain't gonna be people we knowed. For you…"

"I understand, Mr. Woods, and I appreciate your concern." The older man smiled. "But you should understand this: I am not the Steward of their physical selves, but of their souls. What you describe is not, to me, a tragedy, but confirmation that God, in His Wisdom, has called them home. And while I know that what we will see will be horrible, there will be a part of me that wishes I lay among them."

Nathaniel frowned. "I don't reckon that is right."

"Oh, but it is." Ezekiel Fire sighed wearily. "You see, God has showed me what we shall see tomorrow, and all that I shall endure the rest of my days. Believe me when I say that there are some things which are worse than Death, and those very things lay in store for me."

CHAPTER TWENTY-FOUR

13 May 1767
Piety
Postsylvania, Mystria

I n the morning's dead air, nothing moved in Piety.

They'd come in from the east, topping a hill that looked down upon the shallow valley in which the settlement had been raised. A modest stream ran from northeast to southwest, with a small lake at the southwestern end. It wasn't hard to see that the lake had once been larger, but the settlers had drained what had been marshland, reducing it by two-thirds, and had placed that land under cultivation. A wooden dock jutted into the lake and Owen easily imagined boys fishing off it on a warm summer afternoon.

Owen had crouched and taken out a journal to sketch a rough map of the village. The structures had been clustered toward the northeastern end of the valley. They had neither a mill nor a workshop, but a central blockhouse overlooked a village green and served as a meeting house. Smaller houses had been arranged around it, many with corrals and chicken coops built nearby. Four barns served the community, two on each side of the stream, all southwest of the settlement.

Nathaniel sank down beside Owen. "Ain't nothing to see, is there?"

"Doesn't appear to be." Owen sighed. "We might as well go down and investigate."

"Agreed." Nathaniel stood. "Everyone stay together. Makepeace, you'll be watching our backsides. Steward, you'll be with Owen, telling him what's normal and what ain't. Kamiskwa, Colonel, we'll be keeping our eyes peeled and don't be forgetting the sky. Anything comes on bat-wings, I reckon we should send it back to Hell."

The party made their way down into the village from the east and approached one of the houses from the rear. It really wasn't much more than a log shack, ten feet deep and twenty wide. It had a long roof sloping toward the rear, with an overhang that covered a shelf for wood storage. Owen figured it had first been made as a lean-to, with the front face open, but that had later been finished with rough-hewn boards. A plank door hung crooked on leather hinges.

Kamiskwa swung a door to the chicken coop back and forth. "No birds, a little blood, but the coop is intact. Whatever took them wasn't a wild animal."

Nathaniel nodded and pointed toward the goat pen. "They also took time to brush away their footprints."

"Looks wind-scoured to me." Makepeace bent down to take a better look. "But ain't no wind woulda done that good a job, save for a big storm, and we ain't had that."

Owen shivered. "Magick, then?"

He'd expected Kamiskwa to answer, but Fire hung his head. "Evil magick. I can feel it."

Makepeace and Rathfield crossed themselves.

They moved on to the house. Owen entered first, rifle ready, but the small shack proved empty. A sleeping loft considerably lowered the ceiling over the main room. The fire in the hearth on the left wall had long since died. Cornmeal mush had congealed in the base of a cast-iron pot hanging there. The surface had cracked like the mud in a dry lake bed. The porridge had been served up and small mounds of it had dried on four plates set on a table suitable for seating six. Butter had melted and resolidified in a small crock, and the loaf of brown bread on a cutting board had grown stale.

"Do you know who lived here?"

Fire nodded solemnly. "Ben Mason, his wife, four children—a boy, three girls."

Owen quickly mounted the log ladder to the sleeping loft. A large bed with a cradle at the foot of it lay to the right, and three sleeping mats with blankets lay to the left. The beds had been made neatly, with one of the sleeping mats having a small ragged doll in a grey dress and bonnet leaning against the pillow.

Owen descended again and rejoined the others outside. "Family was having dinner, must have come out peacefully because there is nothing out of place. If we didn't know what had happened, a casual look-see and I'd assume they were all coming back inside the hour."

"Miriam always did keep a good house. Encouraged the children that way."

Fire's observation did nothing to make Owen feel any better. The peaceful nature of the village contrasted with the horror of the wounds on the Green woman's body. For all intents and purposes, every living thing had vanished in an instant, and there was no reason Owen could imagine that they couldn't disappear just as quickly. His stomach tightened as the pain of never seeing Miranda again struck him. In its wake came the cold realization that his wife would not miss him. And when he visualized his daughter crying, the woman he saw comforting her was Bethany Frost.

He wished for one moment—one selfish moment—that she had come along with them. He told himself it was because he wanted her insight on what he was seeing. He was missing something and he knew it. She would have seen it. *She will pick it easily from my journal notes.* She would have made short work of the mystery of Piety.

But he also knew he wanted her there for more. Piety, empty and silent, made him feel terribly alone. He harkened back to when du Malphias had kept him captive and how it had been Bethany who nursed him back to health after his escape. And even limiting his recollection to that point in his life, he was cheating, and knew it. He'd resented those men who had paid Bethany court, and secretly delighted when their suits failed—even though he could have no claim on her.

The fact was that he'd felt alone for far longer than he'd been in Mystria. While he had no desire to be alone, he realized there was no escaping that fate. His wife might loathe him, but she would never grant him a divorce. To do so would be to admit, somehow, that she had lost something. He was a possession that she would never let slip from her grasp. More importantly, however, he would never ask for a divorce. He had been solemn and sincere when he made his marriage vows to her. It did not matter that she had abandoned her obligations to him; as an honorable man, he could not abandon his to her.

Owen shook himself and they continued exploring homes, working their way toward the block house. Each home matched what they'd seen in the Mason home. Families at supper had stepped out of their houses and had simply evaporated. No signs where they had gone, and no signs of the horror Becca Green had related.

Then they reached the block house. Rathfield entered first, then turned back and vomited. Hunched over, he still held a hand out, warning the others off. As he went to his knees, Fire comforted him.

The officer wiped his mouth on his sleeve. "Don't go in there. It's…"

Owen swallowed hard and moved upwind of the man's vomit. He glanced at Nathaniel. The scout nodded, Makepeace crossed himself, and the three of them cautiously passed over meeting house threshold.

The single room had been arranged as it must have been for services. A lectern stood at the front, next to a table, facing the door through which they entered. Row upon row of sturdy wooden chairs, each handcrafted, with the family name carved uppermost on the back, faced the lectern. A few chairs without names formed the last row, as if waiting to welcome visitors. The most ornate chairs, being just bit larger than the others, had been reserved for family patriarchs.

The people of Piety had never left. Virtually every chair had been filled, with bodies sitting upright and attentive, hands clasped in their laps. The villagers heads had been cleanly removed, and sat on top of those hands. Time and warmth had begun to desiccate the flesh, but otherwise Owen saw no signs of putrefaction. No bodily fluids had dripped, and all he could smell was dust, no decay. While some of the clothes showed evidence of battle—like sleeves having been slashed during efforts to ward off attacks—the faces had been arranged to look impassive, if not peaceful.

The deacon's body stood at the lectern. His head rested where the Good Book should have been. He stared toward the door with milky eyes.

Owen didn't know how long he stood there. He'd seen horrible things in combat—bodies so thoroughly destroyed that all one could do was to pile bits into a basket and hope they all belonged to the same person. This was worse, far worse, because it had been done deliberately and with great precision. Not only had the people been slain, but their killing mocked who they had been. He could only imagine their horror as their fate befell them, and wept for all the fathers who had watched their children die.

He stuck out a hand to bar the Steward from going past the doorway.

"You can't."

"I must." Fire pushed past, then slumped back against the wall. "Oh, Heavenly Father…"

Kamiskwa stayed clear, as did Rathfield. Nathaniel and Makepeace got as far as the first row with bodies. They studied the patriarch of that family, then withdrew. Owen followed, guiding the Steward out with him.

"I counted fifty-two bodies. How many people lived in Piety?"

Fire glanced back toward the meeting house. "Seventy, last I knew, which was a month ago."

"The two who made to Happy Valley brings that total to fifty-four. That's sixteen unaccounted for."

Nathaniel nodded. "Like as not, tain't more than another two or three escaped the slaughter. Scout about; we could find some bodies."

"So, that's a dozen that vanished. The Mason family was two shy of full. A son and daughter." Owen got out a journal and made a note. "I want to check something at the Mason home."

He ran back, took a quick inventory, made more notes, then returned. His heart ached and he wanted nothing more than to lay down get drunk "It's worse than we imagined."

Rathfield, who still looked grey, sat in the shadow of a house. "How is that possible? Out with it, man."

"We have a dozen people unaccounted for. The Masons were a family of six, but only four places were set at the table. One child was an infant, so it wouldn't have had a plate. But that fifth setting is gone, plate, food, utensils, cup, napkin. And a doll is missing from one of the beds. I imagine, if we go through every home here, we'll find other things missing. These people didn't have much, so we might not notice what had been taken, but I'd imagine there will be empty spaces on shelves, or that things you might expect to find will be gone."

Nathaniel nodded. "I reckon we can confirm that idea for you."

"We could, Woods, but what would it prove?"

Owen closed his journal. "It would prove, Colonel, that we have a big problem."

Rathfield laughed. "The congregation proves that."

"We know it does, but no one in Norisle will see it that way. They'll come and say that the people of Piety went insane. Outbreak of St. Vitus' dance or, given the fact that they followed the Steward here, they'll say he preached a wrong message. They'll say parents slaughtered children, then husbands killed wives. They'll say the deacon then killed the husbands and that the Steward here killed the deacon. They'll make it into a problem that doesn't require a solution because they won't have a solution.

"In pointing out that things are missing, I'm pointing out that someone went through here and collected things, samples—same as those Prince Vlad asks Nathaniel, Kamiskwa, and me to collect. Whoever did this took things not as plunder, but to *study*." Owen thrust a finger at the meeting house. "And given their willingness to kill so easily, does having them study a settlement make you uneasy? It does me, because I can see my wife and daughter headless in some of those empty chairs."

Rathfield struggled to his feet. "What are you saying, Strake? That there is a madman out here who styles himself a naturalist like Prince Vlad? If you are, you're mad. There's only Tharyngians out here, and they hardly need to study Norillians."

Nathaniel spat into the dust. "And you're gonna be telling me that Ryngians done raised that ruin we done explored?"

The Norillian hesitated. "I don't know if…"

"Colonel, someone from Auropa wouldn't have no need to study us. But whoever did create that ruin, whoever did inscribe those tablets, ain't from around these parts." Nathaniel shook his head. "They may have run into the Shedashee before, so when they found Piety, it was something new, something worthy of study. And given how powerful they appear to be in terms of magick, I'd prefer them knowing less about us than more."

Nathaniel slapped Owen on the shoulder. "I don't reckon I'm much suited to thinking the way Prince Vlad thinks, but I am considerable good at collecting them things he likes to think about. I reckon we need to go over this here settlement and look for the things ain't right. Since it seems magick was used to erase tracks, but didn't blow so hard as to make too much of a mess, we might just find us some things could be useful. Let's take it house by house and see what we can find."

What they found didn't amount to much. As expected, a variety of things had been taken from the homes, including candle molds, a fiddle, the Weaver family's copy of the Good Book, and a few other odds and ends. Nothing made of iron or steel had been taken, as nearly as could be discerned, since every home had an ax, cast iron pots and pans, and not a single musket or pistol was missing to the best of the Steward's knowledge. Owen assumed that the Prince would conclude that the creatures who had taken things were highly involved in magick, so iron and steel would be almost poisonous to them.

Kamiskwa, Nathaniel, and Makepeace found the most interesting artifacts out to the southwest. A bent barn nail had trapped a few long hairs, which, as nearly as any of them could discern, belonged to a wooly rhinoceros. They didn't discover any tracks to indicate how the hair had gotten there, but Fire had never heard of any wooly rhinos being in the area.

As odd as that was, the two artifacts Nathaniel displayed in his open palm were far stranger. A claw, hooked, hollow, and black, had caught in the jamb on a hayloft door. Because it was thinner at the base than it was toward the top, Owen imagined that this claw had sheathed another claw below, and when stressed, had broken free. Beside it lay a triangular tooth with a serrated edge. It had a mother-of-pearl pattern to it, akin to the sheen of oil on water. Though it was no bigger than his thumbnail, Owen had no doubt that it would do a fair amount of cutting—and though it would have helped confirm his conclusion, he didn't suggest returning to the meeting house to match wounds to either tooth or claw.

Nathaniel slipped the tooth and claw into his bag. "I ain't sure what to make of these, and like as not I don't want to hear what Prince Vlad will say."

"I agree." Owen closed his journal and replaced it in his satchel. "But the sooner we get back, the sooner he can figure out what we should do next."

"I don't see no reason to delay our departure."

"Me neither, brother."

The five of them waited at the edge of the green as Ezekiel Fire faced the meeting house and offered a prayer. Owen couldn't hear it, so just offered his own. After he finished, Fire crossed himself, then tossed a burning brand into the blockhouse. They waited until the building caught fire solidly, then headed west, letting the blaze light their way.

CHAPTER TWENTY-FIVE

16 May 1767
Prince Haven
Temperance Bay, Mystria

Prince Vlad looked up from his notebook as his wife entered his laboratory. "What is it, my dear?"

She hugged her arms around herself. "Baker just came back from town. He brought a note from Catherine Strake. She begged our pardon, but she will be one more day in Temperance. She is attending a sick friend. Miranda is ours alone for one more day."

Vlad closed the notebook on his pencil, then leaned back. "She expects to be back tomorrow night, then?"

Gisella nodded. "I would not worry, but this is the sailing season…"

"Yes, a legion of ships loading up and heading back to Norisle." Vlad's natural inclination was to think that the woman would not abandon her husband and child, but when Catherine Strake had nothing to occupy her time, she filled it with dreams of returning to Norisle. "Do you really think she would go?"

"It would be easier now that Owen is away. I just cannot imagine her leaving Miranda behind. She's so possessive. If she wanted to hurt Owen, she'd take the child. It would tear his heart out."

"True, so why would she abandon the child? Does she think that returning to Norisle without Miranda would improve her prospects? I gather that being a poor refugee from the Colonies is not something looked upon with great favor in Launston."

"I believe she has an elderly relative—a grandmother, perhaps—who is wealthy. I don't know if the woman approved of the match with Owen. Catherine's leaving him might improve her lot." Gisella shrugged. "And she could be charming, and is smart enough, to play well the person horrified by how primitive the colonies are. Her comments would be most welcome in certain highly placed circles."

Vlad pushed his chair back and stood. "I could stop her. I could have a warrant issued for her detention for abandoning her child."

"You hesitate because you don't know if that would be a blessing or curse for Owen."

He pressed his hands together, then nodded. "I asked him if he was taking the mission west to do his duty, or to escape his wife. His answer was quite frank. I think he did love her once, and part of him may yet. She *is*, after all, the mother of his child and he loves Miranda fiercely. Catherine is profoundly unhappy here. She wants to leave, and he can't imagine leaving. To have to share your life with someone so opposed to what makes you happy..."

Gisella threaded her way between heavily book-laden tables and hugged him. "It is a fate we avoided, beloved, when your aunt and my father thought to foist us off on each other."

Vlad kissed her forehead. "I wish my friends were as lucky as we."

"Perhaps someday they will be." She smiled. "If you issue a warrant and Catherine is not thinking of leaving..."

"She will have one more thing to hate here. If I accept her at her word and she does not return tomorrow night, it will be too late." He shook his head. "If I had worked on the thaumagraph, tested it, and had a copy in Summerland, she could be detained there."

"Many ifs, darling. Besides, your new project is more important." She pulled back from him. "Your son, you may have noticed, has taken to wearing gloves as you do."

"It will be a while before he has a pair of these." Vlad turned toward his desk and the pair of leather gloves arranged so he could sketch them into his notes. The only truly unusual thing about them was the wooden disk assembly that had been riveted to the back of each index finger. The disk, which was no larger than a crown coin, had been positioned to allow easy access with the thumb. The thumb, as with many gloves used by soldiers and huntsmen, had a sheath over the thumb which could be pulled back to expose it.

Building upon the vibrating teacup experiment results, Vlad had fashioned a means to communicate with Mugwump in flight. He placed other disk assemblies into a harness which fitted over the dragon's head. The assemblies settled right over the scales that covered Mugwump's aural canals. Invoking the spell he'd created, Vlad could spin the wheels on his gloves, making the right or left disk click against the dragon's head. While Mugwump had not reacted well to the noise at first, when Vlad was able to moderate the noise *and* remove the bridle and reins, the dragon became far more tolerant of the tapping.

"Are you going to try flying him with them?"

"I will be very careful, my love." Vlad sighed. "I've trained him on the ground, and yesterday we flew and I had the reins. Off the ground the noise needs to be a bit louder because of the air rushing past, but he did respond."

"Yes, you'd been afraid that his magick might interfere with yours." Gisella took his hands in hers and examined his thumbnails. Blood had gathered beneath them. "You should have drained them."

"I can't. I need to measure." He went to the desk and opened his notebook. "Here, you see, I measure the increase in the area, based on how much magick I'm using. If you check this chart…"

Her blue eyes narrowed as her finger traced the descending line. "It looks as if the amount of blood loss is decreasing even though your magick use is remaining the same or even increasing."

"Yes, exactly. And I have good way to measure it, but I find using magick less draining. I theorize this could be because the spell I'm using is one I created myself, so it takes less energy to make it work."

She glanced up. "I am not certain I follow."

"Think of it in terms of language. Norillian is not your native tongue, so reading and translating take more concentration than it would for you to read something written in Kessian. Or, a better example, when a cook with vast experience starts putting something together, they just do it their way, putting in what they know is right, and do it faster because that is their routine. They're comfortable, so they just act, they don't have to think." Vlad opened his hands. "The spell to ignite brimstone, for example, starts with me visualizing the sun. But if I've lived my whole life in a cave and have never seen the sun, I would have to equate the sun to a torch, the torch to fire, and then use that to ignite the brimstone. By creating my own spell, I don't have to work through the model someone else dreamed up, I work directly through what comes most easily for me."

She stepped back, her face darkening. "If this is true, then it would mean that every man could create his own magick."

"I'm not so certain." The Prince opened his hands. "There are plenty of carpenters who can drive nails and saw wood, but ask them to design a set of shelves and that might just be beyond them. Just the act of reading, or knowing how to read and write, may make all the difference. In doing either, you translate from the real world to an abstraction. The word *apple* won't feed you, but reading it will conjure up the right image, and can communicate to someone else what you want to eat."

Gisella stared toward the floor for a moment, then slowly nodded. "Which brings you back to the grimoire hidden in the Good Book. The people most likely to be able to read are going to be clergy. While I want your idea to be correct, I fear the consequences if it is."

"Here is the positive side of it, and why I think it is true. Mugwump is using magick to fly, but no one ever *taught him* a spell that would let him fly. There isn't any, as nearly as I know. And as he has flown more, he has bled less than before. Using magick has to be natural for him, even instinctual. It could be that just as magick that is born of him will not hurt him very much, so magick we each create will take less out of us than spells we learn from another. Think of it: the brimstone spell is at least three and a half centuries old. Who, today, thinks as someone might have then? They believed the world was flat and that you could sail off the edge. That we could craft a more natural spell to trigger brimstone shouldn't be a surprise."

"No, but it should be a secret."

"I agree." *If the Church had any idea what I have discovered, they would go after me as they likely have after Ezekiel Fire.*

He reached over and gathered up his gloves. "I will fly Mugwump briefly today without reins. We will see how that works, then I will work on the next iteration of these gloves."

She took the gloves from him and held them out so he could put them on. "You will be careful."

"Completely. I'll be back well before dusk." He pulled her to him and kissed her. "You know that I love you for more than being the mother of my children, yes?"

She smiled and hugged him strongly. "Likewise, beloved husband. Never forget that."

The Prince entered the wurmrest and walked along the catwalk to the riverside wall. He worked a crank, drawing up the barred gate. Mugwump slowly stretched, then opened his mouth in what Vlad had decided was a dragonly grin. The creature swung his head around so the Prince could fit the disk harness onto his head and secure it in place. He then waited for the bridle and reins.

Vlad shook his head. "Not today. Meet you outside."

Vlad shouldered the saddle, gathering loops of cinch straps in his other arm, and waited on the lawn for the dragon. When Mugwump emerged, Vlad fitted the saddle between his shoulders and tightened the harness in place. The dragon shifted and stretched, requiring Vlad to give another tug or two on various straps, but soon enough man and beast were satisfied.

Vlad held a hand up and then began pacing his way along the lawn. The day before he'd gone twenty paces or roughly thirty yards. He considered that a significant distance because he was fairly certain that the clicking of the wheels on his gloves couldn't be heard at that range. If Mugwump responded to the wheels, it was because of the magick. Because the dragon had responded, Vlad moved to twenty-five paces.

Holding his hands behind his back, Vlad invoked the spell and worked the wheel on his right glove.

Mugwump dutifully turned to the right until the clicking stopped. Vlad spun the wheels left and right in no particular order and the dragon moved as commanded. When Vlad spun them both together, the dragon advanced; when he backed them in three staccato clicks, Mugwump retreated.

Vlad brought the dragon around to face him, then spun the wheels forward. He turned to walk toward the path to the training field and Mugwump caught up in no time.

Vlad glanced sidelong into a big golden eye. "We know this spell works at forty yards. That's a killing shot for a musket. Seems to work quickly enough, but if this magick will make my thaumagraph work, I need to know how fast magick flows."

Mugwump blinked slowly.

"I do get the feeling you understand what I'm saying." Vlad shook his head. "And sometimes you seem to wonder why I'm taking so long to understand things you take for granted."

The dragon swung his head to the right, gently knocking Vlad off course. Vlad stumbled to the side, then looked back. Had the dragon not nudged him, he'd have stepped into a chuck hole.

The Prince laughed. "Is that your way of telling me I overlook the obvious?"

The dragon unfurled his wings and raised his muzzle to the sky.

"Yes—why are we walking when we could be flying?" Vlad laughed and settled his goggles on his eyes. He clambered up into the saddle, strapped himself in, and rolled both glove wheels forward.

Mugwump began a lumbering run that quickly transformed into a graceful lope. With his head held low like that of a hunting feline, the dragon sped forward. Just as he began to gallop, he spread his wings again, then launched himself skyward with a powerful leap and beat of wings. Though Vlad had experienced take-off before, he always grabbed onto his saddle horn. It felt as if he'd left his stomach on the ground.

That little spark of fear died as Mugwump rose through the air. The Benjamin River became a ribbon of silver. Patchy green fields separated by darker green forest swaths covered the ground in a crazy-quilt pattern, which, though lacking regularity, did not lack for beauty. Even the road to Temperance held appeal as it lazily wended its way through vales and around hills.

Vlad spun wheels left and right and Mugwump responded, his wings wide. When the Prince backed the wheels the dragon climbed, and a slow roll forward started a descent. The dragon had learned the commands easily enough, and if the calls he hooted toward the west were any indication, he enjoyed the flight as much as the Prince.

Vlad reached down and patted him on the neck. "You've done well, Mugwump, but shadows are getting long. We need to go home." He slid the wheels forward, then rolled the left one more to turn them back toward Prince Haven.

Mugwump instead turned right, toward the setting sun.

Vlad reinvoked the spell and worked the left wheel. He looked ahead and was pretty sure he could see the left disk rattling away, but he couldn't quite be certain. Then he tried the right wheel, but again no response. Instead the dragon began to climb, his wings beating urgently.

Vlad began to shiver.

It wasn't just from the cold.

CHAPTER TWENTY-SIX

16 May 1767
Happy Valley
Postsylvania, Mystria

Nathaniel lowered his canteen and wiped his mouth on the back of his sleeve. "Ain't more than couple hours now. We'll be there well afore dusk."

"Right, very good, Woods." Rathfield stood in the center of the trail, leaning on his musket. "This will give us several hours of daylight for the people of Happy Valley to pack up as much as they can. Won't be much—wagons won't make it through the mountains."

The Steward looked up from the rock upon which he perched. "My people are not leaving, Colonel."

"Do you not understand the gravity of the situation, Steward Fire?" Rathfield pointed off in the direction where he thought Piety lay. Nathaniel didn't correct him. "Do you want the people of Happy Valley to end up like that?"

"It has nothing to do with what I desire, Colonel. It is what God demands of me and my people." The older man stared down at empty and calloused hands. "God brought the flood to destroy wickedness. He brought the plagues to free His people. He destroyed sinful cities with cleansing fire. He sacrificed His Son to save all of us. If He was willing to do all that, how can I, as His servant, shy from willingness to do the same?"

Nathaniel drank again, wishing the canteen contained whiskey. There was no mistaking the sincerity in the Steward's voice, but his surrendering to what he saw as God's plan didn't make any sense to Nathaniel. He'd always believed in the saying, "God helps those who help themselves." Makepeace had once told him that the saying wasn't in the Good Book, and Nathaniel reckoned it should have been added.

Rathfield smiled. "I understand your thinking, Steward. I respect it. But what if God is testing you? What if He is asking you to sacrifice your people the way He asked Abram to sacrifice his son?"

"I know He is testing me, Colonel. He has showed me many things, many terrible things. It is more than a man can bear—save for his faith in God. So, perhaps I am cast as Abram, or perhaps my lot is that of Job." Fire looked toward the heavens. "Either does not matter because the moral of each Scripture is that faith will sustain us through the most horrible of trials. Our reward for faith is to abide with God forever in Heaven."

Nathaniel stoppered his canteen. "I ain't of a mind to say you're wrong, Steward, and I don't know enough Scripture to tell if you're right. But I seem to remember—and you can correct me—that the Good Lord hisself said that the children should come unto Him on account of they was innocent. I cain't see anybody what loves children that much wanting to happen to them what happened to the children in Piety."

"You must understand, Mr. Woods, that God challenges us so we reaffirm our faith in Him."

Nathaniel frowned. "Now, see, that is something I don't reckon I can figure out. You clearly is a pious man, doing His work, gathering up people that believe in Him, and He goes and slaughters a bunch of them to test your faith? Ain't that like having a sweetheart that goes out a-walking with another man, then comes back and asks if you believe her when she says she is chaste? Once you do, she goes out walking again, but this time they hold hands. How far would you let her test you? Would you wait until you found them naked and under the sheets, and would you believe when she says she's chaste?"

The Steward opened his hands. "The mind of God is not knowable to man."

"I hear you say that, but they's an awful, terrible, powerful lot of preachers who claim they *do* know what God is thinking. They don't skimp on giving you a piece of His mind when they get to preachifying."

Rathfield raised a hand. "You tread perilously close to blasphemy, Woods."

"I is not neither." Nathaniel shook his head. "I reckon religion can give you peace on account of it tells you that there's a reason things happen, terrible things, horrible things. When the good ones happen, you're happy with God; when the bad ones happen, you just count it up as something God don't think you need to understand at that moment."

Kamiskwa raised an eyebrow. "Perhaps my brother would get to the point of his discussion."

"I reckon I might, thank you, Kamiskwa." Nathaniel pointed his rifle off toward Happy Valley. "You don't know if God intends to kill them people, or if He'll tell you it was just a test at the last moment. From the stories you mentioned previous, odds are four to one that blood is going to be shed. Seems to me there was some Scripture stories about great leaders, bringing their people out of the wilderness, to a promised land. Ain't it possible that's how God is leaning?"

"Woods, that will be quite enough!"

The Steward focused distantly for a moment, then hung his head. "You may well be right, Mr. Woods. I allowed myself to succumb to the sin of pride. I elevated the trials I shall face above those of the people who have put their trust in me. That I need to be strong for them, and strong to face these trials, this is an even greater test than I imagined. I am blessed that your insight revealed to me more of His plan."

Nathaniel nodded once. The Steward still wasn't grasping the seriousness of what they faced, but at least he now allowed as how not everyone should be given up to death. As long as Fire held open the door that some might survive, they might be able to evacuate the settlement and get people back over the mountains.

As they shouldered their packs again, Rathfield took off in the lead. Makepeace walked with the Steward, shouldering his pack and sharing some prayers. Kamiskwa watched their back trail, leaving Owen and Nathaniel walking together.

Owen glanced at him. "Do you honestly think he'd let them all die?"

"Being as how he's more worried about their souls than he is their mortal remains, I don't reckon he's seeing death as quite the tragedy we do. Tragedy or not, long as I'm breathing, ain't no way Becca Green's going to the Lord, even if He comes down and invites her to Him. I reckon if He weren't keen on being tacked to a tree and having a spear poked into his side, He surely ain't going to like a bullet punching him dead center."

Surprise widened Owen's eyes. "You seem to bear God some animosity, Nathaniel."

"It ain't I got a hate-on for Him. It's more I got a hate-on for his fol-lowers."

"Like Makepeace?"

"Nope. Makepeace, he goes and prays good times and bad. Sometimes he does what he oughten't to do, but he's sorry and sincere about it and fair good at seeing it don't happen again for a good long time." Nathaniel nodded. "He weren't always like that, but come his meeting with the Good Lord and that bear, he's been sincere since."

"I can't argue with you there, only having known him since. But you're telling it right." Owen climbed up a steep set of rocks, then offered Nathaniel a hand. "But what do you think of God? Do you believe?"

Nathaniel took his hand and pulled himself up. "You really want to know the answer?"

"I believe I do."

Nathaniel swept a hand out over the panorama of the wooded valley below and the hills that defined it. "I look at all this and I know men see the hand of the Creator there. You got your God; Kamiskwa and the Shedashee, they got theirs. I reckon other people gots themselves gods, 'cepting the Ryngians who seem a mite confused and awful willing to take the Lord's name in vain even though they don't believe. And all them Creators get credit for the same thing, but they all has themselves a set of rules 'bout what a body can and cannot do. And the one thing all them rules have in common is that they tend to benefit whosoever is the one telling everyone else what them rules is."

"I can't deny your point there."

Nathaniel patted Owen on the shoulder and they started walking again. "So I got to wondering not iffen there *was* a God, but whether or not any of them people got it right. It would be as if we done heard a big cat calling in the night, and we found pawprints, and we found a tooth, and we brung it all back to Prince Vlad. Now he'd go on and tell us how big the cat was, what it ate and so forth but, being a wise man, he wouldn't tell us what color it was, or that it had wings and horns and two heads."

"But holy men are doing just that?"

"'Xactly so." Nathaniel nodded. "So I might allow as how there is a God. I might even go so far as to say that some things, like the Golden Rule and the whole 'Thou shalt not murder,' sounds like things a God might want us to be doing. Beyond that, I reckon men is inventing more than they ought to."

"So you don't think God let the people of Piety die?"

"Tain't that. I don't think He *wanted* them to die." Nathaniel shook his head. "I don't reckon any Creator what worked so hard to create beauty and life would make it part of a plan to have folks die hard and evil like that. You think he wanted them to die?"

"I really try not to fathom the mind of God."

Nathaniel raised an eyebrow. "Your turn, Captain Strake. You believe in God?"

Owen ducked beneath a pine branch. "I'm afraid the God I believe in is a bit more capricious and nasty than the one you accept. Put it down to being raised in a family where we had our own Church and would sit up front at services, yet where my uncles, father, and grandfather would indulge themselves in cruel ways. And credit it to what I've seen on battlefields, where men pray for God to end their suffering. So simple a thing for Him to grant, and yet it always seemed that he who prayed the most devoutly, suffered the longest."

Nathaniel's thoughts flew back to Fort Cuivre and the aftermath of the battle at Anvil Lake. Shot and sword, bullet and bludgeon, the weapons of war had rendered men unrecognizable. Some did pray as they died, others wept, and still more cried out for mothers and wives living an ocean away. While he understood the injuries, and understood the desire for comfort, he'd never taken the time to fit that carnage into any theological context. Those battles had been Man's creation and weren't something for which he could imagine any god wanting credit.

"Almost sounds to me, Captain, that you're leaning toward thinking there ain't no God."

"I probably would think that, save for something you touched upon earlier. Loving or cruel, capricious or calculating, God being in Heaven means there *is* a reason for everything." Owen sighed. "I might not understand it, but knowing there is a reason is a lot more comforting than believing there isn't. And if God does exist, maybe, just maybe, the next prayer He answers will be mine."

Nathaniel leaped over a marshy stretch of trail. "I reckon this, Owen. Iffen God's going to be answer any prayers, like as not they'll be from someone like you."

"How do you figure that?"

"My hunch is this: iffen you was dying and in a powerful lot of pain, you wouldn't be praying for comfort for yourself, but for your daughter and wife. I reckon most of the others miss that. The Good Lord, if the tales be true, done sacrificed Hisself for others. Praying for yourself kinda mocks all that, don't it?"

"I imagine there are Scriptural scholars who would debate that point, but I agree." Owen laughed. "And I do pray for Miranda, every night."

Nathaniel noticed that Owen hadn't said he prayed for his wife, and that didn't surprise him. Nathaniel found her as welcome as a case of carbuncles. The woman seemed to be mean for the sake of being mean, and took a special dislike to anything or anyone that inspired her husband to remain in Mystria. He'd just as soon see the backside of her on a ship sailing toward dawn, but it wasn't his place to say anything in that regard, so he held his tongue.

The party topped the last rise about two hours before the sun would set. The settlement appeared normal, with people going about their normal tasks. It wasn't until they started down toward the meeting house that Nathaniel noted that the herders hadn't come to greet them but, instead, followed them at greater than gunshot range.

Rathfield appeared not to notice. "When we reach the town, you'll have to give the order, Steward, to get everyone out. They should pack food. We will have ample water."

"You worry too much, Colonel." The Steward, as if revived by having returned home, smiled. "God will provide for us. Not a mouth shall go hungry on our way."

People gathered on the trail into Happy Valley, men in front, women behind, two dozen of the former and all of their wives. One stepped forward. "Ezekiel Fire, you are welcome to rejoin the community. The Steward awaits you in the Temple."

Fire stopped a pace beyond the party. "Deacon Stone, *I* am the Steward."

"No, Ezekiel. God came to us in a vision, all of us. He said you had been tested and tempted and corrupted by these men." Stone opened his arms, turning his hands palm up to the sky. The others aped his posture and raised their faces to the heavens. "Salvation is still open to you, Ezekiel.

So the Steward has said."

Nathaniel stepped up. "I don't reckon I need to be asking who this new Steward is, do I? Where is he? The meeting house, what you's calling the Temple now?"

Stone stared at Nathaniel. "You are not welcome here. If you step into the precincts of Happy Valley, you will not be spared."

Nathaniel leveled his rifle at the man's gut. "I'm a mite more worried about your safety than mine right at the moment, Deacon Stone. Now, you gonna take me to Rufus Branch, or am I going to be asking your widows for directions?"

"Put up your gun, Nathaniel." The men and women of Happy Valley parted down the middle as if a human curtain. "You can't harm them, but the reverse is not true."

Nathaniel recognized the voice more by the venom in it than the tone or timbre. A man came forward, but had it not been for the voice, he never would have known the figure to be Rufus Branch. While the man had retained his height, he had become skeletally thin. Color had leeched from his hair and it had fallen out in patches, as if he had the mange. His eyes had become larger and much darker. He clutched a golden tablet to his chest.

"We will not deny you entry, Nathaniel. It is all part of the plan." Rufus caressed the tablet. "You are meant to be here, so I am told. We shall put you on trial for heresy, and then we will watch you die."

CHAPTER TWENTY-SEVEN

16 May 1767
Happy Valley
Postsylvania, Mystria

Ian Rathfield shouldered his way past Owen and got between the mob and Ezekiel Fire. "I think this has gone far enough."

Rufus Branch hissed at him in sibilant tones that sent a shiver down Owen's spine. "You have no authority here."

"In the name of the Queen, and the sovereign and Almighty God who put her on the throne, I *am* the authority here." Rathfield stood tall, thrusting a finger at Branch. "You'll answer to my authority immediately."

Branch's right hand snaked out, grabbing Ian's wrist. "I answer to no man."

Rathfield made to tug his wrist free, but couldn't. Back when Branch had been thickly muscled, Owen would have allowed it possible that Rathfield might not break his grip. *But he's wasted away, in just days, how can he...?* Branch twisted his hand ever so slightly, and the larger man went to his knees. They locked gazes, then Rathfield shuddered and sagged. When Branch released him, he curled up on the ground, hugging himself with quaking arms.

Branch laughed. "Such a sinner are you, Colonel. You shall burn for a long time."

Fire crouched, reaching a hand toward Rathfield, but looked up at his former charge. "Rufus, this is not like you. What has happened?"

Branch pulled back and smiled easily. "The tablets held the secret. Tell him. Tell *them*."

Stone nodded. "It's true, all has been revealed. God has granted us the gifts denied us when we left the garden. It is as you preached, Ezekiel." The man raised a finger and wrote on the air. Golden sigils hung there,

186

twinkling as if made of stardust, then slowly vanished. Owen could make nothing of them, but he'd seen them before, on the walls of the outpost.

As the sigils drained away, a plant sprouted beneath them. It looked for all intents to be a sunflower, with a blossom eight inches across. It grew to waist height in less than a minute's time, and the flower opened. The blossom appeared very much like cauliflower, but golden-brown on the surface. It smelled for all the world of cinnamon.

"You see, as it was said in the Good Book: Manna, given to us through this Godly gift. These tablets that the Steward has translated were put here for us, so we can lead people to God."

Fire, instead of rising, went down to his other knee. He clasped his hands in prayer. "Father Almighty, please forgive these Your children…"

"Silence! Blasphemy will not be tolerated." Branch thrust a finger at Fire. "Clap him in irons and hitch him to the Post of Shame."

Two men stepped forward, pulled on leather gloves, and dragged Fire toward the center of the green. A stout post had been sunk into the middle of it, and a pair of manacles bound to it by a short length of chain. Fire neither struggled nor protested his treatment. Once secured, he went to his knees again, and the short chains raised his arms to an obviously uncomfortable height.

Owen and Nathaniel exchanged glances. If they attacked now and managed to kill Branch, they still would have three dozen adults to deal with. Not only would the expedition end right there, but whatever had transformed the people of Happy Valley would be free to continue working.

Nathaniel raised his rifle's muzzle to the sky. "You serious 'bout that trial, Rufus?"

Branch scratched over his ear and a clump of hair came away. He looked at it for a moment, puzzled, as if he didn't know what it was. Then he cast it aside and stroked the tablet again. "Yes. A trial. Exactly. I will summon those who will judge you. If you run, Fire will die."

Makepeace bent down to help Rathfield to his feet. "And what if we recant our heresy and accept fellowship and communion here in Happy Valley?"

Rufus looked Makepeace up and down, then snorted. "There may be mercy granted. Go to the workshop. Await the summoning."

Nathaniel led the way to the workshop. It didn't appear as if Rathfield would be able to climb the ladder into the hayloft, so Owen gathered a length of rope and hitched it to a chain and hook. He opened the loft door to thread it through the pulley, but the Colonel had recovered enough to make the trip himself. They positioned him by the loft door so he could watch the green and report if anything unusual was happening.

Owen crouched with the others two-dozen feet away. "Suggestions?"

Nathaniel nodded. "I got me a plan."

"Let's hear it."

"Well, Kamiskwa, the second it gets dark, you're going to light on out of here."

"I am not abandoning you."

Nathaniel clapped the Shedashee on the shoulders. "I ain't sending you off to save your life. It's to save many lives. Did you notice that the workshop here, and near all the houses I could see, they had themselves paper nailed up on the doors. Got that fancy writing that Stone made on 'em?"

Kamiskwa nodded. "I take some of those and get them to Prince Vlad?"

"You got the best chance of any of us to do that."

Owen's eyes narrowed. "Once he's gone, they'll kill the rest of us."

"I 'spect, but see, Rufus Branch, he ain't never really got the best of me. He couldn't never beat me fair and square, so he went to poison and all. I don't got me no idea what's going on here, but he'll jump at the chance to break me his own self."

"You saw what he did to Rathfield. Breaking you is not going to take long."

"Now Captain, I reckoned you had more faith in me than that." Nathaniel smiled. "Rufus, he's playing by some rules here, and I reckon offering a benediction will be part of them. Makepeace, do you reckon you could offer some Scriptural comments to mount our defense for heresy?"

"Iffen you think there is going to be a trial."

"I think there will. He still needs the congregation. If he didn't, he'd gone and kilt us right off."

Rathfield shifted his position by the loft door. "People going into the Temple. All of them."

Owen walked over and watched. The people weren't just walking to the meeting house, they were streaming toward it, like ants on the edge of a leaf. Fathers leading mothers, children following behind in descending order of height. Owen couldn't help but imagine that was how the people in Piety had moved before they were attacked.

He looked down at Rathfield, whose eyes still focused distantly, and whose lower lip trembled. "What happened, Colonel?"

"It got inside my mind. Everything, it knows everything." He stared up with haunted eyes and gripped Owen's forearm tightly. "Even things I never wanted to remember."

As the people continued making their way to the Temple, Rufus Branch emerged from it wearing a long robe belted narrowly at the waist. He carried both tablets beneath his left arm.

Owen turned. "Something strange going on with Branch."

Nathaniel crossed to the door, crouching between Owen and Rathfield. "Kamiskwa, get ready. Almost dark enough."

The new Steward approached the post and said something to Fire, then threw his head back and laughed. He began walking a slow circle around him, and faint snatches of melody made its way to the loft. As Branch began singing louder, the discordant notes and odd phrases made Owen's flesh crawl. Even more eerily, as the volume increased, the song appeared as a black ribbon of sigils trimmed in gold, rising from Rufus' mouth as steam might from a winter's-night conversation. They swirled into the sky, evaporating slowly and mingling with the gloom.

Owen pointed toward the meeting house. "I can't see beyond it. There's a black fog."

Makepeace grunted. "More like shadow done froze over."

Kamiskwa, over by the workshop's side door, called out. "It's around the barn. I can't open the door."

Nathaniel retreated from the window and fetched his rifle. He crouched again and sighted down the barrel. "Hundred and ten yards, give or take."

Makepeace nodded. "I reckon you can hit him, but killing him's another matter."

As if he had heard the remark, Rufus stopped singing and turned toward the workshop. He ran a hand back through his hair as if to smooth it, but instead harvested great swaths instead. He let the hair float in the air for a moment before beginning his approach.

His voice boomed. "I know you too well, Nathaniel Woods. This is why I have taken the precaution of summoning the fog. You would have sent your friend away, but the mist will kill him."

"That doesn't sound like Rufus Branch to me." Owen shook his head. "Too precise."

Kamiskwa, who had joined them, shrugged. "Fire did say he taught him to read and write."

"Different from making speeches, though."

Nathaniel stood. "Well, whatever or whoever, I ain't about to be crouching here like some mouse." He descended the ladder and threw open the workshop door. The others, save for Rathfield, followed from the workshop and took a stand beside him with the workshop's narrow wall at their backs. "I thought we was getting a trial, Rufus."

"Change of plans. Earlier I thought that would be useful, but I can see, now, it is of little use." Rufus smoothed away the last of the hair on the right side of his head. "From you I need something else. A verification. And, I believe, that will require a demonstration on my part."

Rufus had closed within forty yards. He crooked his right index finger. The nail had grown out into a proper talon, which he played over the surface of the tablet. He traced one of the glyphs, an angular one, then flicked with the nail. The glyph came up off the tablet, flying up swiftly, then lazily descending like an autumn leaf.

It burned red.

Rufus caught it on his open palm and allowed the color to pool there. He rocked his hand forward and back. The redness congealed into a plum-size ball, shot through with gold lightning. Some of the bolts emerged to link his fingers with a sizzling web, and the ball rose at the heart of it. He flexed his fingers, letting the web slip from them, and the ball hovered, bathing his pallid face with a bloody glow.

"There is, in this world, power unimagined."

He brushed the ball away as casually as one might swat at dandelion fluff. The ball circled once, caught in the vortex of air his hand had created, then arced up and back toward the meeting house. Owen lost sight of it for a heartbeat, then it exploded beside the door, washing it in a sheet of flame. Before he could open his mouth to shout a warning, flames licked up to the roof.

And despite the sound and light, no one within shouted or screamed, nor made any attempt to escape.

Owen's mouth hung open. "Are you insane?"

Before Rufus could answer, Nathaniel raised his rifle and dropped his thumb to the firestone. Thunder cracked. At that range, there was no way Nathaniel could miss. Smoke blew back over them, but instead of revealing a dead Steward, they found themselves looking at Rufus rolling the bullet around in his palm, much as he had the glyph.

"As I said, power unimagined. Freezing a bullet in the air, plucking it from where it hovered, that is as nothing." Rufus idly examined his talons in the fire's glow. "I wish to understand how you will greet my return."

Nathaniel levered his reloaded rifle breech closed again. "I can give you another demonstration."

"Not you, my friend, but all of you." Rufus raised a hand. "I said a *verification.*"

Owen's eyes tightened. "What would you be verifying?"

"I saw what lurked in your cowering friend's mind. I have visions of Fort Cuivre and Anvil Lake. I know how hard you fight." The hand fell. "Now I wish to know how you will fight this."

Bat-winged creatures boiled out of the darkness. Smaller than men, but not by much, more slender and lighter as befitted a flying creature, they streamed in from the sides and down from the gloom. Their tiny eyes burned scarlet, and jagged mother-of-pearl teeth flashed. They bore no weapons save for those teeth and the sharp claws on their feet and hands.

Without thinking Owen thrust his rifle into one's face and triggered a spell. The bullet blew through the creature's brains and sent another tumbling back through the air. He clubbed a third with his rifle butt and brained a fourth with the barrel. The steel appeared to do more harm, making its flesh bubble and blister. He shifted it to his left hand and drew his steel tomahawk, laying about him with both as quickly as he could.

Makepeace roared, smashing them with a rifle in one hand and snatching them out of the air with the other. He grabbed one by the throat and its wings closed around his hand, knuckles showing through the grey membrane. Bones crackled and the dead thing fell away, but Makepeace bled from where it had bitten and clawed him.

Kamiskwa's warclub made short work of the creatures. It seemed as if the weapon had been designed to crush their brittle bones and slice through their wings. One clung to his long braid, so the warrior whipped his head back and flung the beast hard against the workshop doors.

Nathaniel, too, fought as if the devil had opened the gates to Hell and demons had poured forth. Tomahawk and knife flashed. Dark blood splashed through the night. Ebon bodies littered the ground, twitching and grasping, each creature chancing a last scratch or bite.

So many of them to fight. None of them had inflicted a deep wound, but the scratches stung and the bites wept. The woman who had escaped from Piety had not been subject to one swift attack, but to a series of slow and deliberate attacks. Though Owen fought against a horde of the creatures, no single wound could match any of hers, and taken in the aggregate, they had done less damage.

The sheer weight of the assault, however, forced Owen back, foot by foot. He slashed high and low, kicking creatures away, but could not regain lost ground. Wings wrapped his face and shoulders, blinding him. Things bit at his neck and ears. He'd tear them off, gaining a moment to orient himself, and then they would descend again.

Then he tripped, the leather rustling of their wings accompanying his fall. To stay down was to die, but bloody mud gave his feet no purchase. The demons pounced, piling onto his legs, grabbing his arms and spreading them wide.

Behind him, Makepeace had been backed against the workshop. The demons covered him in a living gray coat. Kamiskwa had likewise fallen and had been buried beneath a writhing gray carpet. Nathaniel lay slumped at the base of the workshop wall, his face a mask of blood.

Rufus strode through the carnage and laughed. "So, I see. This will be easier than I imagined. But time to end this now."

A sudden shriek from above caused the Steward to look up. There, wide-eyed and clearly insane with terror, Ian Rathfield leaped from the workshop loft. He landed on both feet and staggered—Owen thought certain he'd heard a bone break—but it mattered not at all. In his hand, Ian bore the steel chain with which Owen had thought to haul him into the loft, and he whirled it above his head.

The chain's deadly arc swept demons from the air. The heavy hook on its end dashed out brains. Roaring at the top of his lungs, making a sound no human throat was ever meant to utter, Rathfield drove forward and wrapped the chain around Rufus' chest. He trapped the left arm there, warping the tablets. And yet, even as his attack crumpled the Steward, Rufus thrust his right hand toward Ian, and a glowing purple sigil flew from his palm.

The arcane symbol struck Ian in the forehead with the force of a hammer, denting his skull. The man dropped into a heap. One of the demons landed before him, wings spread, clawed hands raised high, ready to finish the work the magick had begun.

And behind it, backlit by the burning Temple, a bat-winged leviathan descended from the sky.

CHAPTER TWENTY-EIGHT

16 May 1767
Happy Valley
Postsylvania, Mystria

Mugwump snatched the demon up in his mouth and spat it, broken and limp, toward a clump of the creatures covering something on the ground. The demon steamed, the dragon's saliva already consuming it. The others screeched and pulled back, smeared mucus already burning holes in their wings. The dragon's tail flicked left and right, snapping demons into clouds of black blood and bone splinters.

Prince Vlad, clinging to the saddle with frostbitten fingers, hunched forward as Mugwump spun. The dragon bit things in half, shaking his head as a terrier might shake a rat, and wetness spattered the Prince. Vlad didn't really care what it was, since it was warmer than he. He dearly wished they were closer to the fire—at least until he realized it was a building.

Then Mugwump launched himself into the air again, up into a black fog that hid the ground, visibly reducing the burning building to a tiny spark. Right wing went up, left down. Mugwump rolled through the sky, flying after the bat-winged creatures. He hissed savagely, a sound the Prince had heard at Anvil Lake, but this time saliva jetted out in a mist. The demons caught in it curled up and dropped from sight. Vlad marveled, never having suspected the dragon of having such a weapon.

Mugwump pumped his wings and twisted again sharply in pursuit. He looped up and over as he chased after a particularly good flier. Prince Vlad vomited. He coughed and retched, doubling over both frozen and miserable, holding on for dear life and wishing he might fall to his death and end the torture. He had no idea where he was, why Mugwump had stopped responding to commands, what the demons were, or why Mugwump seemed so intent on, and skilled at, killing them.

Then one landed on Vlad's back, cloaking him in its wings. It chittered as it lunged for his neck, its fetid breath hot against exposed flesh. Its clawed hands grabbed his shoulders tightly, and toe talons found purchase on his thighs.

Vlad snapped his head back, driving his skull into the creature's face. Bones broke, and a part of the Prince's brain catalogued that fact. It made sense that the creature's bones would be light, even hollow, like a bird's. To confirm that, he grabbed its ankles and squeezed. More bones popped and the creature thrashed. He reached up and back, grabbing it by the wings, then pulled it forward and smashed its spine against the saddle horn.

For a heartbeat he contemplated keeping it as a specimen, but contemptuously tossed it aside. As it fell, Mugwump looked back and hooted triumphantly.

Then he rolled again and dropped from the sky, leaving Prince Vlad's stomach somewhere above the clouds. The dragon's sharp descent pierced the black fog, but it had already begun to dissipate. Wings flared and Mugwump landed softly, snorting and hissing more deadly mist.

A man came running over, remaining well clear of Mugwump's wings and tail. "Highness, what are you doing here?"

It took Prince Vlad a moment to recognize him beneath the blood. "I could ask you the same, Owen. Is this Postsylvania?"

"So the locals say."

Kamiskwa came trotting over, a young girl clutched in one arm, his bloody warclub in his other hand. "Becca was never called to the Temple. She hid. As the demons scattered, one entered the house she was in. She screamed. I thought Rufus might have slunk off in that direction, so I went looking and found her instead."

Mugwump raised his muzzle and sniffed. He roared a challenge.

The Altashee smiled. "Then I leave her to you, Mugwump, and I shall continue seeking signs of our enemy."

Prince Vlad invoked the spell and spun the left-hand wheel. The dragon responded by turning toward a large barnlike building in front of which Nathaniel and Makepeace crouched over a man. "Is that Colonel Rathfield?"

Owen nodded. "Rufus Branch used magick on him, the like of which I've never seen before. Not even du Malphias had this sort of power. Please tell me Mugwump ate him."

"I don't believe so, but I cannot be sure." The Prince slid from the saddle and went to his knees. "I've been riding for hours, maybe five or so."

Owen helped him up and threw an arm around his waist. "We're glad you got here. We were done until you sent them flying."

"Not me, it was Mugwump." The Prince became a bit steadier as they walked to where Rathfield lay. "Magick, you say?"

"Wickedly powerful magick." Owen held his hand out to Becca and she reluctantly took it, hanging back away from Rathfield.

Rathfield had been stretched out and his limbs straightened. He had a few minor cuts—far fewer than any of the others, all of whom looked thoroughly gnawed—and signs of a broken leg. Of most concern, however, was the clear indication of a skull fracture. The flesh over his left eye had already begun to swell and turn purple.

Nathaniel swiped his forearm over his forehead, smearing blood. "He's breathing, but reedy. Tain't going to be long for this world."

A distant voice called out. "I can help him."

Makepeace got up and lumbered toward the center of the green. "Done forgot the Steward."

The Prince raised an eyebrow. "Who?"

"Ezekiel Fire. He's the Steward of Happy Valley, which is the capital of Postsylvania. He founded the True Oriental Church of the Lord." Owen tore a strip off his loincloth and stuffed it against a bite-mark on his forearm. "Did the Count and Hodge make it back to you yet?"

"No."

Nathaniel nodded. "Sixteenth might have been a bit quick to expect, but inside two weeks they'll reach Temperance Bay."

Before the Prince could even begin to catalogue the questions he wanted to ask, Makepeace returned with a small, older man who was rubbing his wrists. Without a word Fire sank to his knees beside Ian Rathfield and held his hands out flat over the man's cracked skull. A faint reddish glow surrounded them, then he looked up. "This is not good. I can help, but I cannot heal him, not fully."

"Well, Steward, I reckon you want to be telling us what you kin do, then we'll figger the rest."

"His leg's broken, but you can set that."

The Prince pointed to the man's head. "Depressed skull fracture."

The Steward nodded. "It is, but it isn't just that. There's still magick there. It's lost lots of power, but is still trying to drive bone into his brain. God willing, I can break that."

Makepeace knelt beside the Steward at the Colonel's head. "I'll be proud to be praying with you."

Fire nodded, then gently lay his hands on Rathfield's skull. He touched thumb to thumb and index finger to index finger, letting the wound appear plainly in that triangle. He took a deep breath, then raised his face toward the Heavens.

"Most Holy and Almighty God, I kneel here before You a most foolish and unworthy servant. Through my sinfulness and pride, I allowed a man to learn things I do not think You meant him to know. He laid this man low. I saw it as plain as I see the results now. But this man, Ian Rathfield, he is a good and righteous man. He came to the aid of his fellow men here, knowing the danger he was in. You made him magnificent, Lord, a Lion of the Faith, facing a man possessed of dozens of demons, a man commanding legions of demons. All because I believed I knew what You wanted. So I beg of you, dear Lord, to lift the magick Your enemy used. I beg You to bring him back from the brink of death. If it is Your will, I will accept from him the burden of his injuries, that he may continue to know life in You, and the joy of communion with You. Thy will be done."

No one said a thing and for a handful of heartbeats, nothing happened. Then the red glow returned to Fire's hands. It intensified, hiding his flesh, yet leaving Rathfield's forehead still visible. And there bones shifted. Though the swelling did not subside, bone rose and snapped crisply back into place. A bit of the glow outlined an odd sigil in Rathfield's flesh, as if a tattoo somehow fading into invisibility.

Fire slumped back on his heels. Makepeace caught him and dragged him away, laying him out on the ground. "He's breathing regular, just exhausted."

Nathaniel moved down to Rathfield's ankle. "Makepeace, grab his knee. Girl, can you go into the workshop and get me two pieces of wood about as long as you are tall?"

Becca stared at him, still shivering.

Owen squeezed her hand. "I'll go with you. It will help."

Once the girl had vanished into the workshop, Nathaniel pulled on the ankle and Kamiskwa set the broken leg. Rathfield remained unconscious throughout. His breathing became more regular and quiet.

Prince Vlad slowly shook his head. "Where do I begin?"

"Telling your story, or hearing ours?" Nathaniel smiled. "Not sure there's enough time for either."

"I'm not sure I follow."

As Owen returned with the splints for the leg, Nathaniel steered the Prince toward the village green. "Bad doings here, very bad. Owen can give you his journal. That will tell you most of it. Plain facts is this: two villages done been destroyed, maybe a third. Yonder fire's all's left of the folks of Happy Valley. It's a blessing we're up wind of it. Ezekiel Fire and his people found some magick which makes that healing he done look like lighting a candle. I ain't sure Fire's in his right mind. And the things we done found up to the mountains, well, if they are just a sliver of what they might be, I ain't sure there's power on this here earth what can even slow them down."

Vlad's mouth soured. "I've been doing some researching myself. What Fire knows would be enough to scare most of Norisle by itself. If…"

"Begging your pardon, Highness, but this ain't time for strategizing." Nathaniel pointed at Rathfield. "Ain't no way he's walking out of here. I reckon we make a stretcher, strap it to Mugwump, and you fly him on back home. We'll fit you with a journal, like I said, and some other things."

The Prince nodded. "Of course. I'll get him back to Prince Haven and the care he needs, then I can come back for you."

"That ain't gonna work, neither. We'll be walking on out of here, bringing the girl and Fire with us. This being the sixteenth, we should be back early June. That'll give you time to be doing some cogitating on all you'll be reading."

Vlad rested a hand on Nathaniel's shoulder. "You want me out of here quickly, very quickly."

"I reckon I do." The man's eyes tightened. "I ain't wholly sure what I done seen tonight, and I don't want you here if Rufus comes back. Iffen I thought the girl could survive the trip back on Mugwump, I'd be giving her to you, too. After what she's seen in the last week, I ain't sure she'll ever be right."

"But what if Mugwump's presence is what is keeping the things at bay? What if Rufus is hiding until Mugwump leaves?"

"Well, since Ian can't make it through the mountains, and Mugwump ain't gonna be no good for hauling him that way, don't see as it makes much difference." Nathaniel shook his head. "You want me to say it, I will. I am pure-D scared at what I seen. Make me feel better a-knowing you're back in Temperance figuring out how to stop it, than it would to have you coming along."

"I agree, but not about the girl. The trip you're suggesting will not be good for her." Vlad walked back over toward where the others had gathered, and spun the left wheel on his glove. Mugwump's head came up, then the beast reoriented himself. The Prince rolled both wheels forward smoothly, and the dragon padded forward.

Vlad smiled. "Owen, how would your friend, Becca, like to meet someone who came a long way to save her?"

The girl shrank back behind Owen.

Vlad crouched down, and offered her his right hand. "Becca, I am Vlad. These are my friends. Mugwump is, too. Do you know where Temperance is?"

The little girl shook her head.

"It's to the east, over the mountains, very far away. That's where I live. That is where we all live. And do you know what I was doing this afternoon?"

"No."

Vlad looked back at Mugwump. "I was riding my dragon. He is the only dragon in Mystria. And he saved all of our lives several years go. And there I was, flying on his back, in the saddle right there, when Mugwump heard you were in trouble. He can hear very well."

"He doesn't have no ears."

"Well, dragons, they can hear well without them. And he heard you needed help. Do you know what he did?"

Becca peeked past Owen at Mugwump, then ducked back when the dragon's head came around. "No."

"He flew here like a bird. Right here. Right here to save you."

"Me?"

"Yes, you, because you're a very special little girl." The Prince smiled. "Becca, have you ever watched a bird fly through the sky?"

She nodded.

"Have you ever wanted to fly like a bird?"

The hint of a smile crept onto her face.

"Well, I'll tell you a secret. Do you know what makes you so special a little girl?"

"What?"

"You will be the first ever girl to fly on a dragon. Never been done before. Not even once. But Mugwump, he came here to get you because you'll be the first. Isn't that wonderful?"

Fear and curiosity fought for control of the girl's expression. She peeked several more times at the dragon, but finally hung back in Owen's shadow.

Then the Steward sat up. "Do not be afraid, Becca Green. God sent this dragon. You will return with him."

Becca nodded solemnly and walked toward Mugwump.

Vlad caught up with her in two steps. "Becca, this is Mugwump. Mugwump, this is Becca Green."

While the Prince performed introductions and showed the girl where to pet the dragon on his muzzle, the others cobbled together a stretcher and bound Ian into it. Linking together every cinch-strap they could find, they fashioned another harness and bound the bed tightly to Mugwump's lower back. Then they found a small saddle, which they padded well and affixed to the rear of Vlad's saddle. They fitted the girl with a safety harness and swathed her in blankets. They provided more of the same for the Prince, and added a satchel full of Owen's journals and as many of the sheets containing the odd sigils as they could find.

Vlad mounted up. "You're back to Prince Haven by June seven, or I'm backtracking you on the route you took getting here."

Nathaniel nodded. "Godspeed and good luck. We'll come back as fast as we can and make sure ain't nothings following us."

On the return flight, Mugwump followed every command perfectly, and seemed to be contrite for his earlier rebellion. He flew lower, keeping above the treetops but not much higher, which meant they remained warmer. The sun was rising by the time they returned, and Mugwump landed gently in the yard, between Peregrine's pen and the house.

Becca had fallen asleep and even the landing failed to rouse her. Vlad freed himself from the saddle, then undid her buckles. By the time he could pull her from the saddle, Baker, Madeline, and the rest of the household had been roused and poured out to help.

Vlad passed the girl down into Madeline's arms. "Baker, don't worry about Mugwump. Send someone over to the Strake house. Get Owen's men over here. We have to get Colonel Rathfield inside."

Baker ran off toward the stables to dispatch one of the stable boys.

Vlad slid to the ground and again his legs buckled. He would have fallen but his wife caught him. "Gisella, I am so…"

She shoved him back against the dragon's flank and kissed him mightily, then hugged him and sobbed within the circle of his arms. "If you ever do that again…"

"Darling, I had no intention…"

She pulled back and thrust a finger at Mugwump's golden eye. "I was speaking to him!"

Vlad slumped against the dragon, and had he not caught hold of a stirrup, he'd have slid down to the ground. "I don't think it will happen again. It's a good thing it did."

"What did you find?"

"Postsylvania and Ezekiel Fire." Vlad stood and tugged the satchel free of the saddle. "And much more. If what we knew before was enough to change the world, what this might reveal could possibly end it."

CHAPTER TWENTY-NINE

16 May 1767
Happy Valley
Postsylvania, Mystria

Nathaniel watched after the Prince for as long as he could. The black fog had lifted, so he could see stars and the dragon silhouetted against them as he flew. He took great delight in being able to see the stars, but wished the dragon would be around to protect them. He didn't know what the things were that they fought, but Mugwump didn't seem to like them, and took great delight in dispatching them.

Kamiskwa ran in from the shadows. "It's too dark to track Rufus. He crawled a ways, but I lost him."

"I reckon he's gonna lay up, rest up. He used a powerful lot of magick."

Owen handed Nathaniel his rifle. "How about us? Do we wait until light to move out?"

"My druthers is to be shed of this place, but the Steward's in serious need of rest, too." Nathaniel pointed off toward one of the many bubbling grey puddles that used to be a demon. "I am thinking we needs to find us some pots or something and scoop up some of that stuff. Smells bad, but might keep them at bay. Take some bones, too, if you can find any."

"Will do." Owen nodded toward the nearest house. "We can barricade it up until daybreak, take one last look, then head out."

"'Bout what I was thinking."

Rummaging around in houses they found a number of pots, pans, and bowls into which they collected the partially digested demon soup. They set them around the small cabin's perimeter. Makepeace dabbed some on the doorpost, citing Scripture, then they closed the door and moved a small chest to block it. Two men stayed on watch and two slept—they let the Steward sleep throughout.

Nathaniel had the first watch along with Makepeace, but didn't strike up a conversation. He and Makepeace silently agreed it was so the others would have quiet, but both knew the truth. They didn't want to be discussing what they'd seen. The less it got talked about, the faster the memories would fade and that was fine as far as the both of them were concerned.

Goosebumps rose on Nathaniel's arms as he ripped a dress into strips and tended to his wounds. He'd been torn up worse running through thorny bushes a time or two—or so he told himself—and none of the wounds ran very deep. The demons had attacked in swarms and seemed bent on just smothering their prey. He'd been hit from all sides and when they got dragging on his legs, he couldn't move fast, then he tripped and banged down against the workshop.

Iffen Mugwump hadn't come along, that woulda been the end of me.

The thought of dying wasn't what sent a shiver through him. It was the memory of being unable to move, of being smothered by the demons. They clawed and bit and tore at him. They just overwhelmed him and yet left him in a position where he could watch Owen and Kamiskwa and Makepeace going down as well. That might not have been deliberate, but if they were acting at Rufus' command, it would have been. He would have known how much that would pain Nathaniel.

The scout snorted.

Makepeace looked over. "You found something by way of amusement?"

"Just hope that we got at least a piece of Rufus in one of them buckets outside. Tain't a bad thing that being true."

"Bit of a silver lining, that is." Makepeace nodded. "Iffen I was a writing man like Owen, I'd be using up a whole page just for that."

They both chuckled, then fell silent again. Their watch remained uneventful. When Owen and Kamiskwa took over, Nathaniel fell asleep quickly. He woke with the dawn, not particularly feeling rested, but he couldn't remember any nightmares. Owen had boiled up some root tea in the hearth and Fire served it out. It warmed Nathaniel's insides and slowly sharpened his focus.

Kamiskwa came in and accepted a cup from the Steward. "Fire's died down. No tracks. No one survived. I cut Rufus' trail again. You'll want to see this."

The expedition followed Kamiskwa back outside. In daylight they picked up Rufus' trail easily enough. He'd gone down and crawled away. The chain had slipped off him a dozen yards to the workshop's north side. A bit further along they found one of the golden tablets glinting in the sun. Makepeace gathered it up. Their course took them to another of the small houses and Kamiskwa pushed the door open with his musket.

The floorboards had been torn up with enough force that the wood around the nails had splintered. Beneath lay bare earth, but it had been freshly turned. One of the iron nails had snagged a piece of the robe they'd last seen Rufus wearing.

Nathaniel crouched at the hole's edge, but didn't reach down into it. "Ain't no shovels hereabouts. He tunneled using magick?"

Both Kamiskwa and the Steward nodded.

He stood up, then sighted back toward the workshop. "The Colonel done hurt him. He weren't thinking straight. Probably didn't notice he'd dropped a tablet. Like a wild animal, he gets in here, burrows away."

"Yes, but a wild animal capable of using magick." Owen frowned. "I made notes while on watch, trying to get every detail down. Rufus, there toward the end, was saying things that didn't really sound like him saying them."

"It was the demons in him."

Nathaniel looked the Steward up and down. "How is you meaning that remark?"

"Mr. Woods, I know you did not like Rufus Branch, and had good reasons not to. When he came here, he was a man consumed by fear. Having spent time with you, I understand why. But you must understand that here, he accepted our Lord as his savior. He worked hard within the community. I spent many hours with him, teaching him to read. Do you have any idea how humiliating it is for a grown man to have children who read better than he can?"

"I just might have an inkling in that regard, yes, sir."

"Rufus did learn to read. He studied Scripture. He became an upstanding and valuable member of our community here. As you saw, he was a deacon. And in tracking us from the ruins, you know that he and I spent a great deal of time together out in the wilderness. This was by my choice." The Steward opened his hands. "You may think me foolish, but I liked the man, and trusted him. What I forgot, however, is that he was but an infant in things spiritual, and that made him vulnerable."

Owen shook his head. "I'm not certain I follow you."

"It should be obvious. The devil laid those tablets on that altar in the Temple. He did so to tempt men. Most would have taken the tablets for their material wealth. But for men who are favored of God, their spiritual value cannot be calculated. Though I could not translate them, I knew they held the secret of magicks older than man. I can see now that these were temptations to lead men to ruin. So it did here."

Nathaniel frowned. "That don't explain what happened in Piety. We know it was these demons what acted there, but there weren't no Rufus. No one from Piety was here, saw the tablets, and got back home, was there?"

"No." The Steward shook his head. "I cannot explain that, nor do I know the moment Rufus surrendered himself to the demons. It is my vain hope it was after we started for Piety, elsewise I shall have to live with knowing that I missed the signs and consequently consigned Happy Valley to death."

The man's shoulder's slumped. "I accept this is God's plan but I..." The Steward covered his face with his hands and his shoulder shook with silent sobs.

Nathaniel looked over at Makepeace. "You'll tell me there's Scriptures what agree that demons could make magick like that?"

The large man nodded. "Revelations 16:14, clear as day. 'For they are the spirits of devils, working miracles, who go forth unto the kings of the earth and of the whole world.'"

"I could have started the day with better news." Nathaniel sighed. "And I ain't much pleased with Rufus' being able to pluck a bullet out the air."

"Yes, but he didn't stop the chain. It's being iron might have been the cause of that." Owen's eyes narrowed. "Or it could be that Rathfield surprised him. He knew you would shoot, so he was ready for you."

"So, iffen he was possessed, leastways part of him is still in there." Nathaniel shifted his shoulders uneasily. "I reckon we want to be quitting this place as fast as we can. Sooner we get back to Temperance, sooner someone might be able to make sense of all this."

They returned to their cabin and discovered that some of the vessels had rotted during the night, specifically a wooden bowl and an iron pot. A copper-bottomed pot appeared in the best shape, and a crock gave it strong competition. Because the pot would not travel well when full, they found a number of small pottery urns and divided the soup among them. They sealed them and packed them in a layer of wet clay. They bound that up in leather and each man added one to his baggage.

They took as much food as they could from Happy Valley and left notes in several houses for anyone traveling there from the Green River settlement. While Ezekiel Fire wanted to visit Green River, he agreed that they couldn't afford the time and that even a warning might not save the settlement. They all hoped the people of Green River would escape destruction, but there wasn't a one of them that didn't believe that it had already suffered the fate of Piety.

It took them a week to reach Dire Wolf Draw. They didn't see any recent signs of wolf activity in the area, but that surprised no one. The wolves would follow herds during their migration. The few tracks they did find indicated the beasts had headed southwest along the spine of the mountains, which would bring them to the point where the great northern migration started. Nathaniel had never seen it, and had only heard of it in tales told by Msitazi of the Altashee.

"That is something I want to see before I die." Nathaniel tossed a stick of wood on their campsite's fire. "To hear your father tell it, Kamiskwa, just an ocean of brown beasts heading north. Mastodons, wooly rhinoceri, bison. Ain't nothing like it in this here whole world."

Kamiskwa unrolled one of the bundles of wolf furs and spread them out for airing. "I think then, my friend, it will need to be next spring. It will be our last chance."

Makepeace laughed. "Ain't nothing gonna be making the migration go away, Kamiskwa."

Nathaniel grunted. "I reckon he's saying we ain't going to be around come summer a year hence."

Makepeace thought for a moment, then nodded. "I reckon that's something worth considering."

Owen sighed heavily. "You know, three years ago I wasn't thinking we'd see the end of summer, and then we were just fighting a Ryngian Laureate and a legion of the undead."

"Hearing you put it that way, Owen, does make it sound kind of ordinary." Nathaniel scratched at the back of his neck. "This is a little bit different, I reckon."

Ezekiel Fire poked a stick deep into the coals. "It's the End of Days. It's the Judgment time."

Owen looked up from his journal. "It's a bit premature to believe that, isn't it?"

Kamiskwa shook his head. "The Shedashee would agree. We have stories, stories that have been forgotten, stories of which I have only heard a phrase or two. They talk of these things coming. I don't know more, but what I do know frightens me. Just as the herds migrate north, imagine a grey mold working east, spreading over the mountains, down to the sea. Imagine Temperance being reduced like Piety."

"Do these things have names among your people?"

"They do, but I do not know them. I do not know if anyone does." Kamiskwa's amber eyes narrowed, reflecting a tiny sliver of firelight. "In magick, to know a name is to have power. As you address a letter to Prince Vlad, so a sorcerer can make a target of your name. Not the name that everyone knows, but your *true name*."

"My true name?" Owen raised an eyebrow. "I don't believe I have one."

"You do, but you do not know it. This can be good because it means others cannot know you." Kamiskwa shrugged. "It is bad because you cannot use it to make magick, strong magick. And, friend Makepeace, you shake your head, but among your people, do you not get a special name when you are confirmed in your faith?"

"I reckon that's different."

"No, it just means there is a second way to find you."

Nathaniel shivered, seeing a grey mold spreading over Temperance, catching up those he loved. "Well, now, I reckon I'll not be sleeping much after this discussion, so I'll take the first watch. After two hours, I'll wake the next man."

Ezekiel raised a hand. "I will take a watch."

"No need for that, Steward." Nathaniel half-smiled. "But if you find yourself awake and want to send a prayer or two off for our benefit, I'd be much obliged."

"God would be pleased to hear from you directly, Mr. Woods."

"Might could be, Steward, but I think we're much better off with you speaking for us."

In the morning they repacked the wolfskins and continued their climb into the mountains. In two more days they reached the Antediluvian ruins. Not much had changed, save that a family of beavers had begun to dam up the outflow, so water had begun to fill the lowest spots. It didn't appear as if anything had changed. The Temple doors still stood open and water lapped at the Temple steps, indicating that the dome which had kept the Temple dry had not reappeared.

"I don't like the idea of going in there but…" Nathaniel shrugged. "We have to know, I reckon."

Ezekiel Fire cocked his head. "Know what?"

"Steward, we entered the Temple after you and Rufus removed the tablets. We found evidence, near the Altar, that part of the floor might provide entry to subterranean chambers." Owen started up the steps. "With Rufus having magicked his way under the ground to get away…"

"I understand. But given what we know, don't you think this place could be a trap?"

Nathaniel, who had reached the top of the steps before the others, held up a hand to stop them. "I do believe that is a distinct possibility, Steward."

There, in the distance, a bent golden tablet glittered from within the tabernacle.

"'Pears Rufus done got here before us, and don't seem to mind our knowing it."

CHAPTER THIRTY

26 May 1767
Antediluvian Ruins
Westridge Mountains, Mystria

Owen took a quick look inside the Temple, then ducked back. "No doubt we're being taunted."

Nathaniel took a couple steps back and down. "I don't know that I think that is true. Seems fair certain that the intention of getting the tablets took was to create havoc. Onliest reason to leave that one there would be to do more of the same. Rufus couldn't be certain we'd come back this way. Heck, we'd not be but Prince Vlad said he'd backtrack us on this trail iffen we was not home quick enough."

Kamiskwa let his pack slip from his shoulders. "You think the tablet is there so someone else will find it and fall prey to it as did Rufus?"

"Like as not. Could figure that we have one, the other would find it, and get us." Nathaniel smiled. "Last Rufus knowed I couldn't read. He prolly thinks this here trap could snare the Prince, which he wouldn't mind at all."

Owen nodded. "That being the case, to leave the tablet here would be more dangerous than getting trapped in there."

Makepeace sighted down his rifle barrel, then thumbed a spec of dust off by the muzzle. "All your thinking don't mean this ain't a trap. More of them demons could spring up out the ground and you're done."

Nathaniel shucked off his pack and dug around, bringing out the urn full of demon broth. "Well, I gots me a plan. Being as how I is faster than any of the rest of you, I'll just run in there, smash this over that slab goes into the ground, and be back with the tablet in no time."

"If it doesn't work, 'I gots me a plan' will make for one hell of an epitaph."

"You have that wrong, Captain." Kamiskwa came up with his urn. "If it doesn't work, there won't be enough to bury."

"What are you proposing, brother?"

"I may not be faster than you, but I feel magick better. I make the run. You three stay here, ready to shoot anything that bothers me."

"Cain't argue as much as I'd like with your logic." Nathaniel levered his rifle's breech opened and pulled out the bullet. Using his knife, he cut a cross on the nose, then extended it toward the Steward. "I know you ain't much on shooting and all, but I reckon a blessing might be of some comfort here."

Ezekiel Fire laid his hand over Nathaniel's. "Let Thy will be done."

Owen similarly opened his rifle and got his bullet blessed, as did Makepeace. Owen saw no reddish glow, felt nothing, but also didn't feel wholly hypocritical about asking for the blessing. What he had seen in Happy Valley and Piety had opened whole new windows in his world. He'd always known magick existed, and knew he could wield it at a strong level, but his abilities were nothing compared to what he'd seen Deacon Stone do, much less Rufus. In the face of that which he didn't understand, asking for divine help didn't seem to be a vice.

He loaded the bullet back into his rifle, then lay down on the stairs and steadied the rifle on the top step. Nathaniel crouched on the top of the stairs, and Makepeace sank down beside Owen. The large man mumbled a short prayer.

Kamiskwa carried a steel tomahawk in his right hand and the urn in his left. He stepped to the doors, then slipped through. He walked casually for a few paces down the middle, glancing back to see if the doors were closing, then put his head down and sprinted toward the stone altar. His body eclipsed the golden tablet.

Owen kept his rifle trained on the spot to the right of the altar where the slab had lain. At the first hint of motion he was going to shoot. He prepared himself for a cloud of demons exploding up, or Rufus rising like a ghost from the grave. He rubbed his thumb over the firestone. *Come on, come on.*

Kamiskwa reached the tabernacle. He smashed the urn onto the floor slab, then grabbed the tablet. Something began to grind behind him, sounding like the low rumbling of an avalanche to those who waited outside. The Tabernacle began to slide backward slowly.

A shaggy grey creature clambered up from the depths, all elbows, shoulders, and a broad head with curled ram's horns. At least, that's what it appeared to be to Owen, in the brief glimpse he had of it. Then Nathaniel fired. Smoke billowed, choking the entrance. Something yelped from within, but without seeing a target, and knowing Kamiskwa was running straight toward them, Owen couldn't shoot.

Then Kamiskwa dove out though the smoke, the tablet clutched firmly in his left hand. His body drew the smoke away, revealing a hazy glimpse of a creature at least ten feet tall. Then the Temple doors began to close, and Owen and Makepeace shot in unison. They couldn't see if they'd hit the creature, but it would have been hard to miss. Yet before the smoke could clear, the doors clanged shut.

Fire grabbed Kamiskwa's pack, and the others retreated, reloading as they went. They moved through the ruins cautiously, then headed down into Little Elephant Valley. They'd have been happy to get further from the ruins, but daylight faded and exhaustion replaced excitement. They found an easily defended spot and set up camp, knowing full well that if the creature from the Temple or any of the demons wanted to attack during the night, they were powerless to stop them. Still, they splashed a little of the demon broth around and set up a rotation of shifts for nightwatch.

Kamiskwa woke Owen in the middle of the night. "Your watch, Owen."

"Thanks." Owen pulled his moccasins on. "Mind if I ask you something?"

The Altashee nodded.

"You clearly do not like whatever exists up there in the ruins."

Kamiskwa laughed. "You are too much a civilized man to say they scare me. They do. I have heard stories since I was a child. An adult may try to pretend those stories no longer have power, but they do. And they do terrify me."

"Then why be the one to make the run?"

"Owen, you have learned much in your time here. You have learned things of my people, but there are some lessons you do not understand." The warrior smiled. "Norillians and Ryngians all treat fear as if it is a shameful thing. It is not. Succumbing to it might be. But fear is just telling you that you face great danger. It tells you that you must take extreme caution. Those who ignore such warnings are foolhardy and die. Those who cannot see past them are cowards. But I am a *warrior*. If I do not honor fear, if I fail to face it with intelligence and courage, I am nothing."

He looked back toward the high mountain peak. "Did I run from that thing as swiftly as I could? Yes, but I did not give in to terror. I showed it I was indeed the most fleet of us. If I was wrong, if it caught me, all I would have lost is a race. I would not have lost what it is to be a man."

"Then it was the creature that yelped."

"No, that was me." The Altashee laughed. "If you have Nathaniel Magehawk pointing a rifle at you and shooting, you will yelp, too."

"I would at that." Owen patted him on the shoulder. "Sleep well."

The night passed without any oddness. In the morning they scouted around for signs of anything that might be following them, but found nothing. Though they did not relax their guard as they moved further from the ruins, they saw no sign of pursuit. Were they not carrying the golden tablets and demon broth—not to mention claw marks and bites—they'd have had no evidence that anything out of the ordinary had taken place.

And then, at the end of the first week of June, they returned to Plentiful. As they'd gotten close they saw ample signs of the flood that had raced down the Snake River. Riverbanks had been undermined and trees had fallen. Large rocks stood in the channel hundreds of yards from where they had been previously, or had been left high and dry on the flood plain thirty and forty yards from the river itself. Yet even these displays of the river's titanic power did not prepare them for what they found at the settlement.

The flood had poured through the valley deep and fast. Owen imagined that Arise Faith and his people, if they had any warning at all, assumed they had angered God in some incredible way. *They would have seen it as the Scriptural Deluge come again.*

A tumble of trees and splintered logs lay strewn over the valley floor. Green fields had been washed away, along with most all the buildings. Three houses on the southwest hillside had been preserved, though the hillside had been nibbled away right up to the doorstep of the lowest. The only attempts at clean up, it appeared, had been half-hearted harvesting of firewood from the wooden tangle that had once been Plentiful.

They worked their way along the valley edge, approaching the houses in the open. They stood off and announced their presence.

A ragged group of people, heads hung in shame, slowly poured out of the buildings. Owen didn't see Arise Faith among them. Half of them were children, two were old women, and the rest adults young enough to be unmarried and uncertain of what they should be doing.

Nathaniel immediately set down his pack and opened it. He pulled out a small bag of flour from Happy Valley. "Looks like you could be using this."

One of the young men stepped forward. "We don't want no charity nor no trouble."

"Ain't charity, boy, just common sense. I am plumb tired of carrying this weight. It would be a sin just to throw it away." Nathaniel advanced a few steps, set the bag down, then retreated. "We would trouble you for word of friends who passed through—Count von Metternin and Hodge Dunsby. Prolly came through two-three weeks ago."

One of the women came forward. "They did, and they were most generous. They said they would send help."

"And I am sure they will. We is in from the west, so we don't got much to share, but we'll share it all."

The rest of the expedition offered their supplies, too, which amounted to a pound and a half of flour and two of beans. It wasn't much, but the old woman found scales and weighed it all. She made Owen write down an account of what they'd been given. She solemnly promised that it would be repaid a hundred fold when Plentiful got back up and going.

Owen made her a copy of the bill of lading, then signed it. "You're going to stay here and rebuild?"

"Don't really have a choice." She folded the paper with skeletal hands. "When God scoured the earth with a flood, He did it so mankind could rebuild. His message for us can be no clearer. Look."

Owen followed her quivering finger as she pointed to the survivors. It took him a moment to recognize it, then he understood. "Two by two."

"That's right, seven men, seven women. Most are too young yet, but they will grow into God's plan." She slipped the bill inside her apron. "Suffering is a terrible thing, but knowing we are doing God's work is a comfort."

She walked away and Owen closed his journal. He went to return it to his pack and found Ezekiel Fire standing off and alone. "Something the matter, Steward?"

"Every so often, when new people found us, they would have a letter or two for me from Arise Faith. I never met the man, but he offered me the blessings of holy fellowship—then proceeded to tell me why my followers and I were damned." The small man stared down into the ruined valley. "My people succumbed to the whispers of an idol and were rightly consigned to Perdition. But these people, they did nothing, and the flood wiped them out—the flood that revealed the ruin that poisoned my people. The citizens of Plentiful believe they are part of God's plan. I believe I am as well. I daresay we would be judged to hold our beliefs with equal strength, yet one of us is wrong."

"Didn't you suggest the mind of God is unknowable?"

He turned back toward Owen. "True. Mr. Woods objected. I find it easy to see why now." He looked at his empty hands, then shook his head. "Do you wish to know the worst of it, Captain Strake?"

"Sure."

Fire's eyes blazed with an intensity Owen hadn't seen before. "With what God has showed me, I know I could clear this valley with the wave of a hand. I could raise crops—not the false manna you saw conjured through demonic instruments, but food that would sustain both mind and soul. I could ease their pain and make life easier for them. I could grant them the prosperity that their agony has certainly entitled them to."

Owen folded his arms across his chest. "Why don't you?"

"Because He has not given me leave to do so." Fire glanced at the ground again. "I do not know if it is to punish me by having me know that were I a better person He would allow me to relieve their suffering, or if it is because He has need for my gifts to be used elsewhere, to greater effect. In Scripture, the Good Lord blessed those who believed without ever seeing a miracle. Is it thus that these people who so need a miracle will be blessed? My failure to please Him pains my soul. If you will excuse me, I must pray."

Owen nodded and left Fire in peace. He worked his way higher up the hill and found Nathaniel standing with Kamiskwa, overlooking the valley. "I can't begin to imagine how much help these people need."

"A fair bit of it. Our supplies won't go far, I'm afraid, but they will do until help gets here."

"How long do you think that will be?"

Nathaniel shrugged. "I reckon Hodge and the Count done made it back to Temperance a week ago. If Hodge got together some help and started back fast, they could be here in another week or so, ten days at the outside."

Makepeace came trudging up the hill and slung his pack at their feet. "I reckon I'm going to stay here, help out a bit. I feel the calling to do it. Onliest things left in there is the tablets, demon broth, and the wolf pelts. Sell mine, send supplies: seed, nails."

"You summering out here, then?"

"Most like." He smiled easily. "When you see help coming up, tell them to go faster."

"Will if we do, but ain't likely." Nathaniel stared off east. "Ain't going back the way we came up."

Owen frowned. "But I thought the Prince said…"

"He did, but Kamiskwa here, he's itching to get to Saint Luke, and I can't blame him." Nathaniel sighed. "And given what the Shedashee might know about what's on the other side of them mountains, I ain't thinking the Prince is going to mind if we make a stop, and you fill a journal with notes."

CHAPTER THIRTY-ONE

28 May 1767
Prince Haven
Temperance Bay, Mystria

Prince Vlad caught the rope Count von Metternin tossed him as the Kessian guided his canoe to the Prince's dock. Vlad dropped to a knee and steadied the canoe as the smaller man got out. The Auropean had become quite skilled at maneuvering the craft and made no pretense of hiding his smile at that fact.

Vlad stood and nodded. "Neatly done."

The Count tied the aft off, then stood and straightened his robin's-egg-blue jacket. "Thank you. Two months in the wilderness and I have learned a great deal."

"You're looking much more yourself as well."

Von Metternin laughed, running a hand across his clean-shaven jaw. The lower half of his face remained pale, where his beard had covered it. He'd also had his hair cut back from when the Prince had first seen him, four days previously. While he now looked quite presentable in conventional clothes, Vlad thought he caught a hint of wistful nostalgia for his wilderness outfit.

"The truth is, I should still be outfitted for travel, and heading back up to Plentiful with Hodge, save that my first duty is to you and the Princess." He bowed briefly. "I apologize for dropping the satchel with you and then vanishing, but there were the supplies to be organized."

"No apologies necessary. Between what you had there and what I brought back from Happy Valley, I have been quite consumed." He waved the man forward. "Come, I can show you."

They'd made it halfway up the lawn, when Vlad turned and stopped his friend with a hand to the chest. "Before I show you what I have learned,

I need you to understand something. I trust you implicitly. What I will share with you not only has implications for our nations, but carries well beyond that. What you will learn today will forever change your vision of the world. Wait—don't say anything yet. It may also put you in grave danger. Men who have a stranglehold on power seldom like to feel their grip loosening, and panic when their prey has escaped."

Count von Metternin smiled carefully. "Highness, I cannot express my gratitude and pleasure in what you have said. And I would answer you the same way no matter what. But you must remember that I was in the mountains. I have seen the Antediluvian ruins. I cannot forget it, and I shall not rest until I understand what it means to the world. In your company I have seen many wondrous things, and I hope to learn many more. It pleases me that you would save me from any danger, but pleases me more to be able to shoulder the burden which this knowledge has placed on you."

Vlad shifted his hand, throwing his arm around von Metternin's shoulders, and steered him to the laboratory. Over the next two hours he explained what he had uncovered in Ezekiel Fire's notes and the Good Book. He delighted in the Kessian's reaction to having wooden disks vibrate in his palm as the Prince fiddled with wheels on gloves. Count von Metternin immediately asked for paper and a pencil, and sketched out a different control set that allowed the dragon to be controlled with only one hand, which left the other free for actually firing a pistol or swivel gun.

Lastly Prince Vlad spread out the paper taken from the doors and walls in Happy Valley. "The writing apparently was taken from a pair of golden tablets which Rufus Branch had retrieved from the ruins. To me it seems a mixture of pictograms and sigils which, I would imagine, represent phonemes. I do not know what is written here. Quite frankly, I don't know if I want to try to translate any of it. If these formulae represent spells, I could trigger something I cannot control."

Von Metternin frowned. "Given what Owen wrote of the people of Happy Valley on his initial visit, I would not think these are spells. If they believed that what Branch shared with them was a secret directly from God, a secret revealed in God's own language, then to display actual spells would make that information widely available. Instead I would imagine that what these are, are key Scriptures copied out by members of the community to prove and promote literacy in the new language. By reading them and understanding them, and knowing that they were right, just, and holy, the people would confirm for themselves that righteousness of the language. They would have ensnared themselves in the trap, then be quite content because they would believe the trap was where God intended them to be."

Vlad nodded. The Count's point did have a logic to it. If any of the writings were traps, the people of Happy Valley could have triggered them and that would have warned the others. "I do understand what you are saying, but I maintain my reticence to pursue translation."

"I would agree except for one key thing." The Count picked up one of the control gloves. "You reported that using the magick became easier and less tiring over time. You attribute that, in part, to the fact that you created the spell yourself, so it is idiosyncratic. It is logical to suppose, then, that the undoing of a spell would be made easier if one understood both the nature of the magick cast and the mind of the person casting it. At least understanding what the symbols mean might provide a benefit in that regard."

"I see your point."

The Count tossed the glove back onto the table. "One other thing we need to do is to prepare a rudimentary version of your thaumagraph— two, really. I shall take one to my house across the river and we shall see how well we can communicate. Key to this will not, however, be my learning your spell for making the device work. Instead, I shall have to come up with my own spell. In this way each operator can be as efficient as possible."

Vlad sat down. "Well, there is the difficulty, of course."

"Yes?"

"Can we let people know they can create their own magick?" He leaned forward, elbows on his knees, holding his head in his hands. "I have wrestled with this question for a number of sleepless nights. Even if we assume that only the most powerful and adroit could actually learn to create spells, and even if we assume they must be literate first to do so, this leaves us with a population of people who could create spells that could do incredible damage. Rufus Branch was a scoundrel and attempted murderer. Were it not for Mugwump's intervention, he would have finally killed Nathaniel, and it was a spell that nearly killed Colonel Rathfield."

The Count pursed his lips. "The question is, my friend, can you possibly prevent that outcome? You are brilliant, but you never saw the connection until Ezekiel Fire's work led you to it. Even if we assume that the Church controls most of those who can make this connection by one means or another, all it takes is one madman to repeat Fire's discovery, or a Tharyngian Laureate to reveal the secret to the world, and whatever you seek to preserve will be lost. Can you imagine a Ryngian Regiment of Riflemen where each of them has created his own magick to make his weapon fire? They might be faster, more accurate, their bullets hit with more power. The cost in blood would be incalculable—and this is just the devil we know. Whatever Branch discovered may not only release such magick to others, but that magick could be so powerful that there is no defeating it."

"But just because we *can* do a thing, and just because that thing's being done might be inevitable, we are not absolved from responsibility if we do it." Vlad looked up. "I had only the briefest description of the magick used to fell Colonel Rathfield. It was a spell that passed ten yards through air and was able to crack his skull. I have no idea the furthest range at which it could have been used, nor the optimal range. What if that spell, used in connection with something that is linked to the target, could make the range immaterial? Warfare would be transformed in ways that I doubt any at Horse Guards are prepared to contemplate."

Von Metternin's brown eyes became slits. "You mean, I believe, that Horse Guards would not fail to find a variety of uses for."

"Yes. John Rivendell would use it capriciously and irresponsibly; Richard Ventnor most viciously."

The smaller man sat back. "Then the question is, how much do you tell your aunt?"

"I cannot answer that until I know how much she knows." Vlad rose and began gathering the Happy Valley sheets. "The destruction of Happy Valley and Piety represent a threat to the Colonies, but the Crown may dismiss their elimination as insignificant since they were not chartered and were beyond lands where the Crown is granting charters. If I say that there is a serious magickal threat beyond the mountains, the best I can hope for is that they will send more people to investigate. That will take a year, and then another year before they send troops."

"And another year before they send *enough* troops."

Vlad laughed. "You know the Crown so well."

"Too well. I suspect your news of slaughter will be transformed into attacks by Twilight People. I also expect that the floods and damage from the earthquake will warrant more attention, since the need for supplies is raising prices on food and lumber, and killing the sales of goods from Norisle." The Count shrugged. "To a certain extent, what you send to Launston is going to be determined by whatever report Colonel Rathfield sends."

"He's promised to show it to me before he sends it. I've offered to correct geographical details."

"How is he?"

"Doing well. We kept him here for the first three days, while he remained unconscious. Catherine Strake has thrown herself into caring for him. When he awakened, she insisted on his being moved to her home. Miranda has remained here with us so she won't disturb him. I went over and saw him this morning." Vlad folded the sheets and tucked them into a folio. "He's lucid and has been dictating notes to Catherine."

"His leg?"

"Healing nicely. He won't have much of a limp."

"What did he say of his report?"

Vlad frowned. "Not very much. I got the sense he was hiding something, but I did not have a chance to get it out of him. Catherine *hovers*, and played the hostess far too well. She sent me away, quite politely, suggesting Rathfield was fatigued."

Von Metternin stood and stretched. "It will be a tricky business to learn if he was sent by the Crown to bring settlers back, or by the Church to bring a dangerous renegade to heel."

"If the Fire documents had not been sent to me anonymously, I would not even suspect enough to ask that latter question. Moreover, there is no reason to believe he might not have had both missions. But if I press him to learn what he knows of Fire's ability to work magick, he could come to suspect what I know. If he knew enough to suspect me, he would certainly communicate that knowledge to the Church."

"And that would make you as dangerous as Ezekiel Fire in their eyes."

Vlad raked fingers back through his hair. "That possibility has not escaped me, which puts me in another delicate situation. What I have learned is information that cannot be lost. I need to show others, like you, how to do what I can do. I would add Nathaniel if he becomes a better reader, Kamiskwa because I am certain the Shedashee have found another path to the same destination, Caleb Frost, and his father."

"Not Owen?"

"No, I would add Owen." Vlad sighed. "My only concern is his ability to keep a confidence from his wife. I fear I have never warmed to the woman. While I appreciate her devoting herself to Rathfield's recovery, it is difficult to trust a woman who so thoroughly wishes to be in Norisle."

The Count smiled. "I agree with you. Every time I see her I wonder if Johnny Rivendell was not accurate when he said she was Richard Ventnor's mistress on the voyage from Norisle. Were that true, then Miranda…"

"I know. I look at the child and she is so good-natured and has been such a help with Becca Green, that I easily see Owen in her. I think I want to believe she is Owen's because he clearly believes it and would be crushed were it otherwise."

"You fear Catherine would use knowledge of your Mystrian thauma-turgy to buy her way back to Norisle?"

"It's a horrible thing to say, but, yes." Vlad nodded. "I am not left with many choices here. If I tell the Crown nothing, and ask for no help, then I risk the colonies being overrun by enemies wielding magick and controlling demons. If I tell the Crown nothing, but gather together an elite cadre of men and train them in new ways of magick, they might be enough to repel the rebels, but in doing so their victory would reveal to the Crown what I have kept secret. I would be seen as being treasonous, the colonies as in rebellion, and Norisle would act to put it down. If I request help to deal with enemies, they will come in to do that and might never leave."

"You have a decision to make, my friend, but one that can be delayed until Colonel Rathfield finishes his report. After that…" Von Metternin's face became impassive. "… you need to ask yourself one very serious question. Do you believe there is anything you could do or say to prevent the Crown from sending troops to Mystria to exert full and direct control of the colonies? If the answer is yes, then you must do those things. If the answer is no, you must still try, because your effort will buy time for people here to prepare for an invasion."

Vlad's eyes tightened. "Doesn't your question require me to decide if my allegiance is with the Crown or Mystria?"

"My friend, were it with the Crown, we would never have had this discussion." The Count slowly shook his head. "The Crown does not realize that you take most seriously your role as Governor-General. That is their mistake. Just how bad a mistake that is remains to be seen, and the answer to that question will forever shift the course of history."

CHAPTER THIRTY-TWO

15 June 1767
Saint Luke
Bounty, Mystria

Aweek out of Plentiful, they reached the Altashee village of Saint Luke. Nathaniel had been surprised at how well Ezekiel Fire had managed to keep up on foot and in canoes. Kamiskwa had taken the preacher with him, and Nathaniel had Owen up front in his canoe. Once they left Plentiful behind, the men didn't say much, each one being given to contemplation of what he'd seen.

As they grew nearer Saint Luke, an urgency built in Nathaniel's chest. He tried to ascribe it to the aftermath of seeing Plentiful. Though the Altashee had never set their village up so dangerously close to a river, it would not take much of a natural disaster to destroy a village. He kept telling himself that his friends and children would be alive, well, and happy to see him, but until he laid eyes on them, doubt lingered.

But that which had destroyed Happy Valley had been anything but natural. Rufus Branch hated Nathaniel and knew where the Altashee could be found. More than once Nathaniel had awakened from a sound sleep while stretched out on the ground. He imagined hearing something beneath him clawing its way to the surface. For Rufus to race ahead through the earth and attack Saint Luke grew in his mind from a faint possibility to a dead certainty, and this pushed him to go further and faster.

None of the others resisted this effort or complained about it.

They spent the last six hours on game trails, moving through forests bright with summer green. The light breeze teased leaves. Meadow grasses swayed and bumblebees darted from orange flowers to yellow and red. The travelers cut around a small pond created by a beaver dam, and surprised a doe and her fawn in the process. None of them raised a gun, however, as the thunder of a shot would have spoiled the late afternoon peace.

Roughly a hundred yards out of the wooded valley in which Saint Luke existed, they came across a series of birch posts running in a straight line from northwest to southeast. The posts stood ten feet tall and were separated by ten feet. The bark had been scored with pictographs of a turtle, all facing back toward the Westridge Mountains. The line of posts disappeared from view in both directions.

Nathaniel signaled a halt. "We don't go no further until welcomed."

Owen took a closer look at one of the pictographs. "The turtle is a symbol of strength and protection, isn't it?"

"It warns enemies that Saint Luke is prepared to defend itself." Kamiskwa shrugged off his pack and began removing his clothing. "You might as well do it now. It will save time."

Nathaniel likewise divested himself of his pack. "Best be doffing your clothes, too, Steward."

Fire lowered his pack, but did not start unbuttoning his shirt or pants. "The Good Lord wishes upon us modesty. None should see us naked but our Creator and our spouses."

"Ain't really the eyes of God you need worry about right now." Nathaniel jerked his head along the trail. Three ancient Altashee advanced. In the lead came Msitazi, the chief of the Altashee. He wore a much-patched red coat that had once belonged to Owen. His right eye shared the amber color of his son's eyes, but the left had the milky color that suggested blindness. Nathaniel, who had known Msitazi for over two decades, often thought that eye saw the most.

One of the two Altashee trailing him bore a warclub. His tunic had been worked with shell in the pattern of a hawk. The other man carried an obsidian knife. A turtle motif had been used to decorate his clothing. They both stopped ten feet from the line of posts, and Msitazi advanced to it along the path.

Nathaniel clasped his hands at the small of his back and bowed in greeting.

Msitazi did not return it.

Ain't no good coming of this. He exchanged a glance with Kamiskwa.

His brother's expression revealed nothing but surprise. The two of them, down through the years, had done things to get in trouble, but never had they done anything that earned a greeting like this.

Msitazi turned on his heel and headed back to the village. The other two Altashee remained where they were, closing ranks to bar passage.

The Steward kept his voice low. "Mr. Woods, what's happening?"

"Iffen I knew, I'd tell you. I reckon tain't no time for modesty, Steward." Nathaniel shook his head. "I don't know what Msitazi has in mind, but I'm going to be trusting it's for the good."

The four of them stood on the trail naked for nearly an hour, as measured by the slow lengthening of shadows. It disturbed Nathaniel a bit that the posts didn't create shadows. It bothered him a lot more that when his shadow crept up to the post line, it did not extend beyond it. By the time Msitazi returned, the line had devoured the shadow of Nathaniel's head and had started on his shoulders.

The Altashee chieftain tossed four leather hoods outside the line, then accompanied each with a pair of buckskin mittens.

Kamiskwa gathered them, then handed a hood to each of his companions. He opened his to reveal that the turtle symbol had been sewn into the interior. "We put these on and it prevents us from working wickedness." He pulled his hood on and tied it tightly so that it would not come off without great effort.

Owen looked at Nathaniel. "How much danger are we in?"

The scout looked at Msitazi's hard expression. "Fact we ain't dead means there might be some redeeming coming our way. Failing that, though, I reckon we'll be about as dead as Happy Valley."

Owen nodded, glanced at his gear, then pulled his hood on. Nathaniel followed suit, tying it snugly around his neck. The hood immediately became hot and stuffy. Nathaniel swallowed to create a little space around the edge, to let fresh air in, but had little success. He shoved his hands into the mittens, felt the beaded pattern inside them as well, and waited.

Rough hands grabbed him, poking and prodding, spinning him one way and back. Fingers jabbed at wounds. A couple reopened. He could feel blood begin that slow, oozing crawl down his forearm and thigh. Then something splashed in the wounds and he yelped. The bag didn't muffle other shouts, so he knew he wasn't alone in how he was being treated.

Hands shoved him forward. At the point where he would have expected to pass the post-line, he met resistance. It felt no heavier against him than a spider-web, but it took heavy shoving to get him through it. He stumbled on the other side, but hands caught him. One man on either side marched him along the trail. A couple hundred yards further on they cut off the path. Grasses lashed his thighs, then he found himself on sand and could hear a stream burbling nearby.

His captors forced him down onto hands and knees, then shoved him forward. He crawled along and felt a leather curtain play over his back. Once inside other hands guided him to the left and shoved him down on his side. Another person, straddled him, grabbed his shoulders and hauled him up into a sitting position. The person loosened the hood's tie and brought the edge up to just beneath his nose, then pressed a narrow-mouthed gourd to his lips.

Nathaniel tipped his head back and drank. Even before the turgid, sour liquid hit his throat, he knew what it was: *salksasi*. The Shedashee brewed it from mashed roots, adding some maple sugar and peppers. The scent immediately filled his head, clearing it, and the pepper burned his tongue and throat. The Shedashee saved it for rituals of all sorts, usually allowing a warrior only a mouthful because it could produce visions more easily than a gallon of whiskey drunk real fast. Nathaniel couldn't swallow quickly enough, letting slender ribbons of the liquid roll down the side of his face like saliva.

Finally the gourd disappeared and the hood descended again. Nathaniel lay back and found himself propped up by skins. He tried to shift around, but his hands were numb and his legs had already been arranged so he sat cross-legged. *I should have remembered that, shouldn't I?* Then he felt heat building against his chest and legs.

Someone pulled the hood off him, an old man wearing a carved turtle mask. A man in a hawk mask had removed Owen's hood, and the man wearing a bear mask had removed Kamiskwa's hood. The other two sat back awkwardly as Nathaniel did, blood trickling from the demon wounds. A small fire burned in the center of the circle, Nathaniel slowly realized, which sat beneath a short dome formed of birch boughs lashed together and covered with hides.

Turtle tossed something onto the fire. The flames shot up, shifting from red-gold to green. A sweet scent, part pine resin, part cedar, filled the enclosure. Smoke drifted down and Nathaniel breathed it in. It erased the last trace of *salksasi*.

Hawk fed a small wooden disk into the fire. Nathaniel found his eyes drawn to it. The surface had been worked with a sigil that reminded him of the squid motif from the ruin. And yet, even as he stared at it, the octopus' limbs straightened and the symbol became that of the sun.

And Msitazi's voice emerged from within the bear mask. "In a time before there was time, when young were the ancient spirits that tread the winding path…"

Msitazi's voice faded, as did vision of anything but the sun. Nathaniel looked down from the yellow ball in the sky toward a valley, a broad green valley through which snaked a slow, blue river. He stood high on a promontory, yet could not see himself, nor feel himself. He was just there, an observer. He believed himself to be as light as a feather, and willed himself forward and down.

He went down because there, in the valley floor, was a vast city, built within a hexagonal series of mounds, just to the south of the river. To the east and west of it, vast fields had been cultivated, clearly made possible through the network of irrigation canals. Forest abutted the cleared areas, and the wood had been used to build many huts and even larger buildings—buildings that dwarfed the meeting houses, with wings added at odd angles which should have struck him as wrong, but seemed proper. They made the buildings stronger, not in the material world, but in the world of the supernatural. As the canals channeled water, so these walls could divert magick. Courtyards allowed it to pool. Towers sucked it skyward, letting it rain down in displays that teased him. They glittered like icy lace that collapsed when he studied it too intently.

In a large courtyard at the city's heart—and Nathaniel knew instinctively that this city boasted more people than Temperance—people had gathered for a massive market. The Shedashee were well represented, with tribes he recognized from the east, and those he had dim knowledge of from tales. He even recognized symbols of tribes that no longer existed, which marked the vision as having taken place a long time ago.

In and among the Shedashee, moving between traders, laughing as did people in Temperance as they strolled the streets, were a golden people. Taller than the Shedashee and more slender, with golden hair and golden flesh, they appeared so achingly beautiful that they made Nathaniel weep with desire. Men and women alike wore broad girdles decorated with jewels and golden buttons. Pectorals of gold, worked with lapis and turquoise flashed in the sun. Nathaniel saw not a single weapon among them.

The golden people named themselves *Noragah* in his mind. They treated with the Shedashee fairly and happily. As the market day ended, the Shedashee retreated to the forests, and the vision vanished in a long night, which passed in an eyeblink. When it returned, the Noragah still strode among the Shedashee, but the Twilight People were not there as friends. They had been enslaved and their bonds appeared fashioned from the same magick that rose in wondrous fountains.

Fountains which now had become fouled and oily, stinking of rotting flesh. Noragah lashed out with magick, killing Shedashee, torturing the land. They forced it to produce food quickly, as had Deacon Stone, but the Noragah never bothered to harvest it. They would let it rot in the fields, then use magick to raise another crop. As they had enslaved the Shedashee, so they enslaved the very world in which they lived.

Nathaniel tried to pull back from the city, for he could feel the evil pulsing from its heart. Fight as he could, however, the city held him. He did not want to watch, but he recognized the need.

Winged demons followed their masters, doing their bidding and inflicting cruelty on slaves for pure amusement. And though this cruelty entertained the Noragah for a while, it was not long enough. Cities raised armies of the bat-winged demons, and the behemoth which had come after Kamiskwa in the Temple. There must have been rules to their wars, but Nathaniel could not bear to study them long enough to learn. If score was kept, if points were earned, it seemed they went for the most spectacular and torturous methods of destroying an army.

One of the Noragah tired of the game as quickly as Nathaniel. He removed his army from sport and used it to conquer his neighbors. From cities hidden in forests and plains across the continent, rainbows of energy arced through the sky and flooded the valley. The Noragah of that valley grew prosperous. Other Noragah sent their daughters as tribute and accepted sons as governors.

And all around, the land sickened and died. What had been lush and green, turned grey. Swaths of forest burned or blew over. The earth became so exhausted that even more magick could not make it fruitful. So the Noragah began killing the Shedashee and irrigating the fields with their blood. Whole tribes vanished to slake the earth's thirst and yet even that was not enough.

So the leader of the Noragah wove great magicks which would allow him to tap the blood of the land, running hot and deep. He wanted to raise stone rivers and cover the face of the earth with molten rock, to make it anew.

And he would have succeeded, save for the coming of the dragons.

CHAPTER THIRTY-THREE

16 June 1767
Strake House
Temperance Bay, Mystria

Ian Rathfield leaned heavily on a stout walking stick in the parlor and smiled as Catherine Strake ushered Bishop Bumble into the room. "So good to see you again, your Grace," Ian said.

"I have been remiss in failing to visit before this." The round man clapped his hands. "Please, you should not have risen. Sit down."

Ian eased himself into a chair. Catherine busied herself adjusting cushions and raised his cast foot onto an ottoman. "Thank you, Catherine."

"My pleasure, Ian." She straightened up. "I shall bring tea, then leave the two of you to your business."

"Most kind, Mrs. Strake. And perhaps some of those cakes my wife sent along, on a plate. Do save some for yourself and your daughter." Bumble smiled. "Where is little Miranda?"

"She is at Prince Haven. It was thought best she stay there so she would not disturb Colonel Rathfield during his convalescence."

Ian chuckled. "By all reports she has been very helpful with Becca Green. She is mature beyond her years, is Miranda."

"And a blessing upon this house and the next, I see." Bumble clasped his hands together in his lap as Catherine swept out of the room. "I apologize for only having sent Mr. Beecher to visit you, but there has been a great deal of work to be done in anticipation."

Ian's eyes narrowed. "I must have missed something. Anticipation of...?"

"Of putting Ezekiel Fire on trial for heresy."

"Really." Ian's flesh tightened. "I must say, Bishop, that I do not remember anything out of the ordinary. No bloody sacrifices, no obscene rituals."

"One could hardly expect they would reveal the same to outsiders." The older man cocked his head to the side. "Still, the Happy Valley community practiced plural marriage, worshipped golden tablets, and was made up of people willing to sacrifice themselves and their children, and did so beyond the borders of Crown-sanctioned holdings. This also placed him outside the jurisdiction of the Church. He had no bishop above him and belonged to no established diocese."

Ian winced as he lifted and resettled his leg. "I don't wish to argue with you, but I believe there are a number of colonial villages in the west in which plural marriage is practiced. I sincerely doubt all of them are formally part of a diocese."

Bumble raised his hands. "There may have to be allowances for what some people do in innocence. Whereas, Ezekiel Fire chose a murderer and notorious drunkard as his lieutenant."

"We were told that Rufus Branch had not touched a drop of alcohol in years."

"Believe me, Colonel, I do not fault you nor anyone else for being deceived by Fire." The man turned. "Mrs. Strake, you really shouldn't have."

Catherine returned with a silver service in hand and set the tray down on a small table. She poured through a strainer for each man, adding two spoonfuls of sugar for the cleric. She handed Ian his tea, strong and black.

Bumble looked up. "You don't take sugar or milk, Colonel?"

Catherine answered for him. "Colonel Rathfield developed a taste for his tea without adulterations in the field. One cannot always be certain to get milk and sugar on the march."

Bumble stirred quietly. "Yes, ghastly thing, being on the march. I joined them, you know, going to Anvil Lake. Mud to my waist, biting bugs, profanity, all quite horrible."

Catherine plated a small cake and offered it to Ian. "To say nothing of the actual fighting, your Grace?"

"Yes, of course. As your *husband* might know, Mrs. Strake, or the Colonel here."

Ian watched Catherine stiffen and leaned forward. "Catherine, if you would not mind. That cushion. I promise, it will be the last I bother you."

"No bother at all, Ian." She straightened a cushion by pulling it to the side then sliding it back exactly where it had been. "If you need anything more, please, just call out."

The Bishop, catching cake crumbs on a plate placed beneath his chins, nodded.

Ian waited for her to disappear before he set his tea down on a side table. "To be honest, Bishop Bumble, I am not at all certain we were deceived by Steward Fire. Branch may well have deceived him, but the man who traveled with us to Piety and back seemed quite sincere. Were he one to mock or tempt, he had more than enough opportunity to do so."

"Really?"

Ian deliberately took a large bite from the cake he'd been offered. He found it dry and largely tasteless—consisting more of sawdust and salt than anything sweet. He would have washed it down immediately with tea, but that would have freed him to speak. He wanted the time that chewing and swallowing afforded him to cover his reaction.

The Bishop clearly was inviting him to talk about any theological discussions on the trail. Save for Makepeace Bone, all of them had made remarks that could have been interpreted as critical of the Church, whether they were meant to be or not. While Ian knew that his companions had tolerated him more than respected him, he didn't want to reveal anything to the cleric which could come back to haunt them.

Ian sipped tea. "Yes, well, of course, as you saw in your time in the wilderness, men can be coarse and crude, even given to profanity. I will admit to uttering a curse or three myself. Had he wished to manipulate our view of him, he could have done so."

"I see." Bumble nodded solemnly. "Now when Mr. Beecher came to visit, he said you could remember nothing of the other matter we had talked about. Has your head cleared since then?"

Ian set his cup and saucer down. "I am not certain, Bishop, that Mr. Beecher serves you in the best way."

"What do you mean?"

"He made a veiled reference to a matter which I had addressed with you, in the confidence of the confessional, if you will recall." Ian allowed a scowl to steal over his features. "I fear the man may have listened in to our conversation. Not thinking him a safe conduit for information, I complained of a headache which clouded my recollection."

"I see."

"I apologize for causing you undue upset about your aide."

The rotund man shook his head, his chins quivering. "Calm yourself on that count, sir. You must understand, sir, that Mr. Beecher did not listen into our conversation. I told him everything you told me."

Ian blinked and sagged back. "You what?"

"Colonel, it is my duty to see to the spiritual life of everyone within my diocese. What you revealed to me is most troubling, and I would have been remiss if I did not inform Mr. Beecher. In the event I am unable to perform my duties, my responsibilities will fall to him."

Ian glanced off toward the room's far corner, avoiding the man's gaze. "But what I told you in the confessional, you used to pressure me into undertaking special work for you in the wilderness."

Bumble, eyes wide, set the cake plate down forthwith. "In the name of Heaven, sir, I apologize if that is how it appeared to you. I merely wished you to understand that as you trusted me with your most closely held secret, so I trusted you with a mission of incredibly great importance. If... if you felt I *coerced* you in any way, if Mr. Beecher gave you the impression that your secret would become public... well, sir, I understand your outrage and I offer you a most sincere apology."

Ian shifted in the chair. "You will forgive me, sir, for making such a mistake."

"Of course, of course." Bumble's smile spread across his face. "I do have to ask, however, if you saw anything concerning what we discussed."

"I do not recall anything which indicated Steward Fire was practicing or causing his people to practice magicks."

"Did you not tell Mr. Beecher that Fire prevented Woods and Strake from shooting Rufus Branch?"

Ian frowned, his head beginning to throb. "I told your aide that Woods and Strake both reported being unable to fire their rifles, but I have no proof that there truly was such a prohibition. To be frank, they had been having me on about all manner of things during the journey. I thought this might well be yet another of their amusements."

"Are you certain that is how you remember it?"

"What are you implying?"

"I imply nothing, Colonel. I am asking if you have had time to reconsider what you remember." Bumble brushed a crumb from his black coat. "You see, you are correct that the evidence against Fire is circumstantial at this point. Were you to recall his using magick in an inappropriate way, or making outright heretical claims, doing what must be done would be much easier."

"But what if he is innocent?"

"I can assure you he is not."

"And how do you know that?"

Bumble fell silent for a moment, then pressed his hands together in his lap. "The man was a promising student of mine many years ago. While he served under me, he seduced my wife. For her sake we have revealed this to no one. To punish us for our vanity, God made her barren. So I know the evil which has curled itself in his heart. I wished to deal with him, but he vanished years ago. I only wish I had acted more courageously. The people need not have died out there."

Ian shivered. He'd seen Livinia Bumble once. She was to Catherine Strake what vinegar was to wine. The idea of anyone seducing her seemed absurd, and he just could not believe Fire would have done so."

The Bishop reached out and grasped Ian's right forearm. "You see, Colonel, this is why dealing with Ezekiel is so important. You may not have seen him use magick inappropriately, but I know he is capable of it. But you saw nothing?"

"No, nothing, not really."

"Tell me."

"Well, when the Green woman and her daughter came to Happy Valley, he laid his hands on the girl and healed her. He was able to help her, but not her mother, who had collapsed beside her and died."

Bumble patted his hand. "You see, there you are, you do remember."

"I just said he healed her, much as the Good Lord did."

"Oh no; no, no, no. That's what you *think* you saw." Bumble nodded confidently. "What you saw was his using magick to drain the life of the mother to preserve the child. The mother knew too much. She came to report to him what happened at Piety, but he could not let her unless the truth be revealed to the strangers. Then he led you off to Piety so Branch could prepare a trap for you. It's all very clear."

Ian rubbed at his forehead. "You're twisting my words."

"No, Colonel. I am helping you remember the truth." Bumble's smile flashed past quickly. "Much as you asked me *before* to help you remember the truth so you could be absolved of any guilt."

Ian stared blankly at the man, his mouth open, words choking him.

Catherine Strake, her brown eyes blazing dangerously, swiftly re-entered the parlor. "So sorry to have to ask you to leave, Bishop Bumble."

The cleric ignored her and picked up his tea.

Catherine plucked it from his hands and set it down on the tray again. "You must come again, your Grace, when your visit will not tire Colonel Rathfield."

Bumble looked up, his face hardened. "We have not finished our conversation."

"Nor will you on this visit." Catherine pointed a stiffened finger at the door. "Your horse awaits."

The fat man stood. "Were I your husband, I should beat you."

"Were I your wife, I should have long since been your widow." Catherine gave him a withering stare. "Shall we be frank, Bishop? You have never taken to me because of your feelings for my husband."

"I have never liked you, woman, because your husband has given you free rein."

"And you don't like him for the same reason you do not like Colonel Rathfield. Each of them has more courage than you will ever know, and they are the men who stand between you and that which terrifies you the most." Catherine dismissed him with a wave. "You may hold sway in Temperance and even in other colonies, but in this household you are unfit to black the boots of the men who make this their home."

Bumble turned to bid Ian adieu, but Catherine caught his arm and twisted him toward the door. She escorted him out. The door did not slam behind him, but it closed with a firm finality. Relief washed over Ian. He refused to look toward the windows and the front yard, therefore he only peripherally caught the Bishop's departure in shadow.

Catherine returned and went to her knees by his side. "Please, Ian, forgive me. I've embarrassed you terribly. I shall go and write a note of apology. I shall say I was concerned for you and for Owen, and I spoke out of turn." She pressed her face to his left hand and he felt tears dampen his flesh. "Do say you will forgive me."

Catherine, I should forgive you anything.

That was what he wanted to say, that and much more, but he dared not say it or even think it. Gravely ill, he had been transported from far away and for every waking moment of the last month, she had been with him. She had bathed him and clothed him, fed him, read to him. She had changed his bandages and helped him work on his report for Launston. She had done for him all the things he could not do for himself, never passing judgment when he fell or soiled himself, when fevers came or the headaches shortened his temper.

For him she had been the perfect wife, and she had healed more than his body.

He brought his right hand over and caressed her brown hair. "Do not cry, Catherine. You have just done for me what a good friend does for one... of whom one is quite fond. I lack the words to express the depth of my gratitude for this. If you wish to write Bishop Bumble on your on accord, then do so, but I should not require it. Were I your husband, I should forbid it."

She looked up, her eyes rimmed with red. "Really?"

"Yes. It would be a lie to suggest that he did not deserve what happened, or that anything you said was incorrect." Ian smiled at her, pleased to see a smile coming back at him. "The soul in peril this afternoon was his, Catherine, and he should see to it before he concerns himself with aught else."

Chapter Thirty-four

17 June 1767
Saint Luke
Bounty, Mystria

For Owen, whose head still throbbed because of the *salksasi* he'd consumed, the rasp of pen nib on paper sounded as if someone were sawing into his skull. Still, he diligently scribbled down details of the visions Nathaniel and Kamiskwa had, adding his own observations. None of them knew how long they had been wrapped up in the visions, but the day following had consisted of a purification ritual. They'd remained in the hut with a fire blazing, sweat pouring off them and dripping into wounds that stung. Only as night fell were they allowed to emerge, remove their mittens and wash themselves in the nearby stream. They drank more *salksasi*, had their wounds bandaged with *mogiqua* poultices, and were allowed to sleep.

Owen rubbed at eyes that burned. "Kamiskwa, I have your name for the golden people as *Noragah*. I heard it as *Norghaest*. Nathaniel, you heard it in the Shedashee way?"

"Up until the dragons came. Then it was as you did."

Owen made a note. Despite hearing some words differently, and having slightly different emotional attachments to the story, the three of them had seen the same thing. The Norghaest had built an empire on magick, employing it to inflict cruelty on the Shedashee and each other. When it seemed they were invincible and at the height of their power, however, dragons came and destroyed their cities.

Even having seen Mugwump did not prepare Owen for the advent of the dragons. Not a one of them that attacked—and the sky had been blackened with them—was anything less than double Mugwump's size. Many were quite larger, and where the Prince's dragon had smooth scales

237

almost like a snake's skin, the larger dragons had thick, heavier scales with ridges that ended in horny protrusions. They fell on the Norghaest as falcons on varmints, devouring them greedily. With long claws, the winged beasts tore open Norghaest towers and rent the earth to pursue them into the undercities. The carnage would have been unimaginable, but Owen had been at Anvil Lake, and had already seen the visions of bloody orgies the Norghaest staged to entertain themselves.

The dragons' assault drove the Golden People underground, deep underground, like termites. As the visions progressed and they witnessed the Norghaest trying to reestablish their cities, the Norghaest changed. The golden hue drained from their flesh leaving the pale grey of a mushroom. Black hair became white, and many of them lost it completely—the men, anyway, for none of the subsequent visions provided sight of the women.

Kamiskwa drank from a gourd, then lowered it. "The visions showed the patterns: first comes the earthquake. That is them opening the gates to their cities below. They send scouts to see if dragons are about. Then the next year, or the year after, they colonize the surface. If those colonies survive, they emerge in all their glory to re-create their empire."

Nathaniel smiled. "Well, now, I done counted four times the Shedashee did some de-colonization. Only once did they get to that emerging. Shedashee hurt them bad, and dragons finished them."

"But, brother, there were more Shedashee then than there are now, and we only have one dragon, a *small* dragon."

Owen looked up from his journal. "The dragons came from the west, didn't they?"

"'Peared that way to me." Nathaniel shrugged. "Don't quite know what to make of that, but I reckon Prince Vlad will. I reckon he ought to be learning what we saw sooner rather than later."

Owen's journal snapped shut. "We can get a full day's travel in today, be halfway to Grand Falls."

"I cannot go."

The two Mystrians looked at Kamiskwa. Nathaniel frowned. "All this coming from you will carry more weight."

"Agreed, but what I saw is not for the Prince." Kamiskwa knitted his fingers together. "The Shedashee need to be reminded of the *Noragah*. They must remember a time when we united to fight them. My father will already have sent runners to the other nations in the Confederation. They will confer and I must be here to tell them what I have seen…"

He held out his left forearm and poked a jagged claw wound with a thumb. "They will all inspect the wound. Scars will not do. And when they believe, they will send runners. The Shedashee will gather and fight the *Noragah*."

Nathaniel nodded. "Well, then, I'll be there with you to fight 'em."

Kamiskwa shook his head. "You say that, my friend, but you will have other responsibilities."

"You're forgetting that your niece and nephews is my children."

"And they are of the tribe, too; so we shall take care of them." Kamiskwa smiled. "I do not say this to hurt you, nor because I doubt that Magehawk would be welcome at my side. It is because I fear that without your people to fight as our allies, we cannot turn the *Noragah*. And if there are no more dragons in the west, all of the world will be as was Piety."

Reluctant though they were to leave Kamiskwa behind, Owen, Fire, and Nathaniel headed south from Saint Luke, making for the Benjamin River right below Grand Falls. They traveled relatively lightly, having abandoned all but two of the dire wolf pelts to the Altashee. Each man wore new clothing, his tattered and tainted clothes having been given to the women to be washed and repaired or burned.

Ezekiel Fire, because he had not been bitten or scratched by the demons, had not been forced through any cleansing ritual. He'd been treated as a guest and honored by Msitazi on the second night. He'd told the Altashee his favorite stories from the Scriptures, and had reported that the audience was more attentive and appreciative than most he had preached to.

By and large they were not given to much conversation as they made the trip back toward Temperance. Below the falls they found a large canoe and started down river. Owen, in the bow, had an unobstructed view of the countryside. The days had grown longer as they traveled, the green grasses tall, and the tree canopy shaded much of the river the first two days. The utter lack of destruction along the Benjamin contrasted with the devastation along the Snake.

Try as he might, Owen could not help but add details from the visions to the landscape. A soft rolling hill became a mound upon which had once stood a Norghaest outpost. He could imagine tunnels running beneath the landscape everywhere. Though he and Nathaniel did not talk about it, when they made camp, they chose to sleep atop large, flat rocks so Rufus couldn't come up from the earth and, to further frustrate him, they did not stop at camping sites that he might know about.

It was, therefore, with great pleasure that they came around the curve of the river and saw the Prince's dock. Owen picked up his paddle and pointed, then waved it high.

A little girl stopped and waved back.

Nathaniel laughed from the aft. "Your little one done sprung up some, hain't she?"

"Three months we've been gone." Owen dug in with his paddle. "Almost home."

Nathaniel started paddling too. Miranda ran from the dock, then returned with the Prince. He, in turn, managed to catch hold of Prince Richard before the toddler ran off the end. With the boy in one arm, the Prince waved.

As they came to the dock Owen caught sight of his wife, Becca Green, and Princess Gisella sitting in the great house's shade, sipping tea. Ian Rathfield, wearing Norillian clothes, save for a cast on his left leg, sat a bit apart from them in conversation with Bishop Bumble. Count von Metternin came to the dock to help secure the canoe. Both he and the Prince wore pants and shirts of Mystrian manufacture, and could have easily been taken for hired help in the employ of those up by the house.

Once the canoe had been tied off, Owen bounded out and scooped his daughter up. Miranda squealed. Tipping his hat back, Owen kissed her, then she pushed his face away.

"Papa, you have whiskers."

"I do, child, but not for long." He shifted her weight to his left arm, then offered the Prince his right hand. "It is a pleasure to see you again, Highness. You remember Ezekiel Fire."

Vlad nodded. "I do." He nodded to the Steward and Nathaniel, then looked at Owen again. "You're missing two companions."

"Makepeace elected to stay in Plentiful to help after the flood." Owen lowered his voice as he saw Bishop Bumble marching down the lawn. "And Kamiskwa remained in Saint Luke to speak with the Shedashee. We can explain…"

"Please forgive me, gentlemen, Highness, but I do believe I spy my old friend, Ephraim Fox."

Fire's smiled died, and he seemed to shrink a bit. "Othniel Bumble, the years have been kind."

"They have." The fat man clasped his hands over his belly. "And now a sad duty, my friend. As bishop of the Archdiocese of Temperance Bay, I place you under arrest. You will, forthwith, be placed on trial for heresy. When convicted, you will burn."

Prince Vlad fought to keep fury from his face. He turned and handed his son to Ezekiel Fire. "If you would be so kind, Steward, to hold my son."

"Honored, Highness." Fire accepted the boy into his arms and moved away from the edge of the dock.

Vlad turned to Bishop Bumble. "You will want to attend me. *Now*."

"Highness, I think this is so lovely a day, it would be a shame to spoil this party by taking the host away from his guests."

"That is a consideration that you might have made before inviting yourself, Bishop, or before you arrested a man." Vlad turned on his heel and stalked off toward his laboratory. He did not wait for Bumble to follow, and did not turn around to see if the man was coming with him or not. The man's huffing and puffing told him all he needed to know.

Vlad threw open the door and did not invite Bumble in, *per se*. The Bishop had seen the inside of the laboratory before the new structure had been built, and had barely dared to get more than a step or two from the door. Vlad had the impression he'd sooner march through the gates of Hell than enter a building filled with animals, specimens in jars, a variety of unidentifiable items, and one of the largest libraries in Mystria.

The Prince stopped at his desk and turned. Bumble remained in the threshold. Vlad was about to demand that he come in all the way, but there, hidden behind the door, was the thaumagraph station that connected Prince Haven to Count von Metternin's River House. There was no way imaginable that Bumble could discern what the device was, but Prince Vlad doubted that ignorance was going to be any impediment to the man's ability to cause trouble.

Vlad pointed back toward the dock. "What you did out there was rude and unforgivable."

"I do not need to be forgiven, Highness, for doing the job appointed to me." Bumble kept his voice even, but his ears burned red, revealing a hint of shame. "That man is a heretic. He blasphemes and traffics in diabolical magicks. He imperils the souls of everyone present. I daresay, were I not here, he would work his foul ways with you and the doom which visited Piety and Happy Valley would destroy Prince Haven."

Vlad turned to his desk and flipped open a journal. That Bumble knew of Piety and Happy Valley didn't surprise him. Catherine had reported that Bumble had visited Rathfield. Exactly what Bumble knew, and what he would make of it was important. While Vlad would have loved to have questioned him closely, to do so would reveal his knowledge of Fire's discoveries, and that would leave him open to the same charges the Bishop was leveling against Fire.

"You have exceeded yourself here, Bishop."

"I think not. I am well within my duty to arrest Fire. I have long since told you that he would be tried."

Vlad nodded. "You did, so I did some research. We've not burned someone for heresy in the colonies in the last century, and in Temperance Bay we've not done it in over one hundred thirty years. In fact, while you can try him, convict him, excommunicate and defrock him, to have him killed requires the approval of civil authority."

The cleric's jowls rippled with a low chuckle. "I believe you will find, Highness, that there is not a local magistrate who will refuse to sign a death warrant in this case."

"But such a sentence would be appealable to me."

Bumble raised a snowy eyebrow. "And you will sign off on it."

Vlad stared down at the smaller man. "I should not be so certain of myself, were I you."

Bumble's laughter grew slightly, and his grin matched it. "Highness, you and I have managed, for the most part, to have a very good working relationship. You deal with matters of the Crown. I deal with matters of the soul. We both acknowledge that my power comes from a higher realm than yours. And I have seen fit, through the years, to ignore many of the things which others have brought to my attention concerning you."

Vlad folded his arms over his chest. "Such as."

Bumble pointed back out toward the dock. "You are known to keep company with a notorious fornicator, Nathaniel Woods."

The Prince raised his chin. "Is he, now?"

The cleric lowered his voice. "Let us not be coy, Highness, it ill becomes you. I know, from a very reliable source, that Woods and a well-respected woman in Temperance have carried on an affair for many years, despite her being married to another. I know that one of her children is not by her husband. I also know that you threatened her husband were he to take action against Woods or his wife. You are aiding and abetting a pair of adulterers. We both know that Woods has bastard half-breeds among the Twilight People though I doubt even he knows how many are truly his."

"Even the ruination of a good man, and a good woman, is insufficient motivation for me to put Ezekiel Fire to death."

"This does not surprise me." The Bishop opened his hands to take in the whole of the laboratory. "I suspect, however, having yourself exposed for your Ryngian studies, and for having abandoned God and adopting their atheist ways would be. Do you think, standing where we are, that you could not be convicted of such charges and that, once you were, you would not burn beside the heretic down on the dock?"

CHAPTER THIRTY-FIVE

23 June 1767
Prince Haven
Temperance Bay, Mystria

Prince Vlad's first impulse was to open his desk drawer, pull out the pistol he kept therein, and place a three-quarter-inch-diameter sphere of lead directly between Bishop Bumble's beetling brows. The Prince knew quite well—from ample studies conducted using rigorous Ryngian methodology—precisely the sort of damage the ball would do. Slightly flattened as it passed through the forehead, it would reduce the man's brains to the consistency of a pudding, and spray them all over the lawn as the shot exited.

He would have been justified; the man had not so subtly threatened his life. Given those present and their general feelings about Bishop Bumble, were any questions asked, doubtless witnesses would all agree that a Ryngian assassin had managed to kill the Bishop, then escape while the others stood there in a state of shock. Repercussions, were there any, would be minor at best.

And Vlad might have killed him save for two things. First and foremost, he was not a murderer. Though Bishop Bumble might invite killing, though he might deserve it and the world might be a better place without him, it was not Vlad's place to kill him. He would not even do what another noble might, and order the killing done, or hint to someone that it should be done. With Owen, Nathaniel, or the Count, he'd really not even need to hint. With the least bit of provocation they'd tie a rock to Bumble's feet, toss him in the river, and claim that they had all told him that swimming after eating was ill advised.

Second, and more importantly, killing the man would not end the threat he posed. Bumble's remark about Nathaniel contained information that only Zachariah Ward could have supplied. For whatever reason, Ward had confided in Bumble—and the Prince shuddered at the idea that the Bishop might use information he gained while in the confessional to coerce others. Vlad had to assume that Bumble kept notes. Were he to die suddenly and suspiciously, others might find a use for his notes.

So Vlad did the only thing he could do. He sat heavily at his desk and refused to meet Bumble's dark-eyed gaze. "I see."

"I thought you might, Highness." The man ventured another pace into the library, the Prince's evident weakness emboldening him. "I know that there are people who, when they think of what you do here, consider it as just 'being the Prince's way, is all, no harm meant or done.' I, however, must worry about the souls of the people within my diocese. To be frank, Highness, you set a poor example for our people. When I hold services, your pew is empty save for high holy days or when one of your children has been baptized. While I know you are a learned man, and that you regularly correspond with your sainted father, your neglect of your faith promotes contempt in the general audience.

"No, I am not finished, Highness. You may not recall how you treated me on the Anvil Lake campaign, but I remember it very clearly." Color worked its way up past the man's stiff collar. "I offered to hold services, but you would not give the men time to attend. You made no attempt to curtail their profanity, and the riotous merry-making in Hattersburg upon their return is unmatched in the annals of debauchery. There are men who regularly attended services before they went to war under your command who have not set foot in the Cathedral since. I am mocked in tavern songs, and if I am mentioned in stories about the war, it is only as a jester."

Vlad forced himself to shrink under Bumble's furious recitation. That the man was stung and hurt could not be denied, but those indignities were years old. Men of accomplishment would have long since forgotten such things, or would have found a way to turn such things to their advantage. Bumble easily could have paralleled his treatment at the hands of the Mystrian militiamen to the treatment the Good Lord got from his tormentors, and turned that into a lesson on the blessedness of humility.

The Prince kept his voice small. "Bishop Bumble, I had no idea."

"Do *not* lie to me." Bumble's eyes tightened as he shook a finger in

Vlad's direction. "You may not have paid much attention, wrapped up here in worldly and diabolical things, but you are too smart a man to have missed what has happened. And you are smart enough now to see that what I am doing here is for your own good because no matter what you have done to me, no matter the trials you have put me through, I am committed to saving your immortal soul. You are in danger of being lost to God's Adversary. By protecting Fox you show your allegiance. You may not even realize this is what you are doing, so gentle and soft is the Ryngian seduction but, God as my witness, it *is*. You need to mend your ways, sir, and do so publicly, so others will benefit from your example. If you do any less, my hands may be tied in regard to your future."

"Yes, yes, of course." Vlad forced himself to close the journal on his desk. He turned in his chair toward Bumble, but did not raise his eyes. He had to appear completely cowed. A tyrant such as Bumble would discipline him and, if the Prince complied with the punishment, Bumble would accept that rebellion had been quashed. This would buy Vlad time both to figure out how to deal with Bumble and to learn how far and wide Bumble's influence actually extended. Vlad usually did his best to remain above political considerations, but now saw this as a failure because it left him vulnerable to someone like Bumble.

The Prince hid his face behind his hands, then sighed, wearily. "What is it you would have me do?"

"It is not what *I* would have you do, Highness, but what God *demands* you do." Bumble sniffed piously. "You will begin by attending services with your family on a weekly basis. You will begin Sunday next. You'll command Captain Strake to attend as well, and his wife and child. Catherine sees Ian Rathfield to the Cathedral each week, but will not come inside."

"Count von Metternin as well?"

"He is most welcome." Bumble's eyes hardened. "You will dine with my family and me, and invite us to dine when you are in town. This will go a long way to rehabilitating me in the eyes of the Anvil Lake veterans. And you will endow a lecture series to be delivered, by me, at Temperance College. You will attend. It will be good for your soul."

Vlad nodded.

"And you will, it goes without saying, sanction the sentence which comes down from the Court Ecclesiastic in the matter of heresy. You will declare Fire and any who follow him an outlaw. They will answer to me."

The Prince looked up. "There's the matter of the girl."

"She appears to be thriving in the Strake household. As long as the Strakes show their commitment to the Church, I see no reason to worry about the child."

"Yes, of course. I shall speak to Owen immediately."

"Splendid." Bumble looked back out toward the lawn. "I shall tell him you wish to speak with him."

"Please do."

Bumble turned halfway toward the door, then chuckled. "You surprised me, Highness."

"Yes?"

"Indeed. I had mistakenly believed you had a spine."

Owen watched Bumble struggle to keep up with the Prince. Squatting, he set his daughter down. "Shall we go see your mother?"

Miranda nodded solemnly, then took Owen's hand. "Come, Papa."

He looked back at Nathaniel. "Leave my stuff, I'll get it later."

Nathaniel straightened up from his own pack. "Reckoned you could give Colonel Rathfield his black wolf pelt. I'll leave the other for the Prince. I can drop your things at your dock. Wanted to head down Temperance."

Owen caught the bound pelt with his free hand. "Have Mrs. Lighter open our apartment for you."

"Obliged. Tell the Prince to save up his questions iffen your journals don't answer them."

"Papa!" Miranda tugged on his hand.

Nathaniel nodded. "Go on. You been away too long. I will see you in town."

"Godspeed." Owen tossed Nathaniel a quick salute, then headed up the lawn with his daughter. Her hand felt so tiny in his, and so soft. There hadn't been a day he'd not thought of her, but she had taken on the quality of a dream, especially since Piety. But here, with such a big smile and those giggles, Owen felt ready to burst with happiness.

"Momma, it's Papa! Uncle Ian, Becca, it's my papa!"

Owen tossed the wolf pelt to Rathfield. "Don't get up, Colonel. We've got this pelt for you. The others are with the Altashee. They'll do them up nice."

"Nicely, Owen, it's nicely." Catherine rose from her chair. "The more time you spend in the wilds, you forget everything of civilization."

Owen plucked off his hat and bowed politely. "Highness, Catherine."

Gisella smiled up from her chair. "I am so pleased to see you healthy and whole."

"And I'm pleased to be that way." Owen settled his hat on his daughter's head. It fell to cover her face, and she laughed.

Catherine whisked it off her. "Owen, it's filthy. Who knows what sort of vermin…"

"The same sort that would be on me, I would guess." He held his arms open, inviting his wife into an embrace.

She stepped toward him, but came at angle and kissed somewhere in the vicinity of his cheek. "I am very glad you are home, Captain Strake."

"As am I, Strake." Rathfield had struggled to his feet and leaned on a stout cane. "I must thank you for the lend of your wife. She has taken very good care of me. Nursed me back to health, in fact. I shall be sorry to quit your home, it has been so inviting, but I've made inquiries about finding a place in Temperance."

Catherine looked at him. "You shall do no such thing, Ian. You were our guest before you left. Owen's return is no reason for you to leave."

"I appreciate what you are saying, Mrs. Strake but…"

Owen rested a hand on Ian's shoulder. "Colonel, I don't know how much you remember about Happy Valley, but there's one image I'll never forget. We were all done for, then you joined the fight. You saved us. I won't reward such courage by turning you out of my home."

Rathfield regarded Owen oddly, then nodded. "Thank you, Captain Strake. In that case, I shall not refuse your hospitality, at least, for a little while longer."

Bishop Bumble appeared at Owen's right hand. "Captain Strake, the Prince would appreciate a word. Oh, my, Colonel, is that a wolf pelt?"

Feeling vaguely uneasy, Owen excused himself and made for the Prince's laboratory. He wasn't certain why he felt out of sorts, but having Rathfield and Bumble flanking him would have been enough to perturb anyone. He entered the laboratory. "You wished to see me, Highness?"

"Yes, please, Owen. Shut the door, if you don't mind."

Owen complied with the request. "Are you well, Highness?"

Vlad sighed, more with resignation than weariness and just a hint of frustration. "I shall put it to you directly. Bishop Bumble ordered me to order you to attend services every Sunday from this week hence."

"*Ordered* you, Highness?"

"That's not all. Owen, I trust you implicitly, but I have a very difficult task to request of you."

"Anything, Highness."

"Don't say that until you hear me out." The Prince hunched forward on his chair. "While you have been away, I have learned some things which some people would find disturbing. I need your help to determine if there is a cause for concern. If you do choose to participate, however, you cannot say anything to your wife. She must remain completely ignorant, for her sake and the sake of your daughter. If Bumble gets wind of what we are doing, he will go after us as he is going after the Steward. The only way your wife and daughter will survive is if they can deny everything. So, there is the question: Can you lie to your wife? Can you keep a secret from her?"

Owen exhaled slowly. "If it were not important, you would not ask. You said you trust me, Highness. I trust you. If this is part of the duty you demand from me, no one will have word from me of anything."

"It could destroy your marriage."

"Will what you ask save Mystria?"

Vlad nodded solemnly. "I believe it may be the only way to save Mystria. From Branch, from Bumble, perhaps from the Crown itself."

"I can keep a secret from her." *For Mystria, for Miranda's future.* He smiled. "To save Mystria, I'll even stay awake during Bumble's sermons."

Vlad stood and clapped him on both shoulders. "I hate putting this burden upon you, Owen. I truly do. The situation is simple: Bumble wants the Steward dead because the Steward has uncovered knowledge about magick which the Church wants to remain a secret. Magick, right now, is limited by the spells we are taught by instructors sanctioned by the Church. We are led to believe these are the only spells, and they're of marginal importance, relatively speaking. But you've seen that the

Shedashee have a different approach to magick."

Owen nodded. "And the Norghaest, they might have yet another approach. I will explain, Highness, but suffice it to say, for now, that Rufus Branch may have been using their magick. Heck, he might even be one."

"Ah, so this becomes even more delicate." Vlad shook his head. "Bumble wants the Steward dead to put an end to the possibility of his revealing the secret. The problem is, I believe I have learned it. This makes me as much of a danger in the eyes of the Church as Ezekiel Fire."

Owen nodded. "Bumble doesn't know that yet, so following his orders will lull him into a false sense of security."

"Precisely. We need time to figure out how to use what Fire knows, and to figure out what happened at Happy Valley."

Visions of blood and fire flooded back into Owen's mind. "I've learned some things which I can share in that regard, Highness. The most important of them is this: if we are going to stop the Norghaest, we have very little time in which to do it."

CHAPTER THIRTY-SIX

Nathaniel wasn't sure if the Tanner and Hound's ale had gotten worse since he'd been gone, but it certainly hadn't gotten any better. Compared to *salksasi* he might as well have been drinking weak tea, but he'd never been given much to drinking to the point of drunkenness. While he could recall, dimly, some memories of fun times he'd had when a bit drunk, he couldn't really remember a time when any *good* had come from drinking too much.

Even so, he raised his mug to Caleb Frost. "You are a most kind gentleman, Caleb, offering to slake my thirst."

Caleb drank, then set his own mug down. "Not wholly altruistic, Nathaniel. I was hoping I could get some comments from you for the *Gazette*."

"Ain't really sure there's much I can contribute."

"I understand there might be confidences involved. I won't have you break your word, but there are some things you might be able to say." Caleb pulled a small journal and a pencil from his coat pocket. "You were there when Bishop Bumble risked life and limb to arrest the heretic Ephraim Fox."

Only through a mighty effort did Nathaniel refrain from spewing ale all over Caleb. He swallowed hard, then wiped his mouth with the back of his hand. "I was there, but I don't remember no risk save maybe the Bishop getting perilously close to water. If he'd gone in, he'd have sunk like a stone." *And I'd have gladly held him under.*

A low growl issued from Caleb's throat. "The Bishop made some comments when he welcomed Bishop Harder from Bounty and Southfield from Blackwood. They praised him for his courage. Bumble described Fox as a notorious and dangerous man responsible for the deaths of hundreds, and a man guilty of sedition, treason, and heresy. While the Court Ecclesiastic can only address the heresy charge, the other charges are going to weigh on the minds of the Tribunal."

"Who all is they having prosecute the Steward?"

"Bumble will head the tribunal, so Benjamin Beecher will prosecute."

Nathaniel raised an eyebrow. "Even with a friendly court, I wouldn't be thinking Beecher's the man for that job."

"He's changed since he went with us to Fort Cuivre, Nathaniel. It may have been slow coming, and isn't much of a change, but he's harder than you'd expect."

Nathaniel shrugged. Not being a churchgoer, if he'd seen Beecher more than once a year in the last three he'd have been surprised. Those meetings were by accident and over very fast. "Anyone going to defend Fire?"

Caleb shrugged. "No one has stepped forward. Bumble got permission to use the old Regimental armory building for a jail. I went over to talk to Fire, but without Bumble's permission, I was not allowed in. No one doubts he'll be convicted, so I don't think anyone wants to risk earning the Bishop's ire by interfering. You could do it, though."

"Well, I reckon you know 'xactly how lettered I is, Caleb. I'd just make it worse for the Steward." Nathaniel traced a finger through the wet circle his tankard had left on the table. "Pity, too, because the Steward, he ain't a bad sort. I look outside, I see Thursday. The Steward, he sees Wednesday or Friday, maybe both all mixed up, but he ain't a bad man. When Bumble arrested him, he could have run off and the Bishop never would have caught him. He didn't. I think he believes God will see him through this."

"You traveled with him. You truly think he's a good man?"

The scout thought for a moment. "He stopped me from shooting Rufus Branch dead, which I could let be judged either way. I guess the man always was looking to help folks and promote peace. And the folks what died at Piety, he done took that on as a burden himself. Now, he was happy they was in Heaven, but sad that they died; and he done saved Colonel Rathfield's life."

"How did the Colonel get injured?"

Nathaniel held his hands up. "I don't reckon I can say nothing about that."

Caleb leaned forward. "Here's the problem. Six weeks ago he arrives home. No one is saying how. We know he didn't walk with that leg. So people are asking questions. When they don't have answers, they make things up."

"I see what you're saying." Nathaniel nodded, then sat back and raised his voice a bit. "Colonel Rathfield? I can tell you this: there was a night out there when there was just five of us trapped in a little draw thick with dire wolves. Packs might run to ten or a dozen, this was three of them, maybe four, all come together. Well Makepeace and me, Captain Strake and Kamiskwa, we all done kilt our share in the past, so we knows what we's facing. And it was a hard fight. We was close to being overwhelmed when Colonel Rathfield he just ups and leaps on in. You ain't never seen a man fight like that. He musta thought they was Ryngian Laureates, the way he went after them. When all was said and done, we skinned so many that we couldn't carry all the hides; and the bulk of them belong to the Colonel."

Caleb dutifully scribbled notes during the recitation. Others in the tavern took in the story while pretending they weren't listening. By mid-afternoon it would be circulating through Temperance and after the *Gazette*'s next issue came out, the story would explain away everything. The heroism of the exploit would smother any questions about how the Colonel got home so quickly.

That was one thing Nathaniel didn't like about cityfolk—their willingness to dismiss important questions when something else more romantic and less confusing presented itself. The Anvil Lake campaign had pitted Mystrian and Norillian forces against a Ryngian contingent made up of *pasmortes*. The fact that they had fought against the living dead had been discounted and forgotten because the greater story was that the Mystrians had won the battle, redeeming a reputation sullied by their previous performance in a campaign in Auropa. And here, the romance of men fighting against beasts that everyone feared and emerging victorious would stop people from questioning how Rathfield traveled over two hundred miles in a night.

Just because the pound sack the miller uses to sell them flour has bright colors, they ignore the fact that he's only giving them fifteen ounces to their pound. Of course, here he was helping Caleb manufacture a story that would pull the wool over their eyes. Granted, it would also cover the fact that Mugwump could fly. Nathaniel had never really been too keen on the dragon, but Mugwump had saved his life every bit as much as Rathfield had, so he felt an obligation to protect him.

Nathaniel leaned forward again. "I will tell you something you can say about Ezekiel Fire iffen you want to."

Caleb turned a page in his notebook. "Go ahead."

"He is pert near the sincerest man I done met, just this side of the Prince and a few others I won't name because they'd be embarrassed by the fuss. Now, funny thing is that for most folks, sincere seems crazy on account of they ain't sincere. Since they got things to hide, they believe everyone else does. And someone who don't is either lying or insane. Ezekiel Fire ain't neither, and that might be rare, but it ain't no reason to burn."

Caleb looked up. "You really want me to print that? With your name attached?"

"Cain't do no harm."

"Bishop Bumble will make you pay for that."

"Well, now, the day I set a lot of store by what he thinks of me is the day I will just walk east and won't look back 'til I'm drying myself off on the Ryngian shore. And if he's thinking about what he can do to me, he's an even bigger fool than I'd have imagined."

"I agree, it's just…" Caleb frowned. "You've always spoken your mind, Nathaniel, but just not so openly. Three-four years ago you'd have spit in disgust and walked west to get shy of this sort of politics."

Nathaniel scratched at his throat. "Tain't I like politics any more than I did. I reckon that if everyone is so a-feared of Bishop Bumble that a man will burn without comment being passed, someone needs to point out it ain't right. Mayhap be that there ain't no winning here, but that don't mean Bumble shouldn't be made to earn his victory."

The younger man nodded. "That's a very good point, and one that extends beyond just Bishop Bumble. Have you heard about the Control Acts?"

Nathaniel shook his head and slid his chair back. "Can't say as I have, cain't say as I want to."

"But they're coming, Nathaniel, and there will be a fight."

"I don't doubt it, but I have learned one thing in my years." Nathaniel stood. "If the enemy is outside rifle shot range, ain't a lot of winning going to be going on. Until then, it's a lot of palaver and I do have better ways to spend my days. Thank you again for the ale. My best to your family."

Nathaniel left the tavern as dusk began to fall. He headed west along Justice, approaching Friendship. The stone silhouette of St. Martin's Cathedral loomed at the corner. Another man might have found it ironic that Fire's trial would be held at that intersection. For Nathaniel it was just another reason living outside the city made sense.

He continued north on Friendship, following it as it curved toward the bay. Just before Faith, he entered a row of houses. A small, apple-cheeked woman who he'd known since before his mother had died, smiled. "I showed your visitor to your parlor, Nathaniel."

"Kind of you, Mrs. Lighter." Nathaniel mounted the stairs and entered the two-room apartment at the top right. The foyer opened into the parlor, and the doorway beyond it into the bedroom, which fronted on Friendship. Since Catherine Strake had decorated the place, it had frilly and lacy things here and there, and colorful jugs and paintings from Norisle on shelves or hung on the walls. Nathaniel couldn't recognize much of Owen in the place, but because he had company, he didn't look that hard.

The woman who turned, smiling, to face him, had brown hair that descended just past her shoulders. Her smile carried up to her hazel eyes. Slender and a head shorter than he, she wore a gray dress, with the white collar of her blouse covering the neckline. She reached out for him with her left hand, the gold band glinting. "I am sorry I could not get away last night, Nathaniel."

He took her hand and brought it to his mouth, kissing it. Then he pulled her into an embrace and lowered his mouth to hers. He kissed her, feeling her press herself hungrily against him. Her hair smelled faintly of rosemary and her kiss tasted so sweet that it banished memories of the ale. He held her tightly, drinking in her warmth and smiled at the little moan she uttered.

He pulled back. "I have been away too long, Rachel, but ain't never you been far from my thoughts."

She smiled and laid her head against his chest. "Nor you, mine. I so wanted to be here yesterday, but Charity had fever and I could not abandon her. Bethany agreed to watch them tonight."

Nathaniel kissed the top of her head. "Please be thanking her for me."

Rachel slipped from his arms, but caught his right hand in her left. "She still does not approve, but she is more… *understanding* these days. And though she would not say it, I've heard that one of her uncle's Captains saw my husband in the arms of another woman down in Fairlee. He spends more time down there now, and Bethany does not like his leaving me with children and the business to run."

"I don't reckon I'm in no position to pass judgment on your husband." Nathaniel fell silent. He'd have been happy to kill Zachariah Ward, and most folks would not be sad to see the man die. But he was a merchant, and a highly successful one, who would never challenge Nathaniel to any sort of a duel. For Nathaniel to challenge him would just be inviting the man to his own murder. Even though Ward had once hired Rufus Branch to kill him, Nathaniel wasn't going to be the instigator in the man's death.

"I don't wish to talk about him." Rachel smiled and tugged on his hand. "I wish to just be with you."

The scout stood his ground. "You said Charity had a fever?"

"Yes, she was the last to get it. Humble had it, but was over it quickly." She stepped back to him and took his other hand in hers. "He is every bit as healthy as his father, and very much as handsome."

Nathaniel nodded, then let her pull him toward the bedroom. She laughed, bumping against a chair in the parlor, then paused in the doorway and kissed him again. "I have been waiting for your return, dreaming of it."

"Me as well, but…"

"Yes?"

Nathaniel looked down. "Bit of wear and tear this time out. Tain't all healed."

"Then I shall have to be very careful." Rachel led him to the bed and made him sit. She went down to a knee to remove his moccasins, then straightened and worked his leather tunic off. She'd gotten the lower hem to the level of his nipples, then slowed down and moved more carefully.

She raised his arms and drew the tunic up by the sleeves, casting it aside on a chair.

"What happened, Nathaniel? You're all bandages and scratches and bites."

"Nothing good, I can tell you." He reached out and pulled her to him, curling his legs around hers. He reached up and began to unbutton her dress. "I'm thinking, however, if you would be so kind, you're the tonic that will heal my wounds, and make me forget how they got there in the first place."

CHAPTER THIRTY-SEVEN

29 June 1767
St. Martin's Cathedral
Temperance Bay, Mystria

As Ian Rathfield sat in the front pew, he was forced to marvel over the efficiency with which the Cathedral had been transformed from House of Worship to House of Justice. The altar had been moved to the side and a high bench had been erected in its place beneath the vaulted ceiling, with room for each judge. Though the finish matched that of the light wood used in the Cathedral's construction, the bench's height and sharpness of line robbed the building of any compassion.

The coat of arms of each diocese hung before the judges, with Bishop Bumble in the middle. Bishop Harder, a large, swarthy man with black curls of hair growing from his ears and bushy eyebrows covering half his forehead, sat on Bumble's right. Blackwood's Bishop Southfield, a small, balding man with a gargantuan red nose, sat on his left. Each man wore a black robe and a black skull cap.

To the left sat the prosecution table. Benjamin Beecher sat at it and shuffled through papers. He wore black pants, white socks to the knee, black shoes, and a black smock-coat. Even given Beecher's slight of build, with thinning black hair, Ian found he could not dismiss the man out of hand. Not only did this come from his earlier encounters with the man, in which he found something disturbingly serpentine about his manner, but because of the way he sorted through documents. The man placed them in distinct piles, squaring them up with themselves and the edge of the table. He did so with the concentration Ian had seen on the faces of men preparing to shoot other men at point-blank range.

Opposite him, another table had been arranged in front of the steps leading up to the apse. Steward Fire sat at it, wearing well-worn grey

258

clothes. He'd been clapped in irons, to restrain him and limit his use of magick. Fire's captors had even gone to the uncommon length of placing him in iron gauntlets. They also fixed a slotted mask to his lower face, presumably so iron could mute magick in his words. Had Ian been so bound, he would have felt as if he was a dog, but Fire bore up as best as could be expected. This, even though the short chains from collar to gauntlets and down to shackles kept him hunched forward.

Bishop Bumble stood. "Your Honors, Mr. Beecher, brothers and sisters in the Lord: we gather here to assess the guilt or innocence of Ephraim Fox. He stands accused of heresy. He did knowingly and willfully, counter to the orders from his Church superiors, lead others into his heresy. He took them beyond the bounds of fellowship in the Church and established them without authority in lands beyond the mountains. His actions did, directly, lead to their worshipping idols, participating in blood rituals, and taking part in ritual human sacrifice. He is a known consorter with demons and a practitioner of Dark Arts."

Bishop Bumble had just begun to warm up, when a voice from one of the pews interrupted him. "I beg your pardon, Bishop Bumble, but I must ask: Are you prosecuting Ephraim Fox, or standing in judgment over him?"

Bumble's jowls quivered with unvoiced rage. "I preside here, Mr. Frost."

The speaker, a tow-headed young man, moved to the aisle and came forward. "I thought I would ask because you seem to be testifying against him."

"I fail to see how this is a concern of yours, Caleb."

"I am a parishioner, as you well know. I've listened to your many sermons on Faith and Justice. I've studied them. I have my degree in Divinity from Temperance College." Caleb Frost stood next to Steward Fire. "In the interest of propriety, I thought I would stand for the accused, so none may suggest, Your Honor, that haste denied Justice."

"Very well, Mr. Frost." Bumble seated himself. "Mr. Beecher, you will proceed."

Beecher stood. "We would call our first witness. Colonel Ian Rathfield."

Rathfield stood and raised his right hand.

"Colonel, do you swear to tell the entirety of the truth, and only but the truth, so help you God?"

"I do."

Beecher moved piles around so one was centered before him. "Colonel Rathfield, when you found Ephraim Fox in Happy Valley, did you see evidence that his settlement there practiced plural marriage, in defiance of the Church's 1567 prohibition against same?"

"I had no opportunity to make that determination."

Beecher looked up. "Is it not true you saw evidence of men living in homes with more than one adult woman?"

"I did not enter any such homes, nor did I speak with any of the people, so I do not know what their living circumstances were."

Bumble pounded a fist on the bench. "Need I remind the witness that he has sworn to tell the truth?"

Ian met Bumble's angry stare openly. "I have taken an oath before God to do so. I can tell you only what I know to be fact and still abide by that oath."

Beecher flipped one sheet over, and then back. "Very commendable, Colonel. Did you ever hear the Steward deny that plural marriage was practiced in Happy Valley?"

"No."

"And did the living arrangements strike you as unusual in Happy Valley?"

Ian hesitated. "There are many things in the west, Mr. Beecher, in all of Mystria, which seem unusual to me."

"You need to answer my question. Did the living arrangements there, or in Piety, seem unusual to you? A simple yes or no."

"Yes."

"Very good." Beecher shifted to another pile. "Did you find the Steward employing Rufus Branch as a trusted aide?"

"Yes."

"Did the Steward prevent him from being brought to justice for crimes he had committed in the Colonies?"

"Yes."

Caleb rose from the pew behind the Steward. "I object."

Bumble's head came up. "On what grounds?"

"Ephraim Fox's association with Rufus Branch might have broken a law, but there are no church prohibitions against such an association. The

Good Lord lived among thieves and fallen women, and prison chaplains actively work to redeem same. This line of questioning is immaterial."

Bumble's nostril's flared. "Mr. Beecher."

"Yes, your Grace." The slender man nodded solemnly. "Did you, Colonel, see Mr. Branch working to translate golden tablets which the defendant said they had taken from a ruin in the mountains?"

"Yes."

"Did he describe these tablets as having been written by God in His own hand?"

"Yes, he did." Ian's eyes narrowed and he glanced at Fire. Ian had never mentioned that detail to Beecher or Bumble, and he was certain neither Woods nor Strake would admit it. *Fire must have told that to them, but why?* Then he looked more closely at the man, the way he hunched down. *He's been beaten. He is protecting ribs. I wonder if the gauntlets hide more wounds?*

"Colonel?"

Ian's head came around. "Please repeat the question."

"In Piety, did you see Ephraim Fox offer an invocation to his Satanic master, then burn the Church."

"What? No."

"He did not burn the Church?"

"Yes, yes, of course he did. The entire congregation was in there. It was the only thing to do."

Beecher nodded, his finger trailing down lines on a sheet. "So you just did not hear the invocation to diabolic forces?"

"I wasn't near enough to hear what he said. None of us were."

Beecher smiled easily, his brown eyes narrowed. "No one but Ephraim Fox and the people who had sacrificed themselves under his influence. Colonel, you were present when he used magick to kill Becca Green's mother?"

"He tried to save her."

"Are you sure, Colonel? He used magick on the girl, didn't he? But did nothing for the woman?"

"He used magick to save me."

Beecher's head came up. "To heal you from a head wound, of which you have no memory receiving, and of which there is no mark on your head, isn't that right?"

Ian frowned. "What are you suggesting?"

"Not that you are not a hero, Colonel. We all know you are." Beecher smiled toward the defense table. "The *Frost Weekly Gazette* made that very clear in its last issue. No, sir, it is the contention of this court that Ephraim Fox knew you were incorruptible, therefore he used magicks, proscribed magicks learned from the same Satanic source which produced the tablets, to alter your memory so it could contain no memory that would convict him of heresy. Moreover, we contend that he did this with each of your companions, in turn, as opportunity allowed while they brought him here."

Caleb stood again. "I object."

Bishop Harder leaned forward. "On what grounds?"

"On the grounds that the Colonel is being asked to speculate about events of which he has no memory. On the grounds that Mr. Beecher contends that the Colonel's lack of memories *proves* that Ephraim Fox used magick to steal those memories. In short, lack of evidence becomes proof that a crime was committed. By that logic, one could conclude that because the Tribunal is not wreathed in flames and reeking of sulphur that you all have been raised to the bench directly from Hell."

Beecher slowly clapped his hands. "You would be correct, Caleb, save for one thing." He raised a thick sheaf of documents bound with twine. "We have a witness to all of this. Ephraim Fox himself has confessed to doing it all, and Colonel Rathfield has just revealed how insidiously thorough he truly was."

Ian reached his apartment by midday and drew all of the blinds. Though he had desired to stay at Strake House just to be close to Catherine, he could not tolerate knowing that she and Owen shared a bed just down the hall from his rooms. He had to get away, so he'd found furnished rooms in Temperance and hid himself away there.

The rooms were not much, and he could have afforded better, but he settled for two small rooms, shabbily painted and floored with dark wood. Most people would have found the rooms quite spare, despite their being furnished with a table, two chairs, a wardrobe, and a bed. For a man used to living in a tent on campaign, the rooms seemed a bit full.

On his trip from the Cathedral he ventured all the way to the docks and procured a bottle of whiskey from a tavern chosen at whim. He carried it home inside his coat, then set it on the parlor table. He sat across from it in the near dark, aching to drink himself into oblivion and yet not daring to risk the consequences.

He had never imagined the trial to be anything less than a sham. From the very first, when Bumble had charged him with the added duty of finding a pretext through which the Steward could be dragged back and put on trial, he understood the danger Fire presented. The man's preaching could lead people astray, and as a man who knew well his own sins, Ian recognized the threat to their souls. He had not thought far enough ahead to imagine that Fire might be killed, but he did realize that separating the man from those he might influence was important.

But the trial was not being conducted to convict Ephraim Fox. Bumble had extracted a confession from him, so conviction was a formality. The trial was about Bumble being able to display himself as a leader protecting the people. He'd had Ian there merely to show that even an officer of the Queen's Army had to answer to him. Had Caleb Frost not offered himself as a focus for Bumble's ire, Ian's reticence to openly condemn the Steward would have had terrible repercussions.

Though he had tried to do the honorable thing, Ian felt soiled. His leg throbbed, and it was from more than just having stood to give his testimony. Bumble had turned Ian's mission to his own advantage, sullying a duty which Ian had performed to the best of his ability. The trial mocked him, and though Bumble had backed away from extorting his cooperation this time, Ian had no doubt that Bumble would use him ruthlessly in the future.

He reached for the bottle, thinking to uncork it and let the amber liquid burn down his throat. It had been nearly two years since he'd drunk any hard liquor—not since the night his wife took her own life. In that time he'd only ever drunk wine, and only if it was diluted with water. But he wanted the whiskey for its ability to steal memories—of the trial. *Of more.*

Someone knocked at the door.

Ian almost ignored it, but his visitor rapped again. He forced himself up and limped to the door. He hesitated, his hand hovering over the knob, then he opened it. *Only one person knows I'm here.*

"Thank God, Ian!" Catherine Strake pushed passed him, then turned and embraced him. "I was there. I saw."

Ian pushed the door closed, but could not escape her grasp. He knew she shouldn't be there, and he knew he should set her back at arm's length, but he felt hollow. He felt as if he would collapse, save for her holding on to him. So he slipped his arms around her.

"I wish you had not seen."

"Why?" She took his face in her hands, her brown eyes brimming with tears. "You were magnificent, Ian. You were more a hero in there than you were killing dire wolves or at Rondeville. You stood up to that tyrant, Bumble. I have never seen a man so brave."

Then she stood on tiptoe and kissed him full on the mouth. Her hands slipped into his hair, pulling him down to her, and he crushed her to him. He held on tightly, kissing her hotly, fiercely. She moaned into his mouth and ground her body against him. He felt himself begin to respond, and then they drew apart only enough for four hands to make quick work of buttons and bows, belts and garters. He lifted her in his arms and carried her to the room's small bed, laying her down there on a quilted coverlet.

She drew him to her, shaking her head to loosen her hair. With nibbles and playful licks, quick caresses, and the long slide of her legs against his, she enflamed him. She rolled him onto his back and grasped him, sliding him into her. They moved together, their hips rising and falling, she a vision of loveliness, her breasts swaying with the fluid rhythm of his thrusts. Her eyes closed and back arched, her mouth falling open, her hands clawing at his shoulders. She cried out, sharply, her body shaking and then, with him still hard inside her, she lay forward on his chest and licked at his neck.

"Let me catch my breath, lover, and then…"

Ian thought, just for a moment, to push her away. *I should not have done this to Owen.* He even grasped her shoulders to do that, but she ducked her head and licked at one of his nipples, then kissed him. And as she brought her head up, he saw in her eyes the light he had once seen in his wife's. In that instant, though he knew himself damned, he also knew himself to be loved. To trade one for the other seemed a wise bargain, and one from which he could not depart.

He smiled. "Yes, lover, catch your breath, and then I need you to show me how much you love me."

Chapter Thirty-eight

29 June 1767
Temperance
Temperance Bay, Mystria

Miranda squeezed Owen's hand tightly as they reached the docks. She stopped moving forward. He looked down and saw fear flash over her face. Then the little girl's eyes began to well up with tears.

Owen snatched her up in his arms. "What is it, Miranda?"

"Mama says that if you don't want to go to Norisle, we shall go anyway." The girl looked at him, her eyes wide. "Don't you love me anymore, Papa?"

Owen's throat immediately thickened. He felt as if his belly had been slashed open and his guts had spilled out. He hugged his daughter tightly. "Miranda, I love you. I have never stopped loving you. I will always love you." He stroked her back as she sobbed, her tears wetting his neck. "Everything shall be fine, princess."

He didn't need to ask what had made her think he didn't love her. Not but an hour earlier Catherine had stormed from their apartment, shouting, "I don't think you've ever loved anyone but yourself, Owen Strake!" He wanted to go after her, but he couldn't leave Miranda alone. He'd looked back and had seen his daughter huddled in the doorway to the bedroom, crouching down so she'd not be noticed.

"Mama said you would go to Norisle, Papa. You said you won't."

Owen found a bench and sat, then placed his daughter beside him. "Miranda, before I went away, I told your mother we would go to Norisle, all three of us. When I got back, the Prince asked me to stay, just a while longer."

"Why?"

"Some of the things I saw while I was gone are scary."

The little girl thought, then nodded, dark ringlets bouncing. "Like wolves and jeopards."

"Exactly." Owen settled his arm around her. "If your papa goes off to Norisle now, many little boys and girls like you and Richard and Rowena could be hurt."

"Then why does Mama want you to go?"

"Do you remember how much you missed me when I was gone?"

Miranda spread her hands as far apart as possible. "More than a hug."

Owen kissed the top of her head. "Your mother misses Norisle more than a hug."

"Then Mama should go."

"But then she would miss you."

Miranda shook her head. "She told me I'm a big girl now. I am big enough to stay with the Princess while she takes care of Uncle Ian."

Owen tipped her head up so he could see her face. "You know your mama loves you."

"I know." Miranda looked down. "I don't want to go if you don't go."

"I don't want to be apart from you, either, Miranda." He gave her another kiss on the top of her head, and they sat there watching the ocean and the ships gently bobbing in the harbor. Owen found himself wishing that, indeed, his wife *was* onboard one, heading toward Norisle. He regretted it instantly, but her refusal to be sensible left him stuck. She made most vociferously plain her desire: that he should honor his pledge that they would go to Norisle as a family. Yet no matter how clearly he explained why he could not go, she came back to the point that he was a liar.

And I cannot argue with that. He had agreed with the Prince that he would keep a secret from her. Given her irrationality, the Prince was right in extracting that promise from him. And he might also have been right that forcing Owen to keep a secret would kill his marriage. It occurred to him that the last time he was truly happy in his marriage was when Catherine had come to Mystria, right before the Anvil Lake campaign. *When we conceived our beautiful daughter.*

"Miranda, do you like Mystria?"

"It's home, Papa. I love you and Mama and Uncle Ian and Agnes and Richard and Rowena and even Peregrine even though we can't get too close and he's stinky." She giggled as she counted on her fingers. "And the Prince and Princess and Becca but not Mugwump. He's stinky, too."

"You should like people even if they are stinky, Miranda."

She looked up, her hazel eyes bright. "I love That Bastard Woods."

"Miranda!"

"What?"

"We don't call people bastards. Where did you hear that?"

Miranda poked out her lower lip, then shrugged. "Mama called him that when you went away."

"Does she mention Kamiskwa?"

The girl nodded. "She calls him 'the heathen.'"

Owen looked her in the face. "Nathaniel and Kamiskwa are very good friends of mine. They have saved my life many times. You will call them Mr. Woods and Prince Kamiskwa. Do you understand."

"Mr. Woods and Prince Kasmirka."

"Kamiskwa."

The little girl screwed her face up with determination. "Kasmirkawa."

"One more time, Miranda…"

"Captain Strake, if I might be so bold."

Owen looked up. "Please, Miss Frost."

Bethany sat on the other side of Miranda. "Miranda, try it slowly. Ka-mis-ka-wa."

"Ka-mis-ka-wa." Miranda immediately looked at her father. "Is that right, Papa?"

"It is, very good." Owen gave the girl a squeeze. "Thank you, Miss Frost."

"My pleasure, Captain Strake." Bethany, clad in a modest dress of grey with a white collar visible from beneath, tucked an errant wisp of blonde hair under her grey bonnet. "I would have expected to find you at the Cathedral for the trial."

"I'd much rather spend time with Miranda."

"I can see why. Miranda, you are a very pretty little girl."

"Thank you, Miss." Miranda, all of a sudden, became very shy and buried her face against Owen's side.

"And why are you not at the trial, Miss Frost?"

"Caleb forbid me to go." Bethany shook her head. "Normally I should not obey, but I believe he has some deviltry in mind. My mother would wonder why I did not stop him."

Owen laughed. "Your brother doesn't seem to mind getting himself into trouble."

"The same can be said of you." Bethany glanced toward the ocean. "I set the type for the story my brother published about Colonel Rathfield. The battle with the dire wolves was quite harrowing."

"The *Gazette* story livened things up a bit." Owen stood and took Miranda's hand. "Come, let us walk, shall we?"

They began to stroll through Temperance, with Miranda between them, holding her father's hand. Owen thought back to a similar walk he had taken with Bethany, before he'd gone on his first expedition. The recollection brought a smile to his face.

She glanced sidelong at him. "The story might have been hyperbolic, but it sounded as if you got away without injury."

"Not entirely, but mostly." He shook his head, understanding the question implied by her comment. "We got gnawed more than bitten. I truly don't remember a single scar from the incident."

"But that reddish line beneath your ear, that's new."

"We ran into trouble in Happy Valley."

Miranda looked up. "Becca is from Happy Valley."

Bethany smiled. "Is she your friend?"

"Yes. She is almost grown up. I let her play with my dolls."

"That's very kind of you."

"You could play with them, too."

Miranda's offer broadened Bethany's smile and pasted a similar one across Owen's face. In an instant he could see the three of them walking along, not a man, his daughter and a friend, but as a family. For just a moment his heart sloughed off the melancholy of the fight with his wife.

"You are very kind, Miranda."

Owen gave his daughter's hand a squeeze. "Miss Frost, once the Prince is finished with them, I would appreciate your transcribing my journals of the last expedition. Whilst I was in the wilderness, I noted a number of things that I thought you might find interesting."

"It would be a great pleasure, Captain, and an honor." Bethany held her head up a bit. "I have always found your stories enjoyable."

"My Papa tells me stories, sometimes, when I go to bed." The little girl marched along happily. "Not scary ones. Well, except the one about wolves on the night I was born. But he rescued me and Mama."

"I should be scared of wolves unless I had someone brave like your father around."

"And yet, Bethany Frost, you never seem to attract a man, brave or otherwise."

Owen turned and found his wife not six feet behind them. "Catherine, there you are. We chanced across Miss Frost by the docks."

"Waiting for a ship full of sailors to come in, was she?" Catherine held her hand out. "Miranda, come here, this instant."

Miranda looked up at her father. "She has her angry voice."

"It was nothing you did, Miranda."

"No, Miranda, nothing you did at all." Owen's wife glared at Bethany. "You failed to steal him once, dear. I tolerated your editing his dreadfully boring prose before, but I am not of a mind to be so tolerant this time."

Bethany bowed her head. "Believe me, Mrs. Strake, when I tell you that the last thing I should wish to do in this world would be to cause you or your family any discomfort."

"Then perhaps you will just find yourself your own man, Miss Frost."

Owen reached out a hand. "Catherine, Bethany is a friend, an innocent friend."

"A *friend*. Interesting use of the word, *husband*. You might protest your innocence, but I already know you to be a liar, Owen Strake." She glanced hotly from Owen to Bethany and back, then snorted. "You have made it plain that you are not going to honor your word. At least now you have abandoned the pretense of hiding behind the Prince in this regard."

"Catherine..."

"No, Owen, I do not want to hear it. Miranda and I shall use the apartment this evening, then return home tomorrow morning. I should appreciate advanced word when you will be coming to Strake House so I can make proper arrangements." His wife spun on her heel and dragged Miranda around with her. "Come, Miranda, we are leaving."

Owen covered his face with a hand. He said nothing as Catherine stalked away. Shame burned through him, first at how his wife treated Bethany, and second at his relief when she departed. He sighed heavily, then looked toward Bethany. He found her hand extended hesitantly toward his shoulder. "Please, Bethany, forgive, forget that. She did not mean…"

Bethany's hand returned to her side. "Captain Strake, she meant every word of it—the words spoken and unspoken."

"She's angry."

"Apparently."

Owen glanced toward the sky. "I promised to go to Norisle. After the trip west, I can't."

Bethany regarded him with cool, blue eyes. "Captain Strake, if you believe that is all which prompted her words, you are far too kind and far too naive. For her, being in Mystria is being made to lay down in a bed of nettles. She has been here going on four and a half years. She has hated every second of it. Each year she has wanted to return, and each year she has been thwarted."

"I know." Owen shook his head. "But there is nothing I can do about it, Bethany. My home is here. My life is here. She may have left her heart in Norisle, but for me to go back would be to tear my heart out and leave it bleeding on these shores. She thinks she will die if she stays. I *know* I will die if I leave."

"Have you told her that?"

Owen half-laughed, throwing his arms open and letting them flap limply to his sides. "How could I? When could I? When she is angry, even acquiescing does not make her listen. And in those times she is calm, to address this would set her off. When I take her down to the river, where we can watch the water flow and moose grazing, all I see is beauty. What she sees are all the ways in which our home is not a Norillian estate."

He glanced down, pressing his hands together fingertip to fingertip. "Perhaps she is right. Perhaps I do have a mistress."

"Owen…"

"She thinks it's you, I know, and I am sorry her suspicions threaten your reputation." He shook his head. "What she doesn't understand is that Mystria is my mistress. Where she sees a primitive, uncivilized land, I see unspoiled majesty. As Catherine offers me less and less, Mystria offers more and more. When the Prince prepared the expedition west, and I agreed to go, he asked if I was doing it for my duty, or to get away from my wife. I guess now I know that I was doing it to spend time with my mistress."

As Owen shaped his emotions into words, he felt as if he was uncovering a treasure which had lain buried for eons. His father had been Mystrian, born of a family cast out of Norisle ages ago. A sailor, he met and married a Norillian noble's daughter. Owen had been born in Mystria, but when his father died at sea, he and his mother had moved back to Norisle, and she had been wedded to Lord Ventnor's youngest son, a wastrel. Owen had grown up thinking that all Norisle hated him for the land of his birth, and in returning he recaptured the life he had been meant to have.

While it was easy to see Catherine as part of Norisle, and recognize the wellspring from which her angry bitterness arose, he could not dismiss her. He had loved her and had exchanged vows with her. Though countless men ignored those vows, Owen would not count himself among them. If he could not be true to his word, then he could never be true to himself or anyone else. The price of being honorable might be pain, but worse would be the price of faithlessness.

Bethany nodded slowly. "You, Captain Strake, are not alone in your love of the land and its people. You should realize that there are people here, many people, who love you for who you are and what you have done. The story in the *Gazette* may have been about Colonel Rathfield, but there was not a man who heard it who did not wish he had been there standing shoulder to shoulder with you. That your wife does not seem to appreciate you is seen by many as a great tragedy. Though no one would ever say a word to you about it, they recognize it and believe you a better man than they for how you deal with it."

Owen nodded. "And probably not a few who think she should get the rough side of my hand."

"Those are the idiots who get supper cold and their beds colder." Bethany graced him with a simple smile. "I must be away, Captain. I apologize for the discomfort I caused. I assure you, I shall do my best never to put you in that situation again."

"Bethany..."

"No, Owen, I made a decision a long time ago, and I have let my resolve erode." She smiled as she backed away. "For the best of all concerned, I must again abide by my previous choice. To do otherwise, to see you in this situation again, would break my heart. I do not imagine it could ever be mended again."

CHAPTER THIRTY-NINE

2 July 1767
Government House, Temperance
Temperance Bay, Mystria

Prince Vlad's mouth soured as Ezekiel Fire shuffled and clanked his way along toward the throne. Two large men, each dressed in the somber black clothes favored by a Virtuan funeral cortege, marched behind him. Fire remained bound as he had been for trial, from mask to the gauntlets and shackles that hobbled him. To the collar had been added a stout chain which one of his keepers held.

Vlad glanced at the man standing beside him. "Yes, Caleb, they do treat him as if he is an animal."

"It is inhuman, Highness."

At trial Fire had been dressed well, but in custody he had been given dirty, ragged clothes and deprived of stockings and shoes. He'd clearly not bathed and given the redness of his eyes, had not been allowed to sleep much, either. Dirt blackened his toenails, proving at least that he still had them. Vlad suspected the same was not true of the fingernails, hidden within the steel gauntlets.

Prince Vlad looked past Fire to the men guarding him. "Remove his mask, remove the collar, unbind his hands."

The man holding the chain shook his head. "Bishop Bumble agreed to bring the prisoner to you, but said, under no circumstances, was he to be released."

"I am the Colonial Governor-General. This prisoner is being kept in a facility by my command. Those chains are government property. I will determine how they are used."

"Bishop Bumble said…"

"If Bishop Bumble wishes this man to remain restrained, he can waddle his way down here and tell me that himself." Vlad knew he'd overplayed his hand at that moment, but he was prepared to pay the price for it. Both men looked shocked. "Go, the both of you, and report to him exactly what I said. The prisoner shall remain in my custody until then."

The two guards exchanged glances.

Vlad thrust a finger toward where the Cathedral stood. "Go. You do not want me summoning troops to enforce my wishes."

The two men bowed and withdrew.

Vlad waved Caleb forward. "Remove the mask."

Caleb unbuckled it and slid it off, revealing Fire's badly bruised face. The knot on one side of his jaw suggested it had been broken. The area around his mouth appeared somewhat clean, as if someone had wiped away blood from his swollen and clearly broken nose.

The Prince approached. "Can you open your mouth?"

Fire nodded and, wincing, complied.

Fewer teeth than I remember. Vlad shook his head and stepped back. "Steward Fire, I am very sorry you have been mightily abused. Bishop Bumble will be made to answer for his treatment of you."

Fire glanced down and shook his head. His teeth remained clenched. "No, Highness."

"I don't think you understand the gravity of the situation, Steward. Later today Bishop Bumble and his confederates will pass judgment upon you. You will be found guilty. They will sentence you to be burned at the stake. They need to have me agree to this. I am given little choice in the matter because, as Mr. Frost tells me, you have resisted every effort at mustering a defense. If you had any mitigating circumstances, anything I could use to put pressure on Bumble, I could ask him to commute your sentence to life. You'd be sent to Fairlee, to the prison at Iron Mountain."

"I thank you and Mr. Frost, Highness." Fire's words came slowly, and his breath shallow, as if breathing pained him. "God has showed me what I must do."

"Caleb, for your own good, you might wish to retire to my office. What gets discussed from this point forward might leave you open to charges of heresy yourself."

Caleb laughed. "What makes you think, since I decided to defend Steward Fire, that I'm not already facing that charge?"

"Fair point." Vlad clasped his hands behind his back. "Steward, I need you to understand that *I* understand. I've read your work. I have studied the King Robert version of the Good Book, and I have seen what you have seen. I have, furthermore, used what you saw and have determined that you are right. I know, therefore, why Bishop Bumble wishes you to be silenced. And I know why Mystria cannot afford to have that happen."

Fire stared at him, then staggered a step forward and fell to his knees. He tried to raise his hands to cover his face, but the chains prohibited him. Tears ran down the man's cheeks. "You understand? You know?"

Vlad nodded.

"Then I'm not mad?"

"No."

Fire hunched forward, sobbing.

The Prince dropped to a knee before him, resting his hands on the man's shoulders. "I can imagine you thought you were. You saw things no one else did. When you spoke to your peers, they couldn't or wouldn't see. When you spoke to your superiors, they were surprised, then told you that you were seeing things. Men like Bumble did things to unsettle you, to undercut your confidence, to make you question yourself and your sanity. But you knew you were right, and knew that to deny what you had seen was to work against God. So you headed west with a select band of followers, to do God's bidding."

The crying man nodded.

"What you failed to see is why I know you're an honest man. You failed to see that Bumble and the Church had to silence you. You were so pleased to be helping others, and you wrote to Bumble to show him a way to join you—not viciously to lord over him the error of his ways, but in fellowship so that he, too, could be saved. But that same motivation convinced Bumble that you could not be bought off or trusted to remain silent. This is why it was important to find you and bring you back for a trial, so that others would be frightened into silence."

Fire looked up, sniffing. "The Good Lord did not resist His prosecutors."

Vlad stood and, with Caleb, helped Fire to a chair by the wall. "I won't argue theology with you, Steward, save to suggest that whatever Bishop Bumble is doing, it's not found in Scripture."

"I know what God has asked me to do. He wants me to share His gifts."

Fire smiled weakly. "You have told me that I have succeeded."

"Not nearly enough. You cannot let Bumble destroy you."

"But you have already said he has not."

Vlad sighed and took a step back. Beaten and exhausted, likely starved and crushed by the destruction of his settlements, Fire couldn't muster enough rational thought to resist Bumble, much less aid Caleb in defending himself. *And it would make no difference if he did.* Even if Fire were able to present himself in a favorable light, the tribunal would still convict.

"Caleb, do you have a sense as to public sentiment in this matter?"

"Half again as many shun me as offer praise, and most of the latter are veterans who remember Bumble poorly. I don't get the sense that anyone believes they could be prosecuted next, so they believe what Bumble is doing will protect us."

Prince Vlad chewed his lower lip for a moment. "I'm not going to be given any choice but to sign off on the death warrant. I can buy time, but little more than that." He thought for a moment, then frowned. "Steward Fire, do you know of any enemies Bishop Bumble might have?"

The prisoner shook his head. "He has always seemed to me to be a well-loved man."

Another question had begun to form itself in Vlad's head, but the slamming open of the doors to his chamber prevented its completion. Bumble burst in, flanked by the two guards, and hurried his way along toward where the Prince stood. Bumble's face had taken on the purple of raging apoplexy.

"What is the meaning of this?"

"I wished to speak to Steward Fire."

Bumble's eyes became slits. "That is not what I refer to, Highness. How *dare* you have beaten the prisoner!"

Fire slumped in the chair and Caleb gasped. Vlad stared. "I beg your pardon?"

The fat cleric pointed a finger straight at the Prince. "My men are witnesses to the fact that the prisoner was not injured when they brought him here."

"You go too far, your Grace."

"Based on our previous discussion, Highness, I would have thought you know that your accusation is a lie." Bumble snapped his fingers. "Get the prisoner back to the armory."

The guards came forward and took custody of Fire. One grabbed the leash while the other buckled the steel muzzle back in place. The one holding the chain yanked it, and Fire staggered toward the door.

The Bishop's eyes never left Vlad's as he pointed at Caleb. "And you, Frost, be gone. And beware what you print in your *Gazette*. Heresy takes all forms, and will be stamped out in these Colonies. I can and will ruin you and your paper."

Caleb laughed. "I'd like to see you try."

"Would you, now?" Bumble's voice dropped into an icy register. "Were I to preach against it, were I to fund Mr. Wattling to reestablish his paper, and then contribute to it, I think you would find your readership greatly reduced. And if my people were to comb through your archives, I am certain there are things there which could be considered seditious, treasonous, or heretical. You are very free in your thinking, Frost, and contributors like Samuel Haste do not help you. So do not test me or tempt me."

Vlad held up a hand. "Thank you, Caleb, but I think you should leave now."

"Yes, Highness, as you wish." Caleb bowed to the Prince and, as he headed for the door, turned back just long enough to stick his tongue out at Bumble.

Vlad waited for the doors to close behind him. "Bishop Bumble…"

"I thought, Highness, I honestly thought, we had an understanding, you and I. I thought I made my wishes clear. I shall be forced to write a letter to the Archbishop in Launston all about your conduct. You give me no choice."

Vlad cocked his head. "I do not mean to sound impertinent or disrespectful, but are you truly that stupid?"

Bumble's pig-eyes widened.

Vlad opened his hands, but let his shoulders slump a bit. "You made it very clear to me that I was to sign off on Fire's being burned at the stake. Now, I ask you to consider Scripture. The Good Lord, once convicted by his own people, was brought before the Remian Provincial Governor, since only he had the authority to put a man to death."

Bumble shook his head slowly. "And you wish to cast yourself as Pilate, and me as one of the High Priests. Do you think I am a fool?"

"No, because that scenario would cast Fire as our Savior. You know that I cannot do that, both because of the pressure you bring on me *and* because Colonel Rathfield was sent from Launston to deal with Fire's having broken the law in establishing his settlements beyond chartered land. You have tried him for heresy. I called him here, clearly, to examine him on the matter of treason—a matter which you were not allowed to address at your trial."

Bumble snorted. "Mr. Frost made that very clear."

"And who do you think ordered Caleb Frost to raise that objection?"

The cleric folded his arms just over his ample belly. "You did?"

Vlad bowed his head. Though he was making things up as he went along, he felt safe. He already knew Bumble was steeped in the ways of conspiracy, and, therefore, would see conspiracy at the slightest provocation. Bumble's vanity also blinded him, so as long as the Prince made certain that he'd only acted because Bumble had him under his thumb, Bumble would believe everything the Prince said. To disbelieve was to allow that Prince Vlad might not be under his control, and his ego would not entertain that possibility.

"You gave me no choice. There are those among Mystrians—Samuel Haste being a prime example—who would criticize me for using civil authority to punish a man for a crime against the Church. By calling Fire here, by examining him myself in the matter of law, and by having his defender here to corroborate and publish my version of the events that transpired, no one will be able to take issue with Fire's fate. He would have been disrespectful and defiant, he would have been said to have cursed the Queen, and all would have thought it fortunate that we were not forced to spend money on a second trial, when one had been already held.

"I would also have you notice that Mr. Frost was willing to play his part—defying you even with no audience—because it bolsters the validity of his testimony about Fire in this regard."

Bumble tapped a finger against his chin, his dark eyes flicking back and forth. "You are saying this was theatre."

"It was politics played out as you demanded. Fire hates you, hates the Church, hates God; there are those who might support him at that. Having him hate the Queen, hate the law and hate me, there are some who would support him in that also. But few are those who will support him in all these things."

Vlad's heart pounded as Bumble silently considered all he'd said. The Prince knew he'd overplayed his hand when he commended Caleb for acting defiant without an audience, but Bumble had let that pass. Vlad just hoped the man had moved from seeing if everything made sense, to figuring out how he would use this new-found knowledge to his advantage.

Bumble's chin came up. "You should have informed me that this is what you were doing."

"I did not think you a good enough actor to manufacture outrage effectively."

"You would be surprised, Highness, as to what emotions I can call upon when needs require." The Bishop's eyes tightened. "This afternoon, we shall pass sentence. I shall want him burned tomorrow."

"Is that wise?"

"How do you mean?"

"If you announce the sentence this afternoon, with the execution to take place on Monday next, your declaration will be in time for the *Gazette*. Moreover, you will be able to preach a message from the pulpit on Sunday which will be heard by crowds swelling the town to watch the Steward burn. With that much advanced notice, you will have people in from Bounty and Lindenvale, or perhaps even down from Summerland and Queensland."

"Up from Richlan, too."

"Exactly." The Prince nodded. "You want to send a message to all heretics, and I need to send the same to anyone who would defy the Crown. Monday next gives us that opportunity."

Bumble slowly smiled, which tightened the Prince's guts. "Yes, very good, you are right. Monday will be perfectly acceptable.

And you will put me through Hell before then. Though he had no idea what Bumble planned, Vlad smiled. "Monday, then. It shall be perfect."

CHAPTER FORTY

Bishop Bumble climbed into the pulpit slowly, measuring his movements for their gravity. Prince Vlad had suggested that he could not have acted to display outrage when necessary. He still stung from having been blindsided by the Prince's ploy. Though the Prince had claimed he did not want to portray himself as Pilate, the Bishop knew that many would see him that way. For his temerity at having tried his little game, Prince Vlad would have to pay.

Bumble grasped the top of the podium and gave himself a moment. He nodded toward Benjamin Beecher, and then turned and nodded to the Prince and his family. He let his gaze wander over the congregation. Vlad had been right about one thing: the delay had packed the Cathedral. *Which is perfect for my performance.*

"Presiding over a heresy trial is a terrible thing, my friends. Reverend Beecher, Bishops Harder and Southfield have been a comfort. At the times when I might have shrunk from the enormity of the situation, they supported me. Their clear-headed counsel kept me focused on one point. The reason for the trial was in the hopes that the defendant would see the error of his ways, would recant his heresy, and again join in communion with the Church."

Bumble looked down, as if he needed a moment to let him get the better of his emotions. "I should like to thank Caleb Frost for accepting the challenge no one else would, of defending Ephraim Fox, even though Fox did not desire defense. Caleb's objections reminded us that we had a grave responsibility to present all the evidence so there could be no doubt as to Fox's involvement with heresy. It was hoped that Fox himself would realize how firmly he was caught, and this realization would be the catalyst for his repentance. Despite Caleb's spirited defense, it was not.

"Even though the case against Ephraim Fox was so overwhelmingly strong, I hoped we would not be forced to pass down the sentence that we did. It is not an easy thing to condemn a man to death. To me, to my fellow judges, that sentence would not only rob him of his *life*, it would rob him of *eternity*. For if he died unrepentant, his soul would forever be consigned to the burning pits of Perdition. While we, my friends, will enjoy Paradise, he will only know unending torment."

The Bishop passed a hand over his forehead. "Even before we passed sentence, I went and spoke with Prince Vladimir on this point. Only he could grant the punishment of death. He had just finished examining Ephraim Fox himself, and what I saw on the Prince's face made my heart shrink. For even though I wished forgiveness for a man who denied and defied God, I saw the Prince was not disposed to grant leniency for crimes committed against the Crown. Though I expressed a wish that he use his power to commute the sentence to life imprisonment at Iron Mountain so that Ephraim Fox would have a chance to reconsider and be saved, the Prince was adamant that insults against the Crown could not go unpunished. And while he could have conducted his own trial, and ordered Fox's execution on criminal grounds, he felt it just as well to save time and allow our sentence to stand."

Bumble turned, nodded toward the Prince. He thought he detected some anger in the man's eyes, but the Prince did a very good job in keeping his face impassive. *That will teach you to defy me, and to try to thrust responsibility upon me.*

"The Good Lord commanded us to love our enemies as ourselves. He beseeched us to forgive and to turn the other cheek. But he also warned us to render unto the government that which was the government's." *And now, Highness, I throw you a bone.* "I know that Prince Vlad's decision was not an easy one for him, and that perhaps his hands were every bit as much tied as mine. I look forward, in the coming days and weeks, to praying with him, so that together we can find peace with the choices thrust upon us. As is said, 'uneasy is the head which wears the crown,' and the same may be said for the mitre. Together, I hope, we can understand and forgive, as we shall hope to be forgiven."

Vlad nodded to Bumble, slightly, but enough to be noticed.

Bumble returned the nod. "And for all of you, for all peoples who claim the Good Lord as their Savior, there is a lesson. Many are the false prophets who come and twist Scripture to deceive you. They wish to bind your thoughts in such a way that you are confused and seek understanding through them. Such a false prophet was Ephraim Fox. He and his work were placed on this earth to do only one thing: to sever your relationship with God and His son. The flames to which he will be consigned are the flames he shall know for all time without end. Look upon him and his fate, weep, and do not follow in his footsteps."

Nathaniel Woods, his face and hands blacked with burnt cork, huddled in the shadows across the street from the old Temperance Armory building. Two men sat before the door and a single lantern burned from where it hung from a nail above the doorway. One of the men, the fatter and older one, had tipped his chair back against the wall and was already nodding off. The other, a nervous young man who had been treated to an extra mug of ale for his dangerous duty guarding the heretic, had taken to bouncing from one foot to the other. He said something to his compatriot, then turned and walked to the alley beside the Armory.

Nathaniel distinctly heard the thump of a body hitting the ground, but the first guard did not notice. Taking one last look up and down the street, Nathaniel darted across. With his right foot he caught a crosspiece on the chair and tipped it forward. As the guard rocked toward the street, Nathaniel dropped a leather hood over his head and pulled the neck tight. The man's hands went to his throat to try and tear the hood off, giving Nathaniel an easy shot at the back of his skull with a leather sack filled with lead shot.

The man pitched face first onto the ground. Nathaniel plucked keys from his belt, closed the shutter on the lamp, then opened the Armory door. He dragged his man in and tied his wrists while Owen did the same with the skinny guard. Nathaniel locked the front door, then the two of them walked to the back and opened a stout oaken door behind which the Steward had been placed.

Fire's prison had once been the strong-room constructed to store supplies of brimstone and firestones. It was fairly sizable for a prison cell, but Fire had been bound in the far corner. The short chain only allowed him to travel five feet. A tray with a crust of bread and a cup of water lay six feet away. Nathaniel thought that was an unnecessary cruelty, since with the gauntlets and the mask, there was no way he could have eaten that last meal.

The Steward's head came up and one eye opened. The other had swollen shut.

Owen crouched next to him, unlocked the chains from the wall. "We don't have much time, Steward. We're taking you out of here. You're not burning tomorrow. You're not a heretic."

"Who sent you?"

Nathaniel worked on the mask's buckles. "Ain't no time for that. God's got more work for you. You know that. We's just making sure you do it. Come with me."

The two men helped the Steward to his feet. Nathaniel took the keys from Owen and carefully walked the preacher toward the rear of the old Armory building. It had been built with its back to the Benjamin River, which made transporting supplies from Norisle easier. Nathaniel unlocked a small door and guided the Steward through.

A twenty-foot-long war canoe waited beside the dock. A slender, clean-shaven man of average height accepted the keys from Nathaniel, then helped the Steward into the canoe. Justice Bone bid the man lie down, then covered him with tent cloth, making the prisoner look like little more than wadded fabric. Nathaniel took his position in the front of the canoe.

Owen came out of the Armory and tossed a strip of cloth into the river, then got into the middle, all but sitting on the Steward. Nathaniel pushed them back from the dock, and Justice guided them into the middle of the broad river. The sliver of a moon half-hid itself behind thready clouds. All three men paddled, keeping their pace steady and serene. They waved to those who saw them passing beneath bridges and excited no alarm.

As they made it past Temperance's western wall, all three men breathed a sigh of relief. Nathaniel turned. "You weren't in there much time at all."

Owen smiled. "They'll get the message, literally. We're halfway done."

They left the city precincts behind, then picked up speed. Within two hours they headed toward the south shore and brought the canoe up against a dock. Justice made the canoe fast while the other two helped the Steward from the canoe and up to a woodshed set back from the river. Once they had him inside, they freed him from the chains. Justice came and got all the restraints, then headed off to sink them in various deep-river channels.

After he departed, Count von Metternin appeared with bandages and ointments. "It is good to meet you, Steward. You will be my guest for some time—until your wounds heal and even longer, I hope."

The Steward looked at the three men, tears welling in his eyes, confusion and fear battling for control of his expression. "Do you know what you've done?"

"I gots me an idea." Nathaniel shrugged. "But don't you be worrying none about us. You're a very important man, and saving you is going to mean a lot."

"I don't understand."

"It is not important that you do, Steward." The Count slowly began to wrap the man's hands in clean bandages. "What is important is that the Prince does, and when the time becomes appropriate, he shall explain all."

Bishop Bumble had been certain that Vlad had arranged for the escape, but his conviction died when he saw Vlad's astonishment and anger at reading the message scrawled on the Armory wall. *It outrages him as much as it does me.*

The cleric offered a restrained smile. "Thank you for coming so quickly, Highness."

Vlad distractedly waved a hand at him and moved deeper into the Armory's front room. A message had been written in ink, clearly scratched there by fingers wrapped in an ink-stained cloth. The vandal had written, "The Croun has no ryte to tak no mans lyfe." Vlad traced some of the letters in the air, then shook his head and turned.

"This is clearly your fault, Bishop."

"What?"

"Don't be coy. In your sermon, you laid the blame for Fox's execution firmly at my feet. You know, you have preached *against* anti-Crown sentiments, and this time you went and stirred them up." Vlad thrust a finger toward the message. "Do you know what I see here? Do you?

Look closely."

Bumble blinked. The anger on the Prince's face, the anger in his voice, made no sense. "It is a message, yes, but I had nothing to do with it."

"No? Is that how you spell *right*? Is that how you spell *life*? No, I bet not." Vlad's eyes tightened. "But in Richlan they *do* spell those words that way. Richlan, where your man Fox traveled before he went beyond the mountains. You thought all his settlements had been destroyed. Apparently not. Or he had sympathizers. Or your trial and plan for a grand execution brought people in, then you set them on me. How do you think this will look in a report to Launston? Have you thought of that?"

"How dare you speak to me in that tone!"

Vlad covered his face with his hands for a moment, then opened his arms wide. "Do you not know what you've done? Let me explain. You laid Fox's death upon me. You made it a matter for the Crown. Now he's escaped. The message is an *anti-Crown* message. Because it is anti-government, now I must act. I must call out troops and have them search. How do you think people will like that? The foment stirred up by this search will increase resentment. It is a spiral that will rage out of control. It cannot be stopped. It cannot."

Bumble's heart began to pound. He understood the Prince's scenario. The idea that things could rage out of control—out of *his* control—sent a cold trickle through the Bishop's guts. *This was not the way things were supposed to go.* "There must be something we can do."

Vlad shook his head adamantly, but slowed the expression and looked up. "Did anyone witness the escape?"

"No."

"And those who discovered it, what have they seen?"

Bumble shook his head. "Just that the guards were tied up and that the cell is empty."

"Then it would be possible…" Vlad frowned. "No, you would never do it."

"Do what?"

The Prince headed back toward the cell and waved the Bishop in his wake. "In the morning half-light, your men likely did not notice the magick circle and forbidden sigils painted there in the corner where Fox sat."

"What sigils?"

The Prince lowered his voice, but stressed his words. "The ones Fox drew with his own blood. One of your men removed the muzzle so Fox could eat. Fox bit his own tongue, then used the blood to lick a circle and sigils. Then he spoke words and his Satanic master stole him away. The devil used imps to capture the guards to humiliate them and you."

Bumble slowly nodded. "And we..."

"Not *we*, Bishop, but *you* discovered the method of escape. I was walking into the cell when you thrust me back and scattered the demons left herein. You cast them out, a legion of them, in a titanic struggle. Were I to tell that tale to Caleb Frost, and were you to deny it, in all modesty, of course, it would be believed."

"Yes, yes it would." Bumble looked back toward the front room. "And of the words on the wall? More deception?"

"Nothing a coat of paint won't conceal."

"But Fox is still out there."

"I know, and a danger to us both, now." Vlad's expression sharpened. "I'll send my best men after him. If Nathaniel and Owen can't find him, he can't be found. And if they do, gunfire will do for him what a bonfire would have. Like as not he's headed west, toward what was once his empire."

"Your plan has merit. I believe we can make this work."

"It better." Vlad nodded solemnly. "If it doesn't, we both will be destroyed."

Bumble hid a smile. *In that, Prince Vlad, you are half right.*

CHAPTER FORTY-ONE

8 July 1767
Temperance
Temperance Bay, Mystria

Clad only with his lover's fading warmth, Ian Rathfield sat at his desk and slowly paged through the report he'd prepared for his superiors in Launston. He had, primarily, stuck to facts that were mission critical. Occasionally he offered insights into the nature of Mystria and Mystrians. Never did he allow himself to speculate about things he could not confirm.

"Could you not sleep?" Catherine Strake, wrapped in a bed sheet, entered the parlor. "You should come back to bed."

Ian shook his head. "I wished to review this one more time. I guess I am trying to anticipate the changes Prince Vlad will suggest."

"Whatever they are, you should make none of them."

"Why not?"

"You know he will be sending his own report to supplement yours." She rested a hand on his forearm. "You know he will do you no favors. His report will stress all the things that you did not see. He will diminish your accomplishments."

Ian smiled. "You need not begin that again, Catherine. I have decided to acquiesce and append a copy of the *Gazette* story about the expedition to my report."

"Good." She drew over a chair and sat, leaning forward to again hold his forearm. "You must learn to avoid the mistakes Owen made, lest you be trapped here as he is."

How could I see Mystria as a prison with you here? "I have agreed with you, darling, but I cannot avoid the fact that I have little or no recollection of parts of the expedition."

"But you have done yourself injury, Ian, by understating what you have seen, and your part in the expedition. You were sent west to find Postsylvania and bring the people back. You did this, at great risk to yourself. And in the process you discovered the Antediluvian ruins. Were you to have centered your report on them alone, you would have done well."

"I know. I recall you telling me to write a book about it, and that my fortune would be assured." Ian flipped pages back atop his copy of the report and squared the edges. "I know that this report is accurate, but it seems lacking, terribly lacking."

"It is modestly presented, as befits the hero you are."

He shook his head. "You say that because you believe it, Catherine, but I know the real reasons for the modesty. The primary one is that the men with whom I traveled impressed me. Awed me, even."

She drew back, her eyes narrowing. "You do yourself a grave injustice with the implied comparison."

"But it is accurate, because I know who I am." Ian's heart began to speed up as memories he'd wished to remain at rest began to rattle around in his mind. "These men, your husband included, took to incredible hardships with good nature that I could barely understand. I could not let them believe they were better suited to things than I, but were it not for Count von Metternin and their respect for him, I doubt we should have called a halt to marching save for nightfall. And the Gazette, it does not do the battle against the wolves justice. We survived not only by dint of courage, but because they had the foresight to choose our campsite carefully and to build a small breastwork to offer defense."

"Beasts fighting beasts."

"I disagree, my dear." He rested a hand on hers. "I know you have no love for Woods or Kamiskwa, and Bone is of a class with them and Dunsby, but crude use of language cannot be mistaken for a dull mind. Though I found his words bordering on blasphemy, Nathaniel Woods proved very capable in addressing a logical argument. Back in Norisle, there's more than one Oxford Don who would meet his better in Woods."

"Still, Ian, you are a more courageous man. Benefiting from breeding and education, you understand more fully the risks you take. This makes your actions far more brave than theirs."

Ian swallowed hard. "I trust you will continue to think that, Catherine, for there is something that I must reveal to you. Something of which I am not proud, for it reveals me to be a coward."

She squeezed his forearm. "I shall never think poorly of you, dear Ian."

He glanced down, unable to meet her gaze. *I must tell her, I will tell her, but just not all of it yet.* "Catherine, you know I was married. My wife killed herself. Many people put it down to her having been quite fragile of spirit, and reports of my death wounded her. My injuries, though I recovered from them, further frightened her. She feared losing me, and that fear consumed her life."

Catherine nodded. "The gist of that story has been communicated to me, yes."

"It's not the truth." Ian's head came up. "You see, I had been cuckolded. Just as I now put the horns on Owen's head, so another man had replaced me in my wife's bed. Replaced me in her affections."

"Who, Ian?"

"It is not important, darling. What you must understand is that when she heard I had been killed, her spirits soared because then she was free to be with her lover. But when I was not dead, and when I was elevated to the status of hero… for her to have left me, for any hint of the scandal to be revealed, would have destroyed her and perhaps even her lover. I gather that he spurned her from that point forward, and this is why she took her life."

"Oh, Ian." Catherine took his hand in hers and raised it to her lips. "It must have caused you terrible heartache, my dear."

He nodded, his throat thickening to block any words.

"Who was it, Ian?"

He shook his head.

Catherine's voice sharpened. "You must tell me, Ian. You are too good a man to see it, but whomever this is, he is your enemy. He will have to destroy you, so you must be careful, and I will help you there. Who was it?"

Ian exhaled slowly. "Duke Deathridge."

Blood drained from her face.

Ian pulled her to him. "I knew I should not have told you, my love. I know you could not have thought evil of Owen's uncle. Some men might have thought it fitting, my taking you to my bed because Richard Ventnor had taken my wife to his, but I am not vindictive. I love you, and that is the reason I cannot give you up."

Catherine pulled back and caressed his cheek. "Oh, darling, you are a noble and brave man. Already he has tried to destroy you. He sent Owen here to win fame and riches for the family. You he sent on a much more difficult mission, hoping to destroy you. And now it makes sense, why you downplay your role. Instinctively you knew that to draw more attention to yourself would be to invite him to work more diligently to destroy you. I should have known. I should have seen. I should have protected you before this."

"You have, my love." Ian kissed her palm. "Deathridge would have had copies of the *Gazette* story sent to him. For me not to include it with my report would be suspect. He must not know that I know. This is the only way he shall think me harmless, and that orders shall be issued that bring me back to Norisle. When those orders come, I shall take you and Miranda with me."

"Oh, darling." Catherine kissed him softly on the lips. "Yes, I shall go with you, happily, proudly."

Ian kissed her more firmly, his arms encircling her in a fierce embrace. He trapped her against his chest, and would have dragged her into his lap, but she pressed a hand to his breastbone and held him off. He loosened his arms. "What is it?"

She looked away. "I will go with you, Ian, but Miranda cannot come with us."

"But she must."

"No, not immediately." She rose from her chair and drifted toward the room's shadowed corner. "From the day of her birth Owen has made her a creature of this place, of Mystria. She would be completely out of place in Norisle. Do you know that on occasions when Woods brings his half-breed children to Temperance, Owen allows Miranda to play with them? Savages, Ian, unbathed, heathen, bastard savages who play at hunting. Miranda can read a track by the river better than she can read letters. Just last week, when the Prince's man, Baker, had trapped several rabbits, Miranda was upset that I would not let her help him butcher them. Right now, at her age, she does not understand why this is wrong."

"But, darling, time in Norisle will break her of these things."

Catherine shook her head. "Oh, Ian, you are too noble a man to even imagine the other side of these things. Were she to come over now, she would be teased mercilessly. She would not understand why, and would cry herself to sleep every night. No, in three years, perhaps five, when she is old enough to reason, then we can send for her. We can prepare her. Perhaps, by then," Catherine turned and smiled at him, "she shall have brothers and sisters."

That idea sent a jolt through Ian. He rose from his chair and went to her, embracing her from behind, pulling her back against him, kissing the back of her neck. "From the first moment I saw you, and again when I woke up and you were my healing angel, I thought, I dreamed, of you someday bearing a child of mine. You were so gentle with me, and are so gentle with your daughter, that I knew I could not want for a better mother for my children."

"Oh, Ian, I shall bear your children, and proudly. Once in Norisle we shall find a prelate who will annul my marriage to Ian, then we shall wed." She turned in his arms, the sheet falling from her, and hugged herself to him. "I already feel I am your wife, and dream of the day our love is sanctioned."

"Nothing will make me happier, darling."

She sighed and laid her head against his shoulder.

"What is it, dearest?"

"Ian, we shall know pain before we know joy." Her hands came up over his back, hooking on to his shoulders, the nails biting in. "I would tell everyone that you are my lover, but we cannot. We will be able to meet here, from time to time—not as often as either of us would desire, but enough, perhaps."

"I will never get enough of you, Catherine."

"Or I of you, Ian. But until the time we can be together, there is something I must do. For your sake, to protect you."

"What is it, darling?"

"Duke Deathridge is a powerful man. Owen is his nephew and his agent in Mystria. Were there to be any suspicion of our love, Deathridge would destroy you." She looked up and kissed his throat. "For the sake of our safety, I will have to make it appear as if my marriage to Owen is as solid as granite. Luckily I am known to be in town when he is not, and vice versa. We will be able to see each other without arousing notice. But I do not want, my darling, for you to be hurt by my being with my husband. If you see my hand on Owen's arm…"

I will imagine you in his bed.

"…know only than I am wishing most fervently that it was you beside me."

Ian shivered. "You will share a bed with him?"

"Does that hurt you, darling?"

Ian swallowed hard. "The thought of it, more than I would have imagined."

"Oh, Ian." Catherine clung to him fiercely. "I shall share his bed, but my body will not be his. I promise you this."

"And if he demands you perform your wifely duties with him?"

"Were I unable to resist, were he to force himself upon me, I should wish it was you and I would count it as a trial to endure to be with you forever." She kissed his chest. "But I do not think Owen will press. And Miranda can always be encouraged to have a night fright and join us—and would anyway in the winter."

Ian shivered. "How odd is it that I, the man who is stealing you away from your husband, begrudge him any time spent in your presence? Seeing you in Church beside him shall drive me mad."

"I shall endure the same torture, darling, knowing that very soon thereafter, I shall enjoy the balm of your love."

Ian held her tightly, his mind racing. He had once believed he was an honorable man. That was how he had been raised. He believed it fervently until the events at Rondeville had proven otherwise. He'd had a window opened into his soul, and he saw himself for who he really was. And since that time he had been very careful to keep that window closed, and to hide it away behind layers of curtains, shaped of lies and denials. Catherine saw that as humility.

Though he loved her dearly, and had convinced himself that this love had sparked when first they met, then roared alight as she cared for him, he could not deny that Owen's relationship to his late wife's lover had not played a part in his pursuit of Catherine Strake. Whenever it occurred to him that what he was doing was wrong, the concept of redress of the grievance Deathridge had done to him had convinced Ian his affair with Catherine was only fair.

And so you deceive yourself yet again, Ian. How long will you deceive this woman you love?

He kissed the crown of her head. There were things she needed to know about him, but not yet. They were not important, yet. When they were together, permanently together, then he could share his innermost secrets. To do it before the time was right would just drive her away. *And then I would be nothing.*

Ian smiled. "Go back to bed, my darling. I shall look at my report one more time, and then I shall join you. We will create wonderful memories to see us through the times we must be apart, and to inspire us when we can yet be together again. I love you, Catherine Strake. Do not doubt this and know, soon, very soon, you *shall* be mine for eternity."

CHAPTER FORTY-TWO

12 July 1767
Government House, Temperance
Temperance Bay, Mystria

Owen turned the last page of Colonel Rathfield's report over, then squared the stack and, righting it, handed it back to Prince Vlad. The sun had set while Owen studied the report in the Prince's office. He'd finished by lamplight and his spindly chair creaked as he sat back.

"Highness, I don't really see anything in there to be overly concerned about. The idea of Antediluvian ruins might attract some attention, but he largely bypasses it. His focus might have some interest to people at Horse Guards, but this is mostly the account of a man's hunting weekend in the country. He'll be asked to repeat the story about the wolf attack, and be congratulated on bringing the people of Postsylvania back into the fold, but he says nothing about the events after our return to Happy Valley."

"Yes, and the slaughter at Piety can be laid at the door of the Twilight People or Ryngian settlers—whichever is more convenient at the time." Prince Vlad smiled and set a small stone on the report. "I liked the piece about his being conveyed 'with all alacrity' back to Temperance, without any mention of how he returned."

Owen nodded. "I saw that. Do you not think that someone will wonder at that?"

The Prince stood and walked to a sideboard, where he poured whiskey into two glasses. "I considered that question, but I believe the statement ends up proving itself. The expedition has been described as conducting a thorough survey, suggesting you were not moving at great speed. On the contrary, his swift return was just that, swift. He certainly has no understanding of how long it took. Outside of my household, or the men who traveled out there, no one else does either. Because the people of Launston think of Mystria as a vast wilderness, they have no idea of the vast distances we travel here."

"I'm not certain I'm clear on that point."

Vlad smiled. "I believe Mugwump flew roughly two hundred and fifty miles each way. How he knew where to go, or why he started going, I don't know. This still concerns me.

"I can understand that, Highness." Owen accepted a glass from the Prince. "What are you going to report to Launston about Happy Valley?"

The Prince rolled his glass in his hands. "This is the greater problem, isn't it? I've read everything you wrote concerning the Norghaest and the visions you had among the Altashee. If we treat their knowledge of how the Norghaest work as accurate, we need to be prepared to repel Norghaest scouts next year and destroy their colonies. If we fail to do that, we face a larger war five or ten years from now. The difficulty is, of course, that if I tell the tale as you have told it, it becomes me using a Shedashee legend to get the Crown to send soldiers and money to fight a war against nightmare creatures. While I am not at all certain I want more troops in Mystria, I am fairly certain that we might not be able to defeat the Norghaest without them."

"But once troops have been sent, Highness, they're not likely to be recalled."

"No." The Prince sipped his whiskey. "I could send back some demon bones, but Mugwump's saliva did a very good job at demineralizing them. They're as fragile as eggshells and likely would not be seen as proof of anything threatening. They'd start a debate about a species of giant bats existing out here, and make Mystrians look silly for mistaking them for demons."

Owen glanced down into his glass, then back up again. "Were you to travel to Norisle to press the case to the Queen herself, you would be believed, but questioning would reveal the fact that Mugwump can fly. Then we'd get lots of troops here, and all of them would be wurmriders, looking to have their wurms transformed into dragons. The Ryngians would bring theirs over, too, and we'd have dragons going to war over the heart of Mystria."

"Exactly. If we invite Norillian troops in to save Mystria, we doom the colonies to warfare. If we don't make the request, we could be overrun." The Prince set his glass down on his desk. "Of course, I have one obvious choice open to me, and I shall have to avail myself of it. I'll prepare a report about the Norghaest and request troops. For me to do anything less would be an abrogation of my responsibility, especially in light of the fact that I truly am uncertain if Mystrian militias can defeat the Norghaest."

Owen frowned. "Are you certain Norillian regulars would be enough to contain them?"

The Prince shook his head. "No. This is why a second course, a very dangerous course, must be taken as well. I will have to rely upon you, Owen, as we discussed earlier."

"Whatever you need, Highness."

Weariness washed over the Prince's face. "This will be an incredibly perilous game, Owen, and one we will lose at one point or another. I know that. Pressure from without, spies from within, somehow our effort will be revealed and there will be no controlling it. The fact is that the Norghaest, from what we saw, from what the Shedashee said, are masters of magick we do not know how to perform. It's obvious that the Shedashee, likewise, are more skilled and powerful than we are. The Church suggests this is because of demonic influences—their way of dismissing that which they do not understand or do not wish to address except with extinction."

Vlad crossed to a cabinet, withdrew a map, unrolled it on his desk, and pinned a corner down with his whiskey glass. He touched the map roughly where the Antediluvian ruins stood. "If we use this as one point, and Piety as another, we can suppose that both places are roughly equidistant from some central point. Exactly how far away that is, I don't know, and I hope it is very far west. Why they chose those two points, we don't know. Happy Valley is a third point, but I would imagine it was Branch's use of their magick which attracted them there. But if you just look at the line between the ruins and Piety, you're looking at an enormous front, and one that is largely unexplored by Mystrians."

Owen came around the desk and studied the map. If the Norghaest advanced along that front, and even if their force narrowed, it would run to the northeast on a line that would split Lindenvale, Queensland, and Summerland in half. *And if they shift to the coast...* With a decent army, they could take what they wanted, kill what they wanted, and reestablish their empire.

"I understand the threat, Highness."

"I needed to stress the nature of it because our counter to it could easily be worse." Vlad picked up his glass, letting the map roll shut, and tossed the whiskey off in a gulp. "It is not enough that I know how to work proscribed magick. We are going to have to teach other men how to do it. We are going to have to teach them to create their own spells, and yet we cannot let them know this is what they're doing."

Owen wondered, for a moment, if that last whiskey had not, in fact, been the Prince's first. "That's not going to be easy, Highness."

"I may have thought of a way." Vlad folded his arms over his chest. "If I ask you to recall the hottest thing you've ever touched, what would it be?"

Owen shivered and stared at his left palm. "At school, in Norisle, some of the boys grabbed me. They held my left hand over a candle. They said I'd cry out in pain. I didn't. Burned myself badly, and then they teased me for being too stupid to pull my hand away. Better that than being a coward."

"Good, very good. Now, think about the spell you know to ignite brimstone. You think of the sun, don't you?"

"Yes, very bright, a noon sun."

"Now think of that candle flame and how hot it was. Use that and rebuild the spell around it."

Owen thought for a moment, then nodded. "I can see how that works, Highness, but I know you're training me to shape my own spell. How do you teach it to men without teaching them what they are doing?"

Vlad opened a desk drawer and pulled out two small vials. One clearly contained brimstone, ground finely, a black powder with the consistency of sand. The other had been likewise prepared, but had a greenish tinge to it. "What we can do is to tell men that we have a new type of brimstone, and that it requires them to think differently. They'll choose the hottest thing they can remember, thinking that the demand is because of the difference in the new brimstone. They'll miss the true significance of what they are doing."

"Most will, but not all."

"And those are the ones we have to watch for, and explain things to."

Vlad shrugged. "Once they have learned the new version of the spell, which should make them more efficient and should tire them less, we can suggest it will work with regular brimstone. If we drill them enough, invoking the new magick will take precedence over the old anyway."

Owen gulped his whiskey down. "Wouldn't you be better off hand picking men and training them fully? Accidentally opening the door to some may be more dangerous than fully training them."

The Prince nodded. "That's the argument that Count von Metternin offers. I think we have to do both. We do have men among us who can be trusted to keep this a secret, and who are intelligent enough to understand the significance of what we show them. Others are not that intelligent, nor are they smart enough to understand the gravity of what we will share with them. I don't like having to deceive them, but if the Norghaest present as formidable a challenge as suggested, we will need more people than we can ever train."

"Or, Highness, we have the other route."

"Yes?"

"The Mystrian Rangers."

"I'm not sure I follow."

"It's simple. When we went to Anvil Lake, we brought with us militia men who had no particular training. We will need them against the Norghaest. But we had the Mystrian Rangers, and they were the elite among us. What if we bring them together and train them in this new way of magick? They become the tip of the spear that we use against the Norghaest. If we are lucky, they will be enough to destroy them. If not, perhaps they will hurt them enough that the militia can destroy them."

"And if we are doubly unlucky, it won't really matter, will it?"

Owen shook his head.

Vlad remained silent for a bit, then slowly nodded. "Your plan has merit. To carry it out, however, will take planning and subterfuge. If Bishop Bumble were to catch wind of what we are doing, we'd best hope the Norghaest are merciful because he will not be. We'll march west to war, and east again to a stake."

"Agreed. We can set up training camps in the west. Come the winter, no one will see or care."

"And we will have to liaise with Major Forest in Fairlee. I will task the

Count with that job."

"I could do it, Highness."

"No. I do not want to spare you and, I'm afraid, you're needed here to blind Bumble." The Prince sighed. "Only seeing us in Church each Sunday will make him think he has the upper hand."

Owen nodded. "He watches you as a hawk studies a field mouse."

"Owen, if we are to make this deception work, you are going to have to continue appearing with your wife in public, at Church and the like. Work on a new book about the expedition. You need to be the hero and be seen."

"Highness…"

Vlad smiled indulgently. "Owen, I know Catherine is angry with you, but scandal will only invite scrutiny. For the sake of Mystria, you have to make an effort. Next year, after we defeat the Norghaest, I shall put her on a ship for Norisle myself."

Owen nodded. "As you desire, Highness."

"Thank you, my friend." The Prince clapped him on the shoulders. "We're doing this because it must be done, for a land and people we love. It's a great sacrifice, but if there is a more noble cause in the world, I cannot imagine it."

Owen walked through the streets, taking a route around toward the docks before heading back to the apartment he let from Mrs. Lighter. Only when he reached the docks did he realize he was looking for Bethany Frost. He knew he'd not find her there, especially after dark. He paused and looked out at the ships at anchor, and the lights swaying from bow and aft. They looked peaceful at anchor, and he sought some of that peace for himself.

Exhaustion threatened to overwhelm him, but pride held it at bay. When the Prince had said that he could think of no more noble a cause than saving Mystria, Owen's heart had swelled. Mystria truly was a land he loved. The people had seemed so different when he arrived and yet now he truly felt himself to be one of them. He would not just be working to save them, but to save himself as well, and the future for Miranda.

That thought made any burden easier to bear.

With a smile on his face he returned to the apartment and slipped into it quietly so as not to awaken Miranda. He looked to where she normally slept on the parlor daybed, but it remained empty. For the barest of moments he thought Catherine had fled on a ship, and had taken Miranda with her.

Then Catherine emerged from the bedroom, wearing a thin nightshirt on which she had failed to tie all fastenings shut. Wordlessly on bare feet, she rushed across the parlor and hugged Owen, clinging to him. She shook with unheard sobs.

Instinctively, protectively, he put his arms around her. "What is it, Catherine? Where is Miranda?"

"Oh, Owen, I have been so silly. You must forgive me."

He took her by the shoulders and held her back. "Of course. Where is our daughter?"

Catherine brushed away tears, then anointed his cheek. "I asked Mrs. Lighter to look after her for this evening. I wanted you all to myself tonight. Please, forgive me."

"Forgive you for what?"

She looked up, surprise widening her eyes. "You truly don't know, do you? You are so good a man, you cannot imagine, can you?"

"Catherine, make sense."

She smiled and kissed him. "Owen, I have been horrible to you. Evil and vile. I never have given you a chance. I haven't given Mystria a chance. I couldn't see what you did in it. And then, today, I saw Miranda staring at things in town, and I asked her why. And she said she wanted to remember everything so she could tell people in Norisle about her home. And when she said it, Owen, she was so sincere that I knew to take her away would be to crush her heart. And a second later, my husband, I realized I had been doing that exact thing to you."

Catherine slipped her hands down his arms and took his hands in hers. "I owe you an apology. I promise, I shall be better, Owen. I shan't be perfect, but I shall try, really try. I will be a good wife to you and a good mother to Miranda. I shall even suggest that we care for Becca and make her part of our family. I just ask, Owen, please, for you to give me this one more chance. Don't say no. I couldn't bear it if you say no."

He looked down at her, not sure if he could trust her, but desperately wanting to believe she was changing. He was too soul weary to fight her, and questioning her would trigger a fight. Though dread trickled through him, his desire for peace pushed him toward believing her. "You will have all the chances you desire, Catherine Strake."

She smiled and pulled him toward the bedroom. "Come, Owen, make me your wife again. Remind me how much you love me, and how much you want this to be our home."

1768

CHAPTER FORTY-THREE

17 March 1768
Government House, Temperance
Temperance Bay, Mystria

The day Prince Vlad had been dreading had arrived. The courier, wearing the uniform of the Fifth Northland Cavalry, had brought him the pouch of dispatches from Launston, then retired to report to Colonel Rathfield. Vlad had taken his time working the worn leather strap free from the brass buckle. At another time he would have found the heavy pouch laying on his office desk pregnant with possibility, but instead he imagined it infested with disaster.

Few had been the ships coming into Temperance from Norisle in the latter half of 1767. Unusually stormy weather off the Norillian coast had been credited with delaying the shipping schedule, but that should have meant the Crown had more time to get messages aboard ships. Even correspondence from his father had slowed to a trickle, and most of it cautioned him against heresy and exhorted him to find "the heretic" as soon as possible. Vlad could not help to wonder if the slowing of communication was meant to send him a message in and of itself, or if governmental uncertainty had caused his father's keepers to withhold all but the most innocuous missives.

Even information from informal channels had been scarce. Prince Vlad felt less that friends were distancing themselves from him than there was just no news to relay. This was remarkable in that it meant the Crown was being exceedingly tight-lipped regarding him and Mystria. That did not bode well.

He poured the correspondence in a pile onto his desk and pulled his glasses on. Each letter had been folded within a sheet of blue paper, bound with twine and sealed with red wax. Vlad sorted them by thickness, being used to guessing at what they contained based on their size. He selected one of the most slender, cut the twine with a knife, then broke the seal. He unfolded the letter and pressed it flat to his desk, relishing the crispness of the paper.

As the courier's uniform had suggested, the packet contained orders for Colonel Rathfield to take command of the Fifth Northland Cavalry Regiment, which was being stationed in Temperance Bay. This doubled the size of the military in Temperance Bay—albeit temporarily. Rathfield would be promoted to Brigadier General and the Prince's Life Guards would be sent south to take up their new duties in Kingstown, Richlan. The notice of change of command included a request for the Prince to requisition enough horses to equip the cavalry, confirming the fact that they'd been sent over without mounts.

And there was no indication of where the Prince was to find the money to pay for the horses.

He set that message aside and picked one of the thicker ones. He selected it because, in addition to the red wax seal, purple twine had been used to bind it. That meant it was from the Crown. By rights he should have opened it first, but he was certain he knew what it contained.

Over his aunt's signature came the response to his request for troops to fight the Norghaest. Embedded within *whereases* and *wherefores* he found a simple message: the Crown does not have money to spend on fighting faery tales. The Crown concluded that the slaughters at Piety and Happy Valley were the result of Shedashee raids, possibly encouraged by the Tharyngians. The deaths should serve to show all Mystrians why they should not stray beyond the Queen's protective reach.

The packet included a proclamation which he was required to publish and have read in town squares and from pulpits throughout the Colonies. In it the Queen came across as a patronizing parent scolding imbecile children for wasting her time crying wolf. She threatened stern punishments were such nonsense to continue. In four paragraphs she managed to call all Mystrians stupid, cowardly, conniving, and dishonest. That single document would not only cause citizens to rally to the banner of anti-government groups like the Sons of Liberty, but would spawn many more, and create impetus for Colonies to break away from Norillian rule.

Vlad shook his head. That single sheet would do more damage than a

Norghaest invasion. He also recognized that it was a test. If he chose not to publish it, he would be revealing himself as a rebel. If he did, he would be charged with incompetence when protests began. *Her response to my petition casts me as a liar. The groundwork is being laid to remove me.*

His fingers trembling, he picked up the next largest packet, one from the Home Secretary. It contained a proclamation of the "Shipping and Commerce Act." It laid the foundation for the Control Acts. It required everyone engaged in the import and export of goods to obtain a license and to register with Her Majesty's government. The legislation had been written as an anti-smuggling law but would require everyone whose products *could* end up on a ship to register. Nathaniel Woods, and all of the Shedashee for that matter, would have to abide by the law or their trade goods could be confiscated. Furthermore, while registration did not cost money, language was in place for the Home Secretary to impose fees and tariffs as necessary to maintain the integrity of the Norillian economy.

Vlad removed his spectacles, tossed them atop the messages, and rubbed his eyes. "Have you any idea what you're doing?" The Shipping and Commerce Act would be more than enough to incite protests. Hunters and trappers would simply ignore the laws, which put pressure on those who bought their furs, subjecting them to possible fines for smuggling. Because the act applied to any product that *could* end up on a ship, the scope of its application knew no limits. The act was designed to remind everyone to whom they were subject.

Adding on top of that, the Crown's reply concerning the request for troops and the Queen was guaranteeing rebellion. It would simmer at a low level, but as taxes and fees got imposed, the heat would rise. *And if the Norghaest do attack... even if they threaten, there is no way the Queen will not be made to look the fool.*

A gentle rapping on his office door caused him to glance at the clock on his sideboard. He got up and answered the door.

"Quite punctual, Miss Frost, thank you."

"My pleasure, Highness." Bethany entered and set the sheaf of papers she was carrying on the side table. She flipped the folio open and handed him a set of sheets which appeared to be ledger pages. He scanned the account names atop each sheet, then smiled. "You had no difficulty with the sendings?"

"Storms did scramble some things, but redundancy allowed me to correct them."

"Any more ghost messages?" The thaumagraphs occasionally produced messages that had a rhythm and cadence all their own, but resulted in nonsense messages. The Prince feared his thaumagraphs were picking up on Church communications through similar devices—which meant his messages might trigger their devices.

"Both your wife and I have heard more of them, but they remain short and appear to be nonsense." The woman smiled. "She can tell you more, but she thinks they might be the result of magick storms."

"Interesting theory. I can't wait to hear more about it." The Prince brought the papers to his desk and then handed Bethany the Queen's proclamation about how her colonial subjects should behave. "Take your time. I'd like your opinion."

"Yes, Highness." She sat at the small desk the Prince had installed for her and began reading.

From the start of the thaumagraph project the Prince needed reliable and intelligent people. He'd brought Caleb Frost into his cabal, and Caleb had suggested employing Bethany. Because she was known to have edited Owen's book, and to edit the *Gazette*, it was easy to make people believe that she was working with the Prince on an immense, multi-volume work on the flora and fauna of Mystria. That fit with what most people knew the Prince for, and quite common was the sight of Bethany hauling papers to and fro.

Where Bethany had proved an incredible boon was not only her facility for working ciphers, but her ability to use the *thaumagraph*. She'd grasped its potential immediately, and in conjunction with Gisella had suggested refinements to the design. Bethany had become far more adept at employing the device than any other operator. The Prince installed a thaumagraph in the attic of the Gazette building and from there Bethany and Caleb were able to gather and send messages from and to the other units.

She looked up at him, her brow creased. "Can the Queen's advisors not see what reading this will do here? Who could have suggested she take a step like this? Bishop Bumble?"

"I have no doubt that bits and pieces of messages he's sent have been communicated to the Queen, and may have influenced her." Vlad shook his head. "Bumble is a grasping man. He'll be more than happy to read that aloud and preach long and hard about it. Still, even he would see that the emotions stirred up by it would not be easily controlled."

"So when rebellion happens, the Church offers to exert control where there is insufficient military to secure it?"

Prince Vlad shivered. "That is far more likely than I would prefer to imagine, though if that were the plan, would the message not be more laudatory of the Church?"

Bethany bit her lower lip. "That is an excellent point. Will you have it read aloud?"

He shook his head. "No. I immediately reply with a need for clarification and another copy. I held the original too close to a candle, can't get the exact wording. It would be June before the duplicate arrived."

"Unless you're anticipated and a second copy has been sent to you or someone else."

"If the seal has been broken on the message, I cannot be certain it is genuine. I would be a fool to publish in that case." Vlad slid his spectacles on again and sat to study the ledger pages. "I know it's a dangerous game, but I have no choice. By June we'll know the nature of the threat from the west."

"Would you like me to draft a response for you?"

He laughed. "Please. Stuffy, stupid, and craven would be the right notes. Fear of the Queen makes me incompetent. It will please her and annoy whoever wanted action to cause trouble."

"My pleasure, Highness."

Prince Vlad glanced at the first ledger page. As with all book code, words had been reduced to digits, with the page number acting as thousands, paragraph number as hundreds and the word being behind the decimal point. Every sixth entry was a number which, when totaled with the five previous, would produce the number ten million. Not only did that provide a way for both the encoder and decoder to make sure they had the right numbers from a transmission, but it provided nonsense-data to confuse anyone attempting to decode the message. Moreover, numbers alternated being recorded in the credit and debit ledger columns, with the totals making running sense, but signifying nothing. Credits formed the first half of the message, debits the second.

The longest message came from Fairlee and Bethany's uncle, Major Forest. He reported no incidences of anything unusual to the south. Moreover, he'd managed to pull the Southern Rangers together and had trained them in the way of "green" powder. He'd had great success and would continue training men, anticipating a call to head west by mid-May.

A second message had come from a training camp Count von Metternin had set up. He reported continued success educating men with the new brimstone spell. He'd also been training more thaumagraph operators drawn from Caleb's Bookworm squad in the Northern Rangers. Once they became proficient in sending and receiving messages, he was going to move to the second phase of their training.

The Prince looked up. "Anything from Plentiful?"

Bethany shook her head. "Double-nought sent from them two days ago, right on schedule. All is well."

The thaumagraph in Plentiful was the unit they'd placed furthest afield. The Prince had set it up such that the Plentiful station would send something at noon and sundown, just to make certain they were still there. When the messages came in, the Temperance operator would note the time, which was always later than noon or sundown. Through this method, and allowing for storms and other delays, Prince Vlad had been able to roughly calculate Plentiful's longitude.

This calculation placed the village just over a hundred miles as the crow flies. Getting there with troops in sufficient quantity and supply to deal with the Norghaest would be the work of weeks. The twice-daily messaging was less to let Plentiful feel it could send for help, than to let the Prince know, by its silence, that the Norghaest had overrun the settlement and were on their way east.

Despite that reality, he did expect some useful information to come from Plentiful. "Please let me know when you hear anything."

"Of course, Highness." Bethany set down her quill, rose, and handed him a sheet with clear writing along even lines. "Make notes and I shall copy it over."

He shook his head. "I'll copy it out myself. It will please my aunt that

I wrote her directly. This is very good. You have a flair for writing."

Color flushed her cheeks. "I merely edit, Highness."

"You edit Samuel Haste, I believe."

Her eyes tightened. "When he makes things available. Why do you ask?"

Vlad handed her the Shipping and Commerce Act. "What would you gauge his reaction to this to be?"

She scanned it quickly, her bright blue eyes flicking back and forth. She chewed her lower lip, then frowned, running a finger under certain sentences. She reread passages, then shook her head. "I don't know how Mr. Haste will react, Highness. I can tell you that my brother and his friends will be very upset. The document tax is nothing compared to this. This is… this is…"

He cocked an eyebrow. "Yes, Miss Frost?"

She handed him back the act, then retreated to her desk. She made some quick notes. "Forgive me, Highness. If you do not put this act in place, you invite intervention. This is far more than our having to pay customs. This requires everyone to keep track of everything they produce, such that Her Majesty's government could figure out who to tax and when, correct?"

"Precisely."

"What if you choose to apply the act universally, and not selectively?"

The Prince removed his spectacles and cleaned them with a handkerchief. "This would invite an immediate revolt."

"Not if you were to focus it." Bethany smiled. "Who are the most educated and literate people in each community?"

"The ministers and priests."

"Exactly. If you ask Bishop Bumble and his peers to not only announce this program, but administer it, anger will focus on them. But, there's something which is even more important. This act, and compliance with it, will force people to create a lot of paper. If Makepeace Bone, for example, was to sell a skin at a trading post, he would need a receipt, the trader would have to keep one, and one would have to cover the sale and be sent to be recorded. And then if that trader sells the skin to a broker in Temperance, more receipts are created and must be recorded. If everyone is doing this, and if farmers would be required to track grain by the bushel, and distillers rum by the gallon…"

Vlad chuckled. "My aunt's surrogates would drown in paper, and that would keep them too busy to pay to much attention to what we are doing."

"And if men like my brother and Samuel Haste urge compliance with the law, pointing out that burying the Queen in paper is better than burning her in effigy, the people will do it for the amusement. When you have countless receipts all signed with a man's mark to sort through, the system will collapse."

"True." Vlad tossed his glasses on his desk. "However, it will still increase resistance to the Crown in the future albeit more slowly than otherwise."

"Highness, do you think you can insulate the Crown from its own stupidity?"

"No." Vlad slowly shook his head. "I just hope I am able to insulate the people from the Crown's ire."

CHAPTER FORTY-FOUR

17 March 1768
Slow Creek
Richlan, Mystria

Nathaniel crouched with Makepeace and Kamiskwa on the crest of a wooded hill. A light breeze carried down from the north across the snow-choked valley to where they waited, blowing their scent far to the south. The light snow clung to their buffalo robes and fur hats, helping to further conceal them. Each man wore double-layered mittens with white rabbit fur on the outside, and a slit thumb that gave them access to their rifles' firestones.

Nathaniel nodded to Makepeace, who smiled happily. Makepeace had seen odd tracks on a patrol to the southwest of Plentiful. He'd described what he thought had made them, but neither Nathaniel nor Kamiskwa believed him. They'd all bundled up and headed out, hoping to backtrack the trail before the snow obliterated it. None of them had expected to see what lay in the little valley below.

Makepeace had been right in that the tracks had been made by a wooly rhinoceros. It was fully grown, making it about half-again as large as Peregrine. Its horn had to be three and a half feet long if an inch, and its thick brown fur was more than enough to insulate it from a March storm. What they'd not expected, however, was a harness holding a copper plate tight to its head. The harness fitted blinders over its eyes, and held a fist-sized stone set in the middle, which looked for all the world like a firestone.

More impressive than that was the creature riding the rhino.

Nathaniel had seen one of them before, in a quick glimpse, in the Antediluvian Temple. Ten feet tall as measured against the rhino's horn, it had ram's horns of its own and a shaggy white coat. Its thick build

311

matched it to Makepeace, if he'd been stretched up, out, and back. Fur shaded its eyes the way it would on a sheepdog, but the black claws on its hands reminded him more of jeopards than dogs. It wore a brown leather girdle and strap that ran from hip to shoulder and back behind, with shiny copper fittings. A flattened warclub with obsidian blades jutting from each edge dangled at its right hip, and it bore a stone-tipped spear in its left hand. Another leather strap bound a copper plate to the creature's forehead, set with a stone that matched the one on the rhino.

Kamiskwa tapped Nathaniel on the shoulder, pointed to the rifle, and raised an eyebrow.

Nathaniel frowned. He figured the target was about a hundred twenty yards out, which would have been beyond the rifle's range save for all the green powder training he'd done over the winter. Prince Vlad had told him what was really going on, and he'd helped train members of the Northern Rangers. The new magick pushed his rifle's range out far enough, and made a killing shot possible at nearly a hundred yards. *Ain't a single bullet going to kill that beast.*

He shook his head.

Kamiskwa shucked his buffalo robe and warclub, then pulled off his tunic. He touched a new tattoo on his left breast, right next to where his medicine bag dangled from a cord around his throat. The tattoo was of a bear paw, yet the large pad had only been done in outline. In the middle of it had been drawn an open eye design. Kamiskwa covered the image with his hand, and when he pulled it away seconds later, the paw remained, but the eye had closed. He picked up his warclub, and worked his way to the right, moving from tree to tree, and down the hillside toward the valley.

Makepeace moved out the other way. Nathaniel waited until Makepeace had paused behind the bole of a tree and brought his rifle to bear before he moved forward. He advanced ten yards and took up a similar firing position. Makepeace then advanced, ranging a bit further out. Nathaniel continued his descent until he reached a fallen log approximately eighty yards from his target. The wind was blowing across his line of fire, but came light enough that he wouldn't have to compensate too much.

Kamiskwa broke from cover, screeching at the top of his lungs. Snow sprayed up with each step—steps which slowed as the Shedashee waded into a deep drift. He held the warclub aloft in one hand, and paddled at the snow with the other.

The troll looked in his direction, then the rhino began to gallop. The rider couched the spear as a lance. Snow flew up and back. The stones in the harnesses blazed with green intensity as the rhino charged. The creature plowed through the drifts as if they were no more substantial than fog.

Nathaniel measured the range with a practiced eye, then invoked the spell to ignite brimstone. Prince Vlad had directed him to think of something hot and burning. Most men thought of embers or the dull, red glow of iron fresh from the forge. Nathaniel allowed as how those things were hot, but he went for something else, something suitable to the winter. He recalled the burning pain of frostbitten fingers slowly warming up, and pumped that through the firestone, adding in, for good measure, the murderous rage he'd been experiencing at the time of that particular recollection.

Makepeace fired a half-second before he did. The man's bullet flew true, hitting the troll high in the chest. It struck with enough force to rock the creature back and tip the spearpoint up.

Nathaniel's rifle bucked against his shoulder. The bullet sped out, but the troll's reaction to Makepeace's shot had shifted Nathaniel's target. He'd been aiming for the throat, hoping to hit higher or lower than that. The troll's being knocked back lowered its head just enough that Nathaniel's shot slammed into its forehead, directly over the left eye. It snapped the leather strap, but the bullet ricocheted to the side, chipping off half of the troll's horn.

With the rhino thirty yards away and in mid-charge, Kamiskwa dove to the left. Nathaniel and Makepeace each levered their rifles open and reloaded, forcing themselves to calmly complete a ritual they'd done hundreds of times before. Nathaniel refused to look at the rhino and trusted to his brother's ability to get clear. If he let worry interfere, he'd never get his rifle loaded for the shot that could save Kamiskwa's life.

He levered his rifle's breech closed, then sighted on the rhino.

Just in time to see the beast rear up and hurl the troll from its back. Churning up a cloud of snow, the rhino turned quickly and ducked its head. The horn came up, and the troll flew again, all limp-limbed, the forehead plate clattering against the whole horn. The rhino attacked the troll again and again, ripping great holes in its torso, then finally trotted off to the side, snorting out great jets of steam. Its course took it upwind of the troll's corpse, which stank of musk and bile, then the rhino shook its head and cleaned its horn in the snow. It pawed at the ground and began to graze peacefully a minute later.

Nathaniel worked his way back up the hill to recover Kamiskwa's gear and met him halfway to the valley floor. Makepeace joined them. The Shedashee pulled his clothes on, but refused to indicate that he'd felt the cold at all.

Nathaniel looked at his companions. "Now I reckon the Prince, he'd like that troll out there."

Makepeace nodded. "I do believe that rhino might dispute our taking it. I ain't of a mind to shoot a beast just to drive it off."

"I agree, Makepeace, but I surely do want to see how much damage our shots did. Don't mind knowing I can crack a horn, but I want to see how much of the skull went with it."

"And knowing how its guts is plumbed would be good." Makepeace smiled. "Though I ain't sure there's much knowing of that to be done from what the rhino left behind."

Kamiskwa pointed. "More valuable will be the plates and stones."

"Cain't get but one of them."

"I think we can." Kamiskwa pulled his medicine bag from within his tunic. "I have just the plan."

Nathaniel, helping Makepeace load pieces of the troll onto a travois, shook his head. "I never would have reckoned that would work."

Thirty yards away, Kamiskwa was unbuckling the rhinoceros' headplate. To accomplish that, he'd taken a small pellet of dragon dung from his medicine pouch, crushed it with a handful of snow to make a muddy paste, which he spread over his hands and face. He circled around wide and approached the rhino from upwind, letting the breeze carry Mugwump's scent to it.

The beast, which had been snorting and digging through the snow for meager mouthfuls of golden grass, had brought its head up. It sniffed the air, then trotted toward Kamiskwa, its shaggy stub of a tail wagging.

It stopped when it caught sight of him, but started grazing again and didn't seem fazed by his getting closer.

"It does beat all sense." Makepeace shrugged and tossed a piece of what appeared to be liver onto the travois. "I do believe we have it all."

Nathaniel gave a low whistle. Kamiskwa backed downwind of the rhino and rejoined them. Nathaniel half-expected the beast to follow him. They took to the woods, working their way along a path the rhino likely wouldn't follow, and just after dark reached Plentiful.

Under Makepeace's direction, and with the help of Hodge Dunsby and the men he brought with him, Plentiful had been rebuilt. They'd leveled off a hilltop and constructed a palisaded fort which commanded the entire valley. They'd also expanded the settlement's graveyard and placed it toward the northeast end, well above the floodline. New homes sprang up between the two points, and had been built as small blockhouses that allowed for overlapping fire and mutual support.

What had once been a peaceful, religiously based town, had become a military encampment. Nathaniel wasn't too certain how Arise Faith would have taken to that idea. Out of respect for him and Plentiful's origins, the fort did include a chapel and services were held twice weekly. Yet the chapel's steeple was manned around the clock, and watchmen kept their eyes peeled southwest for anything coming from the Westridge Mountains.

The three of them dragged the travois into the fort and to the structure where Makepeace made his home. They left the troll under the roofed-over sideyard, warmed and fed themselves, then returned to taking stock of the monster. Nathaniel and Makepeace put the bits back together as best they could. Kamiskwa came in behind them, measuring things and jotting them down in a notebook, just as Owen would usually do.

Once he'd collected some basic information, Kamiskwa retreated to the cabin and prepared to send a sundown message to the Prince. He drew the thaumagraph from a locked cabinet and set it up on Makepeace's table. To Nathaniel's eye, the device looked to be a boxy guitar, complete with hole, and fitted with ten strings, but absent a neck.

From a small drawer built into the side opposite the tuning pegs Kamiskwa pulled a flat, wooden tile. On it had been burned the image of a crown and below it a clock face. Kamiskwa slid that into a slot on the base where it became part of the device's sounding board. That particular tile linked the device to the thaumagraph in Temperance, whereas others would link it to the one at Prince Haven, or at Count von Metternin's home.

Nathaniel understood, in theory, how things worked. Each string represented a number from zero to nine; and all the messages were coded as numbers by matching words to a book or by using a grid to spell letters out. Only just beginning to be comfortable with writing, he left all the coding to Kamiskwa or Makepeace, both of whom had learned to read early on.

Kamiskwa began sending the message by plucking strings. It wasn't much of a pretty song and wasn't one that was going to get itself stuck in Nathaniel's head. Once he'd finished sending part of the message, he'd repeat it. When he'd completed the entire message, he sat back. "Now we wait two days for a reply."

Nathaniel frowned. "Ain't no question what the Prince is going to say."

Musical notes issued hauntingly from the thaumagraph. Kamiskwa turned a page in the thaumagraph journal and got ready to write. "Caleb, from the sound of it."

"He saying anything useful?" Nathaniel thought it kind of queer that one could tell from the way the notes sounded who was plucking the strings. Kamiskwa sent messages with an easy rhythm, whereas Nathaniel's messages came in fits and starts as he worked out what he should be sending. Bethany had a lighter hand. Caleb's messages came fast, but sometimes haste introduced errors.

Kamiskwa shook his head. "Just a message to let us know they got our last." He closed the journal. "You think the Prince will want us to bring this troll to him."

"I reckon he'd rank this up there with that jeopard." Nathaniel looked over as Makepeace opened the door. "Think we can get that thing back to the Prince?"

Makepeace stamped snow from his feet and closed the door behind him. "I kin rustle you up snowshoes and a sledge, that ain't nothing. Most all the lakes is iced over, half the rivers, too. Storms coming in from the northwest. You ain't moving for three days or more. Fighting that storm will kill you sure as anything."

The watchman in the chapel belfry shouted, and something bellowed in the darkness. The three of them ran out and mounted the wall. They looked toward the mountains, hoping they didn't see anything arcane from the site of the ruins. What attracted their attention, however, was a lot closer.

Nathaniel looked at Kamiskwa. "I reckon you got yourself a pet."

The wooly rhino trotted toward the palisade and grunted. "If we could hitch him to the sledge, he could haul the troll, but if the wind shifted so he caught its scent, he would go mad."

"That he would, I reckon." Nathaniel thought for a second, and smiled. "Then again, I reckon I know a way we can fix that and have the Prince his specimen faster than anyone would think possible."

CHAPTER FORTY-FIVE

20 March 1768
St. Martin's Cathedral, Temperance
Temperance Bay, Mystria

Brigadier General Ian Rathfield did not let the fact that his cavalry had not yet received their horses dampen his mood. He held his head high, standing there atop the Cathedral steps, with the Bishop and his family on one side and Prince Vlad and his family on the other. Ian drew his sword and snapped it straight up, letting the sun glint from the silvery steel. A heartbeat later his men did the same, the whisper of metal becoming a unified thunder which drew grasps from the crowd.

There on the government square three battalions of the Fifth Northland paraded. Their captains took them through a complicated series of marching maneuvers, each wordlessly signaled by the twist of an upraised sword. Cavalry normally hated parading without their mounts, but Ian had instilled in the Fifth a love of foot drill.

Many of the men attributed their survival in the Tharyngian war to such training. Muddy ground had made charging impractical, whereas riding hard to a flank and firing with their carbines at close range had made them very effective. They'd been transformed into mounted skirmishers and often had been tasked with harassing enemy columns. It struck Ian fortuitously that they had learned to fight in that manner, since Mystria and its undeveloped terrain largely negated traditional cavalry tactics.

His troops did look wonderful. Their red jackets had black facings which featured two red stripes running from breastbone back and up toward their shoulders. They wore white knickers and tall boots, with silver spurs that shone brightly as they turned sharply back and forth. Their carbines were shorter than the standard issue musket, making them suitable for carrying on horseback. The first battalion had been issued muzzle-loading rifles which took longer to load, but were more accurate and could hit targets at a longer range. Bayonets had not been fixed for drill, but hung on white sashes and slapped against the men's left hips.

He only had three battalions to parade. The Fourth had headed south with the Prince's Life Guards, hoping to round up horses. The Fifth had shipped back north. Squads would be dropped along the coast to likewise gather horses. He would have preferred that either their horses had been shipped, or that bullion had come to finance the purchases. As it was, his officers were authorized to provide scrip which could be redeemed at headquarters. This meant he'd get some horses, but not the best.

It really didn't matter. He could not help but smile as the men, stern-faced beneath their tall hats topped with red fringe, wove their battalions together in a dazzling display of precision drilling. Had all the clouds burned off, and had bayonets been mounted, sunlight would have reflected brilliantly from them as it did an ocean swell. As it was, no one could have looked upon the Fifth and not known fear.

As the men returned to their starting places and stamped to a stop, Ian lowered his sword. His heart pounded against his rib cage. He could not suppress his smile, nor did he make an attempt to. Instead he looked all the men over, meeting their gazes, then raised his voice. "Regiment, dismissed!"

The men broke apart by squads and filed in an orderly manner through the crowds and into the city via all four corners of Government Square. People cheered and a few hats flew—none of those worn by the Regiments, but those of civilians—and children ran and skipped in the soldiers' wake. Each soldier was being temporarily billeted with local families, at least until the Life Guards' old barracks could be refurbished. The citizens had taken to housing troops surprisingly well, despite having just learned of the Shipping and Commerce Act at services.

Bishop Bumble stepped to Ian's side and offered his hands. "I just wish to say, General, that I am very impressed. Not only at the drill, but in the Regiment's choir. Their voices truly made heavenly music today."

"And that, Bishop, is with a number of the best singers gone hunting horses." Ian shook his hand heartily. "I have found that by encouraging the men to attend services, and to join together in things like the choir, they become a tight-knit group."

"And it would keep them out of trouble in the field, I should imagine."

"Yes, sir, it does. One learns to avoid strong drink in the evening when one will be praising God the next morning."

"Splendid." Bumble clapped his hands. "You know, of course, that Beecher and I stand ready to minister to any of the men and address their spiritual needs."

Ian forced himself to smile to cover his wariness. "This is appreciated. I do have Pastor Wrenfold with the Fifth as our chaplain. Until his return, your assistance would be most welcome."

"As you need it, General." Bumble smiled broadly. "I so love hearing that new rank, sir. Most fitting, I assure you."

"You are too kind." Ian greeted Livinia Bumble, their niece Lilith, and Beecher, then turned immediately to Prince Vlad. "I hope, Highness, you found this display pleasing."

"Indeed. Very impressive." The Prince smiled, but it seemed forced. He looked haggard.

Ian lowered his voice. "If you don't mind me saying so, Highness, you look as if you have not slept. Is there something the matter?"

"There is, in fact." The Prince nodded toward Government House. "If it would be convenient for you to join me in my office in an hour, I would be appreciative."

"Of course, Highness."

"Thank you." Vlad led his family away and Ian chatted with others who came to pay their respects. Most were the landed and successful. A few were men who appeared to be shaking his hand on a dare. He suspected most of them were veterans of the Anvil Lake expedition. It wasn't in anything they said, but how they looked him up one side and down the other. They were measuring him against their memory of other Norillian leaders. If they made any judgments, they did not share them.

Ian smiled. "Mrs. Strake, how good of you to stay for the parade."

"I wouldn't have missed it." Catherine had mounted the Cathedral steps. Agnes waited at the base with Miranda and Becca, both of whom were smiling. Ian gave them a salute, which made them dissolve into giggles.

"I noticed your husband was not with you at services this morning. I trust he is well?"

"I trust he is, too." Catherine allowed an apprehensive expression steal over her face. "The Prince sent a messenger in the early hours. Owen had to go west on some urgent business."

Ian managed to smother the smile that tried to burst forth. "You are fortunate the Prince trusts him so. Will he be gone long, do you know?"

She shook her head. "I do not, but he said he would see us again at Strake House when he was able. How far to the west he's going, I don't know, but from the looks of it he will be heading into the teeth of a storm."

"Well, if it would not be inappropriate, I should call upon you."

"You are too busy a man, General."

"Never too busy for friends, Mrs. Strake. And while your husband is gone in the Prince's service, please do not hesitate to ask for help as needed." He smiled. "While my troopers are all gentlemen, some are given to being layabouts and some honest labor would not hurt them."

"Again, you are kind, but I should not take up your time."

"It would be no burden, I assure you." He clasped his hands at the small of his back. "You would relieve me of the tedium of filling out reports, to which there is never an end. Such drudgery will be my nights for the foreseeable future."

Her brown eyes flicked up knowingly. "You poor man. I hope you will find a diversion."

"As do I. Good day, Mrs. Strake."

Catherine withdrew and with children and nanny in tow, headed off to their apartment. Others offered thanks and praise to Ian, which he accepted with a frozen smile and polite replies, though his mind was in no way engaged. He should have been concerned with Regimental affairs, or his meeting with the Prince, but all he could think of was Catherine, naked, her body slick with exertion, sliding over his. He longed to touch her again, to taste her, to feel her nails rake his skin as she bucked beneath him. To yet again see the fierce love burning in her eyes became his reason for living.

Soon enough he extricated himself from the crowd and made his way to Government House, responding to an invitation from Prince Vlad which he'd received before the parade. Clouds began to roll in from the west. His winter in Mystria had taught him how ominous a portent this was. Warm breezes from the sea had melted much of the snow in Temperance, but within a day the city would again be quieted by a blanket of white.

Chandler, the Prince's man, conducted him to the Prince's private office. Ian had not met with him there before. Usually they used the audience chamber, but it had been reconfigured for the Colonial Assembly. The Prince's throne had been pulled out and desks had been arranged. Ian felt certain the Bishop's announcement of the Shipping and Commerce Act would fill the Assembly with oaths and plotting, but he did not believe the potential for rebellion was the reason the Prince had summoned him.

The Prince waited for the door to close before he spoke. "I should ask you for two things, General. The first is understanding, and the second is forgiveness. I realize that social niceties dictate that I spend longer earning each from you, but I fear we have not very much time with which to work. I'd like you to take a look at this."

Removing his hat, Ian approached the Prince's desk. The image of a strange creature almost twice as tall as a man, with claws and horns appeared sketched in a notebook next to the silhouette of a man. "Yes, Highness?"

"I know you've not seen one of these before. This is an image Owen Strake drew. It is a creature he and the others saw in the ruins, in the Temple, on their return journey."

Ian lifted his chin. "Highness…"

The Prince held up a hand. "I do not need you to tell me that this creature cannot exist. I have it on very reliable authority that one was slain last Thursday. It will be back here soon. It exists; it is not the last of its kind. It is the harbinger of a coming disaster which the Crown has already informed me it does not accept as real and will not provide funding to defend against."

The Prince then proceeded to explain to Ian all that Strake, Kamiskwa, and Woods had learned from the point when Rufus Branch grabbed Ian and Ian ceased to remember anything. Ian stood there, listening to point after point, cataloguing everything. Not only were things odder than he could have imagined, but he learned the Prince had withheld from him information that would have proved valuable in his report to the Crown.

"Yes, I know, General, that I did not tell you everything. Consider my position, however. You were a witness to none of this. While you might have reported it, you could not confirm it, which would have made it even easier to dismiss. Not that the Crown needed your help in this regard."

"You could have told me once I'd sent my report in." Ian fought to keep his face impassive. "I am a trained military man, Highness. You could have used my expertise to plan a defense. We've wasted the winter."

Vlad snorted. "Not to be insulting, sir, but if I had asked you to help me plan on how to defeat monsters from beyond the mountains based on hallucinations caused by a Shedashee ritual—which point to a previously unknown people using magicks which we know cannot exist—I suspect you would have been less than forthcoming with your best effort on my behalf."

"I must admit, Highness, that this all still sounds highly improbable."

The Prince nodded, then clasped his hands behind his back. "I've calculated that Happy Valley was approximately two hundred miles, west-southwest from here."

"I am aware of that."

"And you know the date you were felled, and the date you woke up at Prince Haven, yes?"

Ian nodded.

"Did it never occur to you to ask *how* you got back so quickly?"

"Traveling two hundred miles in ten days is hardly unheard of, Highness."

"On the Continent, perhaps, where there are roads." Vlad exhaled slowly. "To demonstrate the gravity of the situation we are facing, I am going to share with you a confidence which I shall consider you honor bound to keep."

"Of course, Highness."

"It did not take you ten days to return." The Prince smiled slightly. "You made the journey in five hours."

Ian's jaw dropped. "Five hours is impossible."

"Not if you are flying on a dragon."

Ian dropped his hat. "A *dragon*. Flying."

"I flew there myself and brought you back. You and the girl."

"Your wurm has wings? This is why you have never invited me to see him."

"In part, yes." The Prince shrugged. "Since Happy Valley Mugwump has been a bit testy. He's been growing, molting several times. I'd planned, in another month, to expand the wurmrest."

Ian shook his head. He'd seen many a wurm in the army, but none had wings or could fly. He wanted to think the Prince was having him on, but the gravity underscoring the man's words did not allow for humor. *If Horse Guards knew...* Suddenly Ian's promise to keep the Prince's confidence choked him.

The Prince nodded. "I know. My exacting a promise from you was not at all fair. If we are able to resolve the situation in the west, I shall release you from it. I make that offer freely, and do not hold it as a condition of your agreeing to help me."

Ian bent and retrieved his hat. "What would you have me do?"

"Assuming the Shedashee tales are true, the Norghaest will attempt to establish a colony in the west. I am attempting to determine where. Our job will be to find it and destroy it. Because we only have one dragon, it will be up to us to prove as hazardous to the Norghaest as were dragons of old. If we cannot do that, and the Norghaest emerge from their subterranean nests, we'd best hope that they can neither swim nor sail. If they can do either, Norisle shall be their first victim in Auropa, and far from their last."

CHAPTER FORTY-SIX

1 April 1768
Bounty, Mystria

O wen firmly clutched the knob on the side of the rectangular surveying box, leaving his thumb free to stroke the single string stretched across the hole in its top. He waited for Hodge Dunsby, who stood a hundred yards further to the west, to raise his left hand. Once Hodge gave the signal, Owen raised his own left hand and strummed the string, producing a mid-range tone. Hodge paced to the south, then back to the north, and on a five count, Owen strummed the string again.

Hodge lowered his hand and took up a position about five feet to the south of where he'd started from. He brought both hands up, then returned them to the survey box hanging around his neck. Owen raised his hand, Hodge followed, and the mid-range tone sounded from Owen's survey box. As Owen stepped south, the tone became higher, then returned to its original middle-C. He paced north and south again, narrowing the field down to the line on which the tone shifted. He stopped on it and the note remained consistently high.

He raised both hands. Hodge aped him, then each man stuck a stick in the snow. Hodge came trotting back to Owen, as Owen shucked his survey box and plotted the points on his map. He looked toward the horizon in both directions and estimated the angle in regard to landmarks. He added notes in his notebook, then pulled mittens on.

Hodge smiled proudly. "That's a strong one."

"Yes it is." Owen smiled. "The Prince, he's a fairly smart fellow."

"I don't like having much truck with Ryngian methods, but I do like being out here doing surveys." Hodge nodded as he looked around. "Might learn to do surveying, I think."

"I don't know if I can spare you, Hodge."

"Oh, I'll always be there for you, sir." Hodge looked away for a second. "It's just, well, since being back, I've been seeing some of Felicity Burns there in town."

Owen dimly recalled a slender slip of a girl, sitting with her family in Church. "Her father is a bookseller, yes?"

"Yes, sir; that's where I bought the journals for this journey and last. Her brother Virtue courted Bethany Frost for a bit. I was thinking that if I had a career, then I might be able to ask her father for her hand, and he'd not think ill of me."

Owen closed his journal. "That's wonderful news, Hodge. If I can help in any way…"

"You have done, sir. Just the fact that you mentioned me so nicely in your book—she liked that."

"Good. We survive what comes, you'll get an even greater mention." Owen laughed. "And I am certain you're right. This land will have need of many surveyors. It's a wise choice."

"Thank you, sir. Shall we do more readings, or go back to camp?" Hodge studied the sky for a moment. "Going to be clear, which means it will be cold."

"I think we go back now, start a fire, stay warm."

"I'll pack up then, sir."

Back in camp, which consisted of a small lean-to nestled against the southern side of a cliff near a stream, Owen set about transferring notes into his larger journal. Prince Vlad had noticed that messages shifted register up or down depending on certain phenomena. Having the check number incorporated helped guard against errors in transcription. The Prince had also dictated that the messages begin with the same phrase, so transcribers could check that known value against what they heard, indicating if they needed to adjust their note values up or down. The Prince was even considering adding the means to quickly retune a thaumagraph so the correction could be done immediately.

Owen's survey, and he assumed that he was not the only one doing such work, had showed two things. When messages flowed across lines—and rivers were the easiest to plot—or upriver, the notes moved lower. The

Benjamin, being a broad and deep river, tended to push them lower than a shallow stream, and the stream's effect might not even be noticed depending on how strong the sender was and the distance the message traveled. Long messages tended to have the tones even out.

If the message traveled *with* the river, the notes rose. A storm, depending on its ferocity, would make the notes rise, but also tended to mute the message, to the point where some notes might not get through at all. Some initial messaging trials with the thaumagraphs had produced evidence of the speeding and slowing effects of rivers, and they had detected something else which had been labeled *ghost rivers*.

The Prince's initial thought was that the disruptions on dry land might have been at the site of ancient riverbeds which had since gone dry and had become overgrown. The difficulty with that idea was that these ghost rivers didn't show up where rivers might have run. Instead of just trailing through a valley, they would cut across it in a way that water would never run. Moreover, they ran in straight lines from point to point, then broke at angles. Some seemed to be very broad, but then became narrower as they split, just to broaden again at another point where others connected up. And, like wet rivers, the ghost rivers definitely had a speed to them, but appeared to flow both directions simultaneously.

Hodge and Owen had been sent west into Bounty to map out rivers, streams, and ghost rivers to create an image of how messages would move over the land. A message that might take two days to go from Temperance to Plentiful, could travel significantly faster if the sending and receiving station were on the same ghost river line. While a message traveling from point to point along a ghost river might actually travel further than a direct-line message, the speed of transmission would still make it quicker, and tended to override interference from storms and streams.

To conduct their survey they'd started from the Count's home and worked west, paralleling the Benjamin River. They would pick a point, then test for ghost rivers in a circle at one hundred yards. If they found something, they'd mark it, then test further along that line. When they lost any sign of it, they'd work to locate the split, then use that as a starting point to see where ghost rivers radiated from there. This method had sent them on a zigzag course to the west, and had produced a trickle of leads for ghost rivers shooting off in all directions along that path.

Owen had hoped the Prince would give them a thaumagraph to take into the field, but he didn't have many of them, and didn't want to chance losing one. Owen understood, but he wanted the Prince to get the information as fast as possible. As it was, they had one more day in the field, and had to be back to Temperance inside a week.

Not having a thaumagraph is likely best. Owen had been one of the first trained on the thaumagraph which, until November, had consisted of wheels that clicked and spun. Depending on the power of the person sending, the wheels might jump about, and recording a message required the operator to watch a wheel, then look at paper to jot the number down, and back to the wheel. That made it easy to miss a number.

He'd trained Bethany Frost and her brother, but she'd been the one to suggest the substitution of notes for clicking wheels. The Prince had recalled thinking of how he first thought the thaumagraph might amount to nothing more than a remotely played pianoforte, so had little trouble redesigning along the lines suggested by Bethany and his wife. Bethany had mastered the new model quickly, and ended up teaching Owen how to work it.

He'd found something soothing in how her messages had sounded. Words encoded as numbers produced discordant music, but she managed a rhythm to the notes which made her messages easy to listen to. There had been times when she was in Temperance and he was in the Prince's laboratory where they abandoned the codes and just spelled words out using a simple five by five grid to relate numbers to letters. To practice they chatted about everyday things, silly things, and he often found himself smiling or laughing aloud, even if a story might take a tortuously long time to unfold or ghost messages interfered.

There had been nothing improper in their chats. Either or both would mention his wife freely. They discussed his family, including Becca, who had become part of his household. Bethany would mention times she'd seen Catherine in Temperance—always at a distance and always polite. The discussions tended largely to be matter of fact, but he found it easy to imagine her listening, smiling, her eyes twinkling. He even took to writing out some messages in his journal in code, so he could send them quickly, and they reduced certain phrases, like common greetings, to abbreviations that only they could decipher.

Catherine really had been doing her best through the winter. She'd stopped nagging him and accepted that he could say little or nothing about his work for the Prince. She devoted herself to caring for Miranda and Becca. She often took them into Temperance—especially when he was traveling for the Prince—and they all sat together in the Cathedral for weekly services.

She had become the wife he remembered, save in sharing the marital bed. Granted, in the winter, when winds howled and the house became very cold, there was little reason to stop Miranda and Becca from joining them in bed. But even when they had time alone, Catherine appeared fatigued. Owen attributed it to her putting out a tremendous effort to make Mystria her home. She always seemed happier after a trip to Temperance. She loved city life and her being forced to choose between it and her husband was exhausting her.

Sex had trickled to nothingness as the winter moved into spring. That wasn't much of a surprise. Their physical relations had always waned as sailing season approached. Even though she remained pleasant and didn't even hint at traveling to Norisle, he suspected past resentment lurked in her heart. Becca's addition to the household obviated the need for another child immediately, but he and Catherine played the game with well-wishing busybodies, claiming they were working on increasing their family one way or another. The lack of lovemaking he could accept as the price of a peaceful home.

Owen shivered, then glanced at Hodge. "Does Miss Felicity know you are intending to ask her to marry?"

Hodge stirred a pot in which he was melting snow. "Well, sir, I'm not sure that she does. Being the winter and all, and half of that spent in Plentiful helping them rebuild, I didn't get to see her much. But Mr. Caleb tells me that, according to his sister, Felicity's not being courted at the moment. I might imagine one of the Fifth might take a shine to her, so I will not lament our returning direct to Temperance. I was hoping, in fact, we might run across a deer or tanner or something I could shoot and bring her a bit of, you know, to show I can be a provider. Do you think that plan will work?"

"It has things to recommend it." Owen stopped himself from chuckling. "Of course, you might ask Caleb to ask his sister what Miss Felicity likes, and you could obtain a sample thereof to catch her eye."

Hodge took the pot off the fire and stirred in some tea leaves. "Now there I was knowing you would know what to do. Was that how you won your Catherine's heart?"

Owen hesitated. At one time he would have answered in the affirmative, but from time to time he'd been given to ask himself why she had married him. That caused him to recall, with a certain amount of embarrassment, that she had actually come after him. It wasn't a question of his winning her heart, but that she let him *believe* he had won it.

"Different circumstances, I think, Hodge, but you can't go wrong there. Women like a provider, but they also like to know a man is thinking of them even when they aren't there."

The smaller man nodded. "Wish I hadn't gone back so soon from the ruin. Ever since the *Gazette* printed that story about the dire wolves, and General Rathfield decided to make his wolfskin into a pelisse, well, they've been all the rage. If I had a skin or two, no question she'd be mine."

"You're welcome to the ones I have in the attic." Owen smiled easily. The Shedashee had cleaned and preserved the wolfskins and had sent them east. Owen had stored them in the attic, figuring to sell them in the spring. "I have five of them, and no real use for them."

"No, sir, I didn't shoot it, I don't want it. Not that I don't mind the offer." Hodge strained tea from the pot into two battered tin mugs, then handed one to Owen. "And I'd not be liking to see any of them wolves on our trip back. If it were to happen, though…"

"I'll give you first shot."

"Obliged, sir." Hodge raised his cup in a salute. "It does surprise me though that your wife hasn't had them skins made into a coat. It would make her the belle of society in Temperance."

"That's why she doesn't do it, Hodge." Owen blew on his tea. "She won't ever let herself show up the Princess. Since the Prince has not made his wife a coat of wolf-pelts, Catherine won't ask me to make her one."

"That the same reason she hasn't told you to make a pelisse like General Rathfield?"

"That sort of short cloak looks good with a uniform, Hodge, not over Church clothes." Owen sipped tea, then sighed. "The General does cut a dashing figure, doesn't he?"

"I think, sir, some will say that, but few will have been at Anvil Lake." Owen laughed.

"What, sir?"

"Hodge, at Anvil Lake, you were serving Her Majesty."

"As were you, sir."

"And that's why I laugh." Owen opened his arms. "Look at us. It's been four years. We're wearing homespun and skins. We're both counting ourselves as Mystrians, and judging men from Norisle by the same standards Mystrians would."

Hodge smiled. "I'm thinking of marrying a nice Mystrian girl."

"Right. What happened to us, Hodge?"

The smaller's face scrunched up a bit, then he nodded once, curtly. "I think, sir, that when we were from Norisle, we spent a lot of time being told what to do by men who thought they knew best what that was. Out here, we're asked to do the best we can, doing the things that are best for Mystria. That kind of freedom, sir, is something one can come to enjoy. And I don't see any reason here and now or hereafter, to be going back to the other way of life."

CHAPTER FORTY-SEVEN

5 April 1768
Temperance
Temperance Bay, Mystria

Prince Vlad leaned forward over the map table in his laboratory, supporting himself on his arms. A million things banged around in his head. He should have been rejoicing. He had a second wooly rhinoceros in his pen, a totally new species of creature scattered over a long table, numerous jars, and a drying rack, and his surveying efforts were proving wildly successful.

The problem is that all of those things point to our being on the brink of a devastating war.

Count von Metternin and Gisella stood on either side of the table. A map of the northeastern region of Mystria covered the table. Plentiful appeared a third of the way in from Temperance, and Happy Valley a third further west-southwest. Rivers and lakes had been drawn in blue ink, and ghost rivers in green. The surveys covering them had been by no means comprehensive, so some appeared as shattered wheels with no rim and broken spokes radiating out for short distances.

Vlad straightened up, rubbing a hand over his jaw, clutching his other arm to his chest. "I'm certain Piety was built on a nexus. I'm certain a survey team would find a line between it and the ruins. You've also noted that both the summer and winter locations for Saint Luke appear to share ghost river lines. Even the preliminary information from Owen suggests lines which would connect known Shedashee settlements and sacred sites."

The Count nodded. "You would suggest, then, that Piety was destroyed because it occupied a nexus point?"

"That, or its location on a nexus point made it easier to destroy." Vlad frowned. "Until Gisella and I discovered that another medium can be used to make magick work, we believed that it worked at touch only. That was one of two constants to magick. The second was that to use magick was to tire and damage the person using it. Experiments suggest that there are magickal currents, energy currents, in the world. They provide a substrate through which magick can move. It is not unreasonable to suggest that if a sorcerer can manipulate those currents, he could produce a bigger effect with less expense to himself."

Gisella nodded. "So that having Piety on a nexus would have supplemented a Norghaest's power."

"Yes." Vlad squeezed his eyes shut, then shook his head. "So many theories, and so much information to sort out."

Gisella moved to his side, stroking his right shoulder. "Beloved, you can only work with the things you know."

"Yes, darling, but there is so much I *need* to know." Vlad gave her a smile, then pointed toward the wurmrest. "We have determined that a thaumagraph can send a message between units at a speed of roughly fifty miles a day. I have been thinking that this is the rough speed of magick. In a tactical situation that's a yard per second. Much slower than a musket ball, but potentially more damaging than a cannon ball. The problem is, of course, that Mugwump flew to Happy Valley, I shall assume, because the use of Norghaest magick attracted him. At the normal speed of magick, it would have taken four days for the magick to reach him, but the only manifestations I can verify happened just hours before we headed off. Have I the wrong speed? I don't…"

Von Metternin shook his head. "That is not something you will know, not immediately, Highness. Perhaps not ever. What you do know is the speed at which the thaumagraph can function. At fifty miles a day, it is much faster than a man on foot or horseback, and ghost rivers can increase that speed. This is why you have been able to issue summonses to the Rangers, to bring them together so quickly. That is what is important."

"You're right, of course. Still…" The Prince moved to the table on which the troll's bones had been laid out. Some sections were missing because the rhino's attack had pulverized them. Others had suffered because Nathaniel's plan for getting the body back without its scent angering the rhino involved freezing it solid in a block of ice. The rhino had no difficulty hauling the block east, but water had seeped into some breaks, had frozen and further shattered bone.

"I am most concerned over the damage, or lack thereof, to the creature's skull. Even with the help of ice formation, Nathaniel's bullet only chipped the skull." He shook his head. "I have no doubt a swivel gun or cannon could kill one, but a musket ball?"

Gisella pointed to one of the jars on a shelf. "At least we know Mugwump's saliva dissolves its tissue, much as it did the demons."

"If I had barrels of his spit and a way to spray it, this should make me happier."

His wife nodded. "I'd rather you had an army of dragons."

"I fear we'll have to make due with one." He glanced up at Count von Metternin. "Are you ready to go, my lord?"

"Yes. I have convinced the Steward that he shall come as my aide, and he has agreed to remain disguised. I do not think any of the Rangers will revolt at knowing who he is, but there is no reason to provoke Bumble unnecessarily." The Count traced a finger along the green ghost river track on the south side of the Benjamin. "A Ranger squad is already at my home, and we shall head out tomorrow morning, find Owen, and push west with all speed. I will have my thaumagraph with me, so I shall send you information to supplement your map."

The Prince turned and plucked a wooden tile from a shelf. It had burned onto it the figure of a walking man wearing a crown. "You should use this for the thaumagraph I will bring with me. I'll leave the other one here, and Gisella will relay information. The thaumagraph from Temperance will also travel with us so we have another way to signal if there is an accident."

"I am packing spare strings, Highness, just in case."

"A wise precaution. We'll be following with the rest of the Rangers and a battalion of foresters to build roads as soon as we can. General Rathfield is organizing to join us, but likely will be several days behind. I hope we will travel faster than we did going to Anvil Lake."

Again his wife squeezed his shoulder. In asking Nathaniel and Owen to recount their visions, both had provided details that suggested the Norghaest would emerge in the late spring and early summer. The presence of the troll indicated the Norghaest were proceeding on schedule.

If the Mystrians were going to locate them and hit them hard before they had raised defenses, they would have to move quickly. *But will it be quickly enough?*

The Count sketched a short bow. "I shall take my leave of you, as much as I would prefer to stay. I am mostly organized, but I wish to double-check the thaumagraph and make certain it is well packed. You will get reports in short form, and I shall send runners back with more complete documents as needed."

"Thank you, my friend."

"It is not just for our friendship or my duty to your wife's family that I do this, you know." The man smiled. "I love this land, and I admire your people. The Rangers have come only because you *ask*, not because you demand or because it is their duty. They are not your vassals; they are your companions. What you have here is unlike anything in Auropa, and fighting to preserve it is a sacred honor."

Gisella crossed to him, hugged him and kissed him on both cheeks. "Go with God, Joachim."

"Thank you, Highness. Your smile shall inspire me."

She closed the door behind, then turned and looked at her husband. "Will you tell him when next you see him?"

Vlad looked up from the map. "Tell him?"

Gisella stroked her stomach with a hand. "That I am pregnant?"

Prince Vlad made no attempt to hide his smile, and even felt the weight pressing on his chest lighten. "I will. I promise he will know before any bullets fly."

"But you have not told him yet because he would argue that you should stay behind."

Vlad shook his head. "It's not that he would argue, it is that I would acquiesce."

His wife came to him and pressed a finger to his lips. "You would not, and you know it. And, no, I do not take that as a sign that you do not love me. At least, not at the moment, but I shan't always be responsible for my feelings in this matter."

He slipped his arms around her and looked upon her smiling face. "It feels as if I am two men jammed together in one body. Part of me knows it is my right, perhaps even my obligation, to choose men like Joachim or

Owen or General Rathfield to act in my stead. Were I a Prince in Norisle, my aunt might let me travel with her generals and field marshals, but she would not give me command. They would not allow it. They would be afraid I was just playing at war and that I'd retire when it bored me or frightened me. And part of me might have done that."

"Not you, Vladimir. You would not be bored or frightened."

"I would become distracted, perhaps, but I would not serve well the cause nor the men fighting beneath me." Vlad kissed the tip of her nose. "But as the Count said, the men going west are not my vassals, they are my companions. The second man inside me is one of them. Four years ago we fought together, shed blood together, and were victorious together. I am calling them together to face a foe who, I fear, makes Laureate du Malphias look like an errant child. The Crown gives me nothing—Ian Rathfield will be sacked for bringing his troops along whether we win or lose. We have too few troops. I could call up the militia, but I haven't funds to pay them or enough brimstone or equipment to provide for them. And, frankly, if we fail in the west, they'll be needed here."

"You won't fail, my love." She slipped from his arms, then opened hers. "Do you know how I can say that?"

"How?"

"You are one of the rare men who looks for truth. Men like Bumble will never understand that because the truth frightens them. I know, when you started to examine magick, you were afraid, but it was your thirst for knowledge that got you past that fear. Now what awaits in the west also frightens you, but you will learn. You will figure out how and where the Norghaest can be defeated. And you will defeat them."

"I shall keep you informed every step of the way."

"My dearest Vladimir, I learned long ago to be patient. There are times when not knowing is fine. I trust you and your judgment. I trust you shall return to me, unharmed."

"Thank you."

She cocked her head. "I do wish you would countermand one order."

"What?"

"You are going off to war. This will be apparent to everyone, and yet Owen is not going to have a chance to say good-bye to Catherine." Gisella hugged her arms around her middle. "I believe they truly have been working on their marriage, but this stress… The last time Catherine was very nervous. I do not know if she will be here when he returns."

Vlad rubbed his hands over his face. "That, I'm afraid, cannot be helped. I need Owen out there. Kamiskwa is off gathering the Shedashee. Nathaniel is in Temperance gathering up the rest of the Northern Rangers. Joachim and Hodge Dunsby know the way to Plentiful, but neither has had sight of a troll alive, or of the demons. I don't wish to cause Catherine or Owen pain, but I cannot spare him. If you think my speaking to her would help…"

"No, beloved, I will do it. I will calm her nerves and distract her."

The Prince went to his wife, sliding one arm over her shoulder and caressing her stomach with his free hand. "I do feel as if I am abandoning you. That would be because I am."

"Vladimir, you are going to fight a foe that would kill your family. If you were abandoning us, you would be sailing to Launston to petition your aunt for troops. I understand the difference and respect it. This does not mean there will not be nights when I cry myself to sleep, or that I do not mumble those angry phrases I don't want our children to learn. I understand, and just because I may not always like it, it does not mean I will think ill of you for the decision you've made."

"I am going to miss you terribly. Every moment."

She slipped her arms around his waist. "I still have the lock of hair you gave me when you went to Anvil Lake. I shall wear it every day you are gone. And I shall have for you a locket with a snip from your son, your daughter, and your loving wife, such that you can never forget us."

He kissed her, fully yet gently, holding her close, memorizing how she felt in his arms. "I could never forget you, Gisella, nor my family. I will love you for eternity and will never let you come to harm."

Chapter Forty-eight

5 May 1768
Prince Haven
Temperance Bay, Mystria

Having entrusted his pack and gear to Caleb Frost for safe keeping, Nathaniel jogged down the drive from the Bounty Trail. He found the Prince taking his leave of his family, Mugwump saddled, and two wagons containing the Prince's headquarters company materiel ready to go. Nathaniel's heart ached to breaking as Prince Richard clung to his father's leg while the Prince hugged and kissed his wife and daughter.

Prince Vlad released his wife, letting a hand trail down her arm to give her hand a squeeze, then squatted to look his son in the eye. "You have to be the man of the house, Richard. It's very important. You're almost four years old. Your mother is going to need you. So is your sister. I need you to be a good little soldier."

The little boy studied his father's face for a moment, then pulled himself together and saluted. Prince Vlad returned the salute, then hugged his son tightly and gave him a kiss. "I love you, and I'll be home before your birthday."

The boy mumbled his reply against his father's neck, so Nathaniel could not hear. It didn't stop him from smiling. He envied the Prince. Nathaniel had taken his own leave from Rachel Ward, but it was different from leaving a child. He'd never met his son by her, Humble. He'd seen him from afar and had watched him playing with other children. The boy seemed a bit on the delicate side to Nathaniel—bookish like Caleb which, Nathaniel reminded himself, showed the boy could have potential in a fight. Still, if Humble didn't need to be shot at, that would be fine, too.

And taking leave of a Mystrian family and a Shedashee family wasn't

338

the same. Nathaniel loved his Altashee children, but the tradition in which they'd been raised placed less emphasis on who their parents were than their place in society. When he left the Altashee, he was missed, but his children would sing songs of his adventures whether he was dead or alive. The entire tribe was their family, which might decrease the role of a single parent, but meant that if that parent died, the children wouldn't be left destitute or forgotten.

Prince Vlad stood and blushed slightly. "I thought you were going to wait on the road."

"Well, that was the plan. Got the foresters out here last night and they done set up camp. Northern Rangers is with them. But come morning, we got us a problem."

The Prince arched an eyebrow. "Yes, Mr. Woods?"

Nathaniel smiled. "I reckon you might want to come see is all, Highness. Ain't nothing I can handle. Caleb, he's getting some information for you."

"I would take this to be dire news, but your attitude suggests otherwise." The Prince sighed. "I just hope this entire expedition is not full of the unexpected."

"I kin understand your thoughts there, Highness, but I reckon you know it will be, 'specially when we meet the enemy."

The two men trudged along to the Bounty Trail, with Vlad picking up the pace and cutting across the fields to where Caleb Frost stood with a tall, slender man. "You're right, Nathaniel, there's definitely something wrong here."

Nathaniel nodded. He'd camped back a bit from the road, over on the north side opposite Prince Haven. Caleb and his Bookworms had joined him without asking his leave, but he wasn't about to tell them no. Four years ago all seven had been at Temperance College and full of book learning. They'd pushed themselves hard, each and everyone, and most had made it all the way to Fort Cuivre and on down to Anvil Lake. Since then they'd returned to college or moved on, each one taking up a profession at which, to the best of Nathaniel's knowledge, they were doing quite well. The fact that most of them were carrying rifled hunting muskets and were wearing fine gear testified to their success.

He'd sat back and listened to them discussing the issues of the day, like the Shipping and Commerce Act. Though he didn't always understand every word they were using, their passion impressed him. Their reasoning did, too, including their thoughts about both when the Crown would pass more acts, and what those acts would do to relations with the Colonies. By the nature of their discussions, and the fact that they were willing to answer the call to go to war, these men stood out as the future of Mystria.

They asked him his opinion of the Shipping and Commerce Act, and remained silent as he expressed himself. "Well, I ain't sure the Queen's got call to expect us to abide by them rules, since didn't nobody ask us, and I ain't sure any of them over there exactly understand Mystria. I reckon they think beaver pelts grow on bushes and we's just out here plucking them on account of we is too bored at chasing after butterflies and drinking whiskey. And I reckon this here Act is her marking her territory, same as a wolf or a jeopard. Just because one of them beasts ain't gnawed on me yet, I ain't going to think they ain't never going to gnaw."

Caleb had looked at him across the little campfire. "Does this mean you won't register?"

Nathaniel had shrugged. "Ain't given it too much mind. I reckon there will be someone, somewhere, what will register a dead man or something, and that dead man will be the producingest man in Mystria. Might be I'd work for him. I don't rightly know if I want to break the law regularly, but I am not of a mind to be abiding it yet."

That comment had been enough to spur another round of conversation. Nathaniel took his leave from it and found it surprisingly easy to fall asleep as they discussed.

Upon waking the next morning he discovered the problem to which he alerted the Prince. A small tent city had sprung up during the night. Men—ranging from boys with their fathers to old men—had joined up. They'd come from near and far, and some had clearly been traveling for days. A few men had come with their wives—the foresters had done that, too—and a few led oxen pulling carts.

Prince Vlad grabbed Nathaniel's arm. "Where did they come from?"

"Everywhere. Heard you was going, wanted to join in."

"But how?" The Prince's eyes tightened. "I asked everyone to keep things secret."

"Well, I reckon that went by the by when all of the Fifth Northland got called back to Temperance. Plus, ain't everyone going to keep their mouths shut. And there's some out there what was with you at Anvil Lake and figure there ain't no way you can go fighting no one without them, asked for or not."

"I should have anticipated this situation." The Prince nodded as he reached Caleb and the tall man. "Yes, Caleb?"

Caleb led a tall man toward them. "This is Horace Longwalk. He's from Jewel, about fourteen miles up on the Bay Thumb. He came with his brother, a son, and his sister-in-law."

"She's a good cook, Highness, and does mending." Horace looked back toward the field. "I met a few others coming along. My brother and me, we done missed Anvil Lake. Wanted to do our part this time."

Prince Vlad nodded sagely. "What exactly is it you think we're doing?"

"Don't precisely know, Highness, but Robert Richards—he's one of your Northern Rangers I guess has gone ahead already—he done left Jewel over a month ago. We was selling some horses to the Norillians when they was called back, so we figured it was big doings."

"I see. Do you have any idea how many people have come in?"

Horace shook his head. "I would have reckoned a hundred or so, but I think more has come in this morning, having camped back yonder."

Caleb consulted a notebook. "I've got it as three hundred, seventeen. A hundred men serve in local militias. Of them, three-quarters were at Anvil Lake. Another twenty-five *say* they were at Anvil Lake. Forty women, thirty children, and fifteen more who are very young men. One young woman toting a long gun, claims she's a dead-eye shot."

"Thank you, Mr. Longwalk. If you could excuse us for a moment." The Prince stepped back south, with Nathaniel and Caleb joining him. "You know they can't go with us."

Nathaniel smiled. "I don't reckon we can stop them."

"This is rather serious, Nathaniel. I don't have the supplies to feed this many people. As much as I would have liked to have called up the militia, I did not in case the Norghaest threat does not materialize. If it does and if we're beaten, I want them here to defend against the Norghaest. This would be an undisciplined group and, my God, there are *children* there. And a girl with a rifle? That just can't be."

Nathaniel scratched at the back of his neck. "Let me ask you a question, Highness, and you answer as fair as you can."

The Prince nodded.

"Are you saying that about the girl on account of you don't think she can shoot, or on account of there ain't no way Norillians would let her on the battlefield?"

Prince Vlad shook his head. "That's immaterial."

"No, it ain't." Nathaniel looked the Prince straight in the eye. "I done listened last night to a mess of educated men. They was all reasonable. They was thinking that ain't nobody in Launston knows us, knows our ways, or *cares*. Now I don't know who that girl is, but I know when she grabbed up her musket and headed on out, there was some folks said she was crazy. But there was other folks knew she'd hit what she aimed at. They knew that's the point of war. Now you may not be comfortable with the idea of a child doing some killing. I ain't full in favor of it myself. But I reckon if she can make it to Plentiful or wherever we end up fighting, I won't mind her dropping whatever's trying to drop me."

Vlad shook his head. "Someday, Nathaniel, I will find your ability to cut straight to the kernel of a problem annoying. Actually, today is that day, but today's not a day when I can say that your insight is not persuasive. That being said, we cannot have *all* of these people going with us."

The scout nodded. "Well, I think I gots me a plan what will make sense to folks. All you have to do, Highness, is…"

Vlad clapped Nathaniel on the shoulders. "No, Nathaniel—or should I phrase that *Captain Woods*—if I do whatever you have in mind, then I shall be responsible for all the people it effects. I'm not trying to duck that responsibility, but I have other things to deal with. You have the plan, you set it up, and when they have a problem, you will bring it to me. I know you didn't ask to be put in the middle, but there you are."

Nathaniel frowned. He could still remember the days when having anything to do with large groups of people—especially citified people—made him itch all over. Still did, but four years previous he'd accepted the responsibility for the Northern Rangers. Even now he still felt the bonds with them. That was why he'd not told the Bookworms to camp elsewhere. It did strike him as a bit funny that they, being educated and citified, didn't think he might want to be alone, but that wasn't really a problem. He could have told them so and they'd have understood.

Mystria was changing. It had been for a long time, longer than he'd been alive. Anvil Lake had sped that up. If the discussion of the Shipping and Commerce Act meant anything, the Norillians didn't seem to mind piling more sheets on the mast for that particular ship. Like as not, that change would sweep him along. If Nathaniel ran from it, he might be safe, but that couldn't be guaranteed. If he stayed, he could protect others and, because he had the ability to protect them, he felt he had a duty to do so.

"I reckon if I do that, Highness, I'm going to need to be *Major Woods* and *Captain* Frost here and all them lieutenants what is Bookworms is going to have to help me out."

"Congratulations, Major, on your promotion." The Prince smiled. "If we ever get uniforms, I'll see that yours is done right. Thank you."

Nathaniel nodded. "Ain't no arguing you's right. We got us a week before we hit Grand Falls and pick up supplies. Two more weeks to Plentiful if we push it. Cain't have those with us what won't make it. I'll fix it, but I reckon I'm going to need you to say a word of thanks to them that don't. Maybe send them home to make sure their militia is ready for when you call."

"I'll do that."

"I reckon from Mugwump's back it'll sound right nice."

"Noted, Major." The Prince offered Nathaniel his hand. "The matter is yours to deal with."

Nathaniel shook his hand heartily. "Thank you, Highness."

The Prince withdrew and Nathaniel returned with Caleb to where Horace Longwalk stood. Nathaniel sent him off to gather folks while Caleb fetched the Bookworms. He briefed them on his plan, then he stepped into a growing circle of people. He bid them to sit, which most did, save for a number of men and one redheaded girl, all at the circle's perimeter.

"I ain't much on speechifying, but the Prince, he done made this a duty. He's going to have a word in a bit with some of you. I reckon you should know that he's touched by you all coming out here. You may wonder why he didn't put out a call for the militia. He'll talk to that, but it ain't on account of he thought you wouldn't be useful. Fact is, we're going off to take a look-see our own selves so as we can figure what's going on. I'd tell you what we know so far, but half of you would just pack up and head back thinking, 'Is *that* all?'"

He waited for mild laughter to subside, then continued. "Fact is, we cain't take you all. The Prince, he's a sharp fellow, and done figured how much powder and vittles we'd be needing. We ain't got enough to feed everyone, and this is going to be some long walking. On account of all that, they's only so many we can take, and so many who has any business going. If you ain't yet in your teen years, you cain't go. We expect your ma or pa will take you home. If you ain't got food for two weeks travel, you cain't go. You need a good knife, a tomahawk, at least sixty rounds of shot and powder, and three firestones. You need one change of clothes, a good blanket, spare moccasins, and it won't hurt if you can read and are toting a book. Preference given to rifles over smooth-bore, experience over not, and if your coming means your ma's got all her children in the grave or on this here march, you are going home.

"Now, I reckon there's a mess of horse-trading to be done. Even if you ain't going, could be your ball wins the day, and that is important." Nathaniel nodded slowly. "We can take a hundred and a half. Me and the Bookworms, we will be deciding. Be quick, on account of we're leaving afore noon."

The crowd began to chatter and shift, so Nathaniel put fingers to his mouth and whistled once, sharply. "One last thing. If you ain't going, don't mean you ain't part of this. You staying here means we get there, and that makes all the difference in the whole, wide world."

Chapter Forty-nine

6 May 1768
Temperance
Temperance Bay, Mystria

Ian, sweatsoaked, arched his back, thrusting his hips upward. He gasped aloud, perspiration burning his eyes and salty on his tongue. His body tensed, then slackened, and he sank into the mattress. Seconds later, breathless herself, Catherine Strake collapsed against his chest. She ground her hips against his, then nuzzled his neck.

"I am going to miss you terribly, Ian."

He encircled her in his arms, his chest rising and falling as he sought to catch his breath. "And I, you, Catherine, and not just for the time we spend together like this."

"I know that, darling, but it makes me smile to think that when you are out there, when you are all alone, you shall remember me, remember *us,* this way." She licked the side of his neck, then came up on her elbows, her full breasts pressed to his chest. "I want you to remember why you will be returning to me."

"I could never forget, beloved." Ian sank fingers into her thick, brown hair, and drew her mouth to his. He kissed her, fully and deeply, urgently and fiercely. He wanted to remember that kiss, and wanted her to remember it. "A down payment on my return."

She smiled against his lips, then her body slipped to the side. Cool air suddenly chilled his loins as she slid under his right arm. She threw her right thigh across his, then traced a nail over his flesh. She curled the damp hair into nonsensical patterns. She kissed his breast, then clung to him tightly. "I know you have to go…"

"Were there any other way, darling, I would take it." Ian kissed the top of her head. "But the world demands we must be apart. By leaving you,

345

I can keep you safe."

"Thank you." She kissed his chest again. "With Owen, I never felt that was his reason for leaving. He left for himself, for adventure. I never thought he cared if I would be here when he came back."

"More the fool, then." Ian pulled a sheet over them. He'd made that comment for her, because he knew it was what she wanted to hear. He had a perspective on Owen that she never would—that no one who had not been under fire would understand. Perhaps if Catherine had been in Mystria to care for Owen as she had for him, she might have understood. Every scar on Ian's body she knew intimately because of their lovemaking, but also because of her caring for him. His scars united them, whereas Owen's scars betokened a part of his life that she did not share.

"I miss you already, Ian." She rolled over, resting her arm on his chest, and looked into his eyes. "I know you must go and gather your troops. I should want to be there and see you off but I am afraid my sadness would betray us."

"I understand. It is, perhaps, for the best." He smiled at her. "I want you to remember that I shall be thinking of you constantly. If I could send you letters, I would."

She pressed a finger to his lips. "No, my darling. Keep a journal if you must, but I will wait for your return to hear your tales of the campaign. I would, of course, send you letters, but anything in my hand would be recognized."

"Of course."

"All I ask, my darling, is that you return to me, safe and whole."

"That I shall do." Ian nodded solemnly. "With God as my witness, and the Good Lord at my side."

Ian, sitting astride a gray stallion, opened his hands. "And what *is* the hold up, Sergeant Morris?"

The beleaguered officer straightened up from inspecting a hoof on a draft horse. "This spavined beast won't get to the edge of town, much less to the mountains."

"Then find another one."

The man's mouth hung open. "Sir, we have done everything but steal horses."

Ian spurred his mount forward. The draft horse in question was one of a pair yoked to a wagon groaning under the weight of supplies. "Sergeant, what, exactly, is all this?"

"The General's table, sir. Thought sure as you knew."

"Please, fill me in."

"I'm afraid, General Rathfield, this is my fault."

Ian looked down at Bishop Bumble. "Good morning, Bishop. How is this your doing?"

"Well, I regret that I can't go with you as I had hoped. I have fond memories of the Anvil Lake campaign with Lord Rivendell. With the Shipping and Commerce Act responsibilities, you see…"

"Quite."

"…and the fact that you've taken Mr. Beecher with you to supplement your own chaplain, I felt it was incumbent upon me to show my appreciation. Really, *our* appreciation, the whole city's appreciation. Lord Rivendell, when he returned to Norisle, had his baggage and appointments stored here. He promised to send for them, then sent me a letter asking me to dispose of them. I didn't have the heart. And I think God put it upon my heart to keep his things together so I can turn it over to you. There's his pavilion and his table, silver service for a dozen, his bed and trunks. You'll be as comfortable in the field as you are here in Temperance."

Ian forced himself to smile, even though he thought he caught a hint of a threat in the very last comment. "Your Grace, your generosity is remarkable, as is the generosity of the people of Temperance. If I might, I should like to write a letter and have you read it, Sunday, from the pulpit."

"Gladly, sir, and any like it you wish to send."

"As I have time, sir." Ian nodded at the wagon. "Alas, I am going to have to leave much of this behind, and for very simple reasons. You may not know, but the Fifth Northland Cavalry is unique among the Queen's forces. We trace our origin back to the Civil War, to King Henry's loyalists. After the Battle of Blackburn, when his army was routed, he elected to travel with the soldiers, not with his baggage train as usual. The Pretender's troops ambushed that train, and would have slain the King. Since that time, the Fifth has always traveled as lightly as possible, with its officers sharing the same billets and conditions as our lowest recruit. So, you understand why I cannot, at this time, accept your gift, and yet I do not want to insult you with my refusal."

The round cleric held up his hands. "It is perfectly understandable, General. You travel in the poverty that our Good Lord knew during his time on this earth. Commendable, sir, bespeaking your virtuous nature. How sad we shall all be that you have departed."

"Your prayers will be appreciated, sir." Ian gave Bumble a quick nod. "Please give my best to your wife."

"I shall, and my prayers shall be with you."

Ian waited for the man to toddle along, then turned to Sergeant Morris. "Unload Lord Rivendell's rubbish."

Morris looked at the furnishings weighing down the wagons. "Begging your pardon, General, but there's many fine things in that load."

"If I wanted *fine* things, Sergeant, I'd be sitting safely in Launston telling stories about battles I imagined I'd won—just like Lord Rivendell." Ian shivered. Rivendell grossly overestimated his military prowess, and his going to battle with a manor house worth of furniture betrayed his lack of focus. "Replace those things with brimstone and shot. Not so much that this horse can't pull, but enough that no man will go wanting. Be quick about it."

"Yes, sir." Morris turned and pointed at soldiers. "Get a move on!"

Ian reined his horse about and started across Government Square, where the Fifth had assembled. His Regiment consisted of five companies of ninety men each. He would have preferred to have three horses for each man, but they'd only been able to buy six hundred worth riding. It was just as well since he didn't have the wagons for hauling fodder, and many of the trails he remembered would be difficult to ride a horse over. Even with the Prince's foresters hacking a road through part of the wilderness, it would be slow going. This meant the mounts, for the most part, would carry gear while the men walked.

As he surveyed his troops, he could not help but smile. Though they'd been in Mystria for only six weeks, some had formed relationships with the locals, as evidenced by tearful good-byes. He'd been terribly thankful that Catherine was not like that. It would have reminded him too much of his wife. Her tears had not been because of his departure, but because she was withholding the secret of her infidelity. She was hoping he would not return, and her tears came at the prospect that he might.

All of his men appeared to be in good spirits, despite the fact that they would be on foot for most of their journey. He'd let them ride out of the city, to give the people lining the streets a spectacle, but once out of sight, they would act with military prudence. War was no place for show and by the time they engaged the enemy, he was certain they would be ready to put an end to the fight.

It struck him as odd that *more* people had not come out to see them off. He didn't sense any outright hostility from the citizens of Temperance, but he could not shake the feeling that they were much like his dead wife. They were less concerned at his leaving than they were about his coming back. Granted that the Shipping and Commerce Act had stirred up some ugly sentiment among the merchant class, but Ian felt that the Act certainly wasn't as bad as it was being made out to be. Any law *might* be turned harmful, but supposing this one would was really projecting trouble.

He shook his head. *Projecting trouble is what I have been doing.* Prince Vlad had taken Ian into his confidence and showed him many things. The troll's skull had been the most daunting. Ian would have decided it was a hoax of some sort save for two things—the presence of a second, larger wooly rhinoceros at Prince Haven and the fact that he couldn't imagine *why* the Prince would perpetrate such a hoax. The man had nothing to gain by it and much to lose by its exposure.

Despite being forced to conclude that the troll existed, Ian had not briefed his men on the foe they were likely to face. To a very great extent it would not matter. A well-placed musket ball would either kill the things or not. Reports of the fight in Happy Valley indicated that the demon creatures fell easily to the touch of steel, and every one of his men had a bayonet for his rifle and a saber at his hip. He'd also encouraged them to obtain tomahawks, which all had. They were as well suited as possible to face their foe.

He seriously considered sharing with his men the Prince's thoughts about the Norghaest, but not while in town. He didn't fear desertion, though he *would* lose some men that way. It was that Prince Vlad's speculation really meant nothing to soldiers. Either the Fifth would win, or they'd be slaughtered. Knowing why they were fighting, and what they were fighting for, provided no strategic, operational, or tactical advantage. In fact, it could distract men from the only reason they fought.

While the story he'd told Bumble about the Fifth's history had been true, he was certain that Bumble had missed its vital import. Soldiers do not fight for Crown or country, cross or banner. They fight for each other, for their friends. No one can ask a man to die for an abstraction, and that had nothing to do with war. War was all about offering men a chance to save their friends by killing the enemy. Glory and honor, rank, medals, and rewards were all afterthoughts. They gilded the real prize: survival. There was never a medal that could grow back a leg or replace an arm. No blind man regained his sight after being made a peer. Yet knowing he'd saved a friend could put a smile on the face of a man whose lower half lay twenty feet away, and could grant him peace as he died.

Ian rode tall in the saddle. "Show some alacrity, men. There's an enemy in the west that needs killing. The job's yours. The sooner we do it, the better it will be done."

Bishop Bumble smiled as widely as he could. "Mrs. Strake, so lovely to see you in town. And you, Miranda, and Miss Becca. I doubt there is as handsome a trio of women in the city as could be found right here before me."

Catherine bowed her head, but eyed him coolly. Her daughter hid behind her skirts and the Green girl sidled halfway there herself. "Bishop Bumble, you are very kind. Out to see the troops off?"

"Of course, as you must be."

Catherine shook her head. "Oh, no, we've just come to town to buy some cloth. Both my girls are growing so quickly. We shall make Becca a new dress and give Miranda an apron to match. They will look ever so cute."

"Indeed, and happy to see their father return." Bumble's smile shrank slightly. "I've not seen him in six weeks. Is he well?"

"Quite, I gather. Prince Vlad had a note from him two weeks back and is very pleased with the progress he's making." Catherine reached down and cupped the back of Miranda's head. "She misses her father, but he sent his love. She wants to learn her letters so she can send him a note."

"Splendid." The man nodded. "General Rathfield looks quite content."

She arched an eyebrow quickly enough to almost account for a moment's hesitation. "Does he? I only ever see him at service these days."

"Well, you've seen quite enough of him. I mean, hosting him and then caring for him when he was injured. You must have quite the healing touch."

"You give me too much credit, sir." Her dark eyes tightened. "Is there a duty you require of me, your Grace? I should hate to be keeping you from something important."

"Me, oh, no, just out to see the troops off, as you said." He cocked his head. "I do trust, even with your husband gone, you will still come to services. I know that your presence will be reassuring to those who have loved ones in the field. You could travel into town with the Princess, I am certain."

"I shall take that up with her, Bishop. Thank you for suggesting it." She bowed. "Now, if you will excuse me."

"Of course, my dear." He smiled and waved to Miranda. "Good-bye."

Catherine turned and did not look back, but Miranda did with widened eyes. She appeared frightened, and this pleased Bishop Bumble.

He watched Catherine Strake walk away. *Go, my dear, go. I already know one of your secrets, and soon I shall know them all. And then, you shall be my creature and do my bidding.* And with that thought in his mind, he allowed his smile to grow wide again, and pleasure burned in his heart.

CHAPTER FIFTY

20 May 1768
Fort Plentiful, Plentiful
Richlan, Mystria

Owen crouched on the crest of a hill directly west of Plentiful. The palisaded fort dominated the Snake River valley. A deep, semicircular trench had been dug around the fort, facing west. The residual earth had been piled high and grassed over to form an oblong berm. More work had been done to dig the pit out toward the west, so the previous depth added height to the berm—to make it more difficult for the trolls to crawl their way up.

He plucked a blade of grass and stuck it in his mouth. "Not a sight I'd want to greet."

Makepeace, standing tall behind him, pointed with his rifle. "Ain't so big a place that an army cain't surround it; and we don't really got no idea what the enemy will bring."

"That's true." That had been the primary difficulty in trying to prepare for the Norghaest. In the visions they'd not seen any cannon, so they'd not added any glacises to deflect cannon balls. Since they didn't know what the Norghaest would use to fight them, planning against them was at best a guess. Fort Plentiful *might* hold off the trolls, but that would really depend on how many the Norghaest brought.

The winged demons presented other problems, but Prince Vlad had thought of things to deal with them. All around the berm, long masts had been erected. Cables ran from them to the fort itself, anchored to the walls. The Mystrian forces would be bringing with them fishing nets, which they'd string between masts and fort, hampering the demons.

And the weight of their bodies could drag it all down.

Hodge and three of the Rangers who'd come with the Count joined them on the hill. The party, which had been out doing more surveying work, had managed to shoot two deer. Hodge looked at the fort and frowned. "Now that's queer."

Owen took another look. A flagpole had been placed at the heart of the fort at the Count's insistence—as far as the Kessian was concerned it was little more than a trading post without one. Someone had produced an old Norillian flag with three crowned golden lions on a red field. As they watched, that flag descended and in its place rose a green flag with a black circle at its center. A red wurm-claw had been worked into the circle, with the talons pointing earthward and shaped to form the letter M.

The Rangers let out a holler at the sight, and Owen found himself smiling. The Mystrians who had marched off to Anvil Lake had done so under the Norillian banner, but by the time they'd returned victorious, it was under the Mystrian flag. Prince Vlad had let it be known that the flag was really the banner of the Mystrian Militia, lest people in Launston become alarmed. Even now, at celebrations and when the Colonial assembly was in session, that flag flew proudly.

"Looks like someone got here. I hope it's the Prince." Owen stood and started down the hill.

Their advance did not go unnoticed. Northern Rangers came out to greet their comrades, leaving Owen, Hodge, and Makepeace to finish the journey by themselves. Owen felt tired and wanted some sleep, but the information he'd gathered through the surveys was something the Prince needed to hear about immediately. Reaching the fort, he asked after Prince Vlad. He was told that the Prince was still a day back, but that he'd sent his staff ahead. Lieutenant Frost was already setting up the Prince's office in what had served as the thaumagraph office.

Owen rapped on the door, then opened it. "Caleb, I've got lots of…"

The room's sole occupant, Bethany Frost, looked up from the table by the thaumagraph. "Oh, Owen, I mean, Captain Strake."

"What are you doing here?" Owen fought surprise. Bethany was the last person he expected to see in Plentiful. "Where's Caleb?"

She stood, smoothing out her dress. "My brother is with the Prince. They should be here this evening. I pushed forward with the Rangers to set up his headquarters." She extended a hand toward him. "What is it you have?"

Owen shook his head. "I was told Lieutenant Frost was here."

"Yes, Captain Strake, that would be *me*." She smiled modestly. "My brother is now a captain, overseeing the First Mystrian Volunteers Battalion."

"What? Who?" Owen pulled of his cap and scratched his head. "Have I been gone that long?"

Bethany pointed him to a chair. "Please, sir, sit. Corporal Brown!"

The cabin door opened and a slender, flame-haired woman dressed in buckskins wearing a floppy-brimmed hat just like Owen's entered. "Yes, sir?"

"See if you can find Captain Strake something to drink and eat. And get him a decent billet."

"Yes, sir." The young woman saluted smartly, a grin splitting her face ear to ear, then went off to follow orders.

Owen's mouth gaped. "Did you, did *she*..."

Bethany laughed. "The Prince assigned her to me after Nathaniel suggested it. Clara is a crack shot and smart, too. She's learning to read so she can work a thaumagraph."

Owen leaned his rifle against the wall and shucked his pack. He laid a satchel on the chair she'd designated for him. "You shouldn't be here, Bethany. It's too dangerous."

"What are you talking about?"

"War. There's no place for women in it."

Her eyes narrowed to blue slits. "Women have followed their men to war for ages, Captain Strake. You just walked through the compound where a dozen women came with their husbands and brothers. There's more coming in with the Volunteers, and General Rathfield's cavalry will have their share, I'm sure."

"But that's different, Bethany. You're not the sort who should be here."

"And what sort is that, exactly, Captain Strake?" She folded her arms across her chest. "Is it you think that the women who follow their men are stupid, or of low virtue? Am I some how too good to be out here, too delicate? Or is that *women* might come to war, but *ladies* like your wife never would? That my being here means I'm not as good as she is?"

Her last two comments—barbed and colder than any winter he'd ever seen—ripped through him. Until that very moment he'd not realized that when he'd seen wives accompany their husbands, he'd taken secret pride that it was always a wife from the *ranks*, not the officers corps, or a foreign woman, a war-bride, who was at home in the land where they were fighting. He'd allowed himself to think less of them not because they deserved it, than it prevented him from questioning why his wife didn't love him enough to want to be with him. Deep down he'd seen that as a failing on his part, not hers, but he'd never taken the time to consider it.

He glanced down at his hands. "Bethany... Lieutenant Frost... I'm sorry. I know you're not stupid, and I have the utmost respect for you. I respect the Prince's decision that places you here, and your decision to be here. It's just..."

"What?"

He drew in a deep breath. "You've seen what war does. You've seen the marks its left on me, on your brother. You've seen your uncle and his empty sleeve. I don't doubt your courage. I just dread what the whirlwind of war could do to you."

"Silly man." Bethany shook her head. "I *have* seen what it did to you and Caleb and my uncle. Do you think I don't dread the same thing? I do. Not for me, but for you and Caleb and Clara and everyone else. Owen, why are you here?"

His head came up. "I have my duty to my home and family, to people I love."

"Do you think, because I am a woman, I do not feel the same duty?" She brushed away a tear. "I am, bar none, the best thaumagraph operator in the world. Clear communication, delivered quickly, is very important. If I were back in Temperance and I thought that something horrible happened because a message got garbled, I don't know what I would do with myself. That line of reasoning—and Princess Gisella's support—is why Prince Vlad allowed me to come. More importantly, Owen, I *earned* my place here because of my skills. I have a responsibility, just like you, so here I am."

Owen closed his eyes for a moment. He could not count the number of times he'd used the same reasoning to explain to Catherine why he had to answer the Prince's call. When *he* did it, he thought it the highest of noble motivations. He could not claim that justification if he would not grant Bethany the same. And not only could he deny it to her, but he felt no desire to do so.

He opened his eyes again and looked at her. She seemed incredibly tiny and fragile, though he knew she was far from either. She held her head up high and her back straight. She was proud of what she'd done so far and yet, in the way she shied from his gaze, she awaited his judgment.

He chewed his lower lip for a second. "I'm pleased, Lieutenant Frost, to have you out here. I'm not saying I won't worry about you being here."

"But no more so than you would any other soldier."

Owen hesitated. "I can't say that, Bethany." He jerked a thumb toward the door. "I don't want harm to come to any of the people here. I'll help any of them I can. But there's people here that I care about, that I care about a great deal. You're at the top of that list. I'd sooner die than see something bad happen to you. I'm sorry, I don't want to embarrass you."

"Nor I, you." She glanced away. "But I should tell you something, so you understand why I will act as I do, why this will be the last time you and I can speak alone behind closed doors."

"Bethany…"

"No, Owen, you must listen." She brushed away another tear. "I remember what it was like when Ira Hill went with the Rangers to Tharyngia. I remember waiting and the worst happened. He never made it home. And I remember when Nathaniel reported you had been captured. The days waiting for your return were pure torture. Then when you went off to Anvil Lake. Every day lasted forever because I didn't know if you would be coming back, but I did know that when you returned, it would not be to me. I think I held my breath the whole of the time you were gone, and returned to life when you came back.

"So my being here, Owen, is to be near you. I know that's wrong. I have no claim on you. I cannot have one while your wife lives. I accept that. But I needed to be here to make sure that you would live, that you would be able to return to her, and to Miranda and Becca. And, yes, I know I am torturing myself. I know I should be smarter than that, that I should forget you and find someone else, but I cannot."

Owen forced himself to remain where he stood. He wanted to cross to her and take her in his arms. He wanted to hold her and keep her safe. He wanted her to feel his presence, for her to feel she could take sanctuary in him.

But he knew he could not. To do so would destroy her. Save for the Prince having chosen her at the insistence of his wife, Bethany would have been thought a woman of curious moral character for going off to war. That her brother was along might offer mitigation and her family's upstanding reputation might shield her, but all that would go away were one person to see them together. Even an innocent remark would be forged into vicious gossip. Catherine would seize upon it and flay her alive. She would be ostracized and ruined, utterly and completely. Traveling south to Fairlee to live with her uncle might allow her to outrun the scandal for a short time, but it would eventually track her down.

Owen studied the floor for a moment, gathering his thoughts. "Anything I say will sound false and will cause you more pain."

She half-laughed. "Then you probably ought not speak."

"Being silent isn't going to help, either." His eyes tightened. "Decisions get made and lives are launched on a course we can't predict. My mother fell in love with a Mystrian sailor. Her decision to marry him, and my father's death, meant her father could decide to marry her into a powerful family. That set my mother up for her life, and made mine miserable. And yet, without any of those decisions, I'd never have come to Mystria. I'd never have fallen in love with the land, the people." *With you.*

"Other decisions put us here," he went on, "under these circumstances. Somewhere out there the Norghaest are making decisions that we'll respond to. There's no telling what will happen. But there is one decision that gives me heart. That's your decision to be here. I can't say I'm not scared for you, but I can say I trust you to do what you have to do. And I understand everything else you said, and I'll respect your wishes."

She nodded without meeting his eye. "Thank you, Captain Strake."

"You're welcome, Lieutenant Frost." Owen shook his head. "It is going to take a bit for me to wrap my mind around having a woman in the militia."

"You're lucky I'm only a lieutenant, and that might change if the Bookworms don't shape up." Bethany smiled genuinely this time. "The Prince has threatened to make me a field marshal if that's what it takes to get them to abide by communication protocols. It's hard to tell their messages from ghost messages sometimes."

"When the Prince promotes you, I'll salute smartly."

Corporal Brown returned with a bowl of stew topped with a hunk of black bread and a small mug with a slug of whiskey in it. She set them on the table, saluted, and made her way out, but left the door open at Bethany's request. Owen moved his satchel, handing it to Bethany, then sat and began eating. "In there's my journal, but it's the map that's the most interesting."

Bethany drew it out, unfolded it, and smoothed it against her desk. She studied it for a moment, then nodded. "Many more ghost rivers. If you project the lines out, the nexuses flow together out here. What's this marking on the map?"

Owen glanced over. "Hodge called it the Stone House. Natural formation at the edge of a woods, nice fort in and of itself. And you're right, lots of ghost rivers come together in that valley about a day's march west. We all noticed it, but I'm not sure of what to make of it."

She shook her head. "Neither am I. I can't wait to hear what the Prince thinks."

Chapter Fifty-one

21 May 1768
Fort Plentiful, Plentiful
Richlan, Mystria

"It almost looks like a system of canals." Standing in the thaumagraph office, Prince Vlad studied the map to which he had added the information from Owen's latest surveys. A strong line running from the direction of the Antediluvian ruins to the northeast—and on toward a geological formation in the mountains in Bounty which looked like a man's face in profile—split near the Stone House. Rays shot out at angles and then bounced back in. Another slightly weaker line ran from the southeast toward the northwest very close to the splitting point. The Prince guessed it was contributing to a formation of which they could only see the edge.

"If you look here and here, you see a similar angle. It is as if several squares are overlapping, rotating by thirty degrees." He tapped his chin with a finger. "That would concentrate a lot of magick in the area."

Owen, who had joined the Prince, Count von Metternin, Nathaniel, and Bethany Frost in the thaumagraph cabin, shook his head. "We didn't see anything unusual out there. Just a valley with those three points on the ridges."

"Not likely you would have seen anything." The Prince smiled. "The Norghaest have taken refuge under the ground. If they were to have planted any devices or tools to help them split and deflect the flow, they likely would have done so from beneath the earth. Without the surveyors you'd likely have passed over the area without noticing anything."

"I reckon we did just that a year ago, on our way into the mountains." Nathaniel tapped a finger on the map. "We'll be needing some eyes on that area. I'm fair sure I ain't the only one what's thinking that if they is going to raise a colony, that's the spot they're preparing for it."

"Precisely what I was thinking." Vlad looked at Owen. "How big is that valley?"

"About as big as this one, but not as much water. Forest mostly, with a bit of marsh in the middle. An industrious beaver could turn it into a lake."

Vlad slapped his own forehead. "Of course. I was insane not to have seen it before."

The Kessian noble cocked his head. "What is it you see?"

Vlad grabbed a sheet of paper from the thaumagraph table and overlaid it on the map. He drew six squares, each with a corner on one of the nexus points at the eastern edge of the valley. "This star shape, it is what we see from the high point of a fortress, with the glacises set to deflect cannon fire. It is easy, then, for us to see these squares as walls, or lines of defense. But what if that is not what it is at all? What if, instead, the magick is being channeled here not as a defense, but to create a reservoir of magick energy? Just as we shipped supplies up the Benjamin to Grand Falls and replenished our supplies there, could the Norghaest look to create a reservoir in the valley?"

Von Metternin frowned. "This would suppose that magickal energy can be contained and that we can draw on that reservoir to make magick work. Unless your studies have carried you much further than even I imagine, neither supposition is supported."

"We do have Kamiskwa's statements that he could feel residual magick in the ruins. Owen, you had your own encounter with it."

"Yes, Highness, after a fashion."

"My Lord von Metternin, please do be so kind as to fetch your servant. He might have an insight into this matter." Vlad studied the map while emotions warred within him. The idea that magick could be collected and somehow could be used by a man alleviated the limitation of magick use. A man who fired a gun would tire. A man who used magick drawn from elsewhere might not. Provided using external magick did not kill him, it might save him from instances where overusing magick *might* kill him. This prospect thrilled Vlad.

And terrified him. A man like Laureate du Malphias, given an inexhaustible source of magick energy, would be unstoppable. If the Church learned of this, or shared knowledge that it already had with various individuals like Duke Deathridge, its control over society would go unchecked. The same knowledge which might give them a fighting chance against the Norghaest could spell doom when their fellow citizens turned it against them.

Von Metternin returned with Ezekiel Fire. The Steward had grown a beard and styled it in the Continental fashion, featuring twin forks. He wore one of the Count's old uniforms, taken in and up, along with hose and black shoes with silver buckles. The Prince found the change jarring. Even though he knew who the aide truly was, he had a hard time reconciling images of Fire and the man before him.

The Prince laid out his thoughts. Fire listened thoughtfully, then nodded slowly. "I don't know as I have a perfect answer for you, Highness, but I been thinking on why in the Good Book, in Genesis, chapters one and two tell the same story of God creating man over again, but different. First time man is made in God's image. Second time around he's made from the dust, has life breathed into him, and God makes him that special Garden, where everything is fruitful and it is a paradise. Now, I am thinking that this garden had four rivers, like the sides of your squares, and inside was paradise. If these rivers were your ghost rivers, then the land inside would be full of magick, which is why it was a paradise and why, within the garden, men knew no pain nor hunger. It's right there in the Good Book, I do believe."

Though he found Fire's comment vague, he did find it reassuring. "And the idea of men being able to use that magick energy?"

Fire smiled. "The Good Lord wasn't the only person who did miracles. His disciples did, too, and their enemies. Seems like it could be used and, being as how there isn't any prohibition against it, I do believe God intended us to be able to use it."

"How?"

The Steward shook his head. "That I do not know. I imagine, however, that Rufus found a way in what was said on the tablets."

Vlad nodded. He had avoided studying or working on translations of the tablets because of what had happened at Happy Valley. Vlad felt certain that whatever Rufus had translated first had, in fact, caused him to invoke Norghaest magick. He suspected, based on what he had later learned about the devices used by trolls to control wooly rhinoceri, that this first magick may have given a Norghaest sorcerer the ability to control Rufus. If the changes in his body were at all accurate, the Prince was ready to suppose a Norghaest sorcerer had actually taken possession of Rufus' body.

"If anyone else has any thoughts on the matter…?"

"Well, Highness, I onliest know about magick what I done learned for green powder, but I have to reckon that if a man is going to use that reserved magick, he needs a couple things. First, he needs access. Second, he needs to know what he needs to be to use it. Could be he just needs to see himself as a pipe and let it flow through, with him directing it. Or, and I beg your pardon Lieutenant Frost, he needs to know what it tastes like going down, then know where he's peeing it out to. I reckon he needs to beware of drowning or being eroded and just figuring out how to start drinking it in would be the big thing."

"Thank you, Nathaniel, for that colorful explanation."

Bethany held a hand up. "Another thought, perhaps?"

"Please, Lieutenant."

"We've noted different transmission speeds of different ghost rivers. We've supposed that it's all one stream, and the only difference is speed. What if, instead, the magick is different? Think of it like the notes in a thaumagraph. It could be that a stream only produces one note, and to be able to use that stream, you have to be attuned to that note. If someone has only one string, he can only use one flow. If he has two or three, more. It may not be, as Major Woods suggests, a matter of drinking all you can, but to learn what to drink."

Owen nodded. "The splitting and diversion might not be channeling all the magick, but only the strains our enemy can use."

"I like that idea. Very clever." The Prince sighed. "Unfortunately I like it because it limits our enemy and suggests vulnerabilities. Until we can prove they exist, however…"

Everyone nodded slowly. Working from any unproven hypothesis and treating it as true was to invite a disaster of an unimaginable magnitude. For a heartbeat Vlad recalled Lord Rivendell and could see him leading troops in a headlong dash for the reservoir, certain he would take it, able to work magick, and vanquish the Crown's enemies.

Vlad tapped the map in the vicinity of the Stone House. "Nathaniel, I will, as suggested, want eyes on this. It's three days out to Stone House, and another to Ghost Lake?"

"That's what I made it mostly. Maybe half a day more to Ghost Lake."

"Take one of the Bookworms and a thaumagraph, a dozen Rangers. Head out after sundown."

Nathaniel nodded. "I will go organize that now."

"Thank you. The rest of you, please, see to your normal duties. If you do have any thoughts on this, let me know." Vlad folded the map up. "I'd be content with a few more solutions and a few less mysteries."

The others left the cabin—save for Bethany Frost. Vlad almost stopped Count von Metternin, intending to fulfill his promise to Gisella to let him know before guns fired that she was pregnant. *There will be ample time yet for that. So much here needs to be done.*

Bethany Frost took her place at the thaumagraph. Vlad tucked the map away in a desk drawer, bid her adieu, then headed out to the large pavilion built against the exterior of the fort's southern wall. It jutted out forty feet and the canvas, peaked roof fluttered in the breeze. Baker sat outside, polishing brass buckles. He started to stand, but the Prince waved him back down onto his stool, then slipped into the tent's dim interior.

Mugwump opened a golden eye.

"You're more ready for this than I am, aren't you?" Vlad approached and ran a hand over the dragon's muzzle. In the months since Mugwump had fought at Happy Valley, his scales had thickened and talons had grown longer with each molt. He still had scarlet stripes and spots, but the color marked where the scales had thickened the most. Though he'd never seen inside a dragon, it appeared as if stripes warded his ribs and spots covered vulnerable joints. The ridges around his eyes had become brightly scarlet, and the bony edges and ribs in his wings matched.

Vlad had wondered for the longest time about the cause of Mugwump's successful molt and growth of wings. He'd put it down to a varied diet, which included plants and berries which were unknown in Auropa. That, combined with Shedashee knowledge of dragons, suggested they may have had their origin in the New World. While all that made it seem like Mugwump's changes were part of a natural process, Vlad had concluded that there was more involved.

Specifically, Mugwump had consumed *pasmortes*—the corpses that du

Malphias had reanimated with magick. He'd gobbled them down quite happily, gorging himself at Anvil Lake. But when du Malphias had killed the spells which animated his corpses, Mugwump stopped feeding and vomited back up the creatures he'd just consumed. Just as greedily, he had snapped demons out of the air at Happy Valley.

Subsequent to both instances of his having gorged on creatures of magick, Mugwump had changed physically. Vlad could not help but surmise that the consumption of magick had provided the impetus for growth and change, but he knew neither how nor why. That the visions had shown the dragons to have an antipathy toward the Norghaest explained why Mugwump would feed on the demons, but Vlad couldn't see any connection between those demons and the *pasmortes*.

"If you knew, would you tell me?" Vlad shook his head. "I need to know because I have a lot of people here who are willing to face *your* enemies. The problem is, I know very little about them. Now, the demons, they seem pretty close to gnats as far as you are concerned. And the trolls, I don't know, bunnies to a hawk?"

The dragon snorted.

"Was that a note of contempt?"

Mugwump shifted, bringing his tail around to hem the Prince in.

Vlad patted his muzzle again. "I'm not worried for you, my friend; I just wish you had a few more of *your* friends to join us. A dozen or so dragons should deal with the Norghaest very nicely, I should think. Then again…"

Vlad leaned against Mugwump's muzzle. Other dragons might view the Mystrians as the same bother as the Norghaest. "I'm not sure how they would deal with my maintaining you as a possession. Would they be wolves looking at you as a dog, or would you be a captive that they would want to free?"

A shiver ran down Vlad's spine. *What if there are no other dragons?*

Auropeans had been on Mystria for nearly three hundred years and had never reported seeing a dragon. The Shedashee had knowledge of them, but always prefaced stories of them with "In the time of the grandfathers," which was the Auropean equivalent of "Once upon a time." The last clutch of wurms born in Auropa had been laid seven centuries before. *Is it possible that there have been none here, since then?*

Mugwump's ears came forward, then his head up and around. Vlad ducked as the dragon looked to the west.

A handful of heartbeats later the ground shook. Not hard nor heavy, just a little tremor. The sort of thing one might feel when standing on a bridge over which troops were marching.

Norghaest troops.

Vlad strode to the opening. "Mr. Baker, please see to saddling Mugwump. The Count will be joining us, and we'd appreciate having our swivel guns ready to go."

CHAPTER FIFTY-TWO

21 May 1768
Fort Plentiful, Plentiful
Richlan, Mystria

Owen ran to the fort's parapet. There, on the cusp of the hills northwest across the river, the ground quivered. Greensward pushed up, like a bubble, then burst. Rich, brown earth geysered into the air, piling up around the depression, as if it were a giant gopher hole. Owen shivered, fearing that analogy was not far off the mark, and knowing foul monsters would pour forth.

I'm sure there's a Scripture that forewarns of such a thing.

A single figure rose from within and easily moved east along the ridgeline. Rufus Branch, with his remaining hair grown long and white, gathered into a ponytail, appeared little changed from when they last saw him. He glanced down as he walked, as if distracted by feeling moist earth and green grasses beneath his feet

Branch wore a black robe secured with a golden girdle around his waist. It had been stripped down from his torso, the arms dangling. The angry red track of a chain scar stood out on his chest and over his left arm. He bore a long staff about a head taller than he was, topped with an ovoid orb which scintillated with golden light.

The hillside continued to boil with undefined forms undulating beneath the sod. Then the earth split facing the fort. White forms, maggotlike, crawled from the wound, glistening wetly. They rolled downhill into a writhing pile. Their skin became translucent and their black heads went from glossy to dull. Mandibles opened wide, then hands thrust up and out through the mouth. The flesh cracked and trolls emerged. The skin folded itself back onto them, and the mandibles curled into their horns.

Vlad appeared beside him on the right. "Dear Lord. There must be hundreds."

"More." Owen pointed toward the west. "Cavalry."

As the Norghaest infantry arrayed itself in ranks, the daunting silhouettes of trolls astride wooly rhinoceri skylined themselves on the western hill crest. Owen only counted fifty, but could imagine more hidden behind the hill. A greater number would just represent overkill, since the rhinos could flatten anything they chose to run over. Sunlight glinted from copper plates on their foreheads, matching the metal on their riders.

"Why there?" Vlad frowned. "He could have deployed on this side of the river."

"No, Prince Vladimir. Our presence did not allow it."

Owen spun, recognizing the voice, but knowing that he had to be mistaken. "How?"

Msitazi, Chief of the Altashee, stood at his left hand. Below, on the fort's parade grounds, a hundred Shedashee braves stood. The air around them shimmered, as if it were a fluid, and seemed to drip from some of them. The drops even fled sideways, back into the shimmer, which quickly evaporated. The warriors—twenty from each of the Confederation's tribes—had painted themselves red and black in a pattern matching Mugwump's markings.

They wore leggings, breechcloths, and bone armor chestplates, as well as feathers and bits of shell as decoration. Msitazi had dressed similarly, but had added a red coat and a proper Norillian hat that had both once belonged to Owen. He bore no weapons, unlike his traveling companions, but Owen hardly thought the man with a milky eye defenseless.

"Your people called us the Twilight People because, in the beginning, they would only see us emerging in the twilight. They assumed we moved through darkness. They were mistaken."

"Great Chief Msitazi, you know far more about the Norghaest than you have told." Vlad concealed his hands behind his back and bowed toward the Shedashee chieftain. "I need to know what you know."

The Shedashee ruefully shook his head. "It is not what you need to *know*, Prince Vladimir, it is what you must *understand*. You have to learn."

Vlad thrust a finger toward the trolls. "We don't have time to learn."

Msitazi smiled in a way which Owen took to be faintly encouraging. "You do. The *Noragah* must learn as well."

"I don't understand."

"What you have yet to learn, they seek to remember."

The sound of a musket-shot spun Owen back around again. "The trolls, Highness, have begun their advance."

Atop the berm, Nathaniel ran over to the man who had fired and smacked him with his hat. "You damned fool. You have a better chance of dropping a moose at that range. Reload."

The trolls, arranged in thick ranks, naked save for their furred pelts, marched forward. Two companies, ten ranks deep by ten columns wide, they kept good pace with each other. Only when they hit the river and started to wade through did their cohesion begin to fray. That would have been the point to hit them, but the river's near edge lay a hundred and fifty yards away, and Nathaniel figured that even with green powder training, that was about five times longer than killing range for a musket.

"Rifles!" Nathaniel pointed with his own weapon. "Ain't a one of you firing a-fore they get halfway up that slope. The rest of you, thirty yards, no more. Aim for something ain't covered in bone."

The trolls splashed their way through the river and came on at a steady pace. They didn't straighten their lines at all, but it hardly mattered. Coming as they did—pretty much the way Lord Rivendell had sent his troops against the Ryngian fortress at Anvil Lake—they presented a wall of fur and flesh that the Mystrians couldn't possibly miss. As they grew bigger and mounted the slope, some of the unseasoned troops began getting antsy, and if their nerves got the best of them, they'd not be able to concentrate enough to invoke the magick that would fire their guns.

Off to the right, one of the two small Mystrian cannons fired from the fort. A cloud of smoke jetted toward the trolls. The gunners had loaded it with canister shot. A dozen fist-sized balls flew in a flat arc and hit the trolls' left flank. Five trolls went down, but two staggered back to their feet. One left most of an arm behind him. He got another thirty feet up the hill before he bled out.

"Rifles, ready!" Nathaniel shouldered his rifle. "Aim. Fire!"

All across the firing line, magick pulsed through firestones and ignited brimstone. The powder burned hot and quick in the chamber, propelling a bullet into the weapon's barrel. The spiral grooves cut into the barrel's steel started the bullet spinning. It emerged from the barrel in a gout of flame, flying on a flat arc, and struck its target.

Blood gushed, staining white fur crimson. A few of the trolls paused, probing wounds with black talons with the same curiosity as a man studying a chigger bite. One or two even watched their blood pulse from deep wounds, before collapsing, but for most the shots had passed without notice.

Nathaniel loaded automatically as the gunsmoke cleared. The volley had dropped some trolls. None had made an attempt to move forward to fill the holes in the line. They just marched forward, relentlessly, remorselessly, and implacably.

"Everyone get ready. Aim low. Fire!"

Muskets and rifles shot, sound rippling from the center out. The fusillade ripped into the trolls, cutting the forward ranks down. The cannon boomed again, felling more of them. Almost a third of them lay on the ground, still or thrashing. And yet the others came on, undaunted by the opposition.

Then Rufus raised his staff and spun it over his head. Light pulsed from the orb and an odd thrumming rattled Nathaniel's bones. The advancing trolls stopped dead in their tracks, then spun and wandered back toward the river with no order or discipline. Their retreat made no sense, but he had no time to figure it out.

Rufus stabbed the staff into the earth. Light flashed in a flat disk that washed over the battlefield. It outlined the trolls for a moment, rendering their flesh and fur and muscle all but invisible. That vision lasted for a heartbeat or two, no more, leaving a carpet of dead trolls in its wake.

Then the bodies began to twitch and quiver. Their bellies swelled as if the creatures were pregnant. The swelling advanced to knees and shoulders, throbbing and pulsing. Then the trolls exploded, their flesh erupting in a shower of ivory maggots. The worms immediately burrowed into the earth, leaving deflated husks behind.

And, across the way, more, larger worms poured from the hole in the ground. They changed as the others had, and filled the back ranks. More light flashed and the trolls began to spread out. Instead of being packed shoulder to shoulder, they opened their ranks. Whereas before a soldier couldn't help but hit a target, now he'd actually have to aim—something Nathaniel was pretty sure most of the volunteers hadn't bothered to do. The lengthened lines also meant the cannon's fire would be less effective. The only counter to that reorganization would be a cavalry attack.

Don't matter none. Rufus gots hisself an endless supply of soldiers, and we ain't got no cavalry.

The reinforced trolls began a second march to the river. Mystrians reloaded. Nathaniel paced behind them, making sure to smile broadly. "Cut 'em down, just the way you did last time!"

Unlike the previous advance, the trolls did not come on in a stately fashion. Once they hit the southern bank they broke into a run. Talons raking the air, mouths open to reveal long, sharp teeth, they sprinted up the slope. The cannon fired again, killing a pair, but not even slowing the rest. Rifles began to bark along the line. Crimson blossomed on trolls, but they kept coming. The muskets spoke in a ragged volley, scattering some of the front ranks.

Mystrians reloaded again, and soldiers atop the palisade fired. Individual muskets shot, but nothing could stop the trolls. They would gain the berm, then claw their way up. As brave as Nathaniel hoped he and his men were, he figured that one of the trolls would be equal to a half-dozen dire wolves.

Then a hiss arose with whiplash fury, and the trolls on the southern flank melted away.

As Mugwump landed and furled his wings, Prince Vlad swung the forward swivel gun to the right and fired. Pain shot through his hand—not as much as had when he fought at Anvil Lake—but igniting the gun's brimstone charge still stung mightily. The shot, each ball being the size of a hen's-egg, knocked a pair of trolls flying. Behind him, in a saddle fitted over Mugwump's hips, Count von Metternin fired another blast. More trolls fell.

Mugwump lashed out with his tail. The tip hit, slicing a troll in half. Then the dragon hissed again. His vaporous breath staggered trolls, dissolving fur and quickly melting the flesh beneath. The trolls, horns evaporating, screamed and clawed at their own skin. It came off in bloody ribbons, their compounding the damage Mugwump had done.

Prince Vlad catalogued their injuries, noting that Mugwump's second hiss did not do as much harm as the first. The natural philosopher put this down to Mugwump's salivary gland running dry. He also realized that the trolls needed more killing than the demons. This did not bode well for Mugwump's entry onto the battlefield, and that prompted alacrity as the Prince reloaded his swivel gun.

Rufus shouted a command in a discordant tongue which made Vlad's flesh crawl. The trolls responded as one, turning and driving toward the dragon. Mugwump, almost catlike, leaped to the side and the south, drawing the trolls away from the fort. His tail flicked, snapping one troll in half, and launching another pair into the oncoming mass. Vlad and von Metternin fired again, this time benefiting from the way the trolls had massed. More fell, torn and bleeding, but others leapfrogged the corpses, eager to get at the dragon.

Mugwump proved too agile for them. He sprang back, then lunged, catching one troll in his jaws. It struggled for a moment, then bones popped loudly. The dragon swallowed and withdrew, baiting the trolls, stretching their lines and parading them before the fort.

From the berm, fire poured into the trolls' flank. Each ball and bullet might not have amounted to much individually, but the sheer weight of metal hurled at the trolls reaped a red harvest. The enfilade fire drove them down the hill, concentrating them, so Vlad's fire could do even more damage.

The trolls hesitated as volleys from the swivel guns cut down their front ranks. For a moment, whatever resolution had driven them dissipated. Forward ranks backed away, some trolls tripping and falling over prostrate comrades. Those nearest the fort turned and started downhill, running and occasionally knocked flying by a lucky shot. Confusion reigned in the Norghaest ranks. Their formation completely disintegrated.

Hissing defiantly, Mugwump leaped into the air again, his wings unfurling proudly. He rose quickly, affording Vlad a glimpse of chaos below. The Prince's heart leapt as the trolls fell back.

Then, from the hilltop, something flashed.

Mugwump jolted, shrieked and, wings flapping weakly, he plummeted from the sky.

CHAPTER FIFTY-THREE

21 May 1768
Fort Plentiful, Plentiful
Richlan, Mystria

As acrid gunsmoke blew away, Owen swiped at a tear. His thumb was beginning to throb. He glanced at it as he levered his rifle's breech open. The thinnest of bloody lines had appeared at the cuticle. Before he'd learned to reshape magick, the three shots he'd already fired would have had blood much thicker. He'd touch his nail to the brass fang on the firestone collar, letting the hot metal melt through to relieve the pressure.

Across the way, Rufus thrust his staff toward the dragon. Fire lanced across the battlefield. What looked like a fiery red comet exploded against Mugwump's breast. The blast knocked the dragon higher into the air and twisted him around. His wings fluttered as he fell. His tail hit first, then his right hindquarters crashed heavily into the earth. A wing bent, then snapped. The ground shook as Mugwump bounced once and lay on his side, very still.

Before Owen could even begin to comprehend what had occurred, two new things happened almost simultaneously. A gray torrent of the demons flew from the troll hole, filling the air. The creatures swirled high, then dove straight at the fort. At the last moment, they split. A third of them swooped toward the dragon, while the rest came straight on at Fort Plentiful. Men yelled orders to deploy the nets, but panic had set in. Even before the demons had reached the fort, the Volunteers had dropped their guns and were running for their lives.

Over by Mugwump, the air shimmered and the Shedashee stepped through. Guns blazed merrily, blasting demons from the sky. The Shedashee cast their guns aside happily and brought their warclubs to bear. The weapons, some long and straight, others curled and knobbed, each set with obsidian blades, swept out in vicious arcs. Bits and pieces of demons flew in every direction. Warriors crushed and stabbed, forming a living wall between the demons and the dragon.

The bulk of the winged gray horde poured over Fort Plentiful. Men fired in every direction, heedless of what they might hit when they missed. Owen buried a tomahawk in one demon's breast, then brained another with his clubbed rifle. He couldn't see past a curtain of wriggling gray flesh, but knew he and his men could never kill enough demons.

But kill Rufus, and this all goes away.

He leaped from the parapet to the roof of the thaumagraph cabin, and from there to the ground. The cabin's door swung open, with Clara Brown brandishing her musket and the foot and a half of steel mated to the muzzle. Behind her Bethany looked out anxiously.

"Stay in there!" Owen batted another demon from the sky. "You're to keep her safe, Corporal. That's an order!"

He waited long enough to see the door close, then ran for the fort's gate. He pulled a demon off a man's back, twisting its head around until its neck popped, then helped the man to his feet. Owen recognized him immediately. "Justice, we have to kill Rufus."

"I don't need asking twice on that."

Makepeace loomed over the two of them. "I'm with you. Let's be quick."

The three of them ran from the fort toward the northeast corner. One of the cannons had been positioned in a little redoubt nearest the fort's northeast corner. As they raced toward the gun, what was left of the crew passed them going the other way, demons clinging to them, biting and tearing.

Reaching the redoubt, Owen grabbed a bag of brimstone, gashed it with a tomahawk, then shoved it into the cannon's muzzle. Makepeace bent down at the other end, lifting the carriage and swinging the gun around to the right. Justice sighted down the barrel, then used a pry bar to shift it back an inch or three. Owen jammed the ramrod into the muzzle and packed the powder in tight, then Makepeace fed a six pound iron ball into the barrel.

Owen looked at the Bone brothers. "You ever shot a cannon before?"

Justice shook his head.

Makepeace smiled. "Cain't be much worse than a swivel gun."

Owen tossed him the ramrod. "It is. I've done it once, and never wanted to do it again."

He ran around to the cannon's closed end and crouched on the carriage. Owen pressed his right palm to the firestone. It seemed cooler than it should have. "Makepeace, get clear!"

"Hurry, Owen."

"I am."

But before Owen could invoke the spell to fire the gun, a furious avalanche of winged demons poured over him and buried him alive.

My left arm is broken. Vlad accepted that knowledge with clarity and surprise, because he didn't yet feel any pain. Still, the odd way that his sleeve hung, and the fact that his hand would not answer commands, gave him no choice other than to realize that he was severely injured and that he *would* hurt incredibly, very soon.

Until then...

He came up to one knee and let his arm dangle. There, between him and the battlefield, Mugwump lay on his side, his left wing canted at an odd angle. He rocked, as if attempting to roll up to the right to cover his belly. Despite his claws churning the earth, Mugwump could not get enough purchase to right himself.

The dragon's effort focused Vlad's attention on the rear saddle. Count von Metternin dangled there, his right foot caught in a stirrup. That leg was broken and the rocking wasn't helping. Clearly unconscious, the Count made no effort to free himself.

"Mugwump, stay down." The Prince tried to shout, but a sharp pain jabbed him in the side. He breathed in carefully and got another twinge. *Broken rib, too.*

He staggered to his feet and ran to Mugwump. He worked his way along to the rear saddle, cut von Metternin loose. The man tumbled into a pile on the ground. Vlad dragged him south by his collar and once he'd gotten him clear, Prince Vlad collapsed next to him.

He watched as the Shedashee drove the demons away from the dragon. They appeared to be Hellspawn themselves, painted up black and red. Though he knew them to be men, he found them very different. Whereas near the fort the Volunteers were fleeing, the Shedashee had pushed the enemy back. It seemed as if the force of their courage, combined with their ferocity, would not allow anything but victory.

Then the Prince watched through the thinning cloud of demons as the trolls regrouped. They turned and drove straight at the fort. With the defenders beset by the demons, the trolls would face no opposition, and would easily tear Fort Plentiful apart.

"Captain Mayberry, first battalion to the fort. The rest of you, on me. One shot at thirty, men, then give them your bayonets!" General Ian Rathfield rose in his stirrups, his saber shining high, then slashed it down. "Charge!"

The Fifth Northland Cavalry entered the small valley from the east and galloped across what had once been flat farmland beside the Snake River. When the Fifth had felt the tremor in the land Ian had ordered his men to saddle up. They left their baggage and supplies to come on as they could and rode quickly west. There wasn't a man among them who didn't feel outraged that the battle had begun before they arrived.

Ian didn't bother to slide his carbine from the saddle scabbard. Through the smoke he recognized their enemy. The winged demons were nothing he remembered from Happy Valley, but he'd seen their like in countless church murals depicting Perdition. He figured them to be a nuisance. The larger figures, the white beasts that walked as men, those he recognized from the Prince's description of trolls. To them, his men would likewise seem nuisances.

That did not cause him to pause, even for a moment. Though it occurred to him that he might be riding to his death, he knew his duty. Retreat was out of the question. So was anything else short of blind obedience to what the Queen demanded of him, which was that he do his duty to protect her realm. He might as well die with failure, because he certainly couldn't live with it.

"For God and the Queen, men, God and the Queen!"

From where Nathaniel stood, the charge of the Fifth Northland Cavalry was both the most beautiful and most futile thing he'd ever seen. They came around the hillside, horses lathered, wide-eyed, and plunged into the troll flanks. Carbines fired and bayonets stabbed. One troll spun away, transfixed by three bayonets, then died as a saber harvested its head.

Other trolls turned and attacked, fangs bared and claws flashing. One lifted a horse and rider and hurled it deeper into the formation. Horses toppled and tangled in a mire of broken limbs and screaming men. A paw swiped through the air, tearing the head clean off a horse. The rider leaped clear, but the troll pounced on him and ripped him in half.

Nathaniel looked for Rathfield, but a troll scaled the rampart in a leap, eclipsing the battlefield. The beast raised its arms high and bellowed. Men ran as if scattered by the sound alone. The troll's lips drew back and its red eyes became slits.

Nathaniel whipped his right arm forward. His tomahawk spun through the air. The steel blade buried itself the troll's breastbone. A small rivulet of blood matted the white pelt, splashing over the monsters belly and thighs. The creature glanced down, tapping a talon against the metal head. The troll looked up at Nathaniel with the hint of a smile. It plucked the tomahawk from its chest, then took an effortless step toward him, clawed hands raised.

Nathaniel leaped back and caught his heels on a discarded musket. He landed on his backside, staring up at the monster looming over him.

Another tomahawk spun through the air. Thrown from atop the palisade, it caught the troll full in the forehead. The blade pierced the flesh and stuck in the bone. The haft, a feather dangling from the end, rested against the top of the troll's muzzle. The creature looked at the tomahawk, crossing its eyes, for a heartbeat appearing confused. It raised a hand to pull that tomahawk free as well, but before it could, the blade quivered. More bone cracked. The head sank deeper into the beast's skull. Three inches, then four, then up to the haft.

The troll staggered. Splitting the bone with a thundercrack, the tomahawk disappeared entirely into the skull. Ruby-gray tissue gushed from the wound. The troll's eyes rolled up into its skull, then it pitched backward and disappeared.

From above. Msitazi smiled.

Nathaniel got back to his feet. "How, Msitazi?"

"You, my son, threw to hit." The elder warrior nodded sincerely. "I threw to *kill.*"

Nathaniel, his mind reeling, bent to retrieve his rifle. *I'm gonna have to learn me that trick.* As he rose, he realized he'd not have enough time.

The troll cavalry charged.

Owen kicked and slashed and bit and pushed to free himself. He spat out bitter demon blood and snarled as more of the gray hellions smothered him. He cut and fought, but their weight shortened his breath. The air got hot and their stink filled his head.

Then, suddenly, cold air poured over him. The demon that had been huddled over his head, jerked upright. A blade flashed around its neck. Blood splashed, adding another coat to the gore covering him, but Owen didn't mind. Another demon got pulled off, then he kicked two more away and stood.

Bethany Frost stood there, bloody knife in hand. Corporal Brown clubbed one demon off Makepeace and Justice dragged another one away.

Bethany fixed Owen with an icy glare. "Not a word, Owen."

"That word would be 'thanks.'" Owen crouched on the gun carriage again. "Give the wedge a tap, Makepeace. Just an inch."

The large man banged his dagger's hilt against the elevation wedge, driving it deeper and lowering the cannon's angle. "You sure that's enough?"

"Four hundred yards if an inch. It's as good a shot as we'll get." Owen grabbed the gunner's handhold, dropped his palm to the firestone, and invoked a spell. Magick pulsed through him, making his senses swim, then ignited the brimstone. The cannon roared and rocked back, almost toppling him from the carriage.

The six-pound ball flew true but short. The ball landed about a dozen yards below Rufus, on a direct line with him, and bounced up. His left hand flicked out by reflex, to swat the annoyance away. The ball did ricochet from him, but the impact knocked Rufus to the side.

His long hair flying in a whiplash, Rufus stumbled and flailed. He drove his staff into the ground again, clutching it in both hands, and leaned heavily upon it. For a heartbeat it seemed as if he would remain upright, but his staggered steps had brought him too close to the troll hole. The earth gave way. He teetered to the left, then disappeared deep into the dark hollow.

The Fifth Cavalry's charge had sliced through the marching trolls' formation. Some of the beasts had continued to fight, but with Rufus' departure, their resolve deserted them. They turned to flee back toward their hole, which would have permitted the cavalry to slaughter them wholesale.

Unfortunately the mounted trolls remained in control of themselves and their rhinoceri. They raced down the hillside, warclubs still slung on their backs. Their mounts' horns gleamed and coats flew. The ground trembled as they came, a wall of muscle and horn.

Owen leaped from the cannon, grabbed Bethany, and turned her face away to the east. "Don't look."

The trollish charge slammed into the Fifth Northland flank, rolling horses and men over as if they were debris caught in a bloody tide. Men's faces twisted with pain or wide-eyed with panic. They'd vanish for a moment, then that same face would reappear, stripped of flesh but still somehow recognizable. By the third time the man's body would have come apart, bloody limbs flying, a skull arcing through the sky with scalp attached by white sinew. Then all that would be ground into a muddy froth, streaked with scarlet, and splashed against the rhinos' breasts and their masters' legs.

The mounted trolls were by no means invincible. Steel sabers rose and fell, particularly potent against the trolls. Owen cheered as a rhinoceros emerged riderless from the fight. Another troll wavered in the saddle and fell, life pumping from a severed limb.

But too few of the trolls died to balance the price paid by the Fifth. The mounted trolls rode through them, curling to the north and on to secure the river. The trollish cavalry's ranks parted, allowing the footsoldiers to pass through to the hole. Half a hundred made it to their sanctuary. What were left of the demons flapped away to the northwest. After the trolls vanished into the earth, the mounted trolls withdrew in that same direction, leaving a half-dozen riderless rhinoceri grazing peacefully on the hillside.

Owen released Bethany as the Fifth's first battalion moved onto Fort Plentiful's ramparts. Blood dripped from Owen's hands. He wasn't sure if it was his or just demon blood. He didn't feel any pain, but figured that would come later. He shook his head. "We didn't kill Rufus. And the cavalry, the troll cavalry, could have crushed us all. Why didn't they?"

Makepeace shook his head. "Don't know. Good question, though. I reckon I'll be thinking on it long past finding the last person out there can use some help."

CHAPTER FIFTY-FOUR

21 May 1768
Fort Plentiful, Plentiful
Richlan, Mystria

Nathaniel upended a bucket of cold river water over his head. He smiled, relishing the chill as it splashed down over him. He stood naked with a number of the Shedashee, washing away blood and inspecting each other for overlooked wounds. Such had been the nature of the battle that those at the rampart had suffered mostly from bites and scratches—though some were down and feverish from the blood poison. Few enough of the Volunteers had died, at least physically. Encampments of those still in shock surrounded the fort, and half the surviving Volunteers had already slunk away east.

Nathaniel couldn't really blame them. Most had been caught up in the idea of a glorious battle like Anvil Lake, and the idea of being able to return home a hero. They'd not thought much about fighting another man, and then they faced creatures from the nether reaches of Hell itself. Just the constant flapping of their wings battering a body was enough to drive men insane, not to mention the biting and clawing. Accompany that with the terrified screams of others, and it was a wonder everyone hadn't gone east fast as they could.

As horrible as all that was, the destruction of the Fifth Northland Cavalry would haunt many nightmares. The cavalry arrived just in time to save the fort from the trolls. Men's spirits rose as the weight of doom lifted from them. They cheered their saviors, these gallant men, riding with bare steel against the horned behemoths.

And then they got to watch as their saviors were churned into blood and mud and ivory bone chips. When Nathaniel had looked out over the area where the cavalry had disappeared, what shocked him was that he didn't see bodies. He didn't see limbs. The tattered scraps of uniforms and scarlet puddles hinted less at their source than scattered autumn leaves described a tree. There wasn't anything he recognized out there as having been of men, horses, guns, swords, or tack.

A few of the riders had survived—mostly from the front few ranks of the charge. The trollish charge had sliced in behind the cavalry's leading edge. The surviving members of the Fifth had turned to chase the trolls, but pursuit languished as their horses galloped through what had once been their friends. Only a handful made it to the river, where they stopped just shy of water running red with blood.

The Shedashee had fared somewhat better than the cavalry, having lost only a quarter of their number. Most of those had fallen to trolls. Kamiskwa had made the best of the opportunity and had slain two with his warclub. The rest of the Shedashee eyed him as if he were a god.

Nathaniel handed him the bucket. "I reckon I have a question or three."

Kamiskwa dumped water over himself, then passed the bucket on and squeezed water out of his hair. "I would keep no secrets from you, my brother."

"Which ain't exactly saying you'll tell me everything." Nathaniel nodded, then knelt in the river and began to wash his clothes. "I reckon there's limitations to your moving from one place to another as you did. Why hain't I never seen that before?"

The Shedashee shook his head. "I had never seen it before. It was my father's doing. I do not know that I could do it."

"Fair enough." Nathaniel grabbed a dollop of lye soap from a small trough and worked it into his loincloth. "Your father, I seen him kill a troll with a tomahawk. Thing done stuck in the troll's skull, then it pushed itself into his brain. Msitazi said that I throw to hit, but he threw to kill. Now you cain't tell me there weren't no magick there, but that blade was steel and he weren't touching it, so that is double reason it shouldn't have worked."

Kamiskwa appropriated some of the soap and began washing his own leggings. "There are magicks you could learn, Magehawk, but you think too much like a Mystrian to believe you can learn them."

"How do you mean?"

Kamiskwa smiled. "You tell me you saw. You tell me there was magick.

But you tell me it could not have worked. How do you know that?"

"Well now, it's pretty well known…"

"By whom, my brother?" Kamiskwa arched an eyebrow above an amber eye. "It is well known that no man alive could shoot and kill a jeopard with a single shot at one hundred yards, but I have seen it done."

"And I've done it." Nathaniel frowned. Kamiskwa was right. Nathaniel had never challenged the conventional wisdom that said magick had to be at touch and that it could not work on steel. Even stories he'd heard about knights of old who had enchanted swords were taken to be, well, just stories. *But if they was true…* "So, now, am I to believe that you knew magick could work on steel and at range?"

"You've known it, too, my friend." Kamiskwa glanced back toward the east. "All the times we have been in the woods and I know where we are, it means I have read what another man has anchored into a tree or rock. In the Antediluvian ruins, there was the writing, and the images on the walls in the Temple. You've known, but because you did not perceive, you refused to believe."

"And you just didn't think to explain all this to me?"

The Shedashee sighed. "You think like a Mystrian, Nathaniel. It is as my father said. You use magick to fire a gun with the *intent* of hitting your target. The ball hits, and does more, but your intent is just to hit. That is enough to do what you need done in most cases. Very few men are those who are willing to study and understand more than what is *enough*, especially if *enough* serves them well."

Nathaniel dunked his loincloth and began rinsing it. "You're saying that if you tried to explain, I'd have said one was as good as t'other?"

"You can be stubborn."

"I reckon I can." The Mystrian's eyes tightened. "Now if I draw some things together here, I'd be thinking that your father done anchored magick in that tomahawk what was meant to kill that there troll."

"Yes."

"Does that guarantee it would work?"

"Do you hit with every shot?"

"Fair enough." Nathaniel wrung out the loincloth, tossed it to the bank, and reached for his leggings. "I reckon it's my intent to be learning more on this here matter, Kamiskwa, and I would be much obliged for your help."

The warrior smiled. "Of course, my brother. Learn quickly. I fear that is the only way we'll stay alive."

Vlad winced sympathetically as Shedashee swarmed over Mugwump. At Msitazi's direction, warriors twisted the broken wing and set it. The dragon's tail thrashed, but hit no one. The Prince smiled ruefully, wishing he'd had a tail to thrash when they'd set his arm, which had then been splinted and hung in a sling. He'd also had his rib tightly bound, and found the treatment bothered him more than the injury.

The Prince withdrew toward the fort as Baker directed men in erecting the wurmrest tent over Mugwump. In addition to having broken a wing, the dragon appeared to have badly bruised his left hip and shoulder. The magickal blast which had knocked him down had blackened scales that had since crumbled into ash. The Prince had seen where the magick had hit. It appeared as if the energy had actually played along the stripes, since those scales had disappeared, leaving others intact.

Count von Metternin sat in a chair someone had fetched for him, his right leg stretched out and splinted straight. Vlad assumed he was in as much pain or more than the Prince, but the Kessian gave little sign of his discomfort. "How are you feeling, Highness?"

"I am well, as are you, I trust." Vlad gave his friend a smile. "I have good news, news which I intended to share before fighting began but…"

"We were preempted."

"Quite. You need to know that Princess Gisella is pregnant again."

The small man clapped his hands. "That is wonderful news. Congratulations. You didn't tell me earlier because you assumed I would insist you remain behind?"

"Yes." Vlad glanced back toward Mugwump. "Part of me wishes I would have had and heeded that advice."

"I never could have kept you away." Von Metternin smiled. "I shall consider that a good omen. Likewise the fact that Mugwump appears no more hurt than those foolish enough to ride him."

"I find myself less concerned over his injuries than the knowledge of dragons Msitazi is displaying. He knows more than Baker does, and Baker's family has been wurmwrights to the Royal House for centuries."

Von Metternin leaned forward, his hands resting atop a thick walking stick a Ranger had hacked into shape for him. "You may have the secret of it there, Highness. Baker is a *wurmwright*. Mugwump is a dragon. It could be that Msitazi does know more."

"But how?"

"I think, my friend, if you are honest with yourself, the question you wish answered is not 'how,' but 'why' you have not been privy to this knowledge. You had signs of it. Msitazi knew when Mugwump would emerge from his molt. That he could show you how scales pointed him to that conclusion allowed you to avoid asking how he knew what the scales would indicate. It was a mystery forgotten when we saw the wings." The seated man shrugged. "And now you feel betrayed, because of the dragon and because Msitazi revealed hidden things about magick."

Vlad nodded. "It is true. I learn what I have learned and hid knowledge of it from the Church for fear of what they will do. And yet I fault the Shedashee for not revealing to us all they know about magick when their motivation clearly is the same as mine. I see the irony, but I feel that if I knew what they know, it would have been easier to prepare troops to face the Norghaest."

"I will suggest two things." The Kessian held up a finger. "It could well be that without the green powder training you've already offered, men would be unable to understand anything the Shedashee might be inclined to teach."

"Good point. The second?"

Von Metternin looked out at the battlefield. "I do not think anything would have prepared men for this."

"No." Bodies were being dragged from the battlements and laid out up hill from the fort. The Shedashee had recovered their dead and moved them toward the west. By custom they would erect platforms and place the bodies on them, so carrion birds would devour them and carry them into the heavens. Later, relatives would collect and clean the bones, then carry them off to hidden caverns where they would be venerated. Plentiful's leader, an older woman, had complained about allowing heathens to desecrate the valley, but Makepeace had cut her off and carried her away mid-rant.

Out on the battlefield nothing moved, save for ravens, crows, and other carrion birds. Vlad spotted a couple of eagles tugging some red fibers apart. The birds picked their way over muddy ground and seemed to have as much trouble finding edible bits as Vlad did recognizing the remains of men. Oddly enough, the birds avoided the troll carcasses, but at the ramparts, tore at the demon bodies with great delight.

Vlad leaned on the back of the Count's chair. "On the parapet, before we saddled up, I had a vexing conversation with Msitazi. He said that I needed to learn, and that the *Noragah* did as well. When I asked for clarification, he said, 'What you have yet to learn, they seek to remember.' I can make little sense of that."

Von Metternin pointed his stick toward the brown scar that marked the troll hole's collapse. "When the trolls first came, they were packed together, much in the way that Lord Rivendell assaulted the fortress at Anvil Lake."

"Yes, but the second time he spread them out."

"Exactly. He learned from what he saw." The Count's brow furrowed. "What if that first assault was set up to show them how we fight, and that the first formation was in keeping with Rufus' experience in mass battle—namely Anvil Lake. But the second time, when the trolls spread out, it was someone trying a more effective strategy against the weapons and tactics we used."

"Do you think Rufus was that smart?"

"I only met the man on a couple of occasions, but his temperament seemed such that he would not have retreated that first time since his trolls could have carried the rampart. He would have wanted to show us all his superiority. Perhaps, and the annals of Church lore would support the idea, he is possessed by a demon which is acting through him. That Norghaest demon, then, is learning about us to know what sort of foe it faces."

"So this was just a test?" Vlad shook his head. "All this to see how tough we are?"

"Yes, my friend, I fear it is so." The Count sighed. "And what the Norghaest learned is that sweeping us from the land will be no trouble at all."

Owen quickly got out of the way as Caleb stormed from the thaumagraph cabin. The young man, fury having reddened his face, didn't acknowledge

Owen. He figured Caleb likely didn't even see him. Owen would have said something, but heard a sob from the cabin's dimming interior.

He entered. Bethany sat at the thaumagraph table, elbows planted on it, hands covering her face.

"Is something wrong, Beth… Lieutenant Frost?"

She glanced at him, then hid her face again for a moment. She brushed away tears and turned toward him, her expression tense. "Don't you start in on me, too, Captain Strake."

"What?"

She stood and pointed a finger toward the door. "Caleb came in here to tell me how stupid I was to go out there. He said I could have been killed. And I know you said…" She leaned against the table. "You told me…"

Owen wanted nothing so badly as to gather her in his arms. He couldn't, so he snarled and pounded a fist against the wall.

Bethany looked up, her eyes brimming. "Please don't, Owen."

"No, Bethany." Owen held his hands up, forcing them open. He'd cleaned the blood off them, though his cuffs remained stained and his clothes still stank. "That wasn't about you. I was, I *will*, go out there and give Caleb a piece of my mind."

"No, let him go." Her shoulders slumped. "He'd been proud of the idea of having me along until it dawned on him that I could end up as dead as anyone else. Now he wants me to go home. He says I can go with the wounded. I told him I wasn't going. He got very angry."

Owen lowered his hands. "That's because he doesn't want to lose you."

"And now you're here to tell me to go, too."

"Huh?"

"Owen…" She took a step toward him, then stopped, her arms wrapping around her middle. "I can't leave. I can't abandon… everyone. But I would do it if you asked, so, please, don't ask."

Owen threw his head back and laughed.

Bethany glared at him. "Don't you dare."

He crossed the room to her. "Bethany, I don't want you to go. I didn't come here to ask you to leave." He reached around to the small of his back and slid a knife in a beaded sheath from inside his belt. "I came to give you this. It's a better knife for cutting. And Justice Bone, he found a couple pistols some people left behind. He figures you can have the lend of them until we get back to Temperance, then you can return them."

She accepted the knife, holding it in her two hands, then looked up. A single tear rolled down her cheek. "You're not angry with me?"

"I don't really like you disobeying an order, or convincing Corporal Brown to disobey with you..."

"She didn't. You ordered her to keep me safe, remember?"

"Right." He smiled. "You saved my life. This is the second time, really, because I'd not have been here except for your nursing five years ago. I came to say thank you."

Owen wanted to brush her tear away, and for half a heartbeat intended to, but he lost himself in watching tension drain from her face. Had she not looked down at the knife again, had she not smiled with childish delight, he would have drawn her to him and kissed her. But the knife's distraction bought him enough time to recover himself,

He took a step back.

"You're probably also going to want to get some leathers. They'll be better for fighting than skirts. Corporal Brown can help you get outfitted."

"What? Yes." Bethany set the knife down. "Owen, you're welcome. And thank you for the knife, the advice, and your friendship."

He gave her a smile, then nodded. "You're welcome." He wanted to say more, but a discordant melody issued from the thaumagraph. "Sounds important, Lieutenant. I'll leave you to your duty."

CHAPTER FIFTY-FIVE

24 May 1768
Temperance
Temperance Bay, Mystria

Bishop Othniel Bumble smiled happily as Catherine Strake emerged from her apartment. "Oh, very good, I feared I had missed you."

"Bishop Bumble, what a pleasant surprise." The smile on her face belied the tone in her voice. "Is there something with which I can be of help?"

"I do believe, yes, very much so." He nodded toward the door. "Perhaps we should discuss this indoors. If the clouds coming in off the sea are any sign, weather will be nasty very soon." *Though not, I suspect, as nasty as our conversation.*

Catherine pointed back up along Friendship. "I was actually on my way to the stable, to get the coach and head back to Prince Haven. Today was just a quick trip, you see, but we shall be back for services again on Sunday."

"I'm certain. And I am afraid I must insist."

"You're scaring me, Bishop."

"Let's hope it does not come to that, Mrs. Strake."

The woman reluctantly re-entered the house and mounted the steps. Bumble followed at a remove and at a dignified pace—that latter largely being dictated by his recurrent gout. He followed Catherine into the apartment. She took up a position in the middle of the room, barely giving him enough space to close the door.

"What is this about?"

"It is a matter of grave importance, Mrs. Strake. Let me assure you of that. Perhaps if you sit…"

"Out with it." She stood her ground.

"Very well. This morning you arrived in town and gave an order for supplies to Peas Whole Goods. Do you know what was in that order?"

Anger smoldering in her eyes, Catherine sniffed and lifted her chin. "The message came from the hand of Princess Gisella. I am not in the habit of reading private missives."

"Well, that does you some credit, doesn't it, Mrs. Strake." Bumble lifted his own chin and clasped his hands at the small of his back. "That order was for food, sundries, and contained an order for shot and brimstone, all to be consolidated and sent up to a town called Plentiful. Do you know where that is?"

"Richlan, just south of the Bounty Border. And how does this concern me, Bishop?"

The man chuckled. "Mr. Peas hired Ichabod Drayman to haul the supplies to Plentiful. He came to me because the form did not include proper identification numbers for the recipient in Plentiful, as dictated by the Shipping and Commerce Act. I had a number for Prince Vlad, having given him the honor of being the first enrollee in Temperance, but I got to thinking and did the math. Given when the Prince left and the time it would take to get to Plentiful, it is impossible for him to have communicated that order."

Catherine shrugged. "Perhaps he just sent a very fast runner, or a relay of them."

"Then why would the Princess use you to bring the order here? No, Mrs. Strake, there is deviltry afoot. The Prince with his Ryngian ways, his secret missions for your husband, the Steward's escape: all much too convenient. The Prince is dabbling with diabolical magicks. He is every bit as dangerous as Ephraim Fox, and you are going to help me prove it."

Her eyes widened. "I will do nothing of the sort. You are an odious little man for even suggesting it."

"I do not believe, Catherine Strake, that you wish to anger me." Bumble removed his hat, slipped past her, and appropriated a chair. He looked up and met her outrage with an open smile. "You see, I know your secrets."

She stared at him with an intensity that should have had his flesh melting off.

"No denial, good. Sit down!"

"Say what you came to say."

"Very well." He inspected his fingernails. "I know that Miranda is not

Owen's daughter. I know you were your husband's uncle's mistress on the voyage here from Norisle, and I shall further speculate that you shared his bed well before that. Don't bother to deny it. Lord Rivendell traveled on the same ship for much of that voyage. He saw a great deal and is not much given to keeping secrets."

Catherine Strake stared down at him, but relief flickered over her face for little more than an instant. Bumble, who had enjoyed long practice of watching people as they confessed sins, understood immediately. Yes, he *had* uncovered a secret, and one she wished hidden, but she had more. He took that as confirmation that she was, indeed, sleeping with General Rathfield. He would have confirmation from the man himself when he returned, one way or another.

"Really, you should sit, my dear."

Catherine chewed her lower lip, then lowered herself to the edge of another chair. "What do you want me to do?"

"Understand that your husband has lied to you, by omission if not outright. He knows of the Prince's magick. That he did not tell you about it may have been a misguided attempt to save you in the event of the discovery of this perfidy, but no Church court will believe that. You and your daughter—a child who is not even of his blood—will face the same flames as Owen does. I don't think you want that."

She shook her head woodenly.

"So, you will convince the Princess to confide in you. She will confirm that the Prince is using unsanctioned magick. You will communicate the same to me, and then you and your daughter will be protected."

"Becca, too."

"That child is beyond redemption already."

Catherine's head came up and her eyes blazed. "You leave her alone or I'll see you in Perdition."

Bumble nodded slowly. He'd anticipated her wanting to save Becca, and he intended to surrender on that point. Her defense of the child increased her stake in the game. It also meant that later, he could threaten that stake again, and force her compliance in other matters. After all, she was not without her charms, as Duke Deathridge and General Rathfield had discovered. She would be very useful to him, on a personal level, or as part of a grander scheme.

"Very well, the child is protected, too, but only if you are able to work quickly. I should want confirmation by Sunday."

Catherine nodded. "By Sunday, yes, I understand. I shall do my what I can."

Bumble stood and caressed her hair. "I know you will, child. It will be for the best. You'll see."

Ian Rathfield sat back in his camp chair and rubbed his eyes. For the first time he wished that he'd taken Bumble up on his offer and had brought Lord Rivendell's baggage to Plentiful. He did not want it for his own comfort, but for the appearance of elegance it would have offered. With the furnishings and the pavilion he could have shaped a Cathedral that would have been suitable for holding a service to honor the men who had fallen.

The Fifth Northland Cavalry Regiment had started west with a full complement of four hundred and fifty men. He'd left the fifth battalion with their supplies, and sent the first to Fort Plentiful. That gave him two-hundred and seventy men—three whole battalions—to throw into battle, and that is exactly what he had done. He had tossed them into danger and thirty-seven of them had emerged from it.

It did not matter that he had little choice. He could not have done things any more wisely. His choices were to do nothing and watch the trolls slaughter the Volunteers, Foresters, and Rangers, or to send his men in to do what they could. Even in Tharyngia an action such as the one he took would have left his troops vulnerable to a counter-charge by heavier cavalry.

But the destruction, so complete. Ian opened his eyes, then closed the ledger book on his camp table. He'd written down the names of every man who had died. He remembered about half the names, and had faces to go with one in twenty—mostly officers. He recalled the drills before St. Martin's Cathedral, and that out of the three battalions that had performed so smartly, only three dozen men remained.

The thing that galled him the most was that people would make excuses for what happened. The horses they were riding had no training for combat, so the counter-charge could not be avoided. Yet, had there been no counter-charge, and had the trolls all been slaughtered, no one would have mentioned the horses' lack of training. Instead his men would have been praised for their horsemanship, since that would have held the key to their success.

The Mystrians—at least, those who had not run off—had been full of honest praise for the cavalry. In the days since the battle men had whittled and planted hundreds of little wooden crosses. Others had gathered flowers to sprinkle over the dried field. People, alone or in the small groups, tended to drift toward where the cavalry had died, offering prayers. Even the Shedashee leader had sung a lament for the dead.

Ian had walked out there alone, and no one had seen fit to interrupt him. He supposed they thought he was praying, commending men to God, perhaps hoping to spot something that he could identify and carry back to a widow or grieving parent. He appreciated the solitude, less than because he wanted to be alone, than he dreaded trying to explain what he was doing out there.

He'd not gone out to pray to God to deliver the souls of his men but to beseech his men to forgive him. He had no doubt that his soldiers had been destroyed because of *his* moral failing. Their deaths were God's punishment for his sleeping with Owen's wife. He couldn't deny that, couldn't escape it. His weakness had doomed them.

And the most terrible thing about that realization was that he could not give her up. Though he had walked for hours across the fields where men who had trusted him had been trampled into gobbets of flesh and splinters of bone, and though he tried to use the horror of their deaths as a wedge, he could not conceive of a life apart from Catherine Strake. God might have punished him here by killing his command, but He had allowed Catherine to bring him back from the dead for a purpose.

Ian bowed his head and clasped his hands together in prayer. "Dear merciful God, peer into my heart. Know I am Your servant. Do with me as You will but, please, let me fulfill a purpose which is pleasing unto You. This is all I ask, in Your name."

He sat there for a moment, holding his breath, hoping God might send an immediate sign. He neither saw nor heard anything. So he opened the ledger again and, confident that he was, somehow, doing God's work, he started down his list and made notes.

Gisella could not help but notice Catherine Strake's agitation. She immediately took the older woman's hands in hers and led her to a couch.

"Madeline, please make some tea. And see if we have biscuit, not the ones I brought back from Mrs. Bumble. Something fun."

The servant nodded and withdrew.

Gisella immediately reached out and tipped Catherine's face up. "What is it, my dear? You've been crying."

Catherine shook her head and looked down again. "No, Highness, I'm just being silly. And I do not wish to bother you. You have so much on your mind already."

"Catherine, please, we are friends. You were the first, after my husband, I told I am pregnant. I would not have any secrets from you."

Owen's wife squeezed her hands. "Thank you, Highness. I just… you *will* think me silly but… well, I went to Temperance and took your message to Mr. Peas. The order will be filled and shipped. Tomorrow morning we will see the flatboats go up the river with it."

"Well, then, that's good news." Gisella made no effort to hide her smile. The message from Plentiful that had come in the night previous had been short and spare, even terse. Bethany had sent it; Gisella recognized that much. The message contained no casualty lists, but the requested supplies left no doubt that a battle had been fought and that people had been badly hurt. She'd immediately sent back a request to know how her husband was, but it would not arrive until tomorrow, and she would not hear until Friday.

"Yes, it is."

"Then why the long face?"

Catherine sighed, her shoulders slumping. "In town, I felt faint. I went to our townhouse and, well, do you remember four years ago, that awful summer?"

"Yes, the Anvil Lake expedition."

"Well, do you remember, I fainted then?"

Gisella did distantly recall Catherine having been under the weather, then the cause came to her. "Oh, Catherine, you're pregnant! Oh, that is so wonderful!"

Catherine glanced at her, then burst into tears. "I don't know what I shall do."

"What do you mean?" Gisella hugged her and stroked her back. "You will have another beautiful child, Catherine. Maybe a son. Owen would like that. I know Richard would rejoice in having a playmate. This is wonderful."

The weeping woman drew back. "No, you don't understand. You see, when I lay down, I fell asleep, and I had a dream. A nightmare, a horrible nightmare. I would think nothing of it but Owen and the Prince had set store by those visions. And I saw Owen hurt and dying and he didn't know he has a son. He lay there and I know it's impossible but, I was certain that if he knew he had a son, he would fight harder, he would come back to us. Please don't think I'm crazy, Highness, I could not bear it."

"No, no, Catherine, no, never." Gisella stroked her hair. "What we are going to do is to write a letter and when the shipment to Plentiful comes up the river, we shall give it to Drayman to take to Owen."

Catherine collapsed into Gisella's arms. "I thought of that, but it will be too late. It's probably already too late. I've prayed, all the way back in the coach I prayed, but I am undone. My Owen will be dead."

Gisella held her and rubbed her back. She would, of course, immediately send a message to Plentiful to let Owen know the happy news. That she could do and then later say she had gotten a message from someone passing through about how Owen had survived a battle and was looking forward to the addition to the family. The delay would torture Catherine, and Gisella would have avoided that at all costs.

Even though it would cause her friend pain, Gisella would not share the secret of the thaumagraph with her. She'd thought her husband perhaps just a bit over-cautious in forbidding Owen to tell his wife about the Mystrian magick. Owen understood the *why* of the prohibition. Catherine's upset over a dream proved she was silly enough to accidentally reveal a secret. Gisella decided to honor her husband's wishes, but she would not let her friend go uncomforted.

Gisella took her by the shoulders and set her back, then clasped Catherine's hands in hers. "I make you a promise here and now, Catherine, that Owen will know about his child. He will know before the supplies arrive. I shall get that message delivered even if I have to throw a saddle onto Peregrine and ride him all the way west myself."

Catherine sniffed and brushed tears away. "Are you certain? You're not just saying that because you want me to stop crying?"

Gisella smiled. "No, darling, because I know when I cry, you do not think ill of me. Our men are at war, so we must take care of each other. So, I shall handle this problem for you, and we shall have no more tears, agreed?"

"Oh, Princess, I cannot tell you how great is my relief." Catherine smiled sheepishly. "I may yet write a note to go with the supplies, but in my heart I now know Owen knows, and that brings a peace for which I cannot thank you enough."

CHAPTER FIFTY-SIX

25 May 1768
Octagon
Richlan, Mystria

Nathaniel hunkered down beside Kamiskwa, the two of them nestled on the lee side of a big granite outcropping. "I ain't thinking that Rufus being right there in the middle of things is the onliest reason Prince Vlad ain't going to be happy about this."

Kamiskwa didn't even nod in response. Immediately after the fight, they'd headed west and a bit north toward where Prince Vlad had predicted the Norghaest were making a magick reservoir. A half-dozen Rangers, including Justice Bone, had come with them. The Rangers remained a mile back, ready to help out if needed.

The weather had turned nasty, with storms blowing in from the northwest. They brought an unseasonable chill and dumped the sharp and icy snowflakes that heralded a long spate of winter weather. It felt like the proverbial cold day in Hell. Nathaniel wasn't ready to bet on what would or wouldn't happen, yet was willing to allow for things to be worse than the worst he could imagine.

He nudged Kamiskwa. "You ignoring me, or is you just froze?"

His brother turned to him with a smile. "Let me show you." Kamiskwa scooped up a handful of new-fallen snow and made to rub it over Nathaniel's face.

Nathaniel drew back. "Now, if this here is a way for you to wash my face with snow, I'm here to tell you I won't be a-laughing."

"I would teach you the magick, but it will take time."

Nathaniel nodded. "Go ahead, then."

Kamiskwa ran his hand across Nathaniel's eyes. The snowflakes thinned to a single layer and locked together into a crystal lace. Light glinted from the angles, sparkling like rainbow jewels. Nathaniel glanced over and saw a fading blue glow from his friend's hand. He was about to comment, but as he looked past him, what he saw stole his words away.

Up to that point all he had seen was Rufus in the bottom of the valley, roughly half a mile down a wooded hillside. Rufus, with the troll cavalry set up to the west, was pacing and gesticulating and acting pretty much the way Nathaniel expected a lunatic to act. He still wore his robe stripped down to the waist despite the cold. The chain scar and some new livid bruises showed up against his pale flesh. He definitely looked as if he was dying of a wasting disease, and Nathaniel's only regret in all that was that it made him a smaller target.

All that shifted with the snowmask. First, ringing the valley, Nathaniel saw eight points at which blue-green energy flows fractured. Half of their flow poured in rainbow streams into the valley, filling it with a fog alive with vivid color, the iridescent hues of a dragonfly's wings. The other bits traveled straightaway to more points, to join and split. From the southwest, on a direct line from the outpost, a larger energy river hit the Octagon, providing most of what was filling the basin.

As amazing as that was, it could not compare to the figures working within the energy. They appeared more substantial than the fog, yet still had a phantasmal sense about them. Rufus clearly saw them, because his words and gesticulations sent them off in various directions. They appeared to be the Norghaest of the early visions, the golden people, all young and carefree, mostly female. They flew through the fog, drawing strands of energy from the eight points of the pool itself. They established thick lines, then split them, stretching and thickening them again. They quickly framed buildings and towers, columns and porticos. The skeletal buildings they raised reminded Nathaniel of the outpost, and some of the Norghaest even bent to creating statues of tentacled creatures.

"I ain't sure what I am seeing."

Kamiskwa turned his back to the construction for a moment. "Obviously they are building a city—a colony. I think what they might be doing is laying it out and planning it. Then wherever they are, they will shape the pieces and, as my father did in moving us to Fort Plentiful, they will bring the city here."

"That's some powerful magick."

"It is, to us. What if it's not to them?" Kamiskwa watched again. "We would survey, then start cutting trees. You would quarry stone. We do what we do because we have the tools to do it. For them, using magick may be easier than using an ax or a hammer and chisel."

He fell silent as one of the Norghaest, a woman, flew around and then up toward where they watched. Her long, dark hair floated gently behind her. She wore a gold loincloth and bracelets of gold, but nothing else to hide her lithe form, long legs, and soft breasts. Nathaniel thought her easily the most beautiful woman in Creation.

She landed at the hill crest, barely a dozen yards away. Rufus looked in her direction and shouted something at her. She dismissed him with a wave, then gathered power in both her hands. She brought them together, forming the energy into an indistinct ball. She patted the edges with the same sort of clumsy motions young children use when packing snow onto a snowman.

Yet at her touch, sharp details sprang out. With a few casual gestures she shaped the glowing energy into one of the squatting guardian figures from the Antediluvian ruins. It grew twelve feet tall and was nearly half that wide and deep. Its flesh rippled with scales and the muscles beneath twitched as if it were alive. Nathaniel would have sworn that the tentacles around its mouth writhed.

The woman caressed the statue's large eyes, much in the same way that Kamiskwa had run his hand over Nathaniel's face. In the wake of her gesture, the guardian's eyes closed.

She sank to a crouch and moved quickly toward the two men, appearing as a ghost. As she drew close, light glinted from a simple gold circlet which had been hidden by her hair, and a slender gold chain onto which had been hung a large, dark pearl. She pulled the latter from around her neck, silently snapping the chain. She held it out clutched between forefinger and thumb, and the air around the pearl shimmered as if it was rippling water.

Kamiskwa reached out and plucked the pearl from her. Their fingers touched, just for a heartbeat. Kamiskwa gasped. He fell back and Nathaniel caught him as the woman rose into the air, then flew down into the valley once again.

Nathaniel dragged Kamiskwa down the hill and behind another snow-clad stone. "What was that?"

Kamiskwa shivered, staring at the pearl in his palm. "I do not know. I... this pearl, it is a puzzle and a key but, to what, I don't know." He pulled his medicine pouch from inside his clothes and slipped the pearl into it. "The sentinel statue, she's blinded it. It won't see us."

"What about the other statues?"

"I don't know."

Nathaniel shook his head. "Why did she do that?"

"I don't know?"

Nathaniel hauled Kamiskwa to his feet. "Who is she?"

"I don't know." The Shedashee shook his head. "She's the woman I'll make my wife, but beyond that, I don't know."

Wind howled outside the thaumagraph cabin. Prince Vlad nodded in Count von Metternin's direction. "Thank you for the excellent summary of our situation."

The plucky Kessian smiled, then painfully lowered himself into a chair. "You are most kind in letting me continue to serve you, Highness, despite my diminished capacity."

"I cannot afford to be without your counsel." The Prince glanced at Major Forest. "Your assessment?"

The tall, slender man from Fairlee had arrived the previous afternoon with his Ranger contingent. He leaned forward to study the map on the table before him. A hank of white hair curled down over his forehead. He swept it out of the way with his left hand, and tapped the map with the hook that replaced his right. "The Norghaest base being here would make me feel good, but the twenty miles of distance did not slow him down in hitting Fort Plentiful. Just from what I saw coming in, I doubt that if my battalion had been here, we would have made that much difference. He had the heavy troops and we did not."

Forest glanced over at General Rathfield. "That's not a slight on your men, General." The Mystrian soldier ran his hook over the misshapen iron ball resting on the table. Owen had recovered it after the battle. The hook bumped over the knuckle and finger impressions stamped into the cannon ball. "Being able to do this to an iron ball makes Rufus far more dangerous than any enemy I've ever fought before."

Rathfield pointed at Fort Plentiful on the map. "This is precisely why I oppose the suggested advance to the Stone House and striking at the Octagon. Here we can prepare for him. No offense intended, Highness, Count von Metternin, but the defenses you were able to throw up were barely adequate for turning a rabble. With professional soldiers here—and I include your men, Major Forest, since they are well disciplined—we can prepare defenses which will stop Rufus."

Prince Vlad shook his head. "I disagree."

"Highness, if you think we cannot prepare adequate defenses here, how will your forces fare when you push them forward to a place where you can prepare *no* defenses?"

Vlad sighed. His was a valid question, and one that the Prince had wrestled with, but for reasons he believed were entirely different than those that gave birth to Rathfield's protest. Prince Vlad did not doubt Rathfield's bravery or that of his men. In fact, he counted on it. But for them, this was an exercise in military science. The Fifth Northland Cavalry, devastated though they were, still could be counted upon as being some of the best troops in the world. Their charge, foolish though it might have seemed, required confidence and skill.

"Msitazi said to me that I had to learn just as the Norghaest did. I have thought long and hard on that. I wondered what the Norghaest were learning when they attacked. What did we reveal about ourselves?" Vlad stiffly held up his left hand and began ticking points off on his fingers. "We showed them that our most fearsome weapon was only partially effective against their troops. We showed them that our use of magick is as a whisper before their bellowing. We showed them that some of our people were ready to break and run. We showed them that we had one dragon, and Mugwump really wasn't much of a threat—less so, now. In short, we proved that we are cowardly, unable to hurt them, and little more than an annoyance."

Rathfield's eyes narrowed. "And moving to Stone House and launching an attack will change that assessment in what way?"

"The reason the Norghaest came at us the way they did is because they based their strategy on Rufus' knowledge of how we wage war. Rufus was present at Anvil Lake, but only after battle had been joined. His sense of how professionals wage war is distorted. Our inability to defend fits in perfectly with the contempt he has for authority. So, the Norghaest are working with that knowledge to determine how to reestablish themselves."

"Highness, you make it sound as if you do not think Rufus is actually running things." Rathfield crossed his arms. "Am I misreading you?"

"I have come to believe, General, that the golden tablets and working with them enabled a Norghaest sorcerer to possess Rufus Branch. I think the changes in him betoken two things. First, he's being changed to be more like them, which enables them to more easily maintain control. Second, I believe he is wasting away because their use of him is consuming him. Rufus, if you will, has the bit in his mouth, but someone else has the reins and is riding him to death.

"Because of that belief, and because the Shedashee have indicated that the Norghaest create colonies before they emerge, I think whoever is riding Rufus is in a difficult situation." Vlad shrugged. "I don't have any of the troops I requested from Norisle because others determined I did not need them. I do not think it is unreasonable to imagine that Rufus' rider is under similar constraints. The one thing I do know is that people in power dislike surprises, and by moving forward to the Stone House and actually attacking, we can surprise him. That might be enough for him or his controllers to withdraw."

Rathfield studied the Prince in silence, then slowly nodded. "I shall have to survey Stone House myself. Woodlands with ravines and hills defeat our ability to charge, but that has proved less than efficacious against the Norghaest. What sort of a role do you imagine for us?"

Count von Metternin rubbed his hands together. "You will find, General, that your men's talents will be quite appreciated."

Vlad withdrew from the conversation and none of the military men noticed. In his consideration of what Msitazi had said, he'd drawn a second conclusion. What the fight had showed him was that both the Norghaest and Shedashee had a substantially different and more greatly nuanced sense of magick than he'd imagined existed. While he was incredibly proud of the thaumagraph, it was little more than a toy compared to what he'd seen on the battlefield. Msitazi's ability to move troops great distances immediately changed the rules of warfare. Instead of troops having to charge or march through the enemy, they could just appear at his rear, capturing the commander.

The Norghaest's ability to resurrect troops reminded him of du Malphias' creation of the *pasmortes*. Prince Vlad and von Metternin had sat at the edge of the redoubt, looking out at Rathfield wandering over the fields where his troops had died. The Count turned and looked at him. "Do you wish now, my friend, that you knew the Laureate's secret for creating *pasmortes*?" Von Metternin had asked. "Think of what could be done if we had the cream of the cavalry back."

"Absolutely not." Vlad had shaken his head. "It's not that they would not be useful, or that their use might not prevent others from dying. That sort of powerful knowledge never remains in the hands of one man alone. Though you or I might use it responsibly, the same cannot be said for everyone else. I would rather that knowledge vanish from the world, than to have it become as common as some other magicks are today."

Vlad still felt that way, but also realized that the only way to meet the Norghaest on an equal footing was to learn how to do what they could do. *Or at least learn enough that I can stop them and make them think I know far more than I do.* He shivered, realizing he was putting full responsibility for victory on himself. But then he realized that he was willing to do it not out of any desire for glory, but because Mystria was his home, and the Norghaest threatened it and his family.

To protect them he would do anything.

Which means I need to speak with Msitazi and get some answers.

CHAPTER FIFTY-SEVEN

26 May 1768
Bishop House, Temperance
Temperance Bay, Mystria

Bishop Othniel Bumble turned the note over and over in his hands. The cream-colored stationery had been folded crisply and sealed in red wax which bore no crest or sign of the person who sealed it. It had been addressed to him in a delightfully delicate hand, written in sepia ink. The letters had been written boldly, with no hesitation.

Livinia, hovering in the doorway to his office, wrung her hands. "All is well, yes, Othniel?"

"Yes, I do believe so." He slid a thumb beneath the flap, but hesitated. He didn't want to tear the paper. He snapped the seal instead, then scraped away what little wax remained with his nail. He unfolded the note, turning it so he could read the three words written there.

"It is true."

"Yes! Yes!" Bishop Bumble pounded a fist against his desk. His inkwell jumped, spilling a black teardrop onto his blotter. He rose from his chair, lifting the letter as he would the Eucharist during services. "This is everything, absolutely everything. I have them and they cannot escape."

His wife had cringed at his outburst. "You have whom?"

"The Prince, his wife, Owen Strake, pretty much anyone I want from that clique." Bumble laughed aloud. "Thank you, God, for delivering Your enemies into my hands. Oh, I shall do Your work so well."

"But how could the Prince have done anything, husband? He is away, in the west."

"Yes, yes he is." He turned slowly to face her, smiling, not wanting to frighten her. "This note confirms that he has a means for quickly getting messages between where he is and Prince Haven—a *supernatural* means.

He is using magick which is, by its very nature, *heretical*. It's worse than Fox, my dear, much worse. The Prince has been seduced by all of this Tharyngian nonsense, his studies and all that. And he should know better."

"How would he have learned…?"

Bumble laid the note on his desk, then composed himself. "It is quite simple, woman, easy enough for even you to understand. He spoke with Fox and Fox revealed to him the details of his heresy. The Prince could not allow Fox to die, so he arranged for his escape. In return, Fox becomes his mentor, teaching him things that a layman was never meant to know."

He clapped his hands. "Do you understand what this means for me? Do you, really? Do you have any idea, the least little inkling?"

Livinia looked down, shaking her head.

"Of course you don't." Bumble snorted. "It means *everything*. You see, when the Prince returns I will tell him that I am prepared to convene another Church Tribunal. I would have him and his wife on charges. Their children would be taken away from them. Owen Strake, the Kessian, Nathaniel Woods and his whore…" He hesitated. He'd almost added in Caleb Frost and Bethany, but Livinia and Hettie Frost were thick as thieves. If he let slip that the Frost children were vulnerable, she'd warn them.

He clasped his hands at the small of his back. "The Prince, to save them all, will be forced to resign as Governor-General. He'll be recalled to Norisle. In his place the Queen will send Lord Rivendell. Who knows the colonies better among her advisors? He's begged for the position ever since Anvil Lake, but the Queen has denied the request because she bears some slender affection for her nephew. With him in disgrace, however…"

His wife smiled weakly. "I recall Lord Rivendell. He was pleasant, if a bit loud."

"Yes, he was." The Bishop made no attempt to suppress his smile. "And the things he told me when I was his Confessor, they will give me a great deal of influence over him. I daresay he will listen to anything I suggest. I will be able to make Temperance Bay and all of Mystria into what it was always meant to be."

He began to pace, spreading his arms, using his hands to conjure invisible buildings out of the air. "Gone will be the grog-shops and taverns, the gambling houses and places where men sate unholy lusts. Sins against men will be recognized as sins against God, and sins against God shall be punished most severely. A hundred years ago an adulterress would have a scarlet letter sewn on the breast of her dress, but we shall have it branded into her flesh. Of course, not all of the Good Book's oldest laws shall be enforced, but just those God means to have guide us now. Drunkards and fornicators shall be flogged, thieves will have their hands smashed, magicians shall have their hands encased in steel, and all of them shall be put to work for the common good until such time as they repent and accept our Savior."

In his mind's eye, Temperance was transformed from a small city built on a series of hills to a gleaming metropolis that shined purely and brightly as a beacon for the rest of the world. Wickedness would be driven from it, and God would bless it. He would provide manna so the people would not need to work, but just worship Him. Thousands of voices joined in prayer would send the joyous sound of their devotion across the continent, converting Twilight People and Tharyngians and whatever else lurked out there, to God's service.

And there he would be, Othniel Bumble, the man who made everything ready for the return of God to the earth. How could God not reward him? How could God deny him the riches He had bestowed upon Solomon? God surely would raise for him a palace and a throne. He would provide gold and wives and concubines. Bumble would be returned to the image of his youth and granted the extended years given to prophets and forefathers who had done considerably less in the service of God.

It will all be mine!

"Othniel."

He turned to face his wife again. "Yes?"

"You seemed lost there for a moment." She managed a timid smile. "What may I do to help you? You seem so happy."

"I am, my dear. All I have labored for is within my grasp." Bumble returned to his desk. "I think I should like tea. And some of your cakes."

She glanced down for a moment. "I shall have to bake you up a batch, if you do not mind. I shall be quick."

He glanced at the clock on his office's mantle. "Take your time, my dear. No premature celebration—God's work must be done first. I shall

406 ✜ Michael A. Stackpole

write up a full report to Norisle immediately. The Archbishop must know what is going on. By the time his reply comes, the situation will have been handled, of course, but I shall not take any chances."

"No, dear, that would not do. I shall prepare the cakes for your tea as usual." She gave him a quick smile, then turned away and disappeared.

Pulling a folio from his desk, and a sheet from that folio, Bishop Bumble never even noticed her leave. He inked a quill, and set about writing the document that would destroy Prince Vlad and make the Bishop the master of Mystria.

Despite the wind driving snow in from the west, Owen didn't crouch down at the southwest corner of the fort's palisade wall. He kept watch, looking out past the tented wurmrest and the big fire around it. The Shedashee had set up their camp around it, living in small domes covered with hides. They'd oriented them with the doors to the east, as if they'd known the storms were coming for days.

"Captain Strake, Lieutenant Frost asked to see you." Clara Brown leaned her gun against the wall. "Said I was to take over for your watch."

Owen glanced at the sky. "Sun's only just gone down. I've got an hour left."

"She said it was urgent, sir."

"Thanks." Owen grabbed his rifle and descended the steps. He crossed the open yard to the thaumagraph cabin. The table upon which Prince Vlad had taken to laying out maps was still there, but the maps had been rolled up. The only thing left on it was the cannon ball with Rufus' fist dent.

Bethany gave him a brave smile when he came in, but said nothing. She extended a note to him, then withdrew.

He opened it and read it twice. "I…"

Bethany held both hands up. "Captain Strake, you need not say anything. I am happy for you. I do hope it's a boy."

Owen set his rifle down and read it a third time. "To Owen. C is pregnant. She thinks she will have his son. Congratulations, G." He looked up. "Did you transcribe this?"

Bethany nodded. "The Princess sent it twice, just to make certain."

"This is a mistake."

"No, Owen, it's not. It's not a ghost message. It's not wrong." Bethany shook her head. "I know what I heard. I transcribed it correctly. You and *your wife* are going to have a child. I don't... I didn't have any..."

Owen crossed to her and took her hands in his. "No, Bethany, you don't understand. My wife and I, we have not... The last time... Last year was... This just isn't, this isn't right."

He turned away, letting the note flutter to the ground. There was no way Catherine could be pregnant, not by him. They'd not slept together for months, a half-year at least. He'd been gone for over two months, and couldn't remember having had sex with Catherine in the new year. *Has it been that long?* Were he the father of her child, he'd have known. She'd be set to give birth before the summer was out and would have been showing before he left.

"This isn't right." Owen turned back. "Are you certain Princess Gisella sent this?"

"Yes, it was her touch." Bethany frowned. "What are you thinking?"

"Too many things, all at once." He hesitated, words catching in his throat. Joy at the possibility of having another child sank beneath waves of shame. He could not be the father, so Catherine had to have taken a lover. She had betrayed him and yet, he felt it was his failing to honor his pledge to her which drove her into another man's bed.

He gathered the message from the floor and stared at it. "Catherine and I have not been together as husband and wife since before the turn of the year. If my wife is pregnant, then it is either a miracle or she has a lover. I cannot imagine, in either case, why Princess Gisella would think that I need to know this information. Informing me of my wife's infidelity is something that could have waited on my return. We do not need the distraction."

Bethany nodded slowly, her eyes narrowing. "Catherine would know that her child is *not* your child. She would keep her pregnancy a secret— for the sake of her reputation and that of her lover if nothing else. She would not confess her infidelity to the Princess."

"Right. So, for the Princess to pass this information along, she had to think it was important that I know. And that means Catherine would have impressed upon her its importance. But why would Catherine have gone to the Princess with what is either a lie or proof of her promiscuity?

What does Catherine gain?"

Bethany shivered and Owen released her arms. "The Princess would not reveal to Catherine the existence of the thaumagraph. If the Princess told her that she'd get a message out as quickly as possible, Catherine would accept that and hope. But why send that message? You know it is false, but will someone else hear it as true?"

"You're suggesting her lover is here?" Owen's guts knotted. "She can't send him a note since someone might wonder what my wife is doing writing to someone else. So she hopes that her lover learns that she's carrying his child through camp gossip about this message?"

"That could be, but who…?"

The hope that Catherine's lover lay dead on the battlefield flashed through Owen. He hated that joyous spark. *It would be too easy for him to be dead.* Then another idea occurred to him. Owen ran a hand over his face. "No, no, it can't be. It can't."

Bethany lifted her chin. "General Rathfield."

"No. No, it couldn't be." Owen wanted to feel certain in his denial, but as he thought back, it did seem that they spent a great deal of time in each other's company. But his thinking did not stop there. It continued back yet further, to when he had returned from captivity and lay helpless in the Frost household. It had been Bethany who had tended to him—*as Catherine tended to Rathfield.* Bethany had literally brought him back to life and had he not been married… *Do not kid yourself, Owen, even in spite of being married, you had feelings for her.*

Anger smoldered within him. *I respected my vows, as did Bethany.*

His fist balled. "Is General Rathfield…?"

Bethany grabbed his wrist. "Owen, you can't do anything. You don't know that your wife has a lover, or that her lover is General Rathfield. You don't know and you have no way of knowing."

"Quite true, of course. She's likely slept with hundreds of men here."

Bethany slapped him, hard, snapping his head around. "Stop it, Owen. I will not have you speak that way."

His left cheek felt hot to the touch. "I beg your pardon."

"You are a gentleman, Owen Strake, a man of honor. You always have been honorable." Bethany half-laughed, then turned away, choking back a sob. She brushed a tear from her cheek. "Too honorable, sometimes, but a man like you should never speak ill of someone else, not when you do not know what is happening."

"Bethany…"

"No, Owen, this is not a problem that requires fixing or attention now. We will be moving forward soon. We don't know how things will turn out, if we will live or die." She turned and caressed the cheek she'd slapped. "Do not think on this, for it serves no purpose."

Owen glanced at the floor, shame burning its way onto his face. Here they were, on the brink of attacking a superior foe, and he was allowing himself to become embroiled in emotions which had no use in the current situation. His frustration at wondering why the message had been sent had opened him to directing darker emotions at Rathfield. Owen never had taken to the man, but Rathfield had been respectful and showed great courage on the battlefield. He had to respect him for that.

He took Bethany's hand in his. "Thank you. I shall not go looking for ghosts where none may exist."

"Good."

His brow furrowed. "There is the other possibility, and this is one we cannot ignore."

"What's that?"

"Someone else believes there is a way to move messages quickly, and believes that message would involve magick that we know would be considered heretical. That person puts pressure on Catherine to find out about it and she goes to the Princess with this outlandish tale, knowing it will be sent. My reply, or even just an assurance by the Princess that things will be handled, would be enough to confirm suspicions."

Bethany nodded. "Bishop Bumble."

"That's my thinking." Owen shook his head. "The Prince needs to be informed. No matter what happens out here, I have a feeling the real battle resides in Temperance Bay."

CHAPTER FIFTY-EIGHT

Prince Vlad eased his left arm out of the sling and worked it up and down. It's didn't hurt as much as feel tight. He couldn't lift much with his left hand—at least nothing heavier than the locket his wife had given him, but he didn't want the limb to get stiff. He smiled as Mugwump twitched his wing sympathetically. Vlad patted him on the muzzle, then turned to Count von Metternin.

"I am sorry, my friend, to be leaving the most dangerous part of this campaign to you."

The smaller man smiled, waving away the suggestion. "No, it makes perfect sense. And you do me credit to say you are saving the mission for me, but I know you are leaving Mugwump in charge of it."

"I am leaving *both* of you in charge."

Mugwump snorted confidently.

In forming a campaign that would surprise Rufus, Vlad had broken down all those things which Rufus knew about how war was waged. The Prince had no doubt that, in his own mind, Rufus saw himself as a grand hero. Whatever possessed him would have no basis upon which to judge otherwise. Because of this, Vlad needed to fashion the sort of campaign that Rufus would not expect him to fashion.

The greatest part of that plan was to use the foresters to cut a road that ran directly from Fort Plentiful to Octagon. Rufus had not been part of the road-building crew during the Anvil Lake campaign, but he had returned along their road on the way to Hattersburg. He'd certainly gotten an earful about how hard it had been, and yet how vital it was to have such a road built. Vlad had every reason to expect Rufus to allow them to waste their time building the road. This would let him know they were coming, and he would have time to prepare his defenses.

Toward this end, Vlad would have von Metternin and Mugwump lead a small group of soldiers and foresters to build the road. The soldiers would be the wounded men and women left in Fort Plentiful, and they would wear the uniforms of General Rathfield's Fifth Northland Cavalry. Meanwhile, ranging widely, troops would swing south and north, converging on Octagon, to strike before the Norghaest were prepared to repel them.

The Count rose from his chair and leaned heavily on a cane. "We will go slowly, Highness. A mile or two a day, no more. At that rate, it will be mid-June by the time we would arrive."

Vlad massaged his temples. "If he strikes at you quickly…"

"There is no preventing our deaths, save by the success of your attack." Von Metternin glanced west. "It is you I pity. You must all have cold camps so that smoke cannot be spotted. You have to move slowly, always alert. You need to prepare the battlefield and haul things with you. You've done much to prepare, but what comes will be the worst."

The Prince exhaled mightily, his breath steaming. "So many elements for which I cannot account. The Shedashee and Msitazi being sent to their death, Ezekiel Fire along with them. Owen, Ian, and the Fifth likewise doomed."

"If you do not succeed, Highness, we all die."

"And even if I do succeed, many of us will die." He looked from the Count to Mugwump and back. "Is this why my father never wished to wear the crown? Having to make plans, knowing men will die, there is a weight to it, you know. A crushing weight. Knowing I might not see my wife, my children, my coming child. I wonder if the pain of Hell is just eternity spent with the gravity of your regrets plaguing you."

"Not quite hellfire, but quite devilish enough."

Vlad nodded. "Joachim, I have a small casket in my tent. In it are papers. There is letter for my wife. There is a packet of papers I wish to go to Laureate du Malphias."

"Indeed."

"What I have learned about magick and the Church cannot be allowed to vanish. I know giving it to du Malphias is a terrible thing, a treasonous thing, but I am reminded that he destroyed his own *pasmortes*. It may be that he did not want us to learn from them. He told Owen he was bored with them. I fear that my aunt and Duke Deathridge would find them endlessly fascinating and of a utilitarian nature."

"I shall, should it come to that, be certain it is delivered." Von Metternin smiled. "I was thinking of sending Mr. Dunsby back with similar packets. He intends to marry soon, and I would not have him die here."

"He's a good man. Wise choice. Tell him it is my bidding." Vlad again stroked Mugwump's muzzle. "Also in that casket you will find a duplicate set of the du Malphias papers. They are for you to do with as you see fit. And there is one more thing."

"Yes, Highness."

"There is a writ of manumission for Mugwump."

Count von Metternin sat down again. "You meant to set him free? I don't…"

"I cannot explain it, Joachim, but I know he is not a beast." Vlad smiled as he looked up into a big golden eye. "What he did as a wurm at Anvil Lake, that is what we might have trained a horse or a hound to do. It took a basic level of intelligence, but since then he has changed. He uses magick, and if that is not the hallmark of being a human, it certainly must be taken as a sign he is of equal intelligence to one."

"It does not take a genius to wield magick, Highness."

"No, it doesn't, but we still consider a person who can to be capable of reasoning, if not sapience and sagacity, don't we?" He shook his head. "So many times, Mugwump, I have wished to know what you were thinking—but I have never questioned *that* you were thinking."

Mugwump's head came up, his jaw opening in a wry grin.

Vlad patted the dragon's cheek. "So, Joachim, if I die, I wish for you to care for Mugwump until he is healed, then to let him go his own way. I feel as if when he has called out, he was looking for the dragons that destroyed the Norghaest in the past. If he is the last of them, then you must find a way to bring more wurms here from Auropa."

"I suspect, my friend, that would be considered a greater act of treason than learning the new magick."

"And yet, if dragons are the only thing which the Norghaest fear, to fail would be treason against humanity."

"Wisely said, Highness." Von Metternin leaned back in his chair. "But fear not. After what we will do here, the Norghaest will learn that dragons are not the only thing they should fear."

Ian Rathfield looked up as Benjamin Beecher entered his tent. The man brushed snow from his shoulders and hat. "Please, General, forgive me, but I wanted to speak with you on the eve of departure."

"Yes, Reverend?" Ian made no indication that the man should sit, but he did so anyway, drawing a camp chair closer to the small stove heating Ian's tent.

Beecher let concern draw his brows together. "General, I wish, this one last time, to prevail upon you to prevail upon the Prince to let me travel with the Fifth. I was the chaplain to the Rangers who attacked Fort Cuivre. I am no stranger to the hardship of campaign, sir. I truly do believe that the men would find solace in my presence."

Ian smiled carefully. "I have spoken to the Prince on your behalf. This is why he delayed our departure until tomorrow evening, so you can hold a proper Sunday service before we leave. However, given the nature of what we are to do, and the presence of the sick and wounded here at Fort Plentiful, I must agree with the Prince that you should remain behind and provide spiritual comfort to those who are so physically tortured."

Beecher appeared to accept that, but Ian expected the man to make one last run at going with them before the Fifth actually departed. Ian knew at least part of the reason the Prince did not want Beecher going along: some of the things he would see on the Fifth's mission would appear to him to be a heretical use of magick. While his reporting it later would cause all sorts of trouble, the possibility that he would try to interfere with the campaign and doom the mission could not be allowed. Were the man to try to stop them, Ian would kill him and think little of it.

"I sense, General, that you might also need some spiritual comfort. If you wish, I will gladly hear your confession and grant you absolution."

Ian set onto his camp desk the slender volume he'd been studying. "Please, Reverend Beecher, do not take this as any sign of disrespect, but I have confessed all of my sins to Bishop Bumble—those I shared with you long ago, and yet others. If it is God's will that I meet my Maker out there, I am confident He will welcome me to His bosom."

Beecher opened his hands and bowed his head. "I understand that, General, but there are times when the devil enters into us not through our actions, but our mere thoughts. It is not that you have, say, lusted after someone, but even that you might have thought of one after whom you have lusted in the past. That would be enough for him. If you bare your soul, if you look deep into your own heart, and you confess your weaknesses before God, He will save you."

Ian lowered his voice and let a razored edge enter it. "I say with great assurance, Reverend Beecher, that I have looked into my heart. It is a far darker place than into which you or any man wishes to venture. That I am content with my standing before God is enough for me."

Beecher lifted his chin. "General, from what I know of your past…"

In a heartbeat Ian was out of his chair and had Beecher's throat in his right hand. "From what you have just said, Reverend Beecher, and from what you have told Bishop Bumble, I have a measure of your heart. As black as mine might be, yours is yet darker. What God forgives, you do not forget."

Beecher clung to his wrist, his voice squeaking. "General, you have it wrong…"

"No, Mr. Beecher, I do not." Ian relaxed his grip, then pushed the man backward, tipping the chair over. "Understand this: I know what you know of me. I have left letters with friends that they are to open in the event of my death or incapacity. Those letters outline the kinds of lies you will tell about me. I have instructed those friends that if they ever hear such rumors—and they would—that they are to seek you out, overtly or covertly. They are to challenge you to a duel, or to have you murdered."

Beecher, massaging his throat, stared up wide-eyed.

"So understand me, Reverend: Go about your calling, the one you have from God, and minister to my people, to the wounded and sick. Confine yourself to those things and see to your own soul. It occurs to me that were I to pray for you, God would listen more closely, than were you to pray for me."

Beecher gathered himself together and stood. "Yes, General." His throat closed after those two words. He bowed and withdrew.

Ian glared after him, then righted the chair. Once they got back to Temperance Bay, Bishop Bumble would make him pay for what he'd just done. "Please, God, take me to You, or deliver me from my enemies." He waited for a reply, but heard nothing above the howl of the wind and lonely hoot of a dragon. He went back to his reading to gain just one evening's peace before he, once again, had to go to war.

Nathaniel Woods, huddled beneath a buffalo robe in the shadow of the Stone House formation, took the birch disk from Kamiskwa. He rubbed it between his hands. Though his fingers were half numb, he ran the tips over the rough surface. He studied the wood and the rings. He even raised it up so he could smell its cloying scent. He'd taken to doing that last on account of the way binding magick worked; it sounded to Nathaniel a lot like animals scent-marking their territory.

As he looked at it and let his nails pick at the bumps and bits, he found a pattern. It reminded him of a little lake up to Queensland. He'd spent time there with some cousins and killed a bear in a dispute over who owned the fish Nathaniel had caught. There'd been some nice salmon on his string. He conjured up the image of one of them salmon and then mixed it with the sensation of the disk. He wove them together, the way he might have woven different colored grasses into a basket or bracelet, all the while trickling magick into the process.

When he figured he'd done enough, he passed the disk over to Kamiskwa. "Well?"

Kamiskwa held it between his hands, then stared at it hard. He looked at Nathaniel, his amber eyes reduced to slits. "What I have is a bear which is a salmon from the waist down, wearing a crown, clawing the earth open."

"How in tarnation did you get that?" Nathaniel shook his head. He knew how. Kamiskwa had not been sleeping well since his encounter with the Norghaest woman. The Altashee had confided that she'd met him in dreams, and that made his sleep less than restful. *It's not helping him see clearly.*

"I got that, my brother, because of what you anchored in the disk."

"Well, magick's damned hard work when your hands is froze."

"Hands have nothing to do with it. Did you imagine weaving again?"

"Yep, just like you do."

"Ah, Nathaniel, you never were a good weaver."

"Well, I ain't no good at painting, neither, and I ain't mastered whittling." He capped his head with his hands. "Ain't much else to work with."

"Why don't you try writing?"

"I'm a better weaver than I am a scribbler."

"Yes, my friend, you are." Kamiskwa handed him a new disk. "But you have worked at writing because writing is necessary for the man you are becoming. So is learning to anchor a spell."

"Right, soes I can anchor all sorts of killing into things."

"I actually think the crowned bear-salmon would likely distract someone." Kamiskwa laughed.

Nathaniel sighed. "Alright, but don't you go complaining about my penmanship."

"I won't, my brother." Kamiskwa looked out into the night where Nathaniel was certain he could see a glowing city and golden woman standing in a tower window. "You must make patterns, and I must break them, and only in this way can we save the world."

Prince Vlad waved his visitors to a pair of chairs in the thaumagraph office. Msitazi and Ezekiel Fire sat, each man nodding respectfully to the other. "I wish to thank you for agreeing to meet with me. I shall be very direct, if you don't mind. Please know I have the utmost admiration for the both of you."

He looked at the Shedashee. "Msitazi, you said I needed to learn as much as the Norghaest did. I believe I understand what they have learned, and have shaped a plan to deal with it."

The Altashee chief clapped his hands together. "I had no doubt."

"What I have learned of myself is that I know far too little of what the Norghaest know. Their power is incredible. I need to know how to counter it. I need to know what the two of you know of magick, and I have a handful of days to master it."

Fire shook his head. "No, Highness."

Vlad stiffened. "Steward Fire, please recall that I rescued you from death, placing myself, my friends, and my family at risk of the same sentence. I am out here with a small force facing the greatest threat we have ever discovered on this continent. If we fail here, nothing will stop the Norghaest from taking all of Mystria and advancing over the rest of the world. For you to withhold what you know is not acceptable."

Msitazi raised a hand. "I think, Prince of Mystria, you mistake what he has said."

Fire nodded. "You don't kneed to know what we know, or to master it. You merely need to know how to undo what the Norghaest do."

"I do not have time to argue semantics, Steward."

"It is not the game of words, Highness." The Shedashee smiled. "You already know what you need to know. In the next six days, we will simply teach you how to do it well."

CHAPTER FIFTY-NINE

4 June 1768
Octagon
Richlan, Mystria

Prince Vlad took a deep breath as he strode to the chosen spot. He'd pulled on the uniform he could, by rights, wear in his capacity as Governor-General of Mystria. Though he would have much preferred to don the simple green coat and buff trouser worn by the Mystrian Rangers, he chose the white uniform with gold buttons and braid, full with a gold satin sash and gold satin waistcoat beneath it. Because snow still fell in thin curtains, or curled up off the ground, chased by winds, he had donned the corresponding cape and a tall white hat, with a plume up over his right ear, which made him look every inch a popinjay.

On the journey from Fort Plentiful, he had spent many long hours in conversation with Steward Fire and Chief Msitazi. Their discussions had confirmed many of the things he had thought to be true, and had opened doors for him to yet other realizations. The two men also learned from each other. A bond formed between them which pleased the Prince, but made him feel excluded, since they understood things between them which he was never sure he would fully comprehend.

The key thing which they both pointed out was that perception could become reality provided one put enough energy into making it so. He'd seen that in politics many times, in situations utterly divorced from magick. Men standing for office, or officers writing their memoirs, would create a picture which, naturally, elevated themselves and usually ran someone else down. The late Lord Rivendell's book *The Five Days Battle of Villerupt* had left many people on either side of the ocean believing that Mystrians were incompetent cowards. Not only did that breed contempt into many Norillians, but it inspired shame in many Mystrians. One man's poorly

418

written and quite fictitious account of a war had caused people to think less of their own capabilities.

Similarly, the fact that most Mystrians came from redemptioneer or criminal stock sent to Mystria in an effort to rid Norisle of undesirables meant that many Mystrians thought themselves inferior to their cousins back in the Home Islands. While Prince Vlad certainly saw little evidence that this idea had any validity, the deference paid to Norillians by Mystrians—even on this expedition—proved that others held it as true. On top of that, Mystrians and Norillians alike obeyed him or Count von Metternin simply because they were nobility. They were primed to feel inferior, and Prince Vlad had to use that.

Because magick could transform perception into reality in a very material sense, a strength of will and confidence aided a magick user. Prince Vlad's mentors encouraged him to think of himself as being Rufus' better. Though Prince Vlad didn't believe Mystrians were of a subrace, he did invest himself in the idea that Rufus was his inferior. What he knew of the man indicated that he was lazy, selfish, stupid, treacherous, a poisoner, given to drunkenness and wife-beating, and Rufus clearly had run after he tried to murder Nathaniel Woods. That marked him as *him* a coward. There was no doubt in Prince Vlad's mind that he was morally superior to Rufus, and well beyond him intellectually.

This last point became a key for Prince Vlad. He accepted that somehow Rufus had opened himself to being possessed or controlled by another creature. That the Norghaest had magick which could enable possession was obvious given the way the cavalry controlled their wooly rhinoceri. No matter how powerful the sorcerer controlling Rufus might be, he would be limited by Rufus. Vlad was certain he could think faster than Rufus, and that he could understand concepts more complex than Rufus could. He counted on both of these things to give him an edge over his enemy.

At the chosen spot, Vlad dug down through the snow with his feet so he stood on bare ground. In learning about magick and perception, again it had become obvious that spells were shaped to transform magickal energy into something that men could control. This was all done through imagery. Visualizing the sun and its heat would allow a man to take magickal energy and alter it into the form he needed to start brimstone burning. Because men drew this energy from themselves, magick exhausted them and hurt them.

But magickal energy could be drawn from elsewhere. With his feet planted firmly on the ground, Vlad calmed himself and sought within. He sought a feeling, a tingle, the sharp crack of a static spark. He visualized it as lightning at first, then changed it into a sunbeam, which he changed again into a cool flowing stream. Once he defined that image, he sought it again, imagining that cool flow passing over his feet, as if he stood in the middle of a stream.

Which, in fact, he did. Thanks to Owen's survey of the area, the Prince had selected a nexus point where two of the energy flows met. Though much smaller than the flow coursing around the Octagon, it sent a cold sensation up his spine. He defined it as invigorating, much as having icy water splashed on him would be. He let the sensation drench him and fill him.

He closed his eyes for a moment, and when he opened them again, the world had changed. Blue was the river of energy that flowed to his feet. It coiled over him and around him, pooling in his hands. Off to the west, a golden glow defined the Octagon, as seen down a wooded hill and back up again to the crest of the valley. Half a mile away as he was, he could see the tops of ghostly towers, its pennants flying in a breeze that the material world did not feel.

A little tremor ran through the gold, humming as if it were a plucked string. It coincided with Rufus' heartbeat, but pounded at a pace that no human heart could sustain for long. It occurred to the Prince that whoever was hagriding Rufus must be hoping to summon to the world a safe haven, so he could again walk beneath the sun. *And my job is to see to it that he fails.*

Vlad turned his head slightly, catching sight of Bethany Frost over his left shoulder. "Everyone is in place, yes, Lieutenant Frost?"

"Even the people at Fort Plentiful, Highness."

"Thank you." He nodded. "I would appreciate if, as we agreed, you would ride back there—get clear. Consider it an order, please."

The blonde woman stared at him defiantly for a moment, then nodded. "I'll be back at the Stone House, Highness."

"Thank you, Miss Frost, for everything." He let the crunch of snow beneath her feet fade before he raised his right hand. Ahead of him by two hundred yards, each atop a small hill, the expedition's two cannons had been set up. The gunner for each raised a hand to acknowledge his signal. Prince Vlad's hand fell. The Battle of Octagon had begun.

A mile to the southwest, Owen waited with Kamiskwa and Justice Bone just beneath the crest of the hills surrounding the Octagon. Somewhere back toward the Prince, General Rathfield and the Fifth Northland Cavalry had set themselves up as a screening force. No matter what Rufus did, their job was to keep the Norghaest troops back and give Kamiskwa time to work. If they failed, the Prince's effort would be for naught, and Mystria would be lost.

The twin cannonade allowed Owen enough warning that he could poke his head up and look into the valley. About a quarter of a mile away, a square berm had been raised and fifty wooly rhinoceri waited within, their breath steaming from their nostrils. Each wore the headdresses that allowed their riders to control it. As the cannon blasts reverberated over the landscape, trolls stirred beneath a blanket of snow. Armed with lances and their obsidian-edged warclubs, they made directly for their mounts.

The two cannon balls arced into the valley. One struck a rock beneath the snow and bounced off toward the north. The second bounded through the trolls. It caught one in the shoulder, ripping its arm off. The ball slammed into another, hitting it firmly in the chest. The second troll bellowed, but the ball bounced off. After a couple of sidling steps, the troll resumed his course for the enclosure.

Off to the north the ground quivered and mud poured up in thick bubbles, staining snow. A geyser blasted skyward, then a hole opened in the ground. Demons fluttered from it, swirling into a black cloud that headed east, and trolls crawled from the opening. Once they reached flat ground, they stood, arrayed themselves in open ranks, and began their slog toward the rising sun.

Rufus emerged, standing tall on a golden disk. It hovered a foot or two above the ground, clipping the tops of snowdrifts here and there. He bore a staff, looking identical to the one he'd carried at Fort Plentiful. His robe fully covered him, but as he flew forward, he slipped his left arm free to display his scars proudly.

Once he passed over the hills to the east, the air shimmered just upwind of the rhinoceros enclosure. Steward Fire emerged through the magickal portal first and ran up the hill as the trolls mounted their beasts. Fire's hands glowed red as he crafted a sphere the size of a pumpkin. Gold highlights shot from within it, and red tendrils drifted up and out. He gave it a shove with his left hand and it floated toward the enclosure as if it were a soap bubble. Then it burst, spraying a red mist over the enclosure.

Though Owen had been instructed on what would happen, he had not let himself imagine it would work so well. Fire, using magick, had reversed the flow from rider to mount. The trolls had used their headgear to impose their senses on the rhinoceri, but now sensory information traveled in the other direction. The trolls, for the first time, perceived the world as did the rhinoceri, meaning that their vision became indistinct beyond fifty feet, and most of their impressions of the world came through their noses.

Which is why the Shedashee warriors who next came with Msitazi through the shimmering portal had painted themselves with dragon dung. Though the trolls could hear the war-whoops and see the Twilight People boiling over snow at them, they simply could not perceive them as a threat. The scent of a dragon meant safety to the rhinoceri, and staring dumbly at the Shedashee, the trollish cavalry met their fate without raising a hand in defense.

Owen could feel no pity for them. The Shedashee moved through the enclosure, their own warclubs blurring. A chop to a knee would topple one of the giants, then warriors would begin the bloody ordeal of hacking all the way through its thick neck. Dark blood splashed steaming over the snow. Trolls fell to the Shedashee butchery, and yet such was the nature of the enclosure's berm that none of the trolls pouring out of the ground could see their comrades dying.

Owen turned back to where Kamiskwa and Justice turned away the last of the earth. "Is it there?"

Kamiskwa nodded, then sank to his knees and reached into the hole they'd carved into the hillside. "I can feel it, the stone and the magick." He took a deep breath, then exhaled a cloud of steam. "Now, to make it work."

Prince Vlad watched as Rufus Branch glided effortlessly down the hill. Behind him, trolls gathered, and above him, the demons circled. *The stick, dammit, I should have gotten myself a stick.* Vlad lifted his chin and drew his hands behind his back. If he wasn't going to have a staff to brandish, he would hide his hands and affect an air of not being concerned at all.

Rufus hovered on a golden disk, keeping himself a bit above eye-level with Prince Vlad, even though four hundred yards separated them.

"You dare attack?" The pure effrontery of the action, and his affected outrage at it, almost completely covered his surprise.

Vlad lifted his chin. "I dare. I more than dare. This is not your land. It belongs to Norisle. You are an intruder here. The one you've chosen to use is singularly ignorant of the world and incapable of understanding the higher concepts at play here. He does not serve you well, except that you must have found his greed quite comforting, likewise his sense of grandiosity and narcissism."

Vlad chose his words carefully, using longer terms that Rufus likely would not have heard before and certainly could not parse accurately. He sensed hesitation in his counterpart. In that moment of inner concentration, the disk dipped and the ordered advance of the trolls faltered.

But only for a heartbeat. The hands settled on the staff, together, at his navel, the orb glowing with a silvery-white light. "Then you have come to negotiate with me?"

"Negotiate? I hardly think so." Vlad shrugged. "I have come to accept your surrender. That is the only way you can avoid your utter and complete destruction."

Rufus' eyes tightened, and his head canted to the side. "You have never before appeared to be mad. Clearly you must be if you have forgotten what I did to your troops so recently. My riders destroyed yours."

"And I have destroyed your riders."

Rufus looked back toward the valley and again the disk wavered for a moment. His head snapped back around and his eyes blazed. "You cannot stop me. You're lost. Your people are lost. Your puny weapons cannot stop us. Your feeble sense of magick cannot stop us."

He raised his hands and spread his arms. The trolls broke ranks and rushed into the forests. The demons plunged down through the evergreen canopy. "Your minions will soon all be dead, Prince Vladimir of Norisle. And I shall save you for the last, so you will know all hope is gone. Once your heart is broken, I shall crush your body and then sweep your people into the sea."

Half-crouched in front of the battle line, Ian Rathfield drew his heavy cavalry saber before the echoes of the cannon shots died. "Steady, men, steady. Just as we planned it." His heart pounded and his mouth went dry, not from fear, but anticipation and anger. These were the creatures that had destroyed his command. He and his men, just like the Rangers, had spent three days preparing the battlefield. As Rufus had caught them unawares at Fort Plentiful, so the Norghaest would find themselves paying for their lack of foresight.

Trolls came up over the hillcrest and fanned out into the woods. Their broad feet kicked up snow. They had to twist to shoulder their way between trees. As they rushed on, their ranks closed. They filtered into easy alleyways that allowed them to speed their advance.

Their clumping together made them simple targets. At thirty yards, a third of a battalion fired. Thirty musket balls blasted into the trolls. Most struck the one in the lead, stippling his fur with dark, bloody wounds. He went down and two others were knocked back, but the rest came on.

"First line withdraw." Ian turned his back to the trolls and marched steadily toward the west as a second line of his troopers took aim. "Ready yourselves!" He glanced back over his shoulder.

"Fire!"

Brimstone smoke gushed out and balls zipped past him. He heard the thuds as they struck home. A troll thumped down behind him, a bit closer than he'd expected. He ran forward as his retreating men fell back to a third line, then stopped and turned. He slashed with his saber, opening a troll's belly, then Ian ran off toward the northwest, as planned, while Captain Cotswold gave the orders to the third line to open fire.

A troll had decided to give chase, and Ian laughed despite the thunder of the thing's footfalls. He ducked beneath branches and relished the crashing as branches whipped across the troll's face. Ian ran for a fallen log which lay between two widespread trees. He leaped it, shearing closely to the tree on the left, then stumbled and rolled. His sword flew a short distance away, snow stained with troll-blood marking where it had fallen. He rolled onto his back and looked at his pursuer.

The troll bounded over the fallen log with ease, landing a good ten feet beyond it. His feet sank through the snow, then punched on through the branches which had been laid over a pit running five feet in depth. Normally that would have been a minor inconvenience for the troll, resulting in a bruise as he slammed against the pit's end, but a handful of sharpened posts had been planted deep into that wall. Three of them impaled the troll, one through a forearm, the other two through the belly, popping free of his back.

More gunfire resounded in volleys as Ian scrambled to his feet. He grabbed his sword and swung it in a grand arc over his head, chopping a demon in half. More flew at him, but they discovered that the nets which had been meant to stop them at Fort Plentiful had been strung through the trees. Demons bit at ropes that had tangled their limbs. Soldiers with steel bayonets thrust up at them, killing them.

Here and there men screamed as trolls caught them or demons attacked, but the Fifth's discipline held. They kept withdrawing, moving from prepared position to prepared position, loading and firing to command. In the woods, at close ranges, they had an advantage, but Ian wondered how long that would last. Most of his men could manage four or five shots before magick began to fail them. In combat on the continent, at that point, they'd be bayonet to bayonet with the enemy, or riding after them as they retreated. This sustained combat, while effective, would only win the day if the supply of trolls ran out before his soldiers' ability to kill them did.

Ian ducked out of the way as a pursuing troll triggered one of many traps the Fifth had labored to construct. The bole of a stout tree had been chopped into a six-foot length. Its branches sharpened into stakes and it had been hauled into the forest's upper reaches. It swung down on ropes, whooshing past him, and branches impaled a troll through the upper chest and neck. Off to the right a deadfall trap broke another troll's legs. As it thrashed on the ground, men bayonetted it to death. Ian split the skull of a demon which clung on one of his men's backs, then thrust the weary man west.

"Falling back, in good order." Ian again raised his sword and laughed bravely. "By God they'll remember tangling with the Fifth, men. Fall back, take aim, and send them home to Hell!"

In an effort to hide his nervousness, Prince Vlad idly studied the fingernails on his right hand. Over the top he studied Rufus. Golden energy trickled up through the ground and curved down, falling over him as if a gentle shower. The disk exuded small etheric pseudopods, keeping it elevated and moving forward. Before the Prince had studied with Msitazi and Fire, the amorphous feet would have been invisible to him. He would have taken greater heart in seeing them, save that the magick that allowed him to do so was the simplest thing he'd learned, and a prerequisite to the greater magicks he'd have to use against Rufus.

Prince Vlad immediately cautioned himself. *You are a fool to think you can stand against him. That's not the game.* Unlike going to war—in which the Prince had always had an academic interest but no desire for glory—a magick duel appealed to him. The victor would be intelligent and have a very strong will—precisely things upon which he prided himself. Were he just fighting Rufus, he had little doubt he'd win. *But it's not Rufus I'm fighting, not yet.*

Vlad made the tiniest gesture with a finger. The way energy flowed through the pseudopods formed a simple cycle, looping back on itself. Vlad cast a simple spell which, at first, joined with the pseudopod and flowed with it. Then, on the third revolution it fragmented, ripping through the cycling energy. A pseudopod vanished.

The disk dipped and that attracted Rufus' attention. With little more than the half-closing of his eyes, Rufus reestablished the foot, and reinforced all four. Instead of flowing fluidly, now they developed a scaled shell, looking very much like Mugwump's flesh.

Rufus momentarily inclined his head toward Vlad. "So, you have learned from the Shedashee, and from another tradition. Young magicks, unforgivably young. And you, so inexperienced."

Vlad looked up, as if his enemy was an annoyance. "You presume much, and have me at a disadvantage. You are not Rufus Branch, not entirely."

"You wish me to talk, to prolong your agony as your men die?" Rufus shook his head. "You could not pronounce my name. The very contemplation of it would damage you. Were I to force this one I wear to say it, his brain would bleed and his mind would shatter."

Vlad shrugged. "Names have power in magick, so I understand your fear."

Rufus threw back his head and laughed, but the laughter died as Vlad cut all four feet from beneath the disk. The right edge hit first, and Rufus staggered through the snow for a couple steps. He didn't touch his staff to the ground to keep himself upright, but energy did stab down from the orb and accomplished the same goal.

Rufus drew himself up, then planted the staff in the ground. "You are bold. Foolish, but bold. Unlike the one I ride, I am not afraid of you. The Shedashee, they once had a name for me: The Sun's Whisper. Think of that as a key, if you wish. See what it gains you."

The Sun's Whisper. The name made no sense to him, but Vlad came up with a multitude of ideas that fit. That first ray of sunlight at dawn, or the last at dusk. The beams of sunlight lancing through the green forest canopy, or a dust mote dancing in the light. None of these appealed to him as being the wholly correct idea, but they were pieces of it.

Rufus gestured. A scintillating blue ball arced in and around at Vlad. He raised a red shield on his left forearm and wove the sunbeam image into it. His arm came up and the ball hit heavily, knocking to the right. But it skipped off and splashed against the ground, draining into the earth.

Not my best idea to use my broken arm to block him.

Another ball arced in. Vlad reshaped the shield, flattening it, then stretching it and rolling it into a cylinder. He widened it at one end, then curved it down. The Norghaest spell rattled down into the cylinder at the top and shot out the lower end, heading back toward Rufus.

The Norghaest twisted his right shoulder out of the way, letting the ball sail past. It struck a pine twenty yards beyond him. In an eyeblink it ignited the tree into a torch.

Vlad stared, having only a moment to wonder what would have been his fate had the spell struck. Flames shot to the sky, the tree a living pyre, and a cold chill ran down Vlad's spine.

Rufus' hands and fingers contorted their way through a more complicated gesture. Energy gathered and crackled. A third blue ball shot toward Prince Vlad.

The tube won't work again. Neither will the shield. Vlad called to mind the glacises used to deflect cannon balls from a fort, and conjured one of them.

Then Rufus' spell split and split again and again. The eight smaller balls swerved sharply toward the north. The last two skipped off Vlad's defenses, but the other six, each now the size of a musket ball, struck Vlad from ankle to shoulder and down to wrist on his right side, spinning him into the snow.

Each strike thrust pain into him without rending cloth or ripping flesh. It was as if he'd had burning thorns driven through his ankle, knee, and hip. His right shoulder, elbow, and wrist refused conscious commands, becoming leaden and useless. He couldn't even stop himself from rolling in the snow. The fire in his limbs matched the burning where snow coated his face and embarrassment flushed his cheeks. His hat flew off, the feather burning.

Agony jolted through him as he struggled to get back on his feet.

Rufus drifted forward, the disk renewed, and peered down at him. "Were you given four of your lifetimes to study, you might prove a worthy amusement, Vladimir. Your grasp of theory was good. You used my name to fashion counterspells. But you did not understand my name, so they could not work."

Vlad slumped back, spirits sinking even as gunfire continued in the forests. "What Rufus does not know is that I am the least powerful of the Mages who have claim to Mystria. Defeating me will mean nothing."

"But it means everything to me." Rufus held out a hand, then closed his fist. Something tugged at Vlad's throat, then snapped. The gold chain and locket snaked from beneath his uniform and floated to the Norghaest. His hand opened again and it came to rest in his palm.

He chuckled. "Names may grant power, but this is much more powerful. I can connect through this back to your wife. Ah, and she is with child. Perfect. I can let her know you're dying, right now, your child, too. I can kill you slowly, and I can even give her the option of accepting your fate unto herself. Would she die to save you, Vladimir? Will she sacrifice herself and your child? Shall we find out?"

The Prince raised his left hand. "No, you can't do that."

"Why not? They will die regardless. As precious as your wife is to you, she would be nothing to me, not even a diversion were I to take her as the spoils of this paltry little war." Rufus held his hand up, letting the locket dangle from the slender chain. "Yes, I think I will let her make that choice. I think I will let her die in your place. And do you know why?"

Vlad shook his head.

"Simply because, Vladimir, I can, and you have no way of stopping me."

Movement through the trees alerted Owen to Ian's ordered retreat. He glanced back. "How are you doing, Kamiskwa?"

The Shedashee looked up from the pit. "Almost there, but I need your lock."

Justice Bone came forward as Owen fell back. Owen went down to one knee beside Kamiskwa and dug into the pouch on his belt. He pulled out a thick lock of the Prince's brown hair. "Here."

The Shedashee took it and twisted several strands into a slender thread. "This should fix it."

In digging down they had uncovered the tip of the stone marker which the Norghaest had thrust up through the earth. It formed one of the points of the Octagon—the point through which energy entered the Octagon from the direction of the outpost. Once they had cleared enough dirt and snow away, Kamiskwa had drawn a crown using pine resin. He'd used the Prince's hair to cover the symbol. The resin stuck the hair fast to the stone. The lock Kamiskwa took from Owen completed the base of the crown.

Owen nervously tucked the rest of the lock away. "Is this going to work?"

Kamiskwa took a deep breath. "It better."

Owen looked up. "Report, Mr. Bone."

"Rathfield's men is drawing mighty close."

Owen patted Kamiskwa on the shoulder. "It will work."

The Shedashee closed his eyes. He raised his left hand to the design, letting his middle finger drift over it. Owen hadn't been told specifically what Kamiskwa was doing, but he knew enough of the new magick to figure it out. The crown represented Prince Vlad. They'd used a similar design to designate his thaumagraph units. The way Kamiskwa touched the design, the directions his fingers took, the pressure, all of these things were linked to his impressions of the Prince. That and the hair, because of its link to the Prince, would combine with Kamiskwa's magick. The spell anchored within the stone gathered power, then split it to other stones, each of which was represented by a symbol. Kamiskwa's job was to substitute one for the other.

Ian's voice echoed from nearby across the hill top. "Ready. Aim. Fire!" His men responded with a staccato rippling of gunshots. Trolls thudded to the ground, but more kept coming.

And we're going to have to stop them.

Ian arrived, breathless, saber slick with blood. "Have we done it?"

Kamiskwa gasped, then sagged sideways. The stink of singed hair rose from the rock. Owen glanced over. The crown had been burned into the stone's gray surface as clearly as if it had been branded into the rock. "It's done."

"Good." Ian laughed aloud and pointed with his sword at trolls squeezing between the trees. "So, I fear, are we."

Owen turned, raising his rifle, and fired a single shot. "Don't give up yet, General. More trolls need killing and we've got plenty of fight left in us."

Vlad stiffened, his back arched, as argent fire poured over his body. "No. I forbid it!"

"You forbid it?" Rufus smiled and made the locket dance on the end of the chain. "You can't forbid it. You completely underestimate me if you think you can."

"Not you. I don't have your measure." Vlad pointed his index finger at Rufus as the first trickle of magick streamed to him. "But I do have the measure of the man whose flesh you wear."

Vlad shaped the energy flowing from the stone around the most basic spell he knew—the spell that would snuff a fire. With a tiny adjustment, it functioned to cancel magick, but to work, it required a key. It required the person using it to know his opponent so well he could wrap it around that thing which would paralyze his enemy. And while Prince Vlad had no idea what that might be for Sun's Whisper, he knew it intimately for Rufus Branch.

Around that spell he wrapped the image and essence of Rufus' mortal enemy, Nathaniel Woods.

Vlad stuck that essence on the tip of a spell like a spearhead on a shaft and stabbed it through Rufus' left eye. The Norghaest's hands rose to his face, an inhuman shriek rising from his throat. Sun's Whisper staggered back a couple of steps. The locket still hung from between his fingers.

The Prince threw his head back and shouted loudly to the world. "Now, Mr. Woods, if you would be so kind."

To be held back as guns cracked in the distance had all but killed Nathaniel Woods. Save for it being an explicit command from Prince Vlad, and its being described as the only chance they had to win, Nathaniel would have refused. He would have been out there on the right, leading the Northern Rangers in place of Makepeace. He would have been shooting trolls dead left and right.

But the Prince had other plans.

As Rufus reeled back not fifty yards away, Nathaniel tracked him effortlessly. Settling his thumb on the firestone, Nathaniel steadied his rifle, and formed the spell in his mind. He pushed it into the firestone.

He shot to kill.

The ovoid lead slug reached its target less than a second after leaving the rifle's muzzle. It blew through Rufus' left hand, burst his eye and shattered bone. It passed into his brain case and hit the back of the skull, cracking it, but it failed to punch all the way through. It ricocheted downward toward the base of the skull, and bounced again to crush the man's first vertebra. It severed his spinal cord even as blood and brain squirted back out through the entry wound.

Rufus' body pirouetted, arms flying out wide. The staff whirled away. The light in its orb died before the staff disappeared beneath the snow. Rufus went to one knee and for the barest of moments Nathaniel feared he'd get back up. The ruin of his face suggested that was an impossibility, but he knelt there, defying gravity even as brains ran down his cheek.

Finally, his body convulsed, then he collapsed in a motionless heap.

Beyond where he lay, trolls poured down the hillside and demons took wing. Nathaniel didn't know if the Norghaest had somehow given them a final command, or had magickally ripped a gaping hole in the earth so more could avenge him, but the legions of Hell raced east. Nathaniel, having no time to reload, ran to the Prince. He knelt and handed him the rifle.

"I reckon you load and can get one shot off." Nathaniel drew his tomahawk. "I got a throw in me, which means 'tween the two of us, we outta kill something."

Ian slashed a troll's thigh, opening a gaping gash. The man spun, bringing his saber back down, and wrapped both hands around the hilt. He aimed his cut at the back of the troll's knee, preparing to hack that half of the limb off.

The troll twisted, roaring in pain, and backhanded Ian with a glancing blow. It sent him flying. He collided with a sapling, then spun into a larger tree. The impact numbed his back and leg. He rebounded from the tree and landed face-first in a snowdrift.

He rolled over and swiped a hand over his face to clear it. The troll, blood leaking from its thigh, loomed over him, paws raised and talons a glossy black. Ian tried to back away, but his right leg wouldn't work. He raised the saber in his right hand to protect himself, but knew it would be to no avail. *I'm done. Catherine, I'm done!* He closed his eyes and thought of her as he waited for death.

But the troll never struck. A mighty shout cut through the din of battle, inarticulate but defiant. The troll roared in response, but a note of pain shot through its voice.

Ian opened his eyes, staring up. A man, he recognized him as Owen, had leaped onto the troll's back. He'd tangled his left hand in the troll's mane and yanked back. His right hand rose and fell, steel knife plunging into the troll's neck. Blood geysered. The creature reached back, trying to pluck the man off him. Owen shifted from its attempts, then sawed the blade through its neck. The troll staggered and toppled. Owen rode to the ground and, standing on its back, lifted the severed head triumphantly.

And then, before Ian could recover his voice, Owen tossed the head aside and was off again.

Captain Cotswold ran to Ian's side. "Are you hurt, General?"

"Get me up, Captain! All that matters is that I'm not dead." Ian gained his feet, then found a carbine with a bayonet attached. "Go, man, kill things!"

His subordinate ran off and Ian snarled. He'd seen a look in Cotswold's eyes, a questioning of whether or not he could continue fighting. *And Owen…* Owen must have seen the fear and resignation on Ian's face. The man, both men, would think him a coward, a man broken, and he could not allow that.

Ian limped into the battle. With every heartbeat, he willfully abandoned civility and reason. It had no place in this battle. Leaving it behind had served him well before, in ways and at times he refused to consciously remember. He reveled in the scent of blood and the howls of pain. He looked inside himself and allowed the *monster* to emerge.

A monster to slay monsters.

Stalking through the forest, he stabbed and slashed, puncturing knees and cutting heel tendons. He thrust through throats and eyes, anywhere he could find an opening. He cut demons from the air. If one of his men fell, Ian was beside him in an instant. He slew the creatures preying on his men, and continued on, letting his soldiers believe he'd been there to save them.

It didn't matter what they thought. Ian's only intent was to prove himself the most lethal creature walking the woods that day.

Yet for all his energy, the battle would have been lost because the trolls kept coming. Though the tight spaces between trees limited their advances, men's weapons could only do so much damage. Steel might hurt the trolls, but it took many wounds to bring one down, and many more to finish them. It became a battle of attrition, which the Norghaests' endless host was bound to win.

Then from the hilltop came a shrieking which Ian was certain, by the chill entering his soul, meant the Norghaest had destroyed Prince Vlad and had unleashed some new horror. It took him a moment to realize he was mistaken, and happily so.

The Shedashee who had avenged the dead cavalry had arrived and attacked the trollish flank. With warclubs a blur, the Twilight People recklessly threw themselves at the trolls. The riders had been besotted and had fallen easily. The Shedashee clearly had to know these trolls were not in the same befuddled state, but that did not seem to matter to them. They, wearing paints that marked them similarly to the Prince's dragon, swept into the trolls and through them. They slashed and smashed with abandon, using speed as their armor, sowing death and confusion in the enemy ranks.

Recognizing the chance to completely destroy the enemy, Ian picked up a discarded carbine and raised it high. "Fifth Northland, on me. Skirmish line. Advance!"

The men of the Fifth dashed forward, forming up into a tight group, the bayonets jabbing forward. Behind them the wounded men reloaded their carbines and snapped off shots here and there. If the line parted around an injured troll, the Fifth's wounded would fall on it and finish it grimly, not gleefully.

The Shedashee made it through the trolls, then slipped back behind the skirmish line. There Kamiskwa joined them and then sprinted up the hill to come around and attack the flank again. The Fifth drove harder, pushing uphill, giving the trolls less and less space to fight. With the Shedashee coming in from the north, Ian stretched his line to the south where they joined Owen and Justice Bone and a few Rangers who had gotten cut off from Major Forest's command.

"Now, damn you, we have them." Ian stabbed a troll in the groin. "For Queen and Country, men. Kill them all!"

Prince Vlad levered the rifle's breech closed and handed it back to Nathaniel. "Your shot will count."

Nathaniel accepted the rifle, then pulled the Prince to his feet. "I'll die on my feet like a man."

Vlad smiled and looked at his hands as the trolls thundered forward. He could still see the magick swirling. He could feel it coursing through him, galvanizing his body along the same pathways that Rufus' magick had used to inflict pain. The Prince directed the magick to quiet angry nerves, and it did.

"I wish I could do more." He shook his head. "To kill Rufus, I learned really well how to cancel magick. Didn't have time to learn much of anything else."

"You did your job, Highness. Ain't no reason for regret." Nathaniel raised the rifle and took aim. "I reckon I'll make the most of the magick I learned."

Nathaniel fired and magick gave the Prince a whole new perspective on his friend's skill. Golden curls of energy rippled through the marksman and shot down through his arm to this thumb. Brimstone ignited in the chamber and the bullet emerged in a fiery gout and cloud of smoke. A slender golden thread played out behind it, tracing a straight line for the lead troll. It struck its neck at seventy yards, shredding an artery. It bounced off the troll's spine, rending more blood vessels as it caromed down into the beast's body cavity.

That first troll pitched forward, leaving a red mist hanging in the air.

"Nice shot."

"I can get one more in."

The trolls stopped in mid-gallop.

Vlad shook his head. "What?" As good as that shot had been, there was no reason they should have stopped.

Then the ground shook as Mugwump landed between the Prince and the trolls. His claws dug deep, scattering ice and snow. He hissed furiously. His breath billowing out in a cloud which shot toward the trolls like an avenging revenant.

And yet even before it could touch them, trolls began to fall as, from the woods on both sides, shooters fired. The volley came raggedly, rippling out in a widening wedge that raked the trolls' flanks. Old muskets and new, blunderbusses and a few rifles, spat fire and lead. It was not so much that any individual shot dealt death, but that the metal ripped the trolls to pieces.

Chaos reigned. Mugwump's breath dissolved any trolls it could reach. Those that could, withdrew, scattering in all directions. Some, panicked, came straight for the Prince. Nathaniel dropped another one, and Mugwump gobbling up his fill.

Those which ran into the woods found men waiting with steel axes and scythes, pruning hooks and swords. The weapons gleamed from just having had layers of rust scraped from them. Vlad immediately recognized the axmen as his foresters. *But how?*

A horse reined up beside him and Count von Metternin cheered. "Yes, Highness, this is going exactly as you explained it would."

Prince Vlad gaped up at his friend. "What are you talking about?"

"The thaumagraph messages you sent. They were in your hand, I know how you send. You told me to gather all the people who had come to Fort Plentiful and bring them forward. You told me how to deploy them on the wings, and you said they were to strike when Mugwump did."

"I still don't understand." Vlad pointed east as people emerged from the forest, shooting trolls and hacking them to pieces. "Where did they come from?"

The Kessian smiled. "That's all Major Woods' fault. When he did his choosing outside Prince Haven, he made it clear what a man had to have to join this fight. And as men went home, they traded for supplies and spread the word. They were a week back of us, and came streaming into Fort Plentiful after you left. I was going to have them ready to oppose the Norghaest as we had discussed, but then your message came through and we came up, advancing this last bit when we heard the cannons go off."

The Prince, his mind reeling, felt power surge through his connection with Octagon. He looked up and caught just the hint of a green-gold glow fading from within the valley. He wasn't certain what it was, but it left him sad. "Nathaniel, find Kamiskwa. He'll need you."

Nathaniel lowered his smoking rifle. "Rangers are peeking on out of the woods both sides, and boys are back at the cannons."

And Mugwump is gorging.

The Count laughed triumphantly. "The enemy is in full retreat, Highness. Some may escape, but we can hunt them down later."

"Yes, very good." Vlad advanced a dozen feet and dropped to a knee beside Rufus' corpse. He pulled the locket and chain from the dead man's hand, then kissed the locket and closed his own fist about it. He visualized his wife and found the connection Rufus had hinted at. He closed his eyes and used magick to convey a sense of relief. He knew she'd get it in a day or two, or perhaps already had it. When didn't matter, just that she knew, did.

Then he opened his eyes again, trailed in his dragon's wake, and began assessing exactly what kind of victory they'd actually won.

CHAPTER SIXTY

4 June 1768
Octagon
Richlan, Mystria

"Well, I ain't of a mind to disagree with you." Nathaniel, as bidden by Prince Vlad, had found Kamiskwa in the Octagon. They both crouched beside a pair of tracks through the snow that worked from the wooly rhinoceros corral on over to where a muddy mixture of snow, ice, and dirt formed a nearly perfect circle. The mud had frozen over, solidifying little ripples and a couple of bubbles that had not yet burst. Dirty snow formed a berm around it and reminded Nathaniel of the tunnel Rufus had dug to escape Happy Valley.

The tracks told one simple story. After dealing with the rhinoceros riders and reversing the magick they used to enslave their mounts, Ezekiel Fire and Msitazi had strolled across the valley floor and into the troll hole. The mud had erased half of Fire's last footstep, and almost all of Msitazi's. Given the length of their strides and the crisp outline of their footprints, Nathaniel could easily visualize them walking arm in arm like old friends, leaning on each other for support, passing serenely through the chaos which, in a few places, overlaid troll tracks on theirs. They had strolled straight through the battle, unconcerned and uncaring.

Kamiskwa looked up from where he traced a finger around the heel mark of his father's last step. "Look again, Magehawk."

Nathaniel scooped up snow, and used magick to fashion the mask Kamiskwa had used on him before. The scene came alive in magick. Whereas the mud lay frozen, glowing blue energy around it still quivered. The hole fairly well seethed with magick, as if it were a pot on the boil. Yet even as he watched, he could tell it was trending toward a simmer. Whatever had opened the hole, and however it had been closed, great

436

magick had been brought to bear, and two men had vanished as a result.

"Your father do that?"

"He did, or they did together." Kamiskwa twisted and sighted back up the hill. "A few of the warriors said my father ordered them to help me. They thought he would come, too."

Nathaniel shook his head. "He knew what he was doing, weren't of a mind to have any of them in the way. Question is, what in tarnation did he do?"

The Shedashee warrior stood. "It feels akin to the portal magick. He used it to send the trolls and demons away from here. What concerns me is this: he has always had to lead the way. Knowing how savage the *Noragah* creatures are, I have to wonder where he would take them."

"And can he get back again?"

"Yes, that, too." Kamiskwa started around the circle's perimeter. "Come take a look at this."

Nathaniel followed, and crouched at the circle's northern edge, almost directly across from where Msitazi's and Fire's tracks vanished. There, preserved in the mud, were two delicate footprints of bare feet, obviously female. No steps led up to that point, or away from it. "You reckon that's the one you seen?"

"Would you recognize Rachel's footprints?"

"I would, but I done seen them a-fore."

"And I've seen hers, in my dreams." Kamiskwa sighed. "Every night, she is there. Not teasing me, but she is a mystery. I can hear her voice, but I cannot understand her words. She's afraid, Magehawk, but feels safe in my company."

Nathaniel ran a hand over his unshaven jaw. "And these just ain't no regular dreams."

"In them she is more real to me than you are right now." Kamiskwa looked at his hands and brushed his thumbs over his fingertips. "She was here, Nathaniel, not the vision she was before, but here. I think she helped my father and Fire deal with this hole."

"So she would know where they are."

"Or she is with them." Kamiskwa glanced down. "I must find them and bring them back."

Nathaniel stood. "Are we leaving right quick now, or will morning be soon enough?"

"Magehawk, I cannot…"

The Mystrian raised a hand. "Now you listen here, Kamiskwa. I seem to recall there was a time when I headed out on a fool expedition while I weren't much better than half-dead, full of hate and stupid. You was the onliest one what stood beside me. Before then and since you done saved my life a passel of times, and I done the same for you. Your pa done took me into your family, and I took a liking to Fire. And if this woman who's gonna be your wife is involved, there's one more reason for me to go. And the reason you want me with you is that aside from being wise, and a better shot than you, it was me made sure the last thing going through Rufus' mind was a hunk of lead. He was the biggest mage I ever done hawked. Where we're going, I reckon there might be a mage or three even bigger what needs some lead poisoning. I'll oblige 'em."

The Shedashee smiled. "Nathaniel, what about the men you led here? You have your responsibility to them."

"Well, I reckon I do, but I reckon there's more of a way to handle that than walking back to Temperance with 'em all. Caleb Frost, good Lord willing he made it through alive, and Makepeace, they done led them in this battle. I reckon they can get them home again. Having me head off with you, providing I go round and visit folks when we's back, will do more for them men than a couple weeks of campfires and tall tales."

"How does that make sense?"

Nathaniel folded his arms across his chest. "For the longest time I didn't want nothing to do with civilization—Norillian civilization, mind. Shedashee civilization makes sense to me. But you was right after Anvil Lake: men was feeling all full of piss and vinegar, like they could whip the world. They'd be expanding Mystria, as Fire did, by pushing on out, and they'd be putting pressure on the Shedashee. But that was when they figured there weren't nothing out here that would push them back, them not reckoning on how hard the Shedashee could push if they was of a mind to.

"See, most of these men love the idea of the wilderness. It makes it safe for them. Iffen a farm fails, they pack up, move west, make a new farm. And me, I is a reminder that the west is always there. Now Caleb has ties to Temperance, and Makepeace is from a Virtuan family, soes they gots more in common with these men than I do. So when I tell the men, and let it be told, that there's some unfinished business out here, and that you and me is going out to handle it, but they should be ready to help. We make them safe again, and important. They'll know we'll be a-calling them, and if you and I is heroes, and we need them, they're heroes, too."

Kamiskwa's amber eyes narrowed. "It is probably best that you remain out here, Magehawk, away from civilization. That kind of animal cunning would make you dangerous in the cities. I think we should depart after we reach Fort Plentiful. We will go to Saint Luke. The Altashee will need to elect a new chief. Then we begin our hunt."

Nathaniel nodded and jerked a thumb toward the southwest. "Start at the Antediluvian ruins?"

"In a practical sense, yes. First, however, we must visit the other tribes. We know what the Altashee know of the *Noragah*. We need to know more." Kamiskwa's lips pressed into a grim smile. "We learn everything we can, then we hunt, Magehawk, killing anything that would stop us along the way."

Owen found Bethany wandering through the encampments on the southern edge of the battlefield. The combatants, exhilarated but exhausted, had grouped together in small meadows and hollows. Pickets had been set out in case any demons or trolls that had escaped decided to come back and raid. Most people believed they'd not stop running or flapping until they reached the far coast, and many were hoping they'd starve to death before they ever got there.

He looped around to approach her from the front. She was completely lost in thought and did not notice him. "Bethany, are you well?"

She looked up, momentarily startled, then smiled as she pressed a hand to her throat. "Oh, Owen, please forgive me."

"What's the matter?" Owen glanced back toward where the Prince had set up his pavilion. "I just saw Caleb. Aside from a couple of cuts, he was fine and happy."

"Yes, I saw him."

He looked around. "Clara wasn't...?"

Bethany shook her head. "She's fine as well. She killed five demons, but won't stop talking about the fact that I shot two with a pistol."

Owen started to comment, but thought better of it. Shooting a demon with a handgun meant Bethany was far closer to combat than she ever should have been. Her having been able to reload to shoot a second time meant she was in danger longer than he liked. Still, the expression on her face—a mix of embarrassment and anger—suggested Caleb had already given her a lecture and she didn't want to hear any more.

"Something is bothering you."

She nodded, her brows arrowing together. "When the Prince sent me back to the Stone House, Clara and I headed off as ordered. But not far back we found Count von Metternin and people, lots of people. We found everyone we'd left at Fort Plentiful, and many of those who had left after the battle. There were even more of those that Nathaniel had dismissed at Prince Haven and other volunteers who had joined along the way. They were just all there, waiting. When the cannons went off, they surged forward, just two wings of an army that I didn't know was there and I'd swear Prince Vlad didn't know was there either."

"How did they come to be there?"

"Count von Metternin said it was on the Prince's orders, but I never sent any messages." Bethany looked up at him. "I thought, then, that the Prince had sent orders independent of me, because the Count said they were in the Prince's hand. But Prince Vlad didn't have a thaumagraph. Or I thought he didn't, but maybe he did, and maybe he sent messages in secret."

Owen reached out, resting his hands on her shoulders, stroking her upper arms. "He couldn't have thought you were a spy."

"No, I know. I didn't think that." She glanced back toward the east. "Before he met with Caleb and the other captains, he pulled me aside. He asked if I'd sent orders independent of him to bring the reinforcements up. I denied it, of course, because I didn't. But he kept questioning me, asking me if I had gotten any messages or had seen anyone near the thaumagraph. I told him I hadn't, and that I'd taken the precaution of removing the identification disk. The thaumagraph wouldn't work without it."

"That was a wise precaution."

"Prince Vlad thought so, too. He thanked me for answering his questions, but I don't think he felt good about my answers." She shook her head, then raised her hands and held his. "But, here I am running off at the mouth about something which doesn't matter. How are you, Owen?"

He smiled. "I can use some mending, but otherwise I'm fine."

"What do you mean?" She stepped back, her expression sharpening. "Are you wounded, Captain Strake?"

"Only the little, tiniest bit." He held his left arm out and cold air poured through the rent deerskin over his ribs. "Troll horn got me there and the one on my thigh was a tenacious demon."

"Is that it?"

"Mostly."

"Owen!"

He laughed, the exasperation in her voice a bit over done. "I'm banged up a bit. Got bashed into a tree or two, but these are the only spots where I'm bleeding."

Bethany grabbed his right hand and immediately marched him toward a small circle of tents with a bright fire in the middle. A half-dozen men wore the green jackets of Northern Rangers. The rest looked to be some of the reinforcements who had joined up, including one family group with the grandmother and her beleaguered daughter-in-law doing some mending by firelight. She had Owen remove his tunic and hissed when she saw the three-inch long gash on his left side.

The old woman called to a boy of ten. She handed him a needle, thread, a cloth, and a crusty green bottle sealed with a cork. "You'll be wanting those, Miss. The liniment, that's *mogiqua* and grain alcohol, with just a bit of honey. Goes on the outside of him. Got the recipe from *At Anvil Lake* by Captain Owen Strake."

Bethany laughed. "This *is* Captain Strake."

"Cain't be. Captain Strake is taller." The old woman pointed a bony finger. "Now get on without foolishness, Miss. Sew him up good."

Behind the old woman, her son shrugged, and the Rangers did their best to hide grins. For his part, Owen moaned a bit and groaned a bit—in a way Captain Strake of the book never would have done. The old woman snorted with satisfaction and went back to her mending.

Bethany wiped away blood and dirt, then scrubbed the wounds with *mogiqua*. It stung, but Owen said nothing. She threaded the needle, then sewed the cut over his ribs closed with neat, even stitching.

What Owen didn't expect was his reaction when Bethany made that final knot, then leaned in to bite the thread off. Her lips brushed his flesh. Despite being in the middle of a crowd, in firelight, his flesh all goosebumps from the cold, a thrill ran through him at the intimacy of the contact. His mind fled back to the days when he lay in the Frost household, days when he had been in a deep slumber. She had tended his wounds then and though he imagined she'd cut thread with scissors, he could not help imagining her lips touching each of his wounds.

He became hyper-aware of her every move as she stitched up his leg. He borrowed a blanket and wrapped it around himself before stripping off his trousers. Bethany dropped to bended-knee to sew the cut closed. Again she cut the thread with her teeth and he could feel her warm breath against his leg. Her lips seemed to linger, not long enough for anyone to notice, but longer than was needed.

He dressed himself and returned the blanket to its owner. He thanked them all, then wandered into the darkened woods with Bethany. In the darkness he offered her his arm and she slid her hand through it.

"What are we going to do, Bethany?"

She rested her head on his shoulder. "We will do nothing, Owen, just as we have been doing. Do not ask me to be your mistress. I haven't the strength to resist. I see what it does to Rachel, to love someone you cannot have. I do not know how she does it, but I know I could not."

"I would not dishonor you, Bethany. And I would not cause you pain." He kissed the top of her head. "I came to Mystria to find a way to create a life for my wife, for the two of us to share. And here I fell in love: with the land, the people, and with you."

"Owen."

He stopped and turned to her, taking her shoulders in his hands. "No, I have to say this, Bethany. In Norisle, I was always the outcast. I think I came to love Catherine because she was part of Norillian life. If I married her, they would have to accept me. They would have no choice, or so I thought. I'm not the first person ever to pretend that others must play by the rules he lays down, and not the first to be deceived by that arrogance. I wanted a life that would give her all the things her friends had, and all the things she desired, because I believed that would mean I was equal with everyone else. But I was wrong.

"I came here, to a land of outcasts—the land of my father, of my birth. Here I found a home among the outcasts. Mystria embraced me not for who I was, but for what I had become, and for what I did. In Norisle I did things to prove I was worthy of being an equal. Here the things I did earned me the respect of others."

Owen shook his head. "You want to know how I got cut with a troll's horn? I was out there, in the midst of battle. I'd fired my rifle, I had thrown my tomahawk. I was down to my knife. I saw a troll knock a man to the ground and prepare to kill him. I leaped and grabbed a hank of hair. Riding his back, I started sawing his head off. He cut me as he was struggling, dying, and as he fell I realized the man I'd saved was Ian. But here's the thing of it: I wasn't fighting to save Ian. I was fighting because I was outraged that these creatures were attacking my home. I'd have killed that troll if it was standing over Johnny Rivendell, or Guy du Malphias or even my uncle."

Bethany stepped forward, slipping her arms around him, and he settled his around her. He said nothing, just feeling her there, feeling the brush of her hair against his cheek. Though he ached and felt exhausted, he wanted the world to stop so this moment would last forever.

Again he kissed the top of her head. "What I want you to know is that I love you. I am bound by vows which, ultimately, led me here to you, and yet keep us apart. A small piece of me wishes we had the courage that Nathaniel and Rachel have, but I understand that there are greater issues which mightily complicate things. While it would be easier to give in to our desires, it would destroy us."

She hugged him a little more tightly. "Promise me you will always let me see your journals, that you will share that intimacy with me. If you will do that, I shall survive."

"I promise."

"Thank you." Bethany pulled back, and starlight glinted from the track of a single tear. "Now, if you would be so kind, Captain Strake, please conduct me to my quarters. I'm certain Clara will be waiting, and I should not want her to fret."

CHAPTER SIXTY-ONE

4 June 1768

Octagon

Richlan, Mystria

Ian Rathfield again cast a glance at the flask a subaltern had left on his camp desk. He felt certain the man meant it as a gift, to ward off the chill and perhaps to celebrate the victory. He couldn't have meant it as a tonic against the void creeping through Ian's guts, eating him up like a cancer. Ian was certain he had given no clue as to what troubled him, and was just as certain that to take a drink would erode the dam behind which his fears pooled.

No matter how he tried to distract himself, he could not escape the certainty of death as he lay there at the troll's ponderous feet. He'd given up. He'd closed his eyes. He was ready to die, his only regret that he would never again look upon Catherine's smiling face, that he would never again feel her caress, or her breath warm against his skin. And even as he thought of her at the very end, he knew he did that because he believed it right and proper. It was the honorable thing an honorable man did as he lay dying.

But he had not died. And even giving free rein to the monster could not erase the image of Owen wrenching the troll's head back, slashing its throat. Ian could see that first spray of arterial blood arc out, each drop like rain softly falling, a crimson mist in the air. The troll's bellow drowning into a gurgle, shrinking to a burbling squeak. The sour scent of fear—both the troll's and his own—still acrid in his nostrils. And Owen, tall, lips parted in a savage grin, acting more savage than any of the Twilight People, his eyes blazing as he saved Ian's life.

As he saved his wife's lover's life.

For a heartbeat Ian wondered if Owen, had he known, would have

444

saved him. The Owen Strake Ian had come to know certainly would have. He was an honorable man, a valiant man, full of courage. He would not have let the troll finish Ian. It was not in his nature to let another do a job for him.

And yet, were our roles reversed, I would not have been so honorable. That realization shook Ian and started his hand reaching for the flask. Had Owen been down, he would not have helped him. He now understood that he moved away from Owen in the battle simply so he would not have been pressed to make that choice. *And so no one would notice if I failed to save him.*

Ian's hand retreated, empty. *Empty, as I feel inside.* He had known for a long time, since he surrendered to the monster at Rondeville and even before, that he was not a hero—not in the way Owen or Nathaniel or Kamiskwa were. Ian had always played by the rules and used them to judge himself honorable. And even when he broke the rules, others allowed him to escape the consequences simply because to expose him would be to expose themselves. They played by unwritten rules, and he was willing to abide by them when the outcome benefited his cause.

He glanced at his shaving mirror, but he had turned it away so he could not see himself. He really didn't want to see himself because he could see the rot behind his eyes. He had long since abandoned any true claim on being honorable. In doing that he had lost himself. He was not worthy of the love of a woman like Catherine. He'd been willing to die so she would never be forced to learn the truth about him. *About the monster...*

He rose stiffly from his camp chair and pulled a cloak around himself. He knew what he had to do. He had to go out into the night and find Owen Strake. He needed to confess having had an affair with the man's wife, and agree to a duel to settle the matter. He expected pistols at dawn, and he resolved that he would not shoot. He had no doubt that Owen would make his shot count, and took some solace in the fact that he could die with honor even if living with it was denied him.

Again he looked at the flask, but eschewed drinking. He would have welcomed the warmth and the false courage, but that would continue his unmanning.

He stepped from his tent and nodded at his men, who sat drinking and mending clothing or themselves. "You all fought splendidly today.

This was the Fifth Northland's finest day."

The men cheered and saluted him with battered tin cups. He smiled and continued on his way. He really had no idea where he might find Owen, but did not stop to ask. He told himself that he needed the time to properly word the confession. He knew that to be a lie. He dreaded the confrontation and was happy for the delay provided by his aimless wandering.

And then he saw them standing together, Bethany Frost clinging to Owen, and Owen kissing her head. He could not hear what they said. He shrank back into the shadows and watched, making certain it was indeed them. When they began to walk off, arm in arm, he forced himself to remain hidden—an act which went against every fiber of his being. And when they had passed into shadows, he discovered he'd clutched the tree behind which he'd hidden so hard that his fingernails had sunk into the bark.

Ian could not believe it. *How dare Owen Strake dishonor his wife? How dare he show her so little respect as to walk freely with his harlot through the Mystrian camp?* His brazenness stunned Ian. Suddenly things became very clear. Owen had used his influence with Prince Vlad to place his mistress in the Prince's entourage. Certainly the Prince must have known of their adulterous relationship—that he would condone it boggled Ian's mind.

He stepped from behind his tree and almost made for them. He would demand satisfaction! Catherine's honor must be upheld. Ian could not allow the woman he loved to be humiliated in this way. No true man could. He would find Owen and challenge him to a duel. Handguns at dawn, and his aim would be true.

A small part of him realized that to challenge Owen in order to defend Catherine's honor was the very definition of irony. Ian didn't care about that—this was about love and honor, respect and chivalry. Had Owen not been carrying on with his Mystrian whore, Catherine never would have sought sanctuary in Ian's arms. This much was so clear that no one could deny it.

What stopped him was his recalling that Owen was Duke Deathridge's nephew. Ian had no love for Deathridge given the man's having had an affair with his wife. He had never gotten any indication from Owen that the two of them were close, or even on speaking terms, for that matter. Still, Deathridge, even if he hated Owen, likely still thought of him as a possession. Killing Owen would invite Deathridge's retribution, and that was an ax Ian had no intention of letting fall on his neck.

He returned to his tent and never gave the flask a second thought. He came to the quick realization that he could not live a life of honor, but that he could arrange things so he could lead a life of pleasure. He might not be the man he once had hoped he would be, but he could be the man who was Catherine Strake's lover. He could do it by framing his Mystrian adventure as a great success, win honors and rank in Norisle. He would get for himself all those things that would make life worth living, and use them to wall off the void in his chest.

He turned the mirror around and smiled at his image. Ian Rathfield *had* died in the wilds of Mystria. With him died the sins of the past. And he had been resurrected. *This new life shall provide everything I desire, and rain misery upon those who would oppose me.*

Prince Vlad returned to the medical station, which had been set up on the very spot where he'd stood to oppose Rufus. He paused for a moment, reaching out, feeling the magickal energy coursing through the earth. He connected to it, adding that flow to the magick that was coming to him straight from the Norghaest Octagon. He should have been exhausted, and could feel fatigue nibbling around the edges, but the energy filled him and kept him going.

The wounded had been sorted long since, and those with minor cuts and bruises had been sent off to fend for themselves. The most serious had been brought to him immediately, but he found he could help precious few of them. Some had had limbs torn clean off. He knew no way to reattach them, nor to replenish their bodies with blood. For most, all he could do was to invoke a spell that dulled their pain and provided them enough lucidity that they could put their affairs in order and bid friends good-bye.

As much as men like Bishop Bumble had accused him of conducting "Ryngian studies," he wished he'd done more of it, especially as concerned medical magick. His understanding of physiology, based on dissections of animals and men, did help him. When an obviously broken arm presented itself, it was relatively simple for him to invoke magick so he could practically see through the skin. He would hold the mental image of a healthy bone in his mind, then use magick to impose that image over the broken bone. Though such magick was not without pain for the patient, it did prove effective in knitting the bone together. Still, he had things splinted and urged the same cautions on them as any doctor might have.

As he progressed through cases, he refined his magick. He learned to confine spells to dealing with the broken bits of bones, not the entire bone. He did the minimal amount of work for the maximum effect. This worked very well on bones, and unfortunately less well on damaged organs, precisely because his understanding of their true function was insufficient to set things completely to rights.

A torn muscle presented little trouble. Using magick, Vlad could weave it back together as a tailor might have used to patch clothing. He could have done the same for cuts, but having someone else use a needle and thread saved him considerable work. Herniated muscles, ruptured bowels, and similar things which required stitching up, he learned how to do efficiently, but this didn't always save his patients.

Only one of them died while he worked on them. A young man had come with his family. His mother sat outside the tent, weeping. He'd been struck in the head by a troll. Vlad's diagnostic spells had found bone fragments driven deeply into the youth's brain. Otherwise he was in perfect condition, without a scratch or bruise on him. He lay motionless, his breathing shallow and getting shallower as Vlad used magick to tease pieces of his skull back into their proper place.

The youth stopped breathing and something changed inside. When Vlad worked, the bodies responded. He found that initiating the healing process was almost like teasing a kitten with a feather. First you used magick to get the body's attention, then you convinced it that it should begin healing. Yet with this young man, the body just quit, as if a stiff wind had snuffed a candle.

And as with a candle, a tiny ember still burned in the wick. Prince Vlad saw it, went for it, improvising. The same magick he used to tease the body into healing he used to tease that ember back to life. It brightened for a moment, and he had hopes, then it began to die again. He tried, shifting to other spells, to those he used to pull tissue together. He tried to grab that spark to hold onto it. He thought he had it and then a force beyond his comprehension yanked it away.

The Prince had stood there, staring down at the young man. Despite the grey pallor, he looked vital. Had he sat up, it would not have surprised Prince Vlad. In that one moment the Prince felt frustration over the waste of that life, and in the next he understood why Guy du Malphias had been willing to raise people from the dead. For Prince Vlad the act would have been one of compassion, so the boy's mother could know joy, but for the Laureate, the boy would merely have been a resource, a means to an end that had nothing to do with who he had been.

Prince Vlad finished dealing with the last of the wounded. Over the course of the day more and more of them had come to address him as Doc, instead of Highness. He smiled at that, and knew others would have been offended. He was not. It was very Mystrian for him to be identified by what he did—and quite un-Mystrian for him to presume to be any better than anyone else. They'd looked at him with gratitude instead of any awe, and that warmed his heart.

Kamiskwa and Nathaniel entered the tent, along with a hobbling Count von Metternin. The Kessian seated himself on the edge of the cot that had served as the Prince's examination table. "You would have time to fix my leg now?"

The Prince shook his head. "No. If I fix you now, you'll be foolish enough to do other things that require fixing." He nodded to Kamiskwa. "I'm very sorry your father is gone."

The Shedashee frowned. "How…?"

Vlad scratched at the back of his neck. "You did your job well. Your magick redirected the Norghaest flow to me. It's how I've been able to help so many. Your magick, however, bears a trace of you. I get a sense of your grief. I had it when I sent Nathaniel to you. I, too, wish your father were here, Steward Fire as well. What they taught me, they taught me well, but they taught me far too little."

"Kamiskwa and me is going to take our leave at Fort Plentiful. The Shedashee have a powerful lot of jawing to be doing, then we're finding Msitazi and bringing him back."

The Prince nodded. "Yes, him and Ythsara."

Kamiskwa's eyes became slits. "Who?"

"The woman, from your dreams. Ythsara is her name." Prince Vlad shook his head. "No, no, no, this is wrong. I should *not* know that. You do *not* know that. Which means, I don't have that information from you."

The Shedashee glanced back to the southwest. "You can only have it from the stone. Which means she helped create it."

"Yes, she did. She did it to help us destroy Rufus." Vlad pointed. "She did it so we have the power to stop the Norghaest."

"I reckon that ain't a bad thing."

Vlad drew in a deep breath, then slowly exhaled. "It is, Nathaniel, a very bad thing. It was Norghaest power that seduced Rufus. It destroyed him and those settlements out west. It's power beyond the imagining of any man, the power to heal and restore, to make bountiful what was barren. A wonderful and terrible power."

Nathaniel gave the Prince a half smile. "I reckon you'll be using the wonderful half of it. Rufus was weak, soes he used the terrible."

"Rufus may have been weak, but no man is that strong." The fleeting memory of his desire to pull that boy back from death flickered through his mind. "Before you go, I have one service I would ask of you, Prince Kamiskwa."

"As you wish it, it shall be done."

Vlad nodded toward the southwest. "Go back out there and destroy that stone. I don't want the power. If we are to defeat the Norghaest, we will just have to find another way."

CHAPTER SIXTY-TWO

9 June 1768
Fort Plentiful
Richlan, Mystria

Prince Vlad returned General Rathfield's smile as the Norillian officer entered the wurmrest. "You wanted to see me, Highness."

"Yes, I wanted to thank you and your men for helping with… everything." The Prince pointed off toward the north side of the valley where a hill had been leveled off and the dead had been buried. "Given that so many of your comrades can't be buried…"

Rathfield clasped his hands at the small of his back. "This place has been watered with the blood of the Fifth Northland Cavalry. Upon my return to Norisle, I shall recommend that we establish a garrison force out here. I should like this to be the Fifth's Mystrian home."

"That would likely be a good idea." Vlad patted Mugwump below his left eye. "I had some questions I hoped you would answer. I want you to answer freely. I shall deal with the consequences of your replies, regardless of what they are."

Rathfield nodded. "I am at your service."

"What will you tell Bishop Bumble about Ezekiel Fire?"

The Norillian officer smiled. "I never saw him. I share Count von Metternin's grief on the loss of his aide, and shall mention the man's bravery in my reports. Bumble may have concerns about Fire, but the man is gone. This is not a matter for me to be concerned with."

One down. "And what will you say to him of my use of magick?"

"Again, Highness, I never saw you using magick. I know many people, including some of my men, benefited from your medical skills. To the best of my knowledge, you set bones and closed wounds, using means less brutal than wrenching and cautery." Rathfield glanced toward the ground. "I understand the Bishop might have concerns, especially as he sees magick use over which he has no control as being heretical. I would say that your use—again, which I never witnessed—certainly fell within the compassion preached by the Good Lord. I have no intention of denouncing you to Bishop Bumble."

"Thank you." Vlad exchanged a sidelong look with Mugwump. "I asked you to swear to keep the fact that Mugwump can fly a secret. I know this information would be of interest in Launston. I said I would release you from your vow if we lived."

"I shall keep your secret, Highness." Ian gestured toward the dragon. "While one cannot deny that this wurm has wings, I have never seen him fly. While he has a martial spirit, as do all wurms to the best of my knowledge, and as is made apparent by how easily his wing was broken; the wings are vestigial, ornamental at best, and of little practical use, much as the wings of a variety of flightless birds."

"General, you know this isn't true."

Rathfield smiled. "And yet, Highness, you know that no amount of sincerity on my part will convince my superiors at Horse Guards that what I've said is other than the truth. If they believe me, what will they do? Let a wurm go to molt and die? They would lay the blame for that death upon me. So then they decide that it only happens here because of food or the air? Can you tell me why Mugwump grew wings? Mugwump has been here for years, and the Crown will never move and station wurms here on the chance that after two or three decades they might grow wings that will never work."

Vlad nodded. "Just as the Crown refused to believe about the Norghaest threat in the west. What will you do with that in your report?"

"I don't know." Rathfield shrugged. "I suppose it is good I have a long journey home to figure that out. Have you decided what you will tell people?"

"Not really. The stories will get outlandish, but our having defeated the Norghaest will keep panic down. Alandalusian troops have reported civilizations in the jungles and deserts south and southwest. Perhaps I will let people believe that these were nomads that we sent home. The demons and trolls can be covered by Shedashee legends." The Prince snorted. "As you've pointed out, it is all a matter of reporting what people are most likely to accept. Luckily I have some influence with the editorial staff at the *Frost Weekly Gazette.*"

Both men laughed, then Rathfield advanced and extended his hand to the Prince. "If you will permit me this familiarity, sir, I wish to tell you I have enjoyed serving under you. I do not believe anyone at court understands what a capable leader you are."

Vlad shook the man's hand. "I'm not a military commander, General."

"I didn't say you were. You're a *leader.*" Rathfield nodded. "With men and women so capable and willing to fight, a leader is all they need. I want to thank you for all your kindness."

"It has been a pleasure."

As they broke their grip, Owen slipped into the wurmrest. He stopped quickly. "Forgive me, Highness, I thought you were alone."

Rathfield turned. "I was saying good-bye."

"Looks like the day for departures. Kamiskwa and Nathaniel are getting ready to leave." Owen offered the General his hand. "Travel safely, sir. Please give my regards to my uncle."

"I shall. And thank you for saving my life."

Owen shook his head. "You'd have done the same for me."

"Pity I didn't have the chance."

The two of them shook hands, then the Prince joined them outside to bid Nathaniel and Kamiskwa farewell. The surviving Shedashee waited across the valley, near the graveyard. As Vlad looked at them and at Nathaniel and Kamiskwa outfitted lightly for quick travel, he wished dearly to be going with them. It was not that he found his responsibilities crushing, but that being able to slip them every so often appealed.

Rathfield shook each man's hand. "Thank you both for seeing to my safety in the wilderness. I dare say my wolfskin pelisse will be the talk of Launston, and you shall be fully credited in my retelling of that adventure. Prince Kamiskwa, please know you have my sympathy at your father's disappearance. I wish you safety in your quest to find him."

"Thank you, General." Kamiskwa smiled. "Safe journey home."

Nathaniel threw the man a quick but casual salute. "Safe travel."

"And you as well." Rathfield turned and marched off to where his surviving men were gathering their horses.

Nathaniel looked over at the Prince. "Something need to be done about him?"

The question's bluntness did not surprise the Prince, but its insight did. Vlad reached into the pocket of his jacket and produced a small handgun he'd been given by du Malphias at Anvil Lake. "I do not believe he will be a problem, and I had anticipated a solution were that not the case."

Kamiskwa raised his musket in one hand and pumped it three times in the air. The waiting Shedashee took off to the northeast, disappearing into the woods. They could have just as easily headed east and ambushed what was left of the Fifth Northland Cavalry.

"Yet another reason why you have my gratitude, gentlemen."

Nathaniel shrugged. "He weren't of the same cut as Johnny Rivendell, but that don't mean I am inclined to trust him much outside of rifle shot."

"I don't disagree, Nathaniel." Vlad sighed. "You will keep me apprised of your travels, yes?"

The Mystrian nodded. "Kamiskwa has convinced me that my boy William is old enough to go with us, least ways for the first part of things. He's been learning his letters, so he'll be keeping one of them journals that you and Owen set so much store by. We got us a thaumagraph, soes we will tell what we know."

"Very good. You'll enjoy having your son with you."

"I reckon." Nathaniel scratched at his throat. "Ain't got no idea how long this will take. Nice that things appear to be warming up."

"Godspeed to you both. I will make certain, Nathaniel, that Mrs. Ward learns that you survived."

"Obliged, Highness." Nathaniel shook the Prince's hand, then turned to Owen. "You keep the Prince safe, hear?"

"Always. And if you need help…"

"First on the list."

Owen shook Nathaniel's hand, then clasped his hands at the small of his back and bowed toward Kamiskwa. "Bountiful hunting."

"Thank you." Kamiskwa returned the bow. "I look forward to our meeting again."

Kamiskwa and Nathaniel headed off down the hill, splashing through the ford and off up in the wake of the Shedashee. Vlad watched them go and the weight of the world pressed in on him. He could never have denied them permission to go after Msitazi, but their absence would make things far more difficult for him. Not that he wanted them to assassinate enemies—though their offer to kill Rathfield indicated just how dangerous they thought he could be. Their practical sense, as well as their knowledge of Mystria and its various peoples, made them invaluable resources.

Plus, he enjoyed their company.

He turned to Owen. "If you don't mind, Captain Strake, I'd like to speak with you in private. Shall we visit Mugwump?"

"Of course, Highness."

Vlad let Owen lead the way. The men entered the wurmrest and Mugwump lifted his muzzle. He sniffed once, then settled back down.

"What is it, Highness?"

"Miss Frost told me of the message which was sent concerning your wife. I believe her when she reports that you said you had not revealed the secret of the thaumagraph to Catherine. I am led to believe two things about the message. The first is that my wife relayed it compassionately, not realizing your wife had tricked her. The second, of course, is that your wife is not pregnant. This leads me to wonder why your wife would have lied to mine, and I must conclude that she was pressured into it."

Owen frowned, then nodded slowly. "I spend a lot of time wondering who would have pressured her, but shifted my thinking to who *could* pressure her. I can come up with only one candidate: Bishop Bumble. I fear he connected me with Fire's escape, and threatened Catherine and my family if she did not cooperate. I have to assume that somehow Bumble guessed that we could communicate more quickly than by runner and used Catherine to confirm that guess."

"Your thinking parallels mine. I will not, of course, allow you to be blamed for any of this. You will, when questioned, claim ignorance. No, Owen, no protest, that is an *order*. If there are negative consequences out of all this, I need you in a position to protect my family and to protect Mystria. Do you understand?"

Owen nodded. "You do me a great honor, Highness."

"No, I do you the lowest of disservices, Owen, because I am saddling you with *my* responsibilities." Vlad looked at the ground for a moment. "A message came in early this morning. I transcribed it myself. Catherine reported to my wife that she miscarried."

Owen gasped, then hugged his arms around himself. "I... I should feel horrible, but I feel, I guess, relief? The child, Highness, if there *was* a child, was not mine. I didn't want to think of Catherine as having broken our vows, but…"

"But you allowed for the possibility."

Owen nodded. "You know as well as I that our relations have been strained, but I'd never let myself think of infidelity. Marriage vows are sacred…"

Vlad grasped the man by both shoulders. "Owen, this is my fault."

"Highness…"

"At least in part, a very large part, because I asked you to lie to your wife. I told you that I did not trust her, and that led you to question whether or not she was worthy of trust." Vlad looked him in the eye. "And now you will have to keep more secrets from her, at least until we sort Bishop Bumble out. You can't ask her who pressured her, but you must be alert for any sign."

"I understand." Owen's eyes narrowed. "If Catherine did have a lover, if she had taken one while I was gone, you would tell me, wouldn't you?"

Vlad hesitated, letting his hands fall to his sides. "Not without good reason. I would not cause you pain, but neither would I allow you to be humiliated."

Owen took a half step back. "I guess, in your position, that is what you must do."

"If you ask me directly, I will not lie to you."

"Does she have a lover?"

I hope to God I am not wrong. "Not to my knowledge."

"Thank you."

"That is not something for which you should be thanking me." Vlad turned and patted Mugwump's flank. "The second matter is of the identity of the person who gave the orders to deploy Count von Metternin and the people from Fort Plentiful. There are three possibilities. The Count said the message had come through in my hand, but I know I did not send it. However, I could not discount that by some trick of magick and location that the message might not have traveled to him before it was sent: a journey through time. So, last evening, I took his transcript and transmitted it, in case that was the solution."

Owen's jaw dropped open. "I never would have imagined…"

"I'm quite certain that is not the solution. Tharyngians have speculated about temporal translocation for a long time and have dismissed it. I hope they are right, or we should be fighting the same wars over and over again. Still, I had to be thorough." The Prince opened his hands. "This leaves us, then, with two other possibilities: an unknown but friendly individual who is known to us but chooses to be hidden, or an unknown person who has access to great magicks and, for purposes unknown to us, chose to help us win the fight."

Owen arched an eyebrow. "Like the woman Kamiskwa saw? Someone who wanted Rufus to fail?"

"Yes. When I spoke with Rufus, he referred to himself as Sun's Whisper, and suggested unequivocally that he was controlling Rufus. I accept that there was someone else inside Rufus. We cannot discount the idea that this Sun's Whisper has enemies among the Norghaest, and that his enemies might have access to messages moving between thaumagraphs." Vlad canted his head slightly. "I do not think this is the solution, but I cannot discount it, nor can I discount the chance of the Norghaest learning of the thaumagraphs."

"Of course, Highness." Owen ran a hand over his jaw. "Figuring out who it was on our side shouldn't be hard. Needs to know magick, have some military training, have access to a thaumagraph, and training on how to use it. And has to know your hand well enough to mimic it. I would think this latter point would be the most difficult."

"Congratulations, you have defined the problem as I did." Vlad shook his head. "Unfortunately, I can't pinpoint anyone who fulfills those parameters."

A grin spread across Owen's face. The Prince found it pleasing and a bit unsettling. "I think, Highness, that's because you are too close to the solution."

"I must be, because I don't understand what you're suggesting." Vlad smiled. "Who is it?"

"The most dangerous military leader in Mystria, Highness. The individual with the longest history of service to the Crown. He uses magick, and likely knows you better than anyone else in the world." Owen looked beyond the Prince. "There's only one possibility. Mugwump himself gave the order to attack."

CHAPTER SIXTY-THREE

20 June 1768
Bounty Trail
Temperance Bay, Mystria

While Owen was anxious to get back to his family, he welcomed the leisurely pace of the return journey for a number of reasons. Each day the party shrank as family groups and squads split off for their homes. The leave-taking was bittersweet and different than it had been after Anvil Lake. These people had lost friends and gotten wounded fighting an enemy they'd never heard of before, and likely never would hear of again. Many of them still had no real idea who the Norghaest were, though the impression that they were from the far, southwest deserts had taken hold. While the people had won a great victory—and probably would never understand how great it truly was—there was no sense of history about it.

They had just come out to defend their homes and support Prince Vlad as he defended Mystria. As causes went, it wasn't a great one and yet, it was one for which people were more than willing to give their lives. That alone made it special, and the grim satisfaction on the faces of those who headed home suggested they understood that fact even if they still weren't clear on all that had happened.

Because the Fifth Northland had ridden ahead, and passed through to Temperance Bay more than a week before the force's main body, local people came out to see the spectacle of returning troops. Because of the odd weather, and it being so early in the year, farmers didn't have much to share with the troops, but they shared what they could. By agreement, the Prince accepted something, and then the children and wounded got offerings, while the rest just watched and cheered. Especially joyous were those times when soldiers found their families waiting for them. Owen secretly hoped Catherine, Miranda, and Becca might be waiting for him, and was certain the Prince's family would greet him before Prince Haven.

The prolonged journey allowed Owen time to wrestle with the problems he'd discussed with the Prince. He didn't think too long on the question of Catherine's infidelity simply because it had become moot. Bumble, or someone else, had pressured her into tricking Princess Gisella. Catherine had to know that Gisella had a secret. Owen had to be on guard not to reveal what he knew, and had to learn what she did know. Until that matter was settled, she had to be considered utterly untrustworthy. In that case, her fidelity and their marriage really did not matter.

What he did realize was that he would never abandon her, nor would he humiliate her. He would endure whatever life threw at him simply because he had taken vows and, more importantly, had two daughters to raise. Mystria was a magickal land that had given him a future. He owed it to his new home to raise his girls to be daughters of Mystria. It didn't matter that Becca was not his blood; she was his responsibility. Just as the Prince had asked him to look after his family, so Owen would look after his own.

The journey gave him a great deal of time to think on the puzzle of Mugwump. Owen had been proud of his conclusion and the Prince's surprised reaction had tickled him to death. Vlad had stammered and stared, then paced. They discussed the facts. Mugwump *had* been born into military service and had fought in wars for nearly seven centuries. He used magick to fly. If his use of magick for flight was a natural process, Owen guessed the dragon might well have been equipped to *hear*, for lack of a better term, the messages being sent. His residence at Prince Haven would have allowed him to experience all of the early messages and, since mimicry was not unknown among animals, it was not hard to postulate that he could have learned to send messages that appeared to have been sent by Prince Vlad.

Supposing that Mugwump had the ability to hear and send messages also accounted for the ghost messages. It occurred to Owen that those might have been Mugwump's first attempts at forming messages, but then an even more interesting and terrifying thought came to him. The Prince had reported that when they flew together, Mugwump would make vocalizations. *What if the ghost messages were magickal vocaliza-*

tions which were meant for other dragons? Messages that men could not understand because they were not meant to be understood by men. *And if they were sent to dragons, did he ever get a reply?*

That question started Owen down into an abyss from which there seemed no recovery. He'd seen adult dragons attacking the Norghaest in his *salksasi*-induced vision. While he took solace in the old adage that "the enemy of my enemy is my friend," he couldn't be certain dragons would see men as friends. Dragons had attacked the Norghaest, and left the Shedashee alone, but Mystrians lived a lifestyle far closer to that of the Norghaest than it was to that of the Shedashee. *If the dragons come, who will they hunt?*

As they drew near to Prince Haven, Owen fell into step with Bethany Frost. Though storm clouds gathered in the east, he refused to think of it as an omen. "Will you stay at Prince Haven, or go straight into Temperance?"

"Home, I think." She smiled and looked back along the line of march where Caleb led the Northern Rangers. "My uncle said some very nice things about Caleb before he and his Southern Rangers left. While Caleb is very pleased and proud, I think he wants to get home again. He asked if I would mind staying one more night in a camp, before we marched in, but made it very clear he hoped I would say no. Given the storm coming in, I think I made the right choice."

"It would appear so."

She lowered her voice. "I've hated that we've not been able to talk much on the march. Your voice carries, though, and I smile when I hear it. I would spend the night out here in a gale, just knowing you were close, wanting you to be safe. It is quite unfair of me to say this, but I love you. I want you to know that, so you can remember me saying it in those quiet times when you need to hear it said."

Owen shook his head. "Thank you. For that. For saving my life at Fort Plentiful. You must promise that when you edit my new book, you will not take out the mentions of your heroism."

She smiled and a hint of color came to her cheeks. "It pleases me to know you'll write another book. That I get to see it first pleases me even more."

So innocent a thing to be discussing, and yet so intimate. Owen wanted to pull her into his arms and hug her, but he held back. They had been completely circumspect on the journey, so much so that Caleb had asked if a rift had developed between them. Owen had no idea what others thought or suspected. He only cared after the pain it might cause Bethany and the ruin it might bring to her reputation.

They came up over a small hill, and Mugwump perked up as the road passed the field in which he had learned to fly. Further on, where the drive to Prince Haven met the trail, a small knot of people waited. The marchers generally moved to the northern side of the road, and draymen under Baker's instructions freed Mugwump from the wagons. They brought horses forward to pull them for the last miles to Temperance.

Owen joined Prince Vlad and Count von Metternin as they headed to the drive. He turned back and waved to Bethany, though many others thought he was waving to them. As they drew closer, it became quite apparent that Princess Gisella was very pregnant. Prince Richard had grown quite a bit and ran to his father once he recognized him. Princess Rowena struggled in her nurse's arms—not to run to Prince Vlad, but to shy from him since she did not recognize him.

Owen's throat thickened as the Prince embraced his wife tightly and Richard clasped the man's left leg in his arms. He marveled for a moment at the love on her face and fierce gentleness of their hug. Try as he might, he could never remember seeing that expression on his wife's face, and longing sliced into him like a knife.

Then Miranda came running to him, arms extended. "Papa! Papa! It's me, Miranda!"

Laughing, he caught her in his arms, lifted her, and twirled her around. "Are you sure you're Miranda? You're terribly big!"

"I'm almost four!" She shrieked delightedly.

He hugged her, then saw Becca standing beside Agnes. He gave Miranda a kiss on the cheek, then pulled Becca under his arm. "It is wonderful to see you, too, Becca. The things which killed your family are gone. You're safe."

The girl slipped her arms around his waist as he looked at the servant. "Where is Mrs. Strake?"

"She went to town, Captain. A day ago."

Gisella twisted in her husband's arms. "When the Fifth came through we learned of your schedule. Catherine went to get wine and supplies to celebrate. She should be back soon, if storms do not keep her in Temperance."

Prince Vlad nodded. "Come with us to Prince Haven. We'll wait things out there."

Owen nodded. "Agnes, if you will take the girls. Highness, I will just head home and change into more suitable clothes. As glad as my wife will be to see me, she will happier if I do not stink of the long walk home."

"An excellent idea." The Prince laughed. "My clothes will have to be boiled or burned, and if I can get a good warm soaking, I don't think I'll care which it is."

Owen found the letter on his dresser, his name neatly inscribed in Catherine's strong hand. He crossed to a desk, sat, lit a lamp, then broke the seal, smoothing the paper against his thigh. He closed his eyes, concentrating on the sound of the paper and the way it felt against his fingertips. He almost raised it to his nose, but he knew it might smell of her, and he did not want that. He resisted the temptation to hold it over the lamp's flame, destroying it unread because he knew what it said.

And he knew the words would be worse than anything he could imagine.

> Owen,
>
> I have been reliably informed of your infidelity while in the west. You arranged for your mistress to join the Prince's staff, and you took no care to keep your affair hidden.
>
> I can understand sinful urges, but I cannot understand how you could embarrass me so. How could you make your family a laughing stock? You must never have loved me, or our daughter, only yourself.
>
> I cannot tolerate this dishonor. Do not try to find me. I shall not return to Mystria if you do. Tell them whatever you must, whatever lie you and your whore concoct. Tell them I was too fragile for this land, or that I found it quite lacking in elegance. Tell them I returned to Norisle in shame. They'll believe it.
>
> But know you this, Owen Strake, I shall never grant you a divorce.

If you pursue me, I shall reveal the true, sordid tale of your affair. Not that it would matter to you, save that your whore would become soiled because of the tawdry nature of your association.

I would have taken Miranda with me, but every time I would have looked at her, I would have seen your face. I would have remembered your beastly conduct. I would have remembered you are a man without honor and I would have hated myself for sharing your life and giving you a child.

You chose Mystria over me, Owen Strake. I see now that you truly were Mystrian. You always have been, and have always been unworthy of a noble Norillian woman like me. I had once harbored hopes that perhaps your mother's blood would be strong in your veins, but now I know your father's mongrel taint has stained you to the core.

You will never see me again, Owen Strake, but I will, forever, remain, your wife.

Catherine

Owen went to sit, but avoided the bed and sank down against the wall. He folded the letter again and clutched it in both hands. Catherine's venom-laden words echoed through his mind. He could almost imagine hearing the scratch of her quill on paper as she wrote, and see her face contorted in fury.

So much anger, more than I ever suspected. Catherine meant the letter to poison his soul. He did not doubt she'd taken a lover, since the letter made it clear that he'd failed her as a husband. He'd failed her in every way. As she saw it, their marriage was long since dead, and only useful as a tool with which she could torture him.

And he realized that no matter how far away she went, she would torture him until the day he died.

CHAPTER SIXTY-FOUR

20 June 1768
Prince Haven
Temperance Bay, Mystria

Prince Vlad, his daughter in his arms, walked happily beside his wife down the drive to their home. He matched his pace to hers and laughed as Richard ran ahead. Miranda Strake caught up with him, scolded him on running too fast, and somewhat chastened, he waited for them to catch up. Even Becca Green appeared happy as she skipped forward, took Richard and Miranda in hand, and led the way.

Vlad shot his wife a smile. She returned it, then stroked a hand over her swollen belly. That gesture, so loving and gentle, shot a thrill through him. The promise of new life nibbled away at the horrors he'd seen. He wished, just for an instant, to work a spell so he could see inside her womb and learn of the child she carried. Was it a boy or a girl?

And yet, even as he asked that question, he immediately wanted to know if it was whole and well, or if a limb might have been twisted. With the right magick, he might be able to fix a club foot or cleft palate. It would be incredibly easy to do and would save him and his wife and his child a lifetime of pain.

To do that, however, would require information no man was meant to know. Vlad caught himself. It wasn't the information that was bad, nor knowledge of the magick to solve such a problem, but the temptation to use it in ways that were not altruistic. Rathfield had said that he'd not had the impression that Vlad had used magick in a way that was not in line with the Good Lord's commandments about compassion, but Vlad could not be certain it would always be that way. And he found it frighteningly easy to imagine a world in which compassion was forgotten, where magick would be seen as the exclusive birthright of the nobility and clergy. They could use it to make sure their children were whole and that their loved ones escaped death. Everyone else would be left to fend for themselves, creating a sharp divide between those who were "cursed" with magick, and those who were damned to live without it.

Even as he found himself pleased that he'd had Kamiskwa sever his access to the concentrated source of Norghaest magick, he also realized that threats to Mystria might require him to reopen that connection. *Can I do that without being consumed by the magick? If I cannot, what could possibly stop me?*

He stopped dead and turned, staring straight at Mugwump. "Now I understand: the *pasmortes*, the trolls, the demons, the Norghaest. Now I understand that *you* will keep an eye on me."

It had all been there in his studies of nature. Everything has a predator. When rabbits reproduce in abundance, foxes, coyotes, bobcats, and dire wolves multiply and consume them. Dragons consumed magick, magick with the taint of evil. To them, the Norghaest were a feast because of their selfish use of magick.

"That's it, isn't it?"

Mugwump did not reply, but simply walked along behind Baker.

Prince Vlad turned and continued, catching up with his family. He passed Rowena on to Madeline, then watched as Baker took Mugwump to the wurmrest.

Gisella came to him, kissed his cheek, and clung to his right arm. "You cannot believe how happy I am to have you home. I appreciated the message you sent letting me know you were well. I've since learned you lied, since you did not mention breaking your arm or rib."

"An oversight."

She slapped him lightly on the chest. "No more oversights. I was so certain… there was a point when I had a very strong impression of your suffering."

Vlad turned and kissed her, caressing her hair. "Shhhhh, don't think any more on that. It's over."

"There's so much I have to tell you. I wanted to send so many messages, but as you requested, I put the thaumagraph in a small casket and sank it in the river." She looked up at him. "Can you tell me what the matter was with it?"

"Yes, of course." He started on his explanation, but the crunch of stone under wheel from the drive caught his attention. "Who?"

A coach drawn by one horse stopped before the main house. The coachman leaped from the box and opened the door, helping an older, slender woman dressed head to toe in black from the interior. She carried with her what appeared to be a thick folio. It look him a moment to recognize her. "Mrs. Bumble, to what do I owe this honor?"

A quick, courtesy smile flashed over Livinia Bumble's face, but died quickly. "You will forgive my intrusion, Highness, but I felt this was a matter which could not wait."

Gisella pressed a hand to her husband's chest. "I've not had a chance yet, Mrs. Bumble, to let the Prince know your husband passed away."

"Yes, nearly a month hence."

Bumble, dead? Vlad gasped. "Please, Mrs. Bumble, you have my greatest sympathy at your loss. Your husband was a pillar of our community. He was…"

The small woman again let a smile fleetingly tug at the corners of her mouth. "He was a man of convictions and great energy."

"Yes, yes, he was."

Mrs. Bumble patted the folio. "I have something here, Highness, I should like to show you. If you do not mind my being rude, Princess, perhaps if your husband and I were to retire to his laboratory, we could dispense with this business quickly and I can be on my way."

Gisella looked at Vlad, then nodded and smiled. "You will, of course, stay for tea and even the evening, if the weather turns bad. The coach house has more than enough room for your horse and coach."

"If it comes to that, yes, thank you."

Vlad kissed his wife, then walked in silence with the widow Bumble to his laboratory. Save for the absence of the thaumagraph, and the notebooks detailing its use, his sanctuary was exactly as he had left it. He offered Mrs. Bumble a chair, but she shook her head and instead handed him the oilskin-wrapped folio.

She turned from him and traced a finger over the curved horn of the troll's skull. "I should have you understand some things, Highness, before you look at that. I am Mystrian. My maiden name was Vale. I am distantly related to Henrietta Frost. We grew up together in very strict Virtuan homes. I did not know my husband then. He went off to Launston to study at seminary and returned full of vigor. He was a much smaller man, then, but just as powerful a speaker. I fell for him almost the instant I saw him, and we were wed within two years. That was a scandalously short time to be betrothed, but everyone figured me the luckiest woman in Temperance Bay."

She continued around the table upon which the troll's skeleton had been laid out, focusing on it. "As a Virtuan I was raised to strictly follow the message of Our Savior and to eschew the pomp and circumstance of the Church. I came to realize too late that Othniel cared less for the message than the trappings of his position, and the power his oratory gave him. By then, however, I had discovered that we could not have children. That was God's punishment on me for my haste. Because we were wed and I hold my vows as sacred, I believed I was forever trapped in a loveless life."

A shiver ran down Vlad's spine. "What are you saying, Mrs. Bumble?"

"It is not something of which I should be proud, Highness, but feel no shame." The older woman smiled, her eyes focused distantly. "Ephraim, he was so passionate a man. He loved Scripture and nature. While Othniel saw to his career, I fell in love with Ephraim. Our affair was discreet, and ended amicably as Ephraim went to do God's work. Othniel confronted me with his suspicions and I confessed. Whenever Ephraim wrote him, Othniel commanded me to destroy his work, as punishment, of course. I could not. I *did* not"

"And so you had them to send to me. That was a brave thing you did." The Prince nodded slowly. "You hoped I could help find him and save him from your husband."

Her head came around and her smile survived a bit longer. "Othniel always thought you were clever, but he never understood how clever. Even in that document, even as he imagined what you had done, he could not understand the implications of it. I am not saying I do, either—the curse skipped me, so this is the stuff of faery stories. Othniel forced Catherine Strake to spy for him. She confirmed that you had a way of getting messages between Temperance and the west more quickly than a rider might."

The Prince stared at the package on his desk. "He intended to bring me up on charges of heresy?"

"That would have been the threat. I think he would have extorted concessions out of you. If you were replaced as Governor-General, he believed he could control whomever they sent to rule in your stead." Her head came up. "Where is he now, Ephraim Fox? He went west with you, yes?"

Vlad nodded. "Using what he learned, he saved many lives. Ultimately he sacrificed himself to save us all—and I do not mean only those in the west. Our enemies had opened a hole into the depths of Hell, and it took a good man to close it."

Livinia Bumble covered her gasp with a hand. "He's gone? I should have thought I would know if he was gone."

"I don't believe he is. I don't know *where* he is, but my best people are going to find him and bring him back."

Her eyes tightened, but no tear glistened. "You are not saying that to an old woman out of pity, are you?"

"No." Vlad frowned. "And I *am* sorry to hear of your husband's unexpected death."

She looked up and blinked. "Highness, it wasn't *unexpected*, not at all. He choked to death on biscuits I'd baked especially for him. For his tea. He liked them so." The widow Bumble slowly shook her head. "Once again Othniel gave in to the sin of Gluttony, and this time God, in His wisdom, meted out swift justice."

Though Vlad protested her leaving, Livinia Bumble chose to return to Temperance despite the thunder and lightning rolling in from the east. He instructed his wife to send Owen to him when he arrived, then ran back to his laboratory and studied the Bumble manuscript. He immediately lost himself in it, doing his best to ignore the man's bombast and ego. That was no mean feat, but beneath all that he found that Bumble had made far more correct deductions than false ones.

The Prince sat back in his chair, trying not to shiver. Had Bumble lived, his manuscript would have provided the Church with unbelievable leverage at court. An ambitious man, like the Archbishop of Launston, might even have been able to force the Queen to abdicate by alleging she condoned and promoted the creation of a heretic state in Mystria for occult reasons of her own. Prince John would be elevated to replace her, the Archbishop would rule through him. Vlad's own compliance could be forced through direct threats to the life of his children.

How much power the Church could wield in Mystria would depend upon the man they chose to replace Bumble. News of his death would be another two weeks reaching Norisle, and it would likely take until September for his replacement to be installed. If he were to guess, Vlad imagined that the Church would send a Norillian-born Bishop to take over—most likely someone from the Archbishop's staff.

A crack of thunder startled the Prince. *I shall worry about that when the man arrives.* He blew out his lamp and as he sprinted through raindrops to the main house he realized Owen hadn't come see him. *Probably waylaid by his daughter.*

The Prince entered through the kitchen door, removed his coat, and hung it on a peg by the hearth. He realized he was still in his road clothes, so he headed for the stairs. As he reached the foyer, a fist pounded on the door. Vlad smiled at his wife in the parlor. "Must be Owen."

The Prince opened the door and stood back, instantly aware that the man before him was not Owen Strake.

The slender man had emerged from a coach and swept off his cloak and hat, spraying water over the floor and the Prince's trousers. Vlad recognized the long face, despite the attempt to make it more jolly through the addition of a wide moustache. *Better he had grown a beard to hide his lack of a chin.* His pouchy belly had not grown nor shrunk since the Prince last saw him, but his gold waistcoat having the lower half of the buttons remain undone, made him look pregnant.

"Surprised you, I did, ain't it true? Ain't it?" Lord Rivendell smiled broadly. "Never expected to see me, did you? Did you?"

Vlad took a step back. "When did you arrive?"

"Just today, just now, came as soon as we hit dry land, which ain't very dry." The man drew a sealed sheaf of papers from inside his black coat's breast pocket. "These are for you. The Queen's ordered you home to Norisle, Prince Vladimir, and I shall be Governor-General while you are gone."

✛

ABOUT THE AUTHOR

Michael A. Stackpole is an award-winning writer, editor, screenplay writer, podcaster, game designer, computer game designer, and graphic novelist. He's best known for his *New York Times* bestselling novels *I, Jedi* and *Rogue Squadron*. In his free time he plays indoor soccer, dances, and occasionally fishes. He also holds weekly chats in Second Life to help other writers learn how to do what they love and make money at it.

To learn more about Mike and his work—including the digital-original novels *In Hero Years...I'm Dead* and *Perfectly Invisible*, please visit his website at www.michaelastackpole.com.